RACE
for the
DYING

RACE
for the
DYING

———

Steven F. Havill

THOMAS DUNNE BOOKS
St. Martin's Press
New York

This is a work of fiction. All of the characters, organizations, and events portrayed in this novel are either products of the author's imagination or are used fictitiously.

THOMAS DUNNE BOOKS.
An imprint of St. Martin's Press.

RACE FOR THE DYING. Copyright © 2009 by Steven F. Havill. All rights reserved. Printed in the United States of America. For information, address St. Martin's Press, 175 Fifth Avenue, New York, N.Y. 10010.

www.thomasdunnebooks.com
www.stmartins.com

LIBRARY OF CONGRESS CATALOGING-IN-PUBLICATION DATA

Havill, Steven.
   Race for the dying / Steven F. Havill.—1st ed.
      p. cm.
   ISBN 978-0-312-38071-7
   1. Physicians—Fiction.   2. Washington (State)—History—20th century—Fiction.   I. Title.
   PS3558.A785R33   2009
   813'.54—dc22

                                        2009017065

First Edition: October 2009

10   9   8   7   6   5   4   3   2   1

For Kathleen

Acknowledgments

The author gratefully acknowledges the assistance of the following muses, whose arguments and debates filled the room, but who claim no responsibility for how the author made use of their knowledge and guidance:

      Dr. George B. Wood (1855)

      Dr. R. V. Pierce (1883)

      Dr. John B. Roberts (1890)

      Dr. Thomas S. K. Morton (1890)

      Dr. William Pepper (1895)

RACE
for the
DYING

I

<hr>

The sea reminded Thomas Parks of his father's neglected tea service. Had sunshine polished the waves and swells, they would have gleamed like lively pewter. But sky met Pacific gray on gray like a sheet of lead. Had there been a way to settle dust on the swells, the match with the pewter service would have been perfect.

Thomas grasped the handrail along the slippery deck until his knuckles were white. Mist soaked his face, plastered his dark hair to his forehead, and found openings in his slicker, running under his woolen shirt to puddle behind his broad leather belt.

It wasn't the gentle roll of the steam schooner that made him nervous—it was knowing that the coastline might be no more than a pistol shot off to starboard. He turned and glanced back toward the quarterdeck. The captain stood with another sailor, his pipe belching rhythmic plumes of smoke. A tousle-headed youngster tended the wheel with a serenity best reserved for sunshine, gentle breezes, and unlimited visibility.

At any moment, a great black rock dripping with foam and kelp and seals would rise out of the sea, and they would never turn away in time. Thomas concentrated on the gray depth ahead, waiting for the first shadow, ready to vault free as the ship splintered and crashed under his feet.

The *Alice* churned on without concern, without interruption of the captain's enjoyment of his pipe, without crashing into the rocks. At one point, Thomas heard the lethargic bell of a buoy come and go, but never saw it.

"We'll be docking within the hour," a voice behind him said, and he turned without releasing his grip on the handrail to see Newell Bassier's pleasant, lined face, water running down the creases and dripping from his gray whiskers. "Thought you might want to fetch your gear," Bassier added. "We're headed on up the coast, and won't be stopping in Port McKinney long." Able seaman, mate, bosun—Thomas had never understood the hierarchy of the ship's crew—Bassier appeared to spend most of his time carving spare belaying pins into elegant figurines.

"I have but the two bags," Thomas replied. "And they're ready and waiting."

"Ah. You travel light, then."

"More is on the way," Thomas conceded. "Shipped overland. A mountain of things, believe me."

"Ah," Bassier said again. "Well, then. About an hour. The fog is lifting quickly enough."

"Quickly?" Thomas said skeptically, and Bassier laughed.

"This is near a sunny day for these parts," he said. "You'll get used to it. Look to the east, there," and he thrust his chin toward the bow. To the east was gray like everywhere else, but now Thomas could see a slender line, a color break above the waves.

"Enjoy the hour, Doctor." Bassier turned. "Shortly you'll be slogging through mud, soaked to the bone, and wishing for a warm bottle." He seemed to be the only one on board who concerned himself even in passing with the needs of the passengers—not that the three paying fares were high maintenance.

One passenger, a priest whose name Thomas had never learned, kept to himself. But the third passenger, a short, florid man named Efrim Carlisle, had bunked with Thomas, and his bulkhead-rending snores had been a wonder. On several occasions the young physician had rested in the darkness, imagining each of the structures in the man's throat as they vibrated and roared to produce such an odd symphony . . . one that never awoke the composer, of course.

An accountant by profession, Carlisle impressed Thomas as an odd duck. To hear him talk, Carlisle dealt with the intricacies of paperwork, but his hands were those of a bricklayer. Stubby fingers, cracked and broken nails, calluses that made his palms dry and hard, he looked no more the part of an office-bound cipher than did the salt-preserved captain of the *Alice*, Robert Kinsman.

As his destination approached, Thomas forced himself to relax. If the crew was not worried, why should he be? He contented himself with watching the constantly changing colors of the water as it broke around the bow. He could not pinpoint the time when they had turned eastward from their northerly route up the Pacific coast. The water told no secrets. From the time they rounded Cape Flattery, leaving the Pacific for the Strait of Juan de Fuca, until the *Alice* docked at Port McKinney, more than a hundred miles would have passed under their hull . . . and he had seen not a single landmark for reference.

When he awakened before dawn that day, long before Carlisle stirred, he dressed quickly and hurried on deck, hoping for the first sight of the new country under a morning sun. Instead, he had been greeted by the soggy, wet wool of the coastal air.

The ship's steam horn vented a note so impossibly long and exquisitely loud that Thomas shut his eyes until the blast died. That symphony was repeated with regularity as they drew closer, although closer to what, Thomas could only guess.

A blink, a glance away, and then his pulse leaped with excitement. The rich line of emerald green, caught by the sun as it finally burned through the fog, outlined the coast perhaps five miles ahead. Thomas could draw no closer to the rail without tumbling overboard, and his eyes ached with the strain. Bit by bit, the coast gained definition. The sun touched his right cheek, and he realized with a disoriented start that the *Alice* was now actually making headway *south*. The ghosts of other watercraft appeared moored here and there, and a great, curving spit of land hooked out into Admiralty Inlet ahead of them.

Once, the strong aroma of burning wood tinged his nostrils, an odd sensation in the middle of the wet gray strait. The gulls wheeled noisily overhead, sometimes hidden in the fog, sometimes diving down to hang on the air currents just above the waves, tiny bright eyes regarding the ship with interest.

Another buoy appeared dead ahead, and the ship swung hard to starboard, its horn bellowing. The hull kissed the bobbing marker. The gentle throb of the steam engine changed pitch, and Thomas felt the deck shudder as the *Alice* slowed, its bow turning away from the open water. They headed toward a dull, dark little community at the base of the curved spit, passing through a fleet of moored ships of varying tonnage and rigging.

The hodgepodge of wharf pilings thrust black and slimy out of the water, and dockside, Thomas could see half a dozen people, some fishing, some no doubt waiting for the *Alice*. A hundred yards down the shore, a trio of children and two mutts played near the water. One of the boys appeared to be flailing at the others with a strand of kelp. Looking again to the wharf, Thomas tried to make out the imposing figure of Dr. John Haines, who had promised a royal welcome.

The *Alice* shuddered again. Black coal smoke belched from the single stack, lifting and mixing with the gray fog. Whoever pulled the steam whistle cord was diligent, and Thomas flinched each time.

The crew galvanized into action at the last moment as the *Alice* sidled her 102 feet of keel and 260 tons up to the wharf as gently as if she were a tiny skiff. Out of habit, Thomas hauled out his watch and snapped it open: 3:17 P.M. on this Saturday, the twelfth day of September, 1891. He had shaken his father's hand in the doorway of his Leister, Connecticut, home at ten minutes after seven on the morning of August 26.

"Absolutely remarkable," he said aloud. The enormous size of the continent, studied and annotated on a score of maps in his father's den, had shrunk to this—eighteen short days, including visiting for two full days with a cousin in St. Louis.

With a final salute from its steam whistle, the *Alice*'s gunwale thudded against the bumpers of Jones's Wharf at Port McKinney, Washington. The schooner rode easy in the dark, greasy water, and Thomas Parks strode back along the deck toward his stateroom, pulse pounding with excitement.

Efrim Carlisle greeted him at the door with a hearty handshake. "So we've made it this far, and we haven't drowned off some terrible reef after all," he announced. He patted his considerable girth. "And the crew tells me we won't be here even long enough for a decent meal."

"I'm the only one to disembark, I think." Thomas extended his hand, surprised once again at the power and hardness of Carlisle's grip. "I hope the remainder of your trip is more pleasant, sir. Drier, perhaps."

"It appears that way," Carlisle said. They made their way back on deck, and Thomas saw that the *Alice*'s bowsprit practically nudged the bay side of a gray-black building, the side facing the wharf open to the weather.

"Charming place, don't you think?" Carlisle asked. "You say your father's to meet you?"

"A *friend* of my father's," Thomas corrected.

"Ah. Well, then, good luck to you, Dr. Parks. I manage to visit Port McKinney now and then. Perhaps our paths will cross again."

Another shattering bellow of the *Alice*'s horn brought a grimace. "I'd best be off," Thomas said. The gangplank was steep and wet, and he waited while two men climbed aboard, neither with baggage. They both nodded at the seaman, Newell Bassier, and one of them shook hands with Efrim Carlisle. The three disappeared toward what passed for staterooms on the *Alice*.

Hefting his black medical bag and the bulky duffel, Dr. Thomas Parks stepped off the *Alice* and set foot on the rough planks of Jones's Wharf. Nothing here matched the genteel, manicured landscape of Leister, Connecticut. No elegant white fences, no smoothly worn cobblestone streets, no houses of cobble or clapboard that had been built before the war of the Revolution, no stately barns. Not a lawn, not a flower bed.

What he could see was brown and gray, dismally wet, wretchedly muddy, and ramshackle, with temporary buildings thrown up in the haste of commerce, many of them no more than canvas tents with slabwood siding. Turning in place, he looked down the coast, his gaze following the curving spit of land. A forest of stumpage studded the hills down to the rocky shoreline. In one sheltered cove, the water itself was brown and corduroy with an enormous floating island of logs that covered a dozen acres. Crowning the tip of the spit itself was another large welter of buildings, perhaps a fishing village.

Port McKinney crowded the harborage, but a scattering of rude shacks stretched farther up the hillside. Dr. John Haines lived somewhere in this settlement of two thousand people, and in his vest pocket, Thomas carried the small card with the address—101 Lincoln Street.

The *Alice* shrieked again and Thomas felt the wharf shudder as the schooner's hull butted it, pulling backward to begin the next leg of the voyage up the coast.

Two fishermen sitting on the opposite side of the wharf watched Thomas with interest. "Could you tell me where I might find Lincoln Street," he said to the nearest man.

"Lincoln," the man repeated. "This be Lincoln." The fisherman jerked his head to the foot of the wharf. "From the warehouse up through town to the good doctor's house on the hill. That's all Lincoln Street." He grinned, showing only one tooth. "Step off the wharf, and there you are."

"Dr. John Haines?"

"That be the one." The man's eyes inventoried Thomas from head to foot, taking in the black medical bag with interest. "You kin, are you?"

"Family friend," Thomas replied. "Are you having luck today?"

The man shrugged and glanced at his stubby cane fishing pole. "Nothing for lunch yet, if that's what you mean. Starfish eat the bait more often than not." He waved a hand toward the heavens as if the answer could be found in the fog. "Good day to you, then," he said, and turned back to his contemplation of the black water a dozen feet below.

The wharf served as a walkway along the flank of the shed complex, and Thomas strolled the length of the building, duffel over one shoulder, able to savor steady footing for the first time since the *Alice* departed San Francisco. That pleasure ended between two enormous pilings marking the entry to Lincoln Street.

His leather boots squelched down into the muck, and he hesitated, both arms spread wide for balance. Half of the Lincoln Street businesses had boardwalks, half did not, and when the street began its steep ascent up the bluff, it was more rock than mud.

Except for the fishermen on the wharf and the children playing near the water down the shore, the village appeared deserted. Thomas trudged across to a length of boardwalk fronting a building marked McKinney Rural Telegraph. He stamped mud off his boots and pushed open the door. Sunshine blasted through one dirty window, and Thomas could see a visored head working behind a large desk.

"Sir," he said politely.

"Yeeeeeess," the voice replied, drawn out like leaking steam. The man stood up, tall and gangling, still squinting at a sheet of paper. He approached the counter. "And what might I do for you, young man?"

"I just arrived on the *Alice*," Thomas said, and thrust out his hand.

"Well, I'm sorry," the man replied before Thomas could introduce himself, and then chuckled at his own joke. He extended his hand. "She arrived in one piece—that's the important thing." His grip was both bony and limp. "Carter Birch, and I hope to be pleased to make your acquaintance."

"I would hope so. I'm Thomas Parks," the young man said. "Dr. Thomas Parks. I've come from Connecticut to work with Dr. John Haines."

"Is that a fact?" The tall man looked sideways at Thomas and tossed the paper he had been reading on his desk. "Does the good doctor know you're here?"

"Not yet. I just stepped off the ship. I'm on my way up there now. What I'd really like to do is send a telegram to my father in Connecticut. He'll want to know that I'm on dry land, I'm sure."

"He'll be relieved, certainly." Birch slid a lined form across the counter and handed Thomas a pencil. "Pleasant trip, on the whole?"

"On the whole, yes. Quite an education."

Writing in neat script, Thomas kept the message brief. "I'm surprised that I don't see more people in town," he said as he signed his name. "I was led to believe that as many as several thousand make their home here."

"Comes and goes," Birch said. "Go down to the Clarissa around nine o'clock tonight, and there'll be crowd enough for you. That's the most popular watering hole, around the point to the south."

Thomas handed the message to Birch, who took it without a glance.

"When do you suppose he might receive that?" Thomas asked, and Birch grinned a show of strong, yellowing teeth.

"A hell of a lot faster than what it took you to travel out here."

"I would hope so."

"You're headed up to one-oh-one now?" Birch asked, and Thomas blinked in surprise. "That's what folks around here call the good doctor's house. Finest one on the hill, beyond a doubt. One-oh-one belonged to one of the mill owners, you know. Had it built board by board, just the way he wanted it. And then one day out in the timber, the butt end of a spruce squashed him like an insect, and that was that. The good doctor purchased it from the widow." Birch grinned again. "Haven't seen her since."

Thomas Parks felt a surge of excitement. "Is Dr. Haines the only doctor in McKinney?"

"Was, until last year. Riggs is the other gentleman's name, I believe. Zachary Riggs. He works with Haines from time to time.

8

I don't know him well, and to tell the truth, I don't know what he does, other than squiring John's daughter about."

"The fair Alvina," Thomas said. "Father has told me about her."

"Most fair, yes, indeed." He held up his left hand, pointing with his right to a long, thin scar that ran around the base of his left thumb, ending low on the fleshy pad of his palm. "She stitched this up, so fine that it looked like an old lady's needlework." He glanced over at the pendulum clock on the far wall. "I could keep you here all day with tall tales, but I suspect you're eager to be on. Stop by from time to time. The telegraph will be off within the hour."

Thomas extended his hand again, and this time Birch's grip was more enthusiastic. "I'll do that, sir. Thanks again."

"Walk up toward Lindeman's place . . . that's the Mercantile at the top of the hill. That's the corner of Lincoln and Gambel. Just across the way, you'll see one-oh-one. It's a three-story that looks like it'd be at home in Connecticut as much as here, all fancy and frilly. That's the place. Oh," and he held up a cautioning finger, "right at the Mercantile, there's a dog that everyone wishes would some day drop dead of lead poisoning. Beware of him. Big brindly looking thing with a bad back leg. Even with it, he's fast enough to catch people. Most of the time, he's locked up in the back of the Merc, but he finds a way out now and then."

"Thanks for the warning."

He turned to go, but Birch held up a hand. "And the telegram is a dollar," he said. "You want to start an account? I do that for folks."

"No," Thomas said, and dug out several coins. "Thanks again."

By the time he stepped back out on the street, most of the fog had lifted, and the strait fairly sparkled as the afternoon sun chased away the last strands of gray.

2

As he walked up Lincoln Street, Thomas Parks found himself turning sideways, even backward, stumbling as he tried to take in a hundred views at once. The clarity of the air was breathtaking as the fog evaporated, as if layers of gauze were being stripped away. Far to the north, a dozen islands daisy-chained through the last tendrils of mist, and the sound was dotted by a myriad of vessels. One of them would be the *Alice*, wending its way north to Bellingham.

The street reached a bench of land, level for a hundred yards along the top of a rock escarpment. The village appeared to be carved out of the trees and the hillsides, an almost random scattering of squat cabins clad in slab wood, and a few stout, elegant houses of multiple stories, looking as if they'd been plucked out of their original eastern neighborhoods and planted here. The pure white spire of a church steeple reached upward, and in that same neighborhood Thomas could see a series of massive brick buildings that might be the true center of Port McKinney commerce. More wharves thrust out into the water, more tall ships waited.

Legs starting to tingle pleasantly from the climb, the young physician approached a major intersection where a carved sign announced Gambel Street. He paused in front of Lindeman's Mercantile, the place in harsh contrast with the neat, prim Sander's Hardware in Leister, where every nut and bolt had its place. This establishment rambled here and there, spreading across the lot from the original two-room building with sheds and additions and corrals and bins. The enclosed portion of the store that fronted both Lincoln and Gambel streets appeared to be constructed entirely of rejected slab wood still carrying the bark. A stovepipe thrust through a tin thimble on the wall, pouring out dense wood smoke.

And the dog. Thomas paused when he saw the animal—sure enough, untethered, unfenced, and intensely interested in this new human being who approached. Large, rawboned, grizzled at the muzzle, and proudly wearing a pedigree that might have included half a dozen parents, the dog sat calmly in the mud.

"How are you today?" Thomas said. The dog blinked and his large ears dropped a touch from the round dome of his skull. The animal's tail was deep in the muck, but there were no raised hackles, no snarling lip. Thomas hefted his medical bag and switched hands with the soft duffel. The sharp, brass-reinforced corners of the bag would make a formidable weapon. The dog yawned and stood up slowly, sucking himself out of the mud. He shook and limped out toward Thomas as if the two of them were old friends. His mucky tail flopped from side to side like a length of dirty rope.

Thomas knew he couldn't outrun the beast, but gambled that the dog's initial display of disinterest wasn't a guise. He stopped walking and ignored the dog, gazing once more out to the southeast. Pressure against his right leg prompted him to look down. The dog had nosed between the medical bag and Thomas's right thigh.

Without moving more than necessary, Thomas reached out with just the thumb of his right hand and scratched behind the dog's ear. The dog huffed a sigh and waited for more.

"I guess you belong here, stranger," a voice said from behind him. Thomas looked over his shoulder. A tiny person stood on the first raised step of the Mercantile, a large mug in one hand, a broom in the other. "You've been adopted by the Prince," the man added, and laughed. "He either adopts you or bites you. Never seems to be a middle ground."

"That's good to know," Thomas said.

"I chain him up, but he always gets loose. Wizard of some kind, I guess. Wants to be out here, not out back. 'Spose I'm going to have to shoot him one day, if someone doesn't beat me to it." He leaned the broom against the wall.

"Perhaps you could move the chain out here, so he can enjoy the view," Thomas allowed.

The man, whom Thomas could see now was quite elderly, settled down on the step. He pushed his woolen cap back on his head, the stubble of gray hair about the same length as that studding his chin and cheeks. "Hadn't thought of that."

"I'm Dr. Thomas Parks." Thomas moved through the mud channel to the steps, placed the medical bag on the wooden planks, and extended his hand. The old man's grip was as bony as Carter Birch's, but fragile, as if too firm a grip would powder his arthritic knuckles.

"I guessed that's who you might be. Dr. John mentioned you were on the way. Pleased to have you with us."

"You're the owner?"

"I am that. Lars Lindeman, in all my sorry old age." He reached out a hand and tousled the dog's ears. "I don't know who Prince belongs to, but I wish he'd go home."

"He's not yours, then?"

"I suppose now he is. Appeared one day last spring. Pain in the ass, mostly." The dog looked up at Thomas, eyebrows arching a bit. "Want some coffee?" Lindeman held up his cup. "I probably make the worst coffee in Port McKinney. Discourages the deadbeats."

Thomas laughed. "Thanks, no. I'm just off the ship, and eager to meet John. It's been a long trip."

"Bet it was. When did you set out?"

"The twenty-sixth of August. From Leister, Connecticut."

"Not sailing all the way, surely."

"No. I came by train to St. Louis, where I have a cousin. Then on to San Francisco and the steam packet up the coast."

"Can be a pleasant enough voyage, I suppose."

"Pleasant only because we didn't sink." Thomas laughed. "Cramped, dirty, awful food, and fog. Lots of fog."

"Yep," Lindeman said, and shrugged. "Well, that's our specialty. The dirt and fog, I mean. A day like this is rare enough. Enjoy it while it lasts." The old man pulled himself to his feet, and Thomas saw the stiffness in the hips, the cramped way the old man's hands tried to grip the railing, the grimace of effort.

Lindeman shot him a glance of amusement at the scrutiny. "Me and the mutt are a pair, eh?" He pointed up the hill toward an impressive three-story home, a house ornate with gingerbread and an entire rainbow of trim colors. "That's one-oh-one. Dr. John ain't to home at the moment, though. I saw him head out when I was dumpin' ashes earlier. Gert will fix you up."

"Gert?"

"His housekeeper. Best cook in the entire world. Makes my coffee taste like kerosene." He looked into his cup as if to check for things moving. "She's been with Dr. John forever. Her brother, too, although you won't get any more words out of Horace than you do Prince here. Don't know if Alvina went with the doctor or not. You met her? No point in asking that. You're just off the boat, for God's sake. Listen to me."

"I exchanged pleasantries with a fisherman, met Mr. Birch and now you. That's the extent of it since I set foot in Port McKinney."

"Well, now. About every soul is either minding his own business or out in the timber . . . or working at the mills. This time of day, it's a quiet place. Come tonight, there's plenty of hell raisin'." He looked closely at Thomas. "I'd ask how you came to know the good doctor, if it was any of my business. But it ain't, so I won't."

Thomas laughed. "He's an old, old friend of my father's. They knew each other during the war. I'm told that I was introduced to him when I was five or six, but I have no recollection. We've had some correspondence recently, and he expressed interest in my studies." Thomas hefted the medical bag. "And then convinced me that there were opportunities here for me. It's really that simple."

"Good enough to have you, then. We'll be talking." Lindeman held out a hand. "Prince, get your worthless carcass in here." The dog shot a glance at both of them, then turned and slowly plodded out into the middle of the street, where he stood with head down, looking into the distance as if engaged in deep thought. "See what I mean? Worthless, flea-infested . . ." The old man went inside, muttering to himself.

As soon as Thomas stepped away from the porch, the dog's head came up, and he followed the young man up the street, remaining a couple paces behind.

So spotlessly clean were the front steps of 101 Lincoln that Thomas hesitated. Seeing no boot scraper, he set his bag and valise on the steps, then looked about until he found a sharp chip of gravel on the walkway. Balancing on one leg with a hand on the step rail, he dug the worst of the mud off his boots, sticky chunks with the consistency of artist's clay. He was standing thus, one-legged, like some odd kind of shore bird, when a horse and rider appeared, charging up Lincoln Street.

Thomas straightened, amazed that the animal could keep its footing. It was then that he saw it was actually a mule, hooves throwing great clots of mud. Prince, who had been sitting quietly in the middle of the street, pulled his rump out of the muck. He stood unmoving for a few seconds until it became obvious that the mule and rider were headed his way, then grudgingly stalked across the street.

The rider was a rough-looking young man perhaps a year or two older than Thomas, dressed in heavy, greasy clothing with a black knit cap jammed tight on his skull. The mule jarred to a halt in front of him, and Thomas saw that the young man's eyes were wild with excitement.

"Gotta have Doc," he shouted. The mule danced clumsily to one side, fighting the bridle, not ready to stop. "Out to the mill."

"I don't believe that Doctor Haines is here at the moment," Thomas replied. "I just arrived myself, and I don't know—"

The young man jerked the reins impatiently, and the mule thrashed its head and managed a small crow hop to one side, nearly dislodging his rider. "Had a bad'n out at the saw, and got a man crushed," he shouted. "He's gonna die for sure if we don't find the doc."

"Listen, I'm a physician. Perhaps I can help."

"Well, if you can, you gotta," the young man said. "You got a horse or buggy, or are you afoot?"

Thomas held out both hands helplessly. "I'm . . . I'm as you see, sir."

Grabbing a fistful of scruffy mane, the young man wrestled his stout boots out of the stirrups, then slid down, squelching into the mud. "Take the mule," he said. "You can ride?"

"Well, yes, although I've never—"

"Take him. I'll fetch me a ride from the Swede." He held out the reins, and as soon as Thomas had them in hand, the young man turned and started toward the Mercantile.

"Wait," Thomas shouted after him. "Where?"

"Schmidt's mill, yonder," the young man said. He pointed southwest, toward the spit of land. "You can see it from here."

"There's a road?"

Stepping backward, the man gesticulated down the hill. "Just slide down to the wharf, then follow the coast trail. It's the only one. I'll be along right behind you. If I can find the doc, I'll bring him, too." He turned and plunged off, arms flailing for balance.

Leaving his duffel bag on the front steps, Thomas gathered the reins and stepped closer to the mule. The animal had settled some, and Thomas searched until he found two loose leather thongs behind the saddle that had once been adequate for lashing a bedroll. He tied them through the grips of his medical bag, then swung up into the saddle.

"I hope you know the way," he said aloud. The mule apparently did, since at the first touch of the reins, he wheeled about, nearly dumping his rider.

The mule's gait was jarring, and for the first few minutes Thomas fought for balance. As they turned off the bluff and started down the steepest portion of Lincoln Street, he clung to the saddle horn with both hands, leaning as far back as he could. The mule trotted with his head down, kicking great projectiles of muddy earth in all directions.

The street narrowed to a rough, rock-studded trail angling to

15

parallel the shoreline. Birds rose in frantic, noisy clouds at his passing, and he could smell the rich vegetation. In a moment, he heard the thunder of hooves.

"Just ahead, there!" The young man urged his bay mare past the mule. "Just ahead, there" was still a mile or more away, and Thomas urged the mule on. The trail circled inland around a great buttress of jagged rocks that reared fifty feet out of the placid waters of the sound, then plunged down close to the water, in one spot crossing a broad tidal flat. The mule drove across the dark sand and Thomas had a brief instant to enjoy himself in the rush of salt-tinged air.

Thomas discovered that if he trusted the mule and didn't try to second-guess the route the animal chose, they could almost keep up with the young man on the mare. A stream trickled out of the rocks, and the mule hopped the first pool of standing water, slid across the open ground for a step or two, misjudged a second puddle, and splashed not toward the trail as it turned right, but toward what appeared to be more sure footing near the shore.

The choice caught Thomas off balance, and he pulled the reins hard, trying to turn the animal. The reins pulled the mule off balance, and he missed his footing for the first time. One hoof drove down between two sharp rocks, exploding the animal's lower leg as his weight twisted. Thomas tried to twist free and couldn't, and mule and rider crashed down through the brush and rocks to the placid water ten feet below.

The impact against the rocks pounded the breath out of his lungs as the mule thrashed over him. His head cracked against a black, wet rock, and then he was in the icy water. In an odd moment of clarity, he could see the bottom, the tiny grains of black sand shifting this way and that. "And now I'm going to drown," he thought, but could do nothing about it. He allowed the water to cushion him, numbing the pain that first crept in and then seeped away.

3

B e careful," the voice commanded. The words drifted out of the rocks from somewhere behind him, and Thomas Parks tried to shift his head. "Hold still," the same voice barked. Thomas was no longer trying to breathe salt water or strangle on kelp, and he hurt too much to be dead.

"Give me that," someone said. "I'll see to it." Then a single explosion pealed out. He started, and that brought such an onrush of pain that he cried out as if a bullet had struck him. Each time he tried to let a breath seep into his lungs, the shafts of bright agony cut his innards to mush.

"Yer gonna hafta," a voice close to Thomas's ear said. *Hafta what?* His left leg was moved in an impossible direction. He bellowed and thrashed against the hands that held him down. All the commands and suggestions were gibberish.

Finally he felt himself being lifted by a dozen hands. He tried to hold perfectly still, to hold himself rigid, absolutely certain that they were going to drop him back into the sea like one of those shipboard deaths that go sliding off the plank to disappear beneath the waves.

The rocks that he could feel digging into his back were replaced by something hard and flat, and then he was hoisted upward. "Careful now," that same voice warned.

He tried to bring a hand up to his face as his world spun, knowing that if he could just *see*, some of this might make sense.

"Easy now," the voice said, and then pulled away. "Where's Jake?"

That brought more unintelligible conversation. The stretcher on which he was bound slid onto a hard surface with a thump that brought a choking cry, his voice sounding as if it belonged to someone else.

"He going to ride all right like that?" someone asked.

"Gonna have to," the voice said.

"Jake said to take him direct to one-oh-one."

"Heard him. Get a move on, now."

For a brief moment of relief, the board underneath him did not move. Breathing was so difficult that Thomas fought the fear of suffocation, as if a wad of dripping, foul seaweed was being thrust down his throat. Once more he felt hands holding his shoulders. "Just lay easy," the voice said. "Ain't no point in struggling."

"Need to see," Thomas tried to gasp. "Can't breathe."

"Ain't nothing to see. We got you all sitcheeated in the wagon, and we'll be gettin' you up the hill directly. Just rest easy."

Wagon. Thomas knew what that one awful word meant, and he groaned in anticipation. He remembered the mule's plunging run down the coast trail, over the hummocks of sedge and through the wet, slick rocks. A wagon on that same trail? But they weren't listening. With a creak of leather the wagon jerked under Thomas.

"I can't," he tried to say, but that thought ended as he passed out.

A dog barked somewhere. "Okay, he's back," a calm voice said. Thomas felt a cool touch on his right shoulder, skin on skin, not through his wet, fragrant woolens. "Thomas, you're going to be all right."

"I . . ."

"Yes, you did," the voice agreed with an easy chuckle. "Most spectacular, I'm told. If you were planning on a downright Shakespearean entrance to our stage, you did a most credible job, but the worst is over now. You're safe at one-oh-one, and you have nothing to do but mend. You're a lucky young man."

Thomas tried to picture the face that went with the reassuring voice. The hand patted his shoulder again. "Doctors make the worst patients," the voice said. "I have no reason to think you'll be an exception. Let me give you something to ponder before the laudanum takes effect, and that may help you avoid some foolishness later in the mending process."

"Ribs," Thomas managed to say.

"Oh, indeed, ribs. Spectacular bruises, I must say. And more pieces than there should be."

Thomas sensed the figure beside the bed pull away, and could not make out the quiet conversation that didn't include him, but shortly the voice returned.

"You have a messy laceration that runs from just in front of your right ear all the way across the top of the right orbit to the bridge of your nose. I'm told that you found a seaside rock with your face." Thomas felt a finger near his lower left eyelid, and the bandage was gently lifted a fraction. The room was dim, and he could make no sense of light and shadows. "Your eyes will be all right, but I want to make sure about any concussive injuries." The hand returned to Thomas's shoulder. "Do you remember anything of the fall?"

"No."

"I'm not surprised. I think what we have is a whole symphony of lacerations and bruises. At first I thought that your left hip had been shattered, but now I'm not so sure. Certainly there is some tendon and ligament damage that will give you something to think about. The battered skull, the broken ribs . . . and oh, your left thumb is fractured."

The hand moved away and Thomas felt his right hand taken in a firm but gentle grip. "Welcome to one-oh-one, Dr. Thomas Parks. I regret that I wasn't able to meet you when you stepped off the *Alice* earlier. Somehow I was expecting the little towheaded child that I remember that summer in Leister. We'll put all these pieces back together, and then, in a few short days, we'll raise our glasses in a proper toast of greeting."

"Thank . . ."

The hand squeezed again. "Not at all. In a day or two, we'll talk. For now, let the sedative work." The voice drew closer to Thomas's left ear. "Picture each bone, each muscle, each ligament, Doctor. Picture them all back in place, and picture them mending. The mind is our best medicine. If you should need anything, there will always be someone near at hand."

This time, Thomas could smell the pungent aroma of tobacco smoke that clung to clothing. As the opiates found the nooks and crannies of his body, the voices receded and he sensed little else.

4

Thomas Parks concentrated on lying absolutely still, letting his mind do the wandering as the morphine wrapped his body in soft flannel. He drifted in and out of consciousness, never quite knowing when he crossed the boundary nor when one hour blended into another.

He awoke with nothing to tell him what time it might be. He wasn't sure *which* night it might be, if night it really was. With nothing to provide an anchor to time or place, disorientation became nausea. He tried to picture himself lying in the bed, as if he were the attending physician calmly assessing the battered patient.

The gash on the right side of his skull throbbed under the mound of bandage. The fire in his left hip smoldered. No matter how he experimented, he could not flex so much as a single toe without skewering himself with a great, saw-toothed lance. He could not bend ankle or knee without the same result, yet he could not determine what the center of the injury was.

When the pain struck, his natural reaction was to suck in a breath, and when he made that mistake, it took his mind off head and hip. The lance stabbed him through the torso so savagely that even the opiates provided no more relief than sucking on a piece of willow bark.

He found that the solution was absolute immobility. But Thomas's natural curiosity fed his impatience. He recalled the most recent harangue by the dynamic, animated British physician, Dr. Marcus Hester. In the noted doctor's guest lecture at the university, Hester had maintained that physicians were ill advised to allow patients to lollygag about in bed, waiting for joints to heal themselves. A joint must move, Dr. Hester had argued. A joint must not be allowed to freeze into uselessness. "If we surrender to pain," Hester had said, one index finger pointing toward the heavens, "we resign ourselves to immobility, and then, without fail, uselessness. If we wish to create cripples, let them languish in bed."

Thomas had listened in rapt attention, sitting in the comfort of the university's medical school theater—imagining along with the other students the frightful damage to *other* people's joints.

He could imagine Hester exhorting him. The healthy always knew what was best for the hurting. Thomas lay in the darkness, thoroughly depressed. He might end up walking like some peg-legged survivor of Gettysburg, scarred face startling the ladies.

Thomas experimented with his right hand, inching his fingers across to the great pad of bandages that corseted his torso. *I am still alive, and I am breathing,* he thought.

That was small consolation, since the world outside was passing him by. The raw excitement of arriving in this new country grew stale and distant. It was not possible to lie in this bed, in this room, for days, weeks, maybe months. He was but twenty-six years old. He had things to do.

Yet every time he so much as twitched, the lance promptly stabbed him into pathetic, gasping submission. At one point, shortly after a particular vicious attack had left him drained and on the brink of passing out, he heard cautious footsteps enter the room. *Don't touch me,* he thought, but could not bring himself to risk uttering the words.

"Can you hear me?" a soft, feminine voice asked. Its owner bent down so close that he could feel her breath against his left ear.

"Yes." He let the word out as nothing more than a whisper.

"I want to open the window and the curtains," she said. "It's impossibly beautiful outside today, and the fresh air would do you good."

"Wonderful," he said, or thought . . . he wasn't sure which.

"I didn't want to startle you," she said, and a wash of sunlight sliced across the room. He willed himself to lie like the dead, and listened as the girl—he assumed it was but a girl, the voice sounded so youthful—lifted the window. He felt the stir of breeze.

"Now you'll feel better," she said. The bandage around his head allowed him to see only her bottom half, silhouetted against the light. Tall, perhaps. Thin enough that hip bones marked her apron. She stood quietly, and he assumed that she was examining him. "The doctor said that the mule rolled right on top of you, and that you would have drowned if Jake hadn't been so quick-witted."

This would be Alvina, he thought.

"We're going to try some broth this morning," she continued. "But that's going to take some planning. We don't want you gagging."

No, we don't.

"Let me adjust that bandage a little," she said. "How can you see like that?" He heard her turn away, then the sound of a cabinet opening. In a moment she was beside him again. "I'm just going to trim around your left eye a little. They got carried away, didn't they? But then again, there wasn't much to see, and you weren't in any condition to see it. Alvi will be in later to do a more artistic job."

He closed his eyes, feeling the feather touch of her fingers, the gentle snick of the scissors. So this *wasn't* Dr. Haines's daughter, Alvina. The housekeeper? The owner of the Mercantile had mentioned her name. Gertrude something.

"There. That's better."

He opened his left eye—the right one was buried under a mound of bandages. The light was still behind her, but he could see that his first assessment had been right. Despite the wonderful voice, this woman was thin as a scarecrow.

"What do you think?" she asked. "Are you in terrible discomfort?"

Discomfort. That word appeared in a myriad of textbooks and lectures, written by someone who wasn't in any at the time.

"Yes."

"Well, I would think so," she said. "I know exactly where the accident happened. My soul, you couldn't have chosen a worse spot."

"What happened at the mill?"

"One of the sawyers slipped and managed to become hung up in the log carriage somehow. I don't know more than that. I'm afraid the poor man passed away."

Thomas closed his eye. "I was close," he whispered.

"Yes, you were. Everyone thinks you were so heroic to do what you did, riding out like that. I'm told that even Mr. Schmidt wants to meet you."

"Who?"

"Mr. Bert Schmidt. He owns the mill out on the point. We're just about a company town here in Port McKinney. He said he might stop by this afternoon to meet you."

"I don't need . . . a circle of mourners," he managed.

The woman reached out and rested her hand on a small patch of exposed forehead above Thomas's left eye.

"You're one of his nurses?"

"My, no. I'm Gertrude James, Dr. Parks. I'm the housekeeper. Gert, most folks call me." She said something to herself and then adjusted the thin blanket. "The doctor will want to talk to you here in a little bit. Then we'll see about eating something."

We'll see, Thomas thought dismally. He watched Gert as she worked in front of the glass cabinet across the room. "I shall return in a moment," she said, and left. Thomas reached up carefully with his right hand, delighted to discover that his arm worked freely. He wiped his lips and held his fingers close, examining them. Then a twinge of apprehension tightened around his gut. Gertrude James had returned, this time carrying a small hypodermic needle in a white enameled pan. He watched her closely.

"What is it?" he whispered.

"We're trying to keep you from coughing so much," she said.

"The morphine helps. You breathed in about half of the inlet, and Lord knows what else. Every time you cough, it sounds as if you're trying to turn inside out."

With deft, practiced hands, she arranged his arm, found the vein, and slipped the needle in before he could think of anything else to say. And in seconds, the warm fuzz of the opiate pressed him deeper into the soft mattress. He let his body relax, his initial apprehension about a housekeeper administering injections drifting away. The morphine didn't actually do much for the pain itself, he observed. Rather, the drug simply made the pain not matter.

Her light touch settled on his shoulder. "I'll be nearby, should you need anything."

"Better luck," he whispered.

She laughed pleasantly. "That's true for us all, Dr. Parks." She stood for a moment, looking at him. "Mr. Lindeman told me that Prince didn't bite you . . . That's something, at least."

He lay quiet, wishing the window were a foot lower so that he could see something other than bright light. Far in the distance, a steam whistle shrieked, a reminder that the world was continuing its commerce without him.

He dozed off, then awoke listening to muffled voices. For how long he had done so, he had no idea, nor did he remember—if he had known in the first place—what the gist of the conversation was. As his consciousness clarified, he tried to distance himself from the battered creature who lay in the bed with weak, shaky breaths coming in agonizing little stabs.

The door clicked open, and Thomas opened his left eye to see who he assumed was the man who had been his father's closest friend for more than sixty years. Thomas knew that his father, Fredrick Parks, and John Haines had been delivered by the same midwife within hours of each other in the tiny village of Essex, Connecticut. He'd heard that story a dozen times. John and Fredrick had shared a childhood that had been one of pastoral delights, and Thomas had listened to his father tell endless tales, most of them no doubt tall, of childhood escapades.

The distinguished physician moved one of the large, heavy chairs close to the bed. He sat down heavily and regarded Thomas in silence.

Thomas turned his head a fraction so he could see Haines without effort. The old man's white beard and mustache were tinged from years of enjoying pipe and cigars, but his lively blue eyes, framed by deep crow's-feet, twinkled. His large, fleshy nose showed the signs of good living, the tiny capillaries running close to the surface.

"So," Haines said at last. "How's my boy this morning?"

"I don't know," Thomas managed. "I don't feel . . ." He stopped, the list too long.

Haines leaned forward a little. "Well, for what it's worth, *I'm* pleased, young man. You have the most damnably remarkable set of bruises I've ever seen—and a laceration or two that required stitching. Two or three broken ribs, perhaps. But that's the extent of it . . . I think. I want to take another look at that right eye. That's worrisome."

"Fracture?" Thomas asked.

"It's hard to tell, with all the swelling." He reached up and touched his own right eye, at the outer end of his bushy gray eyebrow. "That's where you and the rocks collided first, I think. It's fortunate you have a hard head." He watched Thomas's face.

"The mule rolled over you, and that explains the rib damage," he went on. "You're bruised from clavicle to hip to sternum and back again."

"How long have I been . . ."

"Useless? I understand that you were off the boat less than an hour before your spectacular dive into the sea. That was Saturday, the day before yesterday, shortly before the dinner hour. Now I feel all the worse for not having met you on the dock."

"Then we might both have ended up—"

The older physician waggled a finger. "I have a policy, you see, and you might well adopt a similar one. I do my patients no benefit by *not* arriving, Thomas. I take my time, you see. Better to arrive at the scene of carnage five minutes tardy than not arrive at

all." He leaned forward and patted Thomas's left forearm. "But"—
he shrugged expansively, straightening his gold-brocade vest—
"that's not the concern at the moment." He pulled a gold watch
from one vest pocket and snapped it open. "I have a number of
calls to make. Then, late this afternoon, I'll be back to inflict a
little torture. I want another look at that eye. You rest. Then we'll
see what we find."

5

Thomas dozed fitfully. The opiates prompted bizarre, troubled dreams, often of the *Alice* floundering. After one such
episode, he awoke to an oddly textured gray sky. Then he realized he was staring, not at an expanse of sky, but instead at an
expanse of waistcoat. He focused on the watch chain that decorated the spread of tweed. The individual gold links formed an
interesting pattern against the vest.

"How's the nausea? I was called out, and when I returned Alvi
reported that you'd had a bit of a bout."

"I don't remember," Thomas managed. Neither the nausea
nor Alvi. He reached down and worked the thin linen sheet up
toward his chin.

"Well, that's good, then. Unpleasant things are best left un-
recalled." Haines bent over the bed, scrutinizing the white bandage around Thomas's skull. "Let's take a look, now."

The physician took off his jacket, and once again Thomas
smelled the rich combination of tobacco, alcohol, and pharmacy. "I've sent a telegram to your father," the physician continued. "I thought that he should know the particulars."

"He'll just worry," Thomas whispered.

"Ah, he will. But that's his due, I think. I promised to send
him a complete report on a regular basis. Perhaps if you wanted

to compose something, I could include that. Paper and pencil."
He pointed at the table beside the bed, within easy reach.

"I think I can get up," Thomas said.

"No, you can't," Haines countered. "Not yet, anyway. Let's
have a look, now. You took a fearsome rap on the head, my boy.
That's my major worry at this point, along with those nasty rib
fractures. The rest of you is one big bruise, but bruises will
heal."

He clipped the end of the bandage and with a light touch un-
wrapped his nurse's handiwork. A little tug brought a flash of
pain, and Thomas winced.

"Ah, those stitches," Haines said, "but that's getting to it now."
He fussed some more, humming to himself. "You want to examine?" he asked, pulling back. "Of course, you do. Professional
curiosity, if nothing else." In a moment he returned with a large
looking glass. With an odd mix of eagerness and apprehension,
Thomas stared at the apparition in the glass.

His right eye was swollen shut. A patch of hair the diameter of
a teacup had been shaved forward from his right ear. The sutures
nestled in a path of black and blue that began just over his ear,
arching upward and then down to cross along the ridge of his
right eyebrow, finally curling upward toward his hairline in the
center of his forehead. The sutures secured a large flap of his
scalp that had torn free. Haines brought the mirror closer. The
sutures were magnificently tiny and uniform. Still, it would be
impossible to judge the scar until the swelling and bruising subsided. He was a purple and black mess.

"My guess is that your hard skull took most of the force of the
blow. Now, whether there's a fracture, we won't know." The physician laid the mirror back on the dresser. "Let's get a fresh dressing
on this," he said. He cocked his head as if measuring his patient's
hat size, then fashioned a neat, light pad that he deftly held in
place with two strips of gauze around Thomas's head.

"We'll want to guard against sepsis, but there's no point in
turning you into an Egyptian mummy," Haines said, and flashed

an engaging smile at the young man. "But you know that, I'm sure." He stepped back, admiring his handiwork. "Headache?"

"Nothing that I wouldn't expect," Thomas replied.

"Ears ring?"

"No."

"Any throbbing in that eye?"

"Some. Mostly in the rest of my head."

"That's good, then."

"I need to get up."

"Ah, well, you shouldn't, you know," Haines said. "Give it another day or so. Just for the sake of the head and the ribs. There's nothing to be gained by rushing things. For one thing, you won't have the balance of a two-year-old for a while after a rap like that. Your hip took a nasty wrenching as well. So, indulge in our hospitality, Thomas. Let yourself be pampered. Then, when you're fit, working twenty-four hours a day will be the norm." His beard bobbed. "We need your help here, you see. No doubt about that. I can't tell you how eager we've been, anticipating your arrival. Perhaps not such a spectacular arrival as you provided, but . . ." He shrugged and thrust his fingers into the small pockets of his waistcoat. "You're here now. Take the time to heal properly. Before you know it, you'll be up and about."

The door behind the physician opened just far enough to allow Gert James to peer into the room.

"Dr. Haines, Dr. Riggs wondered what time you'd be by the clinic."

"Ah," Haines said. "Well," and he turned back to Thomas, "as you can see, life goes on, my young friend."

"And Mr. Schmidt wanted to stop by. I invited him for dinner at eight," Gert added.

Haines grinned affectionately at the angular woman, then winked conspiratorially at Thomas. "She rules my life, you see. Soon enough, yours, too."

"Well, *someone* has to," Miss James sniffed. She withdrew, leaving the door ajar.

The physician pointed at the paper and pencil. "Write your

father, if you feel up to it, Thomas. I'll see that it's wired promptly. He'd like to hear from you."

Alone in the room after they left, the silence exacerbated Thomas's impatience. As his vision cleared a bit, he examined his surroundings, from the lace curtains to the brocaded wall covering that stretched from the walnut wainscoting to the white plaster ceiling. A single cabinet with glass doors stood in the corner, a small bureau against the far wall. More of a guest bedroom than an examining room, it was the perfect place to tuck an invalid—out of sight, out of mind.

With care, Thomas moved his right foot a fraction, easing it toward the edge of the bed. The ache in his left hip was instant and deep, but he clenched his teeth and gained another inch. The light blanket pulled with the movement, and he turned it down a bit, grateful that his right arm worked passably well. He held the arm up, cocking his head for a clear look. Other than a dark bruise just below his elbow, the arm was intact. Like a man hanging from an invisible trapeze, he lifted his left arm and held it parallel with his right. A cast locked left wrist and thumb, leaving four fingers free.

Using his right hand, he lifted the blanket away and saw that he was wearing only a pair of red flannel bottoms. A wide swath of bandages bound his ribs, and as he ran his fingers along the field of cotton, he found the tender spot centered over his fifth and sixth ribs.

He could not pinpoint the source of the deep, dark ache in his left hip, but when he tried to move his left foot, the ache turned into a trident, skewering him from shoulder to toe.

Relaxing, he tried to slow his breathing. He could hear the traffic of the village outside, and each sound beckoned him. "This is absurd," he said aloud. He found a purchase in the flannel fabric above his right knee and began to pull, trying to flex his right leg at the knee. An inch at a time, he was able to draw his right leg up until his foot rested flat on the mattress. He would be able to rest the pad of paper on his thigh. If nothing else, he could spend his time writing and studying. Sometime within the month, his trunk of books and materials would arrive, shipped overland. Within a month. He groaned, unable to imagine lying helpless in bed for so long.

Laying his right leg flat again, he shifted and tried to roll on his side. That was impossible, and he lay back, sucking air in little gasps, furious.

The door opened again and Gert James reappeared. One eyebrow shot up as she saw the linen blanket pulled aside. Thomas hadn't the strength to cover himself, and Miss James accomplished the task with a casual flip of the coverlet.

"I heard you thrashing about," she said. "You oughtn't to do that."

"I can't stay here like this."

A raspy, dry chuckle greeted that pronouncement. "I don't see many choices at the moment," the housekeeper said. "Maybe something to eat is in order."

Thomas stared at the ceiling, aware now of an urgency in his bladder that promised all manner of complications. Gert James moved closer to the bed and gazed down at him. As if reading his mind, she bent slightly and with just the tip of her finger flicked the enameled metal bedpan that rested on the sheets within easy reach. Thomas hadn't seen the pan, and he nodded in both relief and resignation.

"If you're needing help, you'll have to say so," she said. "I'll be back in a few minutes with some nourishment."

"Thanks, Miss James."

"'Gert' is fine, Doctor." She squeezed his foot and turned to leave.

"Maybe you'd help me sit up," Thomas said.

"That I can do." She opened the armoire in the corner to the left of the bedstead and drew out three large pillows. "Now then," she said, and paused at Thomas's bedside. "What hurts the most?"

"Every bone in my body."

"Oh, stuff and nonsense. Here now," and she piled the pillows on the bed within easy reach, then returned to slip a hand behind Thomas's shoulders. She was surprisingly strong, and Thomas couldn't contain a gasp as his hip and ribs protested. Gert hesitated long enough to reach for one of the pillows and slide it down behind him. "Far enough?"

"Once more," Thomas panted. He could smell the fragrance in her wiry hair as she bent close, wrapping both angular arms around him.

"Just relax now," she said. "Let me do it." He sucked in a breath as his hip once more flexed, and his head pounded anew. "There," Gert said with satisfaction, and patted the stack of pillows. "Is that better?"

" 'Torture' is the word I would have chosen."

She had rescued the bedpan and held it out. "Give you something else to think about." Thomas laughed in spite of himself, and instantly regretted it. "I'll be back," Gert promised.

"You need to tell me about this place," he said.

"Oh, I can do that, all right," she said, nodding with approval. "Take care of things, and we'll see."

He waited for a moment after the door latched behind the housekeeper, and tried to cope with the awkward shape of the bedpan. One leg he could move in tiny increments, the other was a dead log. Eventually he managed, and as he lay with his eye closed, trying to relax enough to accomplish a simple bodily function, he became aware of voices that drifted in through the open window. Outside—perhaps across Gambel Street at the Mercantile—the voices rose in argument, and were punctuated now and then with loud thumps and a dog's heavy, insistent barking.

A still louder crash was followed by a howl of pain, another flurry of barking, and then a report, flat and muffled. Something struck the side of the house below his window, and then another shot pealed out.

He slid the bedpan out from under the blanket and set it on the bed instead of reaching for the nightstand. More voices babbled outside, and the dog's barking grew wild. Thomas managed to swing his right leg to the edge of the bed, and then, dragging his left leg with both hands, he let gravity do the work. In a flash of panic, he realized that the bed was higher than he had expected. The pillows cascaded off the bed, and Thomas fought to regain his balance.

With a cry, he crashed from the bed. His head cracked the edge of the nightstand and bright lights danced across the wood floor. He lay absolutely still, crumpled on his right side, trying to breathe. He could feel a warm, wet trickle running down his cheek to the corner of his mouth. For an instant, he imagined that the bedpan had upended, but then the coppery taste told him otherwise. He reached out his left hand and grasped one of the pillows, hugging it to his ribs. He rested his head on one corner of the pillow and closed his eyes, letting the throbbing sink into the goose down.

6

W ell, for heaven's sake," the voice said, and Thomas Parks awoke with a painful start. "How did you manage this, old man? Ah, now look at that. You've done a workmanlike job of it." Thomas's vision was blurred, but the pillow appeared to be wadded partially under a piece of furniture.

"Here, fetch Alvina," the man said, his speech touched with a light accent. As he bent close, his powerful cologne wafted ahead of him. "How do you feel, my good man? It looks like you've cracked the old pate open."

Thomas mumbled something, disoriented by his odd position. He could see one of the lower legs of the mahogany nightstand and the little curl of dust wrapped around its back foot. Equally obvious was an ugly, dried puddle on the oak flooring and a stain that spread across the crumpled pillow.

"There must be more comfortable places to take one's rest," the man observed. "Ah, here we are."

"How did we manage all this?" a feminine voice said. Thomas tried to turn his head, but two powerful hands held him in position.

"Just wait a moment," the man said, then added, "I'm afraid you're not going to appreciate this, old man." From floor to bed was a mere thirty-six inches, but it seemed miles and hours as hands lifted him up from the floor and into the bed.

Once more flat on his back, Thomas forced himself to lie absolutely still, trying to find his wind as skilled fingers fussed with the bandage on his head. "You don't want to do that again," the girl's voice said, her tone a simple statement of fact.

"You won't need me, then?" the man asked. "I'll be off." Thomas opened his left eye and saw only the broad tweed back as the burly figure left the room.

As she worked, the young woman's face was inches from his own, her forehead furrowed with concentration. "Do something useful and hold that," she said. Her breath was lightly touched with peppermint. She guided Thomas's right hand up. "Right there," she said. He held the bandage pad in place as she fussed with the gauze binding. "You nearly ruined my stitching."

"I'm sorry." He didn't have a clear view of this girl, but her hands were strong and deft. "You're Alvina," Thomas whispered.

"Last I looked. What exactly were you trying to do? Are you one of those mountain men who is more comfortable sleeping on the floor than in a perfectly fine bed?"

"I heard something out in the street. A ruckus of some kind."

"And you got up to see what it was," Alvina said, and touched the side of his face lightly, just a casual, informal stroke of affection. "Don't do that again." She was Thomas's age, dressed entirely in white linen, her figure compact, even stocky. She regarded Thomas critically, and he felt naked to her gaze. After a moment, she reached out and pulled the sheet up a bit.

"What happened outside?" Thomas asked. "I heard a gun-shot."

Her lips pursed thoughtfully. Her eyes were a brilliant blue flecked with sea foam green, set wide in a face with a flawless complexion and broad, pleasant features.

"It's my understanding that Mr. Lindeman had some trouble with one of his customers. Other than that, I couldn't tell you. I was down at the clinic, and have only rumor on which to rely. I didn't suppose any of it was my business."

"I heard shots," Thomas persisted.

"Yes, no doubt you did." She reached out and rested the back of her fingers against his right cheek. "But you're nice and cool," she said. "If we can convince you to behave yourself, you'll heal nicely."

"Was anyone hurt?" he persisted.

"Apparently so. I'm told a fatality. I didn't see the incident."

Thomas emitted a loud, groaning sigh of frustration. "I can't just lie here all day. I'll go insane."

"Well, now," Alvina said, and she folded her hands on the edge of the bed. "Perhaps 'convalescence' was included in your curriculum at university?"

Gentle as it was, the taunting surprised him, coming from this girl whom he had just met. Her tone turned serious. "Father is concerned about your right eye, Dr. Thomas Parks." Moving down the bed slightly so that he could see her without effort, she touched the margin of her own eye at the end of a shapely blond eyebrow. "He thinks that there might be a fracture of the orbit itself. There's no displacement, but he's concerned that there might be bleeding and pressure. It would be *most* helpful if you'd let things mend a bit before you indulge in any more heroics." The eyebrow rose like a schoolmarm's silent discipline.

"It wasn't a question of heroics," Thomas said. "I didn't travel three thousand miles to lie abed like some invalid. I want . . ."

She reached out and patted the back of his right hand and he stopped abruptly, embarrassed at sounding like a petulant child.

"I'm sorry," he said lamely.

"This evening, Mr. Schmidt would like to call. Do you think you might manage a visitor?"

"Of course. He's—"

"Mr. Schmidt owns the sawmill on the point. Where you were headed Saturday."

"Ah."

"Perhaps about eight," Alvina said. "If you're awake."

"I shall try to be."

She regarded him fondly for a moment. "When we heard you were coming to join father's clinic, we all were delighted. In just a few days' time, you'll be working so hard you won't remember this misfortune. But give yourself those few days, Dr. Parks."

"Thomas, please. And believe me, I will welcome the work."

"Dr. *Thomas*, then."

"The sooner that I can be of use, the better."

She hesitated, and he saw the speculation in her eyes. "Suppose I bring you something to occupy your mind, Dr. Thomas. How would that be? You might find some difficulty reading, but we'll see."

"Even a journal or two," he said. "I'd appreciate that, Alvina."

"Alvi." This time she smiled, revealing even, white teeth. "Give me a moment." She gave his arm a final pat and left the room.

Alvina Haines. The young woman took command as a veteran nurse might, Thomas thought. He lay with his eyes closed, and gradually the walls closed in once again, the room growing stuffy. True to her word, less than ten minutes passed before she returned. Thomas felt an odd surge of relief as she entered the room, this time carrying a newspaper that she placed on the nightstand.

"Let's elevate you just a bit more," she said, and in short order and torture he was propped up, cradled by fluffy feather pillows. "How's that?"

"Better."

"Is the pain troublesome? If you can manage without sedation, we think it best to keep it at a minimum. Perhaps later this evening we'll give you something to help you sleep."

"I'll be fine."

Satisfied, she patted his knee again and nodded at the newspaper. "I'll leave this on the nightstand at your right."

"I neglected to ask," Thomas said. "The gentleman who so deftly moved me from floor to bed? We haven't met."

"Well, my apologies," Alvina said. "I'm sure he'll be in to chat with you when you're feeling more like yourself. That's Dr. Zachary Riggs. He works with father and me at the clinic."

"Ah." Then she *was* a nurse. He reached out to pull the newspaper closer.

"It arrived in the post on Friday," Alvina replied.

"I thank you," he said. He saw the San Francisco banner on the paper.

"Well, it's a start," she said. "Don't strain your eyes."

A young woman with a good deal of self-confidence, Thomas thought, guessing that she was in no way intimidated by the physicians who orbited around her.

"I'll check back from time to time," she said, and nodded toward the nightstand. "If there's an urgency, someone will be within hearing." She reached across and lifted a short, fat tumbler that was half full of liquid. "Father left you brandy," she said skeptically. "But let me suggest that it be sipped only enough to taste it on the tongue. Otherwise, it's apt to make you cough, and you don't want that."

"No, I don't," Thomas agreed. "Really, I'm fine."

"That's good. Gert will have some light dinner for you in a little bit. I should imagine by now you're about inside out with hunger, but just take your time. Your body needs time to adjust, and you'll find chewing painful."

For a few minutes after Alvina had left the room, Thomas lay still, his left eye closed.

7

The newspaper promised some curiosities, and Thomas spent five minutes with it, annoyed both by the difficulty of folding it neatly and by the news that didn't apply to his world. It did nothing to assuage his frustration.

Thomas did not recall the details of his plunge into the cold waters of the inlet, but he *did* recall the excitement he had felt when he responded to the initial summons for help at the sawmill. That was immediate. That was medicine on the front lines. The throbbing in his right temple increased as he tried to force himself to lie still, to relax, to mend. What if he could no longer walk? What if the ligaments and tendons in his hip had been so torn and twisted that they would heal in a frozen, useless lump, forcing him to hitch along with crutches or a cane? What if he were blind in one eye, unable to manage the intricate feats of depth perception necessary in the surgery? He heard a loud groan, and realized with a start that it had issued from himself, frustration mixed with self-pity.

He turned his head, reaching up with one hand to hold the bandage.

"I can't do this," he said aloud.

"Do what?" The voice startled him, and he pulled his hand away to see Alvina standing in the open doorway. "You're talking to yourself. I'm not sure that's a good sign."

"I'm sorry." He tried a smile. "I was remembering all the wrong things."

"That's what lying about accomplishes, I think." Alvi stepped up close to the bed. "I looked in on you earlier, but you were asleep. I didn't want to wake you."

"I was asleep? I would have been grateful for the company. I can't lie here like some dead fish, rotting while the world goes on without me." He touched the newspaper. "I wasn't taken to the clinic after the accident . . ."

She reached out and touched his cheek. "And I don't think you're rotting, Dr. Thomas." She withdrew her hand and regarded him with amusement. "I've heard Father say that physicians make the worst patients. I see now that he is correct."

"I want to get up, and I want to eat, and I want to go outside . . . Shall I go on?"

"If it gives you pleasure, Dr. Thomas. You slept through dinner, but Gert has prepared a plate for you. Do you think you can sit up a little straighter?"

"Slept through?" he asked. "How is that possible? And yes, please . . . anything," Thomas replied fervently.

"My goodness, yes," she chided. "We're going on the third day now, after all." She stood back and watched. Thomas waited. "You see?" she said after a moment.

"See what?"

"If you want to get out of bed, the first step will be to sit up by yourself."

He grimaced with impatience. "Of course," he said. "I just thought . . ." He pushed carefully, trying to turn this way and that, finding an impasse with each movement until he could feel the sheen of sweat on his forehead.

"Now, let me—" Alvi said, moving close.

"No," he snapped. He held up his left hand.

"At least let me manage the pillows," she said, and in a moment he rested back against the feather pillows. "So," she continued, "right after you've had a bit to eat, we'll go for a bracing stroll down to the harbor and back."

He saw the twinkle in her eyes. Again her fingers ran down his cheek. "You fancy a beard?" she asked, and he stumbled over an appropriate reply, unused to young women so forward in nature.

"No. I had one once," he said. "I looked like a dog with the mange."

She laughed and smoothed the sheet a bit, pulling it up over his chest. Her face became sober. "The meal will be modest," she said. "I know that you could eat a banquet right now, but moderation is prudent. With injuries such as yours, nausea is a common companion. We don't want that."

"No, we don't," Thomas said. "I *am* a physician, you know."

"Yes. For better or worse, you are." She patted his thigh with a familiarity that made him blush. "Gert will be in in a moment." She pointed at the corner, and for the first time Thomas saw that the wicker chair there was actually a wheelchair. "If you tolerate food well, then in the morning, we'll see."

As she turned to leave, it seemed urgent to Thomas that Alvi Haines remain, if even for an instant more. "You mentioned that the mill owner might stop by," he said. "I don't recall his name."

Without so much as a pause, she said over her shoulder, "He did. We enjoyed a fine dinner, but you were asleep. Perhaps when you're up and about." She stopped in the hallway. "Mr. Schmidt wishes you well, Dr. Thomas. He looks forward to meeting you." She disappeared from view, and Thomas let out a long exhalation of resignation.

8

————

Well, well," Dr. John Haines said, and his full beard bobbed. "You're going to repair very nicely." He tilted his head back so he could see through his half-glasses. One massive hand rested on top of Thomas's skull, turning the young man's head this way and that.

"Close your left eye, now," he instructed, and Thomas did so, trying not to scrunch up his face. "You know, I've seen probably a million sutures in my time. The very best of them were tied by my daughter. Little old ladies who labor over quilts have nothing on her." He peered into Thomas's right eye, his thumb applying just enough gentle pressure on the underside of the swollen eyebrow to lift the lid. He hummed to himself thoughtfully. "Am I hurting you?"

Thomas murmured an untruthful no.

"I'm sorry I missed your excursion this afternoon. Alvi tells me it was spectacular." With the one hand locked on Thomas's head, he held the other out at arm's length, index finger pointing upward. "Follow my finger, Thomas." His breath was strong with tobacco and brandy. "Focus?"

"I think so."

"Read that sign on the opposite wall for me."

"There is no sign on the opposite wall, Doctor." Thomas felt Haines twist, and the grip on his skull released.

"Well, now. So there isn't. I used to have one there, back in the old days, when we used this as an examining room. Well." He stood up, hands on his hips. "I'm pleased, Thomas." He pulled a gold watch from his vest and regarded it judiciously. "Alvi tells me that you were able to keep down some supper."

"Yes. It tasted good."

"Oh, that's a guarantee. Gert does magical things with the simplest food." The physician turned and hooked the wheelchair out of the corner with his toe. He turned and sat in it carefully. "Handy thing, this," he said, patting the wicker arms. He pushed closer to the bed and rested his chin on his hand. "We haven't really had the chance to talk, have we? I've been in and out, and we could say that you have been as well. You've slept most of the time, and I've been loath to wake you, sleep being the perfect restorative."

"Enough is enough," Thomas replied.

Haines laughed. "Ah, the impatience of youth." He lowered his arm and leaned forward, picking up one of the small tumblers on the nightstand. "Nightcap?" he said as he hefted the brandy bottle. "It's really very nice. Have you tried it?"

"I haven't." The glass on the nightstand was empty, but not by his doing.

"Well, then." Haines decanted a small amount in one of the glasses and held it out to Thomas, then splashed a generous half tumbler for himself. He held up the glass. "To your arrival on our shores, Thomas. My God, it's good to see you."

"Such as I am," Thomas replied, and touched his glass to the other. "It's *going* to be good to be here." He touched his tongue to the liquor. Haines polished off the first glass and refilled.

"So tell me," he said finally. "What's your passion, Thomas?"

"My passion, sir?"

The beard bobbed and more brandy disappeared. "Yes. Why travel some what, three thousand miles or more?" He held up a hand quickly. "And please. Don't misunderstand me. We're delighted that you've come. It's a dream come true for us, I assure you. But what is it that you seek? What spurs you on, Thomas?" He held up both fists and shook them dramatically, endangering the brandy that sloshed in the glass. "After all, you've studied in the very heart of modern medicine, Thomas. That must have been exciting, was it not? To listen to all the greats? To be at the very core of all the marvelous debates and developments and discoveries that are surely changing the course of modern medicine?" He took a deep pull of brandy, his eyes going to half-mast with pleasure as he did so.

He lowered the glass and looked at Thomas. "Leaving all that for our miserable little village . . . that must have been a difficult decision." Before Thomas could comment, the doctor waved his glass and continued on. "I mean, here we are, soaked in the mists, mucking along, right in the middle of the most amazing squalor, right in the middle of some of the most *lunatic* undertakings that man ever imagined. My God."

He ran his finger around the rim of the glass thoughtfully. "You know, I received the June issue of *Journal Medica* last week. That's how far from the center of things our little world is, Thomas. My journals are three months out of date when they find this soggy place. Delivery of pharmaceuticals, of equipment, of anything you might imagine, is sporadic and always delayed."

He waved a hand with impatience. "Listen to me prattle on like an old woman." Haines drained the glass and reached for the bottle, adding another inch.

"So I ask you, tell me about your dreams. What is your passion, my good young man? What are you looking for here? Thank God that you did, but why have you come to join us?"

"You invited me, sir."

Haines tipped his head back and bellowed a laugh. "That's a fine thing," he said, regarding Thomas fondly. "You've inherited a measure of your mother's directness, bless her soul. Indeed I did invite you here. And now I want to know why you accepted the offer with such alacrity. You could stay in Philadelphia and become a wealthy man . . . but I suppose you may be that already."

"There is wealth everywhere, sir, just as there is pain and suffering everywhere, but the excitement is on the fringes. That's what I saw on my trip. Once things become established, something in the excitement is lost."

"Really. The old frontier-spirit business."

"I suppose so."

"And excitement? That's what you seek in medicine? Some sort of frontier?"

Thomas reached over and carefully set the glass on the nightstand, clutching one of the pillows tight to his chest with his other arm. He settled back and took a slow, deep breath, right to the point where the battered ribs said "no more."

"Exactly what happened to me," he said.

"A certain irony there," Haines observed.

"Yes, I see that. But what excites me are the decisions to be made immediately following a catastrophic event . . . and more than just a few cuts and bruises, I must say. But when the patient's life hangs in the balance, when there are but moments, perhaps even seconds, that decide whether he bleeds to death or lives. Whether his next faltering inhalation will be his last."

"My word," Haines said. "You bring back memories."

"Of the war, you mean?"

"Indeed, and not such welcome ones, either." He drained the glass again, and then rolled it between his fingers, watching the

42

patterns in the glass catch the light from the single gas wall sconce behind the nightstand. "That was a long time ago," he said, and dismissed the recollection. "Well," he said, and dropped one foot to the floor, pushing his chair back away from the bed. "You need some rest."

"That's all I've had the past days, sir."

"Ah, then *I* need some rest, Thomas." He stood up carefully and returned the wheelchair to the corner. "Tomorrow I want you out and about. We'll help you to this chair, and then I need to evaluate that hip . . . troublesome, I think. You can spend the day exploring the house. Without doing more damage to yourself, by the way. You'll find my library of interest. We'll have dinner at eight sharp, and we'd be pleased if you would join us, providing you don't wear yourself out."

He moved close to the bed and extended his hands, taking Thomas's in both of his. "Welcome to one-oh-one, Thomas."

"Thank you, sir." Dr. Haines reached up toward the gaslight. "I'd prefer you left the light, sir."

"Certainly." Haines saw the newspaper and cocked his head. "Perhaps you'd prefer a journal or two? Not that I have any that you haven't already seen months ago."

"That would be welcome . . . and the wheelchair as well. I look forward to visiting the clinic."

"Ah." Haines nodded. "I hope you won't be disappointed. It's rather modest."

"Is it far from here?"

"In your condition, it might as well be on the other side of the world," Haines replied. "Six blocks only. That gives you something to strive for, doesn't it? Let's take it one step at a time, shall we? There's no need to rush nature, Thomas. You and Zachary will get on famously, I'm sure. You have much in common."

"I look forward to meeting him," Thomas said. "I have him to thank for rescuing me from my most recent embarrassment, but he didn't remain in the room long enough for us to exchange words."

"He's a busy man, Thomas. I know he'll welcome your assistance. He and Alvi have more to do with the clinic's success than anything I do. Rest easy, young man." He nodded good night, and pulled the door closed as he left the room.

9

The house was dark and silent when Thomas awoke on his right side, his right hand balled under his head. The head wound both ached and itched, and the young man eased onto his back.

The gaslight had been turned off. The outline of the window gradually coalesced, but with no street lamps, the village was as dark as the inside of a closet. After a moment, Thomas realized that the door of his room was open. He could see the outline of the jamb, highlighted by a gas lamp left on far down the hallway.

Moving with the utmost care, he pushed himself farther upright, sitting crooked to favor his left hip and ribs, supporting himself on his hands. He sat thus for a long time. To feel his pulse thumping at the same time from head and hip was an odd sensation. Shifting his weight again, he maneuvered his right leg over the edge of the bed and paused, trying to calm his breathing. The pain in his ribs was sharp and stinging, more acute than it should be.

It seemed so simple to just slide down, taking the weight on his right foot. Simple enough—but exactly the way he'd ended up in a fetal position in the corner after his first excursion.

For a time he sat on the edge of the bed, considering his predicament. " 'Returning were as tedious as go o'er,' " he whispered, but Macbeth was no help.

From somewhere deep in the house came a deep, harrumphing cough. Thomas could picture John Haines tossing in bed, his sleep floating in a sea of brandy. The window curtains behind him stirred, and the air that wafted into the room was damp and cool across his bare shoulders. His eyes had adjusted enough to make out the outline of the wheelchair in the corner.

Keeping his weight on his right hip, he let himself slide off the edge. His right hand shot out to grasp the nightstand. Standing up straight was impossible.

Bent at the waist, both hands now on the edge of the nightstand, Thomas worked away from the support of the bed. He hopped once, rewarded by a stab of pain so agonizing that he gasped aloud. He hopped again, closing the distance toward the chair.

He leaned his weight hard against the nightstand, balanced on his right arm, reaching out for the wall with his left. An inch at a time, he crabbed along the wall. A final, ungainly lunge brought him to the chair, and it rolled backward a few inches until its back thumped the wall.

Hunched over, both hands clinging to the wicker, he considered how to turn so that he might sit down. He realized that he could now see the chair, including the woolen blanket spread over its back. He turned ever so slightly and looked toward the light. The figure stood in the doorway, lamp in hand.

"You are a determined young fellow." Alvina glided into the room on bare feet, wearing a long nightgown and robe. She lit the gaslight and turned it up, the shadows dancing around the room. Satisfied, she turned back to Thomas, who waited by the chair like a desperate hunchback.

"So," she said.

"I'm almost there." Thomas tried to sound lighthearted and gallant.

"Indeed you are. Here," she said. As she drew close, he could smell the fragrance that enveloped her as if she stood perpetually in a field of blossoms. "Put your arm over my shoulders." As skillfully as if she had practiced that very maneuver dozens of times, she hooked the chair with a toe and turned Thomas at the same time. She was strong and practiced. "Now," she said, and he sank into the wicker seat.

He could feel a tear running down his left cheek, and wiped his face with the back of his hand to bring her into focus.

"Are you going to be all right?"

"I think so." He leaned his head back against the blanket pad.

"Let's make that more useful," she said, and in a moment the blanket was draped around his shoulders. She stepped back, hands on her hips. "Nearly human, now," she said.

"What time is it?"

"Just after five."

"Are you certain? It's that late?"

"I'm certain. I heard you thumping and bumping around and was afraid you were exploring the floor again."

"Almost. I'm sorry if I woke you."

"Oh, you didn't. We don't often have patients here at the house, but when we do, I tend to sleep with one ear open. Father wouldn't awaken if the entirety of Puget Sound turned upside down. Do you need the bedpan?"

Thomas found himself blushing, and pulled the blanket around himself . . . and then blushed again at the ridiculousness of it all. He was a physician, after all. The body held no secrets.

"I suppose I do," he said.

"Now that you're on wheels, let's do something easier," she said. "Mind your feet." She pushed him out of the room, and the sense of liberation was amazing. They reached the doorway centered at the end of the hallway, and Alvi stepped around the chair.

The toilet was spacious and for a moment, as he watched her adjust the gaslight and check the water pitcher beside the sink, Thomas was sure that Alvina Haines proposed to assist him all the way.

"The pitcher is full of hot water," she said, patting the edge of the marble sink, "and I'll bring you more in a minute. When you're finished with the toilet, just pull the chain." She turned and touched the brass chain that hung from the suspended water reservoir for the toilet.

46

"I know how they work," Thomas said, more testily than he would have liked.

"That's good. I wasn't sure if Philadelphia was as up-to-date as we are out here in paradise," she said with a straight face. "I'll leave you then." She patted him on the shoulder like an older sister, and bent slightly, hand still on his arm, eyes searching his. "May I get you something for the pain?"

Thomas shook his head carefully, lest it fall off at her feet. "No. I'm fine, really. Thank you." He knew that in all likelihood he was as pale as porcelain, and he could feel the sweat on his forehead.

"I'll be listening for the crash, then." She eased the door closed, leaving him alone.

By the time he struggled back into the wheelchair he was exhausted. He sat for a while, panting, then dabbed himself as best he could with the water from the pitcher. Anything more required balance, and he had none of that.

The hallway was empty when he opened the door and pushed the wheelchair through. Alvi rounded the corner at the end of the hallway, dressed now as she had been the day before, pure white with a white apron, her hair drawn up tight against the back of her head. She carried a white porcelain cup.

"Well, now, you clean up quite nicely. I thought you might like some coffee," she said. "Gert will have breakfast here in a little bit." He drew the blanket up around himself and accepted the cup.

"You're an early riser," he said.

"It's just easier," she said. "I like to have a few moments to myself."

"And now here I am."

"Yes . . . and an incredible nuisance, I might add." She laughed and moved behind his chair.

"I enjoyed talking to your father last night."

"Yes. I noticed the level in the brandy bottle. But he's pleased, Dr. Thomas. He says that you're healing well. You're a very, very lucky young man."

"Sometimes it's hard to see that."

"Well, you are. Now, let me take you on a little tour. And let me know if it's too much."

Shortly, Thomas saw that he had been occupying only one tiny corner of 101 Lincoln Street. Keeping up a steady narrative, she pushed him from room to room, all polished opulence, lighting the gas lamps as she did so.

"Let's see how the air is this morning," she said, and opened a set of double doors. A long, wide porch, well furnished with wicker, graced both sides of the house that faced Lincoln and Gambel Streets.

"This is my favorite place," Alvi said. She let the chair nudge against the ornate white railing. "When we don't have the fog, you can see all the way across to the islands. It's magnificent."

The fog was so dense that he had difficulty seeing the Mercantile across the street. "And the clinic? Where is that from here?"

"Just down the hill. Follow Gambel Street down past the grove of evergreens that the loggers somehow missed."

Thomas pushed the wheel forward. "I've . . ." He interrupted himself and pointed. The dark shadow plodded across toward them, head down, the rise of each bony shoulder marking his steps.

"Oh, that awful dog," Alvi said. "I've never known such a disreputable creature. He seems to have an affinity for the muck." She walked to the head of the steps. "You can just turn around and go home, Prince." The dog ignored her, hesitating only when it appeared that his nose might actually bump against the first riser. He stood thus—whether pondering or calculating or simply blank, Thomas couldn't tell.

The door behind him opened, and the housekeeper appeared. "My soul, Alvina, what are you trying to do, kill this young man?" She pulled her own wrap more securely around her bony shoulders. "It's the damp of the grave out here. For heaven's sake, come in, now. Breakfast is ready."

"It's wonderful out here," Alvi countered. "He needs some relief from being cooped up."

"Well." Gert James started to argue, then saw the dog. "Oh, for heaven's sake. Will you go *home*," she said, and clapped her hands sharply. "If Mr. Lindeman would feed you once in a while," she added. Taking Thomas's chair, Gert spun it around and pushed him toward the door. "Let's get some food in you, too," she said.

IO

Thomas Parks was astonished to find the prospect of bed welcome. The excursion to the bathroom and then managing an enormous breakfast had all been agonizing work.

Back in the room, he found that his clothing had been neatly hung in the armoire and arranged efficiently in two of the drawers of the bureau. Wheeling the chair next to the wardrobe, he pushed the empty duffel to one side and searched for his black medical bag. It was missing. Perhaps it lay at the bottom of the inlet.

An instant after struggling into bed, he awoke with a start, surprised and disoriented. The pungent fragrance of cooking seafood filled the house, and in a moment Alvi Haines appeared, her wrap showing signs of rain.

"Oh, good, you're awake," she said. As she approached the bed, Thomas could smell her damp woolens. "It's positively nasty out. So tell me, what's Connecticut like? It's coastal, too, is it not? Is it the same as this, like the inside of a water bucket?"

"You're joking, of course," he said.

She turned to look at him, eyebrows raised. "Why would that be? I've never been there."

"Never back east? Good heavens. Well, it rains a good deal in Connecticut, too, of course," Thomas said, "but more sunshine than here, I should think. By the way, I'm a bit concerned about my medical bag. There are some things . . ."

"Bertha has it, down at the clinic," Alvi interrupted. "I'm afraid it took a nasty bashing. She wanted to clean all the instruments and see what she could do with the rest."

"Ah. I'm indebted, then. I haven't met the young lady."

"Oh, you will," Alvi said. "So . . ." She stood in what Thomas had learned was a characteristic pose, hands balled into fists on her hips, elbows akimbo, ready to confront the world. "You found your luggage." She nodded toward the armoire. One of its doors stood ajar.

"I did, and thanks to whoever took care of it all. But then, apparently I fell asleep. What time is it?"

"Just after noon."

"My God."

"Shall I help you up for a little while?"

"I can manage," Thomas said.

"I know you *can*, Dr. Thomas. Here." She pulled the wheelchair closer to the bed. "What kind of flexion are you getting with that leg now?"

"None. The progress is that I can move it a bit by hand. It's been busy at the clinic?"

"Always," she replied. "Always. And father was called up the coast to one of the camps to tend a difficult birth, I think." She smiled at the expression on Thomas's face. "He has delivered half the population of Washington, I imagine."

"I had hoped not to spend my practice in obstetrics," Thomas said, and realized immediately how stuffy he sounded.

Alvi laughed. "I'd be interested to learn how that's done."

With no clear idea himself, he changed the subject. "How many patients have you at the clinic?"

She cocked her head. "We have eight beds, and at the moment one of them is occupied. At least until dinnertime."

"Eight beds."

"Yes."

"I had imagined the clinic as considerably larger than that."

"Oh, it will be," Alvi said, "but one sure step at a time. So," and she picked up the robe that lay on the corner of the bed, "are you feeling strong enough to venture to lunch? I could smell the chowder the instant I walked into the house."

"Indeed," Thomas said. "I was thinking of getting dressed today." He fingered the large flannel nightshirt that Alvi had found for him, a cozy thing that encouraged sloth. Even with the rain, he thought, what a fine, invigorating outing to make his way across the rutted street to Lindeman's Mercantile. Or somewhat less ambitious, to walk the length of the front porch. Or to dress himself.

"May I collect your clothing?"

Thomas started to refuse, then thought better of pointless heroics. In a moment, with the clothing lying on the bed, Thomas waited until the door had closed behind Alvi Haines and then rolled onto his right side and hip, working off the baggy pajamas. Pulling on a clean pair of his own long johns was a second endurance contest, but he persisted, an inch gained here and there. He had selected a woolen shirt that he had purchased in San Francisco, and working his arms into the sleeves prompted optimism. Trousers would be impossible, but the huge robe borrowed from John Haines worked perfectly as a housecoat.

Exhausted but quite proud of himself, he wheeled out toward the kitchen. A lanky man whose face appeared to be set in a perpetual grin nodded at Thomas, and the grin spread to bare a prodigious expanse of gums and crooked teeth.

"Well, glory, look who's up," Gert announced.

"Good day to you, sir." The man nodded as if that settled that.

"Good day," Thomas replied. "I'm Thomas Parks." He extended his hand.

"This is my brother, Horace," Gert James said. Horace smiled agreement and shook Thomas's hands with a grip that would have made a blacksmith take notice. "If it weren't for Horace, this big old place would fall down around our ears."

"Oh, go on," Horace rasped. "You going to feed us or yap?"

"As much of both as I please," Gert replied easily. "Here, then." She set a huge earthenware bowl at his place, and slid a loaf of dark brown bread onto the board. "Start on that." Pointing with the wooden spoon, she directed Thomas to the open spot beside Alvi. "Over there, if you please," she ordered, and Thomas wheeled his chair into place. The chowder was thick, a savory deluge of flavors and spices that made his nose run.

"What's in this?" he asked.

"Everything that swims." She patted his shoulder. "Have some bread. I made it just this morning."

The four of them ate in companionable silence, sopping chowder with bread. "I'd best get back," Alvi announced as Gert poured more coffee, first for her brother and then for Thomas.

"You haven't mentioned who your patient is," Thomas said, loath to see her go.

Alvi leaned back. "At the moment, we have one young man from Gershon's Mill up north. He ran afoul of some piece of machinery that removed several necessary body parts," and she grinned as Gert grimaced at her language choice. "I've been stitching on him all morning." She leaned back and looked at the ceiling. "None of his injuries are as serious as they look. And a bit earlier, we had Clarissa. She decided she did not want her baby and—"

"Oh, for heaven's sakes, Alvina," Gert snapped.

"Well," Thomas said, but Gert cut him off.

"I can't bear to imagine what dinners are going to be like," the housekeeper groused. "By the time we have all four of you around the table, serving up these choice tidbits of information that we don't need to hear? It's going to be absolutely repugnant."

"Is there some way that I may be of assistance?" Thomas asked.

"Your time will come." Alvi brightened suddenly. "Oh, and Father received a telegram this morning. His books have shipped. We should have them . . . ," and she made a face. "Someday. Hopefully before we're all old and gray."

"His books?" Thomas said.

"A labor of love," Alvi said. "A 'compendium of helpful medical advice and counsel.'"

"He has written a book?"

"Oh, he has indeed, with Zachary's help. A tome. A volume of weight and dignity." For a moment Thomas could not tell whether Alvi was speaking in jest, but her excitement seemed genuine as she continued, "*The Universal Medical Advisor.* He hasn't mentioned it?"

"No, indeed. He hasn't."

"Well, he's too modest. We have one of the presentation copies in the library. You may find it a delightful way to pass the afternoon, Dr. Thomas."

"I would be in your debt." He pushed himself away from the table. "Thank you so much, Gert. You are a magician."

"You stay warm, now," she admonished.

"I have my robe, and my blanket," Thomas said. "I can steam the day away." Alvi wheeled him to the spacious library, where an impressive collection of volumes rested on shelves towering to the ceiling. "My word," he whispered. An enormous leather chair presided behind a dark, polished wooden desk, its great, carved legs ending in massive claw-and-ball feet.

"Here we are," Alvi said. She indicated a massive volume that rested on the corner of the desk. With leather binding, gilt-edged paper, and a sewn-in ribbon for a bookmark, *The Universal Medical Advisor* was a magnificent book. "Here," Alvi said, and pushed the monstrous leather chair to one side. "You can wheel in here, and just enjoy yourself," she said.

Thomas did so, and pulled the book toward him. "This must weigh ten pounds," he said. "My goodness, what an accomplishment."

"He's very proud," Alvi said. "As you look through it, you'll come to see what he expects of the clinic, and what we're all about."

"I'm enchanted," he said. "You're sure he won't mind me working here?"

"Of course he won't mind. He'll be honored. In fact, he mentioned this morning that you should."

"I was wondering," Thomas said, resting his bandaged left hand on the book. "Do you have a set of crutches I might use?"

"Of course. Do you think that's wise, with your ribs as they are?"

He grinned. "It would be helpful, I think. Some gentle therapy will be just the thing."

"I'll fetch them, then." She stepped across the room. "And this is the shelf that matters, as Father would say." She pushed open a small, carved folding door to reveal a generous decanter and a silver tray holding six glasses. "He would tell you to help yourself."

In a moment she reappeared with the crutches. "I'll leave them here," she said, placing them in the corner within easy reach. "That door?" and she pointed off to Thomas's left. "That leads to the porch as well. Perhaps a safe promenade for you."

"All the town can cheer as I crash down the front steps."

"You'd best not. That would make us very unhappy indeed," Alvi said. "Perhaps if you don't wear yourself out, we'll see you at dinner?"

"Would you make sure?" Thomas said. "I seem to be doing a prodigious amount of sleeping of late. If you'd wake me in time, I'd appreciate it. Will Dr. Riggs join us today?"

"I would think so."

"Good. I look forward to thanking him properly. We haven't had a chance to do so much as say a how-do-you-do. He must think me a terrible imposition."

"I don't suppose he thinks that at all," Alvi said, and left him with a bright smile.

Thomas pulled the enormous volume closer and fingered open the weighty cover. After two blank pages of marbled paper that was a delight to the touch, he turned to a tissue-protected engraving of John L. Haines, M.D., gazing out at him with an expression of benign wisdom and beneficence. Thomas bent close to read the tiny print that bordered the bottom of the picture: Northern Alliance Bank Note & Eng. Co. Chicago. Dominating the page below the portrait was the physician's signature, executed with a broad-nibbed pen.

Thomas smiled with delight and turned his attention to the title page, where bold lettering announced *The Universal Medical Advisor, In Common Sense Language, the Medicine Clarified for Universal Understanding, by John Luther Haines, M.D., founder of Haines Clinic and Vital Research Center.* The bottom of the page bore the date 1891, along with the legend that the volume had been published by The Research Center Printing Office and Bindery, Port McKinney, Washington, and subsidiary facilities, Gruenberg, Austria, and Port Darkling, Ontario, Canada.

Another engraving filled the facing page, this one of an elegant edifice, an imposing, multistory clinic building that appeared to be a bustling medical center. Carved stone over the front doors announced the Haines Clinic. The place was the equal of any that Thomas had seen—even in the medical centers in major eastern cities.

"One patient . . . he must rattle around a bit," Thomas mused. He turned past the title page and found the dedication, although printed in simple font on an unadorned page, to be just as grandiose:

To my patients, who have sought the services of this clinic and research center as guardians of their health and well being, from every hamlet, village, or city of the Union and Canada; and to those dwelling in Europe, Africa, Asia, and other foreign lands who have likewise benefited from our treatments; I respectfully dedicate this work, hoping that it includes those aspects of medical knowledge and advice most profound and most important in the pursuit of a healthy and productive life.

"My goodness," Thomas said, and turned to the two-page preface, attributed to "The Author," and written from "Port McKinney, November, 1890."

II

Time evaporated, and when a clock somewhere deep in the house chimed three that afternoon, Thomas sat back, puzzled. The book's opening hundred pages addressed a simplified description of human anatomy. The material, including a generous number of engravings, was shared by other texts of similar kind—generic and traditional. The second section, grandly titled "Human Temperament," examined the much debated forces that molded behavior—including a lengthy discussion of the relationship inherent between skull shape and human character.

Once the reader could look himself full in the mirror and decide that his physiognomy did not hide the most base motives or unpleasant personal characteristics, he could then turn to the sections on foods, household maintenance, and the pursuit of healthy activities guided by the most common conventions of the past half century.

Having skimmed the first three hundred pages, Thomas arrived at a section titled "The Thoughtful Physician," in which Haines proposed the foundations upon which his medical practice was based, borrowing freely and without apology from the work of "allopathics, homeopathics, eclectics, and hydropathics, all to be sifted and selected by the rational physician determined to practice to full effect in the approaching twentieth century.

"The able and creative physician must stand ready," Haines had written, "to employ every weapon in his arsenal, recognizing that there may even be times when an agent that is poisonous in health may clearly prove curative in the battle against disease."

Thomas stopped and slipped the silk bookmark in place. He stretched carefully. Rain still pounded outside, an oppressive drumming that reminded him of the paragraphs that had discussed the "salubrious, healing nature of sunshine." His left eye watered and his joints felt stiff and wooden. Across the room stood the tempting, large decanter of brandy, a medication that several times had earned special mention by Haines: "Alcohol, although in abuse clearly noxious, holds special station as a curative against the morbid state."

Pushing back from the desk, Thomas wheeled over to the curtained doorway leading to the porch. A rush of sweet, wet air greeted him as he opened the door, and the sensation of a million tiny fingers massaged his skin. He pushed forward until the wheels nudged against the low sill. The porch ended a dozen feet to his left, but to the right, it extended all the way to the front corner of the house, then circled to the broad steps. He watched the rain as it curtained in gusting torrents to spew off the eaves of the Mercantile. He could see to the intersection of Lincoln and Gambel, but no farther. If there was a sawmill out there on the spit, or a waterway beyond that, or a grand clinic down the street, all was well hidden by an impenetrable gray curtain.

Thomas regarded the broad, smooth, expanse of wooden porch decking, with the handy railing running full length. He nodded to himself, and wheeled back into the room to fetch the crutches. Balancing them across his lap, he eased the wheelchair across the doorsill, then turned left and wheeled into the corner where he could brace the chair against the walls of the house. By levering himself against the railing with his right arm, he was able to push himself out of the chair and hunch over the broad railing.

He balanced thus for a moment, and then reached out to secure first one crutch and then the other, edging around until his right rump rested on the railing. Easing forward, he tried to push himself upright. When his weight rested on the leather crutch pads, the action pushed his shoulders upward, which in turn tugged torn ribs.

Gritting his teeth, he edged the crutches forward, shuffling his right foot a few inches. Across the street, a figure darted through the rain toward the store, splashing across a growing, sludgy lake. How simple such a thing used to be, Thomas thought. He looked ahead and saw that fifty feet of porch separated him from the front steps. Impossible. He calculated the distance, counting the carved columns that supported the porch roof, one every ten feet. "Just one, then," he said aloud.

A slicker-cloaked rider sitting a miserable-looking mule rode out of an alley and then down Gambel. Somewhere off in the distance a pair of dogs traded news. The side door of Lindeman's Mercantile opened and Lars appeared, throwing something out into the street. He paused when he saw Thomas, but the young man didn't dare lift a hand from his crutches in greeting. The eight feet to the first column wasn't possible . . . not and be able to return to the chair. He cursed and turned enough to lean against the rail, breathing through his teeth.

The chair was but six feet away, and seemed a mile. *Six feet*, he thought. All right, if that's the way progress is to be measured. Three days ago, he couldn't roll over in bed. He had tried to stand up and been rewarded by falling on his face. Six feet was progress.

A dark shadow appeared from behind the Mercantile, and Prince plodded out into the middle of the street, looking first left and then right, as if traffic might be a threat. Thomas watched the dog limp through the mud, head and tail down. Surely the rain was uncomfortable, beating on his broad skull, pounding his kinky fur flat so that it parted along his back as if that were the seam where his coat was taken on and off. The dog apparently knew where he was going, though, and disappeared around the corner.

The brandy beckoned, and Thomas turned the chair back toward the library. The rush of wet air followed him inside, soothing his aching head. In a moment, the brandy's bloom erupted through his mouth, nose, even his sinuses, and he sat with his eyes closed, letting the sensation roll around his tongue.

"Oh, my," he sighed, and splashed a full inch into the tumbler. He turned the chair away from the cabinet and stopped. The rank aroma of wet dog wafted into the room. The creature stood on the porch, a pace from the library doorway, watching Thomas.

"What deep thoughts are going through your mind?" Thomas said. "I would think you'd be curled up in a dry corner somewhere." He pushed the chair forward, and the dog retreated a step. He saw that its body from belly to claws was thick with mud, a second coat that would harden to armor should the sun come out.

"What a remarkably disreputable creature," the young man observed. He heard the clang of a pot somewhere in the house, and immediately remembered Gert James. "I'd invite you in, old man, but Miss James would have our hides." He wheeled closer, and this time the dog simply stood there, a soggy, gray statue, only his eyes interested.

"What's wrong with your leg, then?" Thomas asked. He set the brandy glass on the desk, pushed back through the door and then turned the chair so that it was broadside to the animal. The dog remained motionless. The coating of mucky fur was enough to hide a multitude of ailments or injuries. Reaching out slowly, Thomas rested his right hand on the large dome of the dog's head, then stroked his thumb along the top of the dog's left eye, lifting the eyebrow slightly. "You've had better days, I'm guessing," he said. He withdrew his hand and the dog immediately took a half step closer to the chair, standing sideways, expectant. His fragrance was more than that of wet dog.

Fingers gently probing, Thomas ran his free hand along the dog's spine, feeling the ribs. "You could do with a bit more flesh on your bones," he said. As his hand neared the animal's rump, the dog shifted slightly, as if to turn away. He didn't, but his head swung around, eyes half-lidded. With but one good hand, Thomas's intent was to stroke down the animal's left hind leg and follow the line of bones to the source of discomfort. The moment his hand passed the bony promontory of the dog's rump and started downward, the animal contorted enough to reach Thomas's hand. His large jaws opened and snapped around the young man's wrist, the massive canines locking on the far side.

59

Captured thus, Thomas froze. He did not try to pull his hand away. The pressure of the animal's jaws was impressive, but Thomas noted with an almost detached astonishment that he wasn't being bitten . . . only held. The dog didn't growl. He just stood there, eyes searching Thomas's face.

"It's back there, then," Thomas said quietly. "Hurts, does it? What have you got there?" Twisting slightly, he tried to grip the right arm of the chair with his left hand, but that was impossible. In a moment, the dog released him with a deep-throated huff. Thomas hooked the wheel rim to twist the chair a bit. "Let me," he said to the dog as if its understanding of English was perfect. He touched the dog's left hip and this time immediately felt the swelling that extended from just behind the animal's knee to the base of its tail. Before he could probe more, the animal stepped away.

Thomas grimaced at the rank odor. "My God, old man, I'd think you could at least walk belly deep into the sound for a bit of a bath," he said. "I'll speak to Mr. Lindeman," he said. "We'll see what can be done." Thomas straightened up and rubbed the silky underside of one of the dog's ears. "I'll see what can be done," he said again, and rolled the chair back away from the door. The dog took a couple of steps as if he might leave, then apparently thought better of it. With a loud grunt, he lay down on the porch on his right side, back snuggled up against the house. For a moment Thomas watched him, but the animal no longer seemed interested in him.

The rank odor lingered despite a trip to the bathroom to wash his hands, and Thomas sacrificed a bit of brandy as hand lotion. He refilled the glass and returned to the desk, leaving the door to the porch ajar. Returning to the impressive *Universal Medical Advisor,* he soon forgot weather, brandy, and dog.

12

"W hat a marvelous occasion," Dr. John Haines said. He stood at the end of the table, wineglass raised. "A toast to our young friend, now well on the road to recovery." He raised the glass a little higher, and Thomas saw that the older man's balance was precarious. "That's a good thing, since very shortly we plan to work him to death." Those around the table laughed.

Thomas felt more weary than recuperating, but he gamely lifted his own glass in thanks, fascinated by this assemblage of contrasting personalities. Dr. Zachary Riggs sat at the end of the table opposite Haines, with Alvi Haines on his right, and Gert James on his left. Gert's brother Horace took his place beside his sister, and Thomas wheeled his chair close to the table on Haines's left. Horace James smiled at everything, but kept his eyes deferentially averted, paying close attention to the business of eating.

Thomas found Zachary Riggs enormously likable and attractive. Stocky, powerfully built, Riggs exuded energy and enthusiasm, as well as an easy laugh that often swelled to a bellow. Rather than the huge, spade-shaped beard favored by Dr. Haines, Riggs sported a close-cropped beard and mustache that matched his ruddy complexion. A pair of gold half-glasses hung from a vest pocket, and a heavy gold chain circled his paunch. He had greeted Thomas with delight, making sure that the young man was comfortable at the table before taking his own seat. The physician was deferential toward both Gert and Horace, and Thomas noted that Gert attended both Riggs and Haines as if they were visiting royalty.

Exactly what the relationship was between Zachary Riggs and Alvina Haines was unclear, but Thomas noted that Riggs's right hand now and then would stray across to touch the back of Alvina's. Thomas was surprised that he noticed at all, and even more surprised that he felt a little stab of disappointment.

"Here you've been under our roof for nearly a week, and we haven't had a chance to exchange more than a word or two," Riggs said. "But I see that you share something in common with most of John's patients . . . and that's a speedy, complication-free recovery. We're all thankful for that." He raised his glass to Thomas.

"Hear, hear," John Haines said, refilling his own. "I repeat my original toast." He drained the glass, and rested his elbow on the table as he regarded Thomas. "So. Alvi tells me that she has inflicted the book on you."

"And may I say," Thomas replied, "it's an incredible accomplishment."

"Well, authors other than myself deserve much of the credit," Haines said off-handedly. "Were it left entirely up to me, I'm afraid I wouldn't have managed beyond page two."

"This is a collaborative effort, then?"

"Indeed," Haines replied. He pointed his fork down-table toward Riggs, and then swept it back and forth to include both his daughter and the physician. "These two have convinced me that such a publication was necessary," he said. "Something that the patient can hold in his two hands and use to make sense of all the folderol and jargon that we physicians spout." He cocked his head, regarding the almost-empty wine bottle. "And, you know, I think they're right. I've had a number of patients tell me the same thing." As he poured the last of the wine, Gert rose, removed the empty bottle, and headed for the kitchen.

"As I see it," Riggs added, "it's more an archival thing, Thomas." He nodded toward Haines. "A way to record for posterity the amazing medical knowledge this good man enjoys." He smiled affectionately at Haines.

"An incredible endeavor."

"How far have you read, then?"

"Well, I only began the journey this afternoon, you understand," Thomas said, "but at the moment, I'm about to embark on part four, I think it is. The section touching on diagnosis."

"Good heavens, man. You've been busy."

"A bit. I thought to devise a system of therapy and exercise for my injuries. I'm sure that your text is a good place to begin my studies."

"Really." Riggs's fork halted halfway to his mouth, his expression one of genuine interest. "I trust you're proceeding with care. I picked you up from the floor once, you may recall. You're a bit heavy to be lugging about."

"I shall try my best not to do that again, sir. But I found that the porch was ideal for my needs."

"Hmm," Haines said, and accepted the fresh wine bottle from Gert.

"I managed some six feet today with the crutches." Thomas laughed ruefully, "and back to the chair. So that's twelve, but it's a start."

"I dare say it's a start," Riggs said, impressed. "What are you taking for the pain?"

"Nothing is best," Thomas said. "At this point, it's to my advantage, I think. Not masking the source of discomfort helps me understand the nature of the injuries."

Riggs nodded, although a bit skeptically. "John tells me that you're a graduate of the University of Pennsylvania?"

"Yes. Just this past spring."

"Then you've heard Lamchert's lectures," Riggs said.

Thomas frowned. "I'm afraid not. The name is not familiar," he said.

Riggs frowned in puzzlement. "I thought Lamchert was at that institution. Perhaps I'm mistaken." He stabbed a piece of beef, forked it to his mouth, and chewed thoughtfully. "Now that I think on it, I believe it was Johns Hopkins. Anyway, little matter. His point is well taken in your case. An injured joint must be exercised with care, but with regularity and persistence. Otherwise it will wither on the vine, so to speak. You concur?"

"I'm in complete agreement," Thomas said, "and above all, what I see clearly *now*, if not before, is that the pain of an injury must be managed in such a way that recuperation isn't put in jeopardy. I confess, before last week, I hadn't considered that a factor."

"You hadn't considered pain?" John Haines said, and covered his mouth with the back of his hand. "My God, man."

"What I mean is, in a *personal* sense. As students, we're told that patients suffer discomfort, even excruciating pain. I suppose we witness that very thing in the wards. But *we* didn't feel it, and so we say wonderfully ridiculous things like, 'Bite the bullet, old man. That leg has to come off.'" Thomas saw Gert frown. "When it's over, if the patient lives, we say, 'Strong man, that.'" He took a sip of wine. "I can imagine someone familiar with my case saying, 'Well, my God, so he ripped a ligament in his hip. Why doesn't the lazy fellow get on with it? A little limp, and even that will disappear in a few days' time.' I found it not that simple. That's all I'm saying."

"With a busted head, a broken rib or two, a broken thumb, lacerations and contusions by the potful, and who knows what damage to your hip joint, I can't imagine anyone gainsaying your progress, my young man," Riggs said.

"Thank you. I didn't want you thinking I was uninterested."

"Hardly."

Thomas looked at Gert, and then Alvi. "I had the opportunity this afternoon to attempt a preliminary examination on a somewhat foul patient."

Again, Riggs's gaze was riveted on the young man. "You don't say."

"I hope you didn't let him in the house," Alvi said, and she held her linen napkin up to her nose as answer to Thomas's startled expression. "I can smell him yet."

"What's all this?" Riggs asked eagerly.

"Most remarkable in some ways," Thomas explained. "I was reading in the study this afternoon, and turned to see Mr. Lindeman's dog standing in the doorway. What a truly disreputable, homely beast he is."

"Oh, my soul," Gert piped. "You *didn't* encourage him inside, I should hope."

"No, indeed I did not. I rolled myself outside to the porch.

Now what interests me is that he has an injury of some kind to his left hind leg. Perhaps the reason he prefers to sit with his hindquarters squelched in the mud is that the muck is somehow soothing. Anyway, a most remarkable thing happened. He was standing beside my chair, and I ran my right hand down his back, impressed with how little flesh there is on his ribs. As I ran my hand down his back leg, he turned with such deliberate speed that I had no chance to move." Thomas held up his right hand like a jaw, and clamped it around the bandages of his left wrist. "He closed his jaws around my right wrist, like so."

"My God, he bit you?"

"No, he *held* me. And let me be the first to say, that dog has a *big* mouth. His canines were on the far side of my wrist."

"It didn't break the skin, then," Riggs said.

"No, indeed. As I said, he *held* me. And gently, now that I think about it in retrospect. I suppose he could have crushed my wrist as one snaps a twig."

"So what did you do?"

"Well, I thought it best not to pull away. In a moment, he let go and allowed me to continue my examination as best I could. I found what appears to be an enormous abscess of some kind. On the inner thigh."

"And he let you do that?"

"He did."

Riggs threw back his head and roared with laughter, smacking the table with the flat of his fingers. "My word. Extraordinary."

"The animal is literally caked in muck, and I didn't have the freedom to probe and poke."

"What do you propose to do now?"

"Well, if I could manage it, I'd walk him down to the Sound and give him a thorough bathing in salt water. We're not going to be able to see much of anything through an inch of mud and a tangle of rank fur. Then I'd go from there."

Riggs filled his glass as the wine bottle was passed to his end of the table. "Alvi tells me that injuries resulting from trauma are what interest you highly—but I had assumed human patients." He smiled indulgently. "I jest, of course."

"Yes, sir."

"The logging country should provide you with plenty of opportunity," Riggs said. "Although most of the cases that come in from the camps go on over to St. Mary's."

"And that is?"

"St. Mary's Hospital," Alvi offered. "Perhaps thirty miles south, in Pesqualmie. It's so much easier than the journey to Seattle. They have facilities to treat the more serious cases."

"I would think little would compare with the treatment offered by the Haines Clinic," Thomas said.

"Oh, we do fair enough," Riggs said, "but we're short-staffed at the moment." He smiled engagingly. "One of the reasons you're here."

"So I'm to understand that you're looking to expand," Thomas said.

"We're expanding *everything*," Riggs said grandly. "That's the aim. Without income, there's little we can do. Eventually, this area will become a center for the training of physicians."

"That's ambitious," Thomas said. "You were at Johns Hopkins, then?"

Riggs shook his head and held up one hand as if he'd heard a base rumor. "No, no. A lecture or two, and a symposium last year. Nothing more than that."

"You studied abroad?"

"Have you read Lucier's work?" Riggs asked.

"I confess I haven't."

"Ah, well . . . Claude Lucier's studies have been revolutionary. More even than Tessier's in Austria, and I had thought that Tessier was the benchmark for the rest of us."

"I . . . ," Thomas shrugged helplessly, feeling somehow provincial.

"Let me tell you," Riggs said, saving Thomas from his discomfiture. "In these small, out-of-the way corners of the world, we're

66

so removed from the advances and studies of Europe. I was fortunate enough to travel extensively recently, and spoke with a score of learned professionals." He made a large globe-shaped figure in the air with both hands. "A world of ideas is out there." He jabbed a thumb at Thomas. "You're most fortunate to have studied at a center such as Philadelphia. That's the pulse of things. We'll be eager to hear your thoughts on a variety of difficult cases."

"Hear, hear," John Haines said. He placed his empty glass carefully on the table, as if he wasn't sure of his target. "And I think I shall retire to the study for a cigar and brandy. You'll join Zachary and me?"

"I'm afraid if I do that, I shall have to spend the night there," Thomas laughed.

"Of course. How stupid of me. We've exhausted you. Tomorrow's another day." He stood unsteadily.

"Let me help," Riggs said, rising quickly. He maneuvered the young man's wheelchair away from the table. Fatigue, alcohol, and too much rich food had numbed Thomas well beyond the desire to fend for himself. He allowed himself to be wheeled back to the room. With an assurance that Thomas could manage his clothing by himself and make his way from chair into bed, Riggs left him with a final, warm salutation.

Wheeling himself close to the bed, Thomas paused. He had no desire to face another struggle. He reached out and pulled two of the feather pillows into his lap. Hugging the pillows with both arms, he cradled his head in the softness and fell asleep.

13

What's this?" Dr. John Haines asked. Thomas had awakened just seconds before the physician appeared in the doorway of his bedroom and hadn't yet figured out how to relieve the kink in his neck. "You wouldn't prefer the bed?"

"I was too tired and sore," Thomas said. He pulled the pillows away from his torso where they had molded themselves. He saw that Haines was dressed in robe and slippers, his eyes alert, redness of nose subsided. Gone was the mellow, tipsy host of the evening previous. Thomas turned and squinted at his watch on the nightstand. "My God . . . is it really?"

"I'm about to go to the clinic," Haines said. "I like to be there by seven, or they think I'm slacking."

"I slept the night through, then," Thomas said.

"Indeed you did. We've been doing a good job of ignoring you these past days, but it seems you've been healing nicely. Let's have a look at you, then." He patted the bed. "Let me give you a hand."

Pushing himself to his right foot, Thomas gained the bed and sat shakily on the edge, leaning on his right arm. Haines stepped close, and Thomas could still smell the liquor on the physician's clothing and the heavy aroma of the cigars. With deft, practiced fingers, Haines peeled away the bandage around Thomas's head, humming to himself. "Well, well," he said at one point. He arose, reached out, and turned up the gas lamp.

"Close your left eye now," he instructed, and Thomas did so. "What do you see?"

"I can see the wall and the doorway, but I cannot distinguish the small details," Thomas said. He reached up and pushed tentatively at his right eyelid, trying to move it upward out of his line of sight.

"Don't do that," Haines said, and caught him by the wrist. "The swelling will subside day by day. Let nature take its course." He pulled a small card out of his pocket. "Can you read this with your right eye alone?" The print was fine, and Thomas turned so that the light fell on the card.

"No. I can't make out the individual letters."

"Do this," and Haines held up his hand, curling his fingers to form a tube, then holding it to his own eye like a short spyglass. "Does that improve it?"

Concentrating on the tiny hole, Thomas eyed the card, opening and closing his fingers until the print appeared almost comprehensible. "It helps."

"Ah. That's good, then," Haines said. "I've no doubt that the eye is going to give you fits for a while, but with rest and care, I think it will straighten itself out. You're going to have a scar on your pate that will be a fascination for all the ladies." He touched the young man's head lightly, turning him this way and that. "No disfigurement . . . just a touch of dash and swashbuckle. That's good." He stood back and regarded Thomas's face critically. "That's good," he repeated. "But I wasn't truly concerned about that." He watched Thomas for a moment. "How's the breathing?"

"As long as I don't do it, fine."

Haines ignored the jest. "You feel movement?"

"I'm not sure."

"Well," Haines said, "*I* am. Let's have a look." He managed the fine knot of the bandage under Thomas's right arm and unwound the linen. "Lie back now if you can." A pad of gauze remained, and he tugged it gently, revealing a nasty wound over the fifth rib on Thomas's left side. The gouge was deep and ragged, surrounded by a spectacular field of color that extended down to the eighth rib and across to his breastbone.

"I think we have at least two fractures, maybe three," Haines said. "I pulled pieces of the sea bottom out of that gouge for the better part of an hour. Rib healing is really problematical." He smiled at Thomas. "Unless, as you say, we can just keep them perfectly motionless for a month or so." He touched the field of black, blue, and yellow, a touch featherlight. Thomas still flinched. "You can feel the slight depression of a fracture of the fourth rib through the swelling here. The sixth and seventh here." He sat back. "You can understand why we're a bit apprehensive about your adventures out of bed, Thomas. You've got a piece of bone essentially floating free there. If you were to fall on it . . ." He made a face. "Nothing would prevent a ragged end from skewering your insides."

"I thought about that."

"But not enough, apparently." Haines made a circular motion. "Roll on your right hip if you can."

Thomas gasped at the first attempt, free as he was of the tight bandaging that had supported his ribs. Haines made a series of puffing noises as he examined the left hip. "Spectacular," he said. "Is there any portion of your left leg where you have lost feeling?"

"I almost wish so," Thomas managed. "But no."

"When your hip attempted to dislocate backward, you did significant damage to some of the suspension for the joint," Haines said. "Right here?" He touched with forefinger and thumb the area over the front and back of the iliac crest. "There are any number of muscle attachments that might be torn from here down to the head of the femur," he said. "Deep within the joint itself. I think the damage is significant, since you're deeply bruised. Really quite spectacular." He took a deep breath. "But I don't think there is a fracture. Everything is in line, as it should be."

"I've managed a bit more movement with it," Thomas said.

"Good," Haines said. "I can give you something for the pain if you prefer."

"No. Although I admit I made considerable progress with your brandy yesterday afternoon."

Haines laughed. "You just help yourself. Between this hip and the brandy, you might develop a quite entertaining stagger. Let's protect that gash now." In a few moments, he had rebandaged Thomas's ribs. With a somewhat lighter bandage around his head, Haines left the right eye exposed.

"I am curious about your pharmaceuticals," Thomas said as Haines finished with the last closure.

"Oh? How so?"

"In particular, the Universal Tonic," Thomas said. "I couldn't help but notice the abundant uses mentioned for it in your volume."

"Ah," Haines said. The corners of his eyes crinkled, and one eyebrow raised. "You've made good use of your time."

"Indeed. I spent most of yesterday engrossed."

"It's important to remember that the book's purpose is not for the physician," Haines said. "It's a book intended for every household. As Zachary says, it is intended as an advisor, so to speak—for those who have no inkling as to which way to turn." He stood away from the bed. "It still amazes me, after all these years, that the basic dictum of clean air, clean habitation, and plentiful, wholesome food escapes most of our population. If we could change only those habits, we would eradicate most disease."

"I agree absolutely," Thomas said. "I mention the tonic simply because I had not encountered a preparation with such manifold uses. You mentioned in the book an entire factory devoted to production of useful materia medica, and a knowledgeable chemist and pharmacist in your employ. Most impressive, I must say. I'm eager to visit your pharmacy, John."

"Well." Haines shrugged. "We do what we can. Zachary has been an astonishing help to me, I must say." He looked upward toward the ceiling, closing his eyes. "I'm trying to recall his description of the very drug to which you refer." He frowned with irritation. "But I cannot. Tonight at dinner, we must ask him. He has a way with words."

"I liked him immediately," Thomas said.

"Engaging gentleman, isn't he," Haines agreed. "We're all fond of him."

"Where did he study? I know that I asked him last night, but somehow missed his answer."

"That man has toured the world," Haines said with admiration. "I don't suppose I've ever met a man who has taken such advantage of opportunity. In fact, just last month, he returned after a week spent in San Francisco. So many new ideas about the import of Oriental medicines that my mind was completely flummoxed. Really quite remarkable."

"He must have had the advantage of an enviable schooling," Thomas said. "His original work was at a university here, or in Europe?"

Haines looked at the ceiling again. "Undergraduate at Yale University, I believe. Medical school at Vanderheide Institute in Delaware. A considerable stint in Vienna, and again in Bonn."

"How did you come to make his acquaintance?"

"A chance meeting. I had traveled to San Francisco myself, to visit an ailing sister—she has since passed, bless her soul. I don't believe that you ever knew her . . . considerably older than myself. Anyway, at the time I took the opportunity to attend a symposium and made his acquaintance there. He wired me shortly after that and suggested that he was now seeking a position of some permanence. I happened to be entertaining the idea of finding assistance with my practice, and as it so often happens, our ideas collided. I confess, I was astonished that he would even consider a tiny, out-of-the-way community like Port McKinney, but I guess we have our advantages. He's been with me now for the better part of five years, and I must say, to our mutual benefit."

"Your practice appears to be thriving," Thomas said.

"Indeed. And you shall be a part of it." He touched the young man lightly on the shoulder. "In due time. Your first job is convalescence."

"Still, I can't bear simply lying here," Thomas said. "I was entertaining the idea of having Horace drive me to the clinic."

Haines glowered. "Under no circumstances," he said. "I absolutely forbid it. Good God, man, think of the consequences of one misstep. Fall against something with that broken rib, and it would be a spear through your heart. No helping you then." He held up an admonishing finger. "Don't be foolish, Thomas. Don't let a little impatience ruin a good start on the journey to recovery."

"I was merely considering," Thomas said. "Once at the clinic, perhaps I could simply remain there. With this wonderful chair, I could wheel about the wards. I could talk with patients, and as I become stronger and more ambulatory, I could be of some real assistance."

"Next you'll want to be driving out through the big timber," Haines snorted. "We'll find you crushed under a pile of logs somewhere."

"I need to earn my keep."

"Hardly." He pulled out his gold watch and snapped it open. "Make me this promise, Thomas. Give yourself another full two weeks. You know that's not enough time for the ribs to heal, but it's a start. By then the eye will be out of trouble, and you may have gained some flexion in the hip. You won't be quite the disaster you are currently. Right now, you have the balance of an infant."

"I . . ."

"Let me confer a bit with Zachary. It may be that we have some work we can bring to the house. It may even be . . . ," and he paused, face thoughtful. "Let me talk with Zachary. We'll speak more about it at dinnertime this evening. You'll feel well enough to join us again, I hope."

"Most certainly."

Haines patted the bed. "Good. Be patient, Thomas. Be a *good* patient. You're otherwise comfortable?"

"More than that," Thomas replied. "Pampering into sloth."

Haines laughed. "Perfect. Eat and rest your way to health. That's what we want you to do. A year from now, when you're lying in bed exhausted from working half a dozen eighteen-hour days, you'll look back on this time and wish for a bit more serenity and relaxation. Take advantage of it while you can."

"I'll try."

"Have you finished the book? What do you think?"

"I am nearing the end. I am most struck by the chapter you present on mechanical aids. I had never seen such a wide range of helpful devices."

"Ah," Haines said. "A direct result of one of Zachary's visits to Vienna." He nodded enthusiastically. "We'll talk at dinner."

14

Wondered how you were getting along," Lars Lindeman called. He leaned on his cane and watched Thomas's progress along the porch toward the second column.

"At this rate, I'll be at the front steps by Christmas," Thomas replied. "How are you doing, sir?'" He turned and let the sun beat on his face. The vista today was as remarkable as it had been nonexistent the days before. Straight to the west the rise of the Olympics marked the horizon, and south, white-toothed and improbable, Rainier looked far closer than he knew it to be.

Lindeman carefully stepped off his own boardwalk, taking his weight first with the cane. He chose his path thoughtfully, chuffing on his pipe at the same time. "Well, I'm all right," he said. "I've been meaning to come by for a visit, but I didn't know if you were so disposed."

"You should see the other fellow."

Lindeman laughed. "Hell of a way for a town to greet a new arrival."

"It was my own fault," Thomas said. He placed the crutches a few inches forward and lurched a step, keeping close to the railing. Lindeman stopped directly below him, and Thomas could smell the strong aroma of the older man's pipe. Looking up at him, Lindeman shook his head slowly, clearly amused.

"You ain't the first that's gone off them rocks." His laugh was a hacking cough. "So what'd you do to yourself?"

"Head, ribs, hip," Thomas said succinctly. "Cracked, broken, and dislocated."

"That's right, you're a damn doctor, ain't you. They say they make the worst patients."

"I've been told that. I don't mean to be impolite, but I can't stand here long, by the way." He nodded off to the left toward the wheelchair. "There are chairs around front. Join me for a few moments?"

It took more than a few minutes, but Thomas finally glided the wheelchair down the length of the porch, feeling each thump of the decking seams. Lindeman had taken his ease, both hands folded on the handle of his cane.

"Thought you'd forgot," Lindeman said. "Makes me feel downright spry, watching you."

"I'm pleased to be of some value," Thomas said, and spun the chair so that he was out of the wind drift from Lindeman's pipe.

He pointed at the dog who had been sitting in the street directly in front of the store. Prince heaved himself out of the mud and limped toward them. "Your dog has an abscessed hip, by the way. I thought I should mention that."

"Is that what's wrong with it? I saw he had himself a limp."

"I'm quite sure. I could feel the swelling."

Lindeman looked at him quickly. "Surprised you still got all your fingers."

"We came to an understanding, he and I."

"That so?" They watched Prince shuffle to the bottom of the steps and stop, head down, reflecting on the barrier before him. "You don't need to come up here," Lindeman said. The dog's wedge-shaped eyebrows twitched.

"I was thinking that we could take him down to the shore and clean him up."

"Well, I don't think that's going to happen," Lindeman said. "He might have blood from half a hundred breeds running in his veins, but I don't see no waterfowl retriever in the mix."

"If we could clean him up, the abscess could be treated. That's why he sits with his rump in the muck. It brings him a measure of relief."

"Huh. You think so, do you? I thought he just sat all the time 'cause he was old and lazy. Well, hell. Clean or not, he's not going to let you go rooting around in his bunghole with a cutter."

"Under anesthetic, he wouldn't have the choice."

Lindeman laughed loudly, choking on a cloud of smoke that he'd been about to exhale. His eyes teared and he leaned forward, whooping for air. "Now that, I want to see," he managed finally.

"You'll agree, then?"

The merchant looked at him sideways. "You're serious?"

"Yes, I'm serious. He's obviously in discomfort." They both looked down at the dog, who had turned enough painful circles to enable him to lie down by the steps.

"He's never mentioned it to me," Lindeman said, and he sounded so earnest that for a moment Thomas thought him serious. "Maybe if I just feed him about a gallon of that syrup that the good doctor hawks, it'll take his mind off it."

"It'll take more than syrup," Thomas said. "You're familiar with that, then?"

"With what?"

"The doctor's line of medications. I was just reading an early edition of his latest textbook. They're mentioned frequently, especially his Universal Tonic."

"Sell a lot of it, that's for sure. Got a whole shelf of self-helps, his included. I don't use the stuff, but there's some who swear by it." He shrugged. "The way I see it, a good stiff drink now and then don't hurt anyone. Does some good."

"I would agree with you. Be that as it may," Thomas persisted, "I was thinking about the dog's discomfort. It would be relatively easy to give him an injection of morphine, and depending on what I find, perhaps some ether to put him out entirely. Then we can excise the abscess and give him some relief."

"Don't know as he's worth it," Lindeman said. "Then again, he isn't my dog, so I guess I don't care. You want him?"

Thomas grinned. "No, I don't want him. I mean, it appears that he has a home already. I'm just saying that he's suffering a bit, and we can relieve that. Perhaps he wouldn't be so quick to bite."

"Well, have at it. Lemme know when you're going to clean him up—or try to. I want to be on hand to watch." He relit his pipe, ignoring the gurgle of fluid in the stem.

"The shooting the other day," Thomas said. "I thought I heard a ruckus of some sort at your store. Was that my imagination?"

"Nope."

"What happened?"

"Well, simple enough. I got a boy who works for me—Charlie Grimes. You haven't met him yet?" He regarded the pipe critically. "A good boy, in most ways, Charlie is. Even Prince doesn't pay him any mind. Well, one of the whistle punks who works for Bert Schmidt's outfit *don't* like him, not one little bit. Charlie's got a stammer, and he's got a temper, and this sprout—his name's Harvey something, I think—he likes to push and push and push."

Lindeman sucked on the pipe, made a face, and whacked the burl against the porch railing, some of the dottle spewing down on Prince. "This time, he pushed a bit too far. Him and Charlie went at it right there in front of the store, and damned if this worthless mutt here didn't take offense at *that*. I don't know which one of them he was going to bite first. Charlie and Harvey are goin' at it right smart, both of them mired down in the mud. Well, first thing you know, he's got this little revolver in his hand, Harvey does. Didn't know he kept that. He lets fly at Prince, but *that* didn't work."

"I thought I heard something hit the house," Thomas said.

"Ain't surprised, bad as his aim is. Well, the dog's got Harvey by the leg, here, and Charlie's got him by the arm, and they're all wrapped up in a heap, with me about as useless as tits on a boar hog. Damn pistol got all twisted around, and there you go." He jabbed the pipe stem into the soft triangle of flesh under his chin. "Right there. Dropped old Harvey like a sack of rocks. He had the damnedest look of surprise on his face." He shrugged philosophically.

"My word. Dr. Haines said nothing of this."

Lindeman shrugged. "There's plenty that gets killed all sorts of ways, young fella. Harvey had it comin', as far as I'm concerned. Lot of folks agree with me. That's what I told old Eastman, when he came around."

"Eastman?"

"Butch Eastman. He's one of the constables. Good enough man. Not the sharpest tool in the box, but a good enough man. He's had a run-in or two with Harvey, come a Saturday night. The boy sure liked to drink. Guess he don't now, though. Not with half of his brain matter mixed in the mud."

"Astounding," Thomas marveled.

"Hate to say it, but it weren't much of a loss. Glad it wasn't Charlie. He's got his faults, but I like him well enough. Hard worker. And I should ask, 'cause I've always wondered . . . What do you figure makes a boy stammer like that . . . like Charlie does, I mean. Fancy medicine got a cure for that?"

"I'm afraid not. There's a new theory out of Switzerland that it has something to do with nutrition of the infant, but unless the affliction is cured in early childhood, there's nothing to be done. I think that's nonsense, myself."

"You do, eh."

"Well, yes. Think of the number of undernourished infants there are, and the relative rarity of people who stammer."

"I don't know how *rare* they are. Seems to me I could come up with a couple myself. Charlie for one. Bert Schmidt's payroll master for another. Seems pretty common to me."

"But not numerically common," Thomas said. "Not out of an entire population."

"Don't know what all that means, but it's a damn shame, no matter what. Ruins a man's life, in some ways." He held two fingers pinched together in front of his lips. "Why can't a fella just *say* what he wants? Just spit the word out?"

"Something gets in the way that we don't understand." Thomas tapped the side of his own skull opposite the bandage. "Something in here."

"That's what I think," Lindeman said. "Not a damn thing he can do about it, old Charlie. That gets him all riled up, too."

"Which makes it worse," Thomas observed.

"And he don't take to teasing, not one little bit. As Harvey found out."

"I wanted to ask you. If I wanted to buy ice, who would I see?"

The abrupt change of subject seemed to take Lindeman by surprise, and he spent a moment carefully reloading his pipe as if it were a difficult question that required considerable pondering. "That would be me," he said. "Don't have a whole lot left, not this time of year, but some."

"I would like to employ a cold pack on my hip. Alcohol and water isn't sufficient. If I had some chipped ice . . ."

"Nothing's easier, young man. You just say when." He dragged the match up the underside of his britches' leg and lit his pipe.

"Doc," and he puffed, interrupting himself, "Doc Haines about used what I had in July. Had an outbreak of the typhoid up at Clallam Creek. Maybe he told you about that."

"No, he hasn't mentioned it."

"He lost two." Lindeman held up two fingers. "Just two. At one point, he had upward of forty in one village. Lost two. That just about made him a hero. We was hauling ice up there by the wagonload, and Doc, he paid cash money right up front. Don't suspect he got any of it back, either, them Indians bein' what they are."

"It was in an Indian village? The outbreak, I mean."

Lindeman nodded. "And spread into one of the loggin' camps."

"He brought them here to the clinic for treatment?"

Lindeman looked puzzled. "Don't suspect he did. They're going to be sick, they're sick in their own way. Don't need to be bringin' them into town."

"I've never seen an Indian," Thomas said. "I mean other than catching a glimpse out of the train window as we passed through the stations. They seem to gather there."

"I expect they die of the typhoid just like anybody else," Lindeman said, "but this time, they only lost two. Doc Haines used the ice baths, I'm told. Force that temperature down."

"That's the trick," Thomas agreed. "You have a wagon, then."

"'Course I have wagons. Got four of 'em. Don't imagine you need that much ice, though."

Thomas laughed. "No. I was thinking about how I might manage to make the trip to the clinic."

Lindeman coughed. "Doc's got a carriage, you know."

"He doesn't want me to leave the house yet."

"Smart man, no doubt. You're movin' about as spry as a hundred-year-old cowpuncher."

"That's why I was thinking about the wagon, Mr. Lindeman. I could just lie back on the tailgate, rather than trying to climb up into a carriage. For such a short ride, what could it hurt? I might find something to do at the clinic. Something to make myself useful."

Lindeman tapped his pipe thoughtfully on the railing. "I don't think I want John Haines angry with me," he said. "He says you should stay put, then that's what you should do." He grinned at Thomas, showing half a dozen teeth. "Anyways, you're a long, long way from walking down these steps to a wagon. I sure as hell ain't about to carry you." He pushed himself out of the chair. "I got to get before Charlie loses the store." He offered his hand to Thomas. "Good talking with you, Doctor. We'll do it again. When was it that you wanted me to send that ice over?"

"How about each morning at nine o'clock for a few days," Thomas said. He held his hands out, bowl fashion. "A pound or two, crushed up?"

"Easily done." He took the steps carefully, and Prince hauled himself to his feet. Lindeman paused, looking down at the dog. "Don't know how I come up with that name. Must have been in my cups. 'Useless' would be better," he said. "And I ain't wasting ice on *his* useless ass, I can tell you that."

"He might appreciate it."

"He might," Lindeman conceded. "Might be sunny two days in a row, too."

15

———

Zachary Riggs held up the large ripe peach between index finger and thumb. "Behold the wonders of the late summer fruit," he announced. He let the words hang in the air for a dramatic moment. Thomas had the feeling that Riggs had carefully prepared for this moment.

"I'll want a good, substantial napkin, of course," Riggs said as an amused aside. "Now," he continued, "even the *anticipation* of this wonderful thing is pleasurable. You agree?"

"Certainly," Thomas said.

Riggs brought the peach to his nose, brushing it in his whiskers. "Ah," he sighed. "What a fragrance. What a bouquet. Am I thinking of anything else? No, of course I'm not. Just the *anticipation* cures me of some of my ills. The worries of the day are lessened." His tongue flicked out to moisten his lips, and he turned to Alvi, lowering his voice. "I can't stand it. Pardon me while I indulge, will you?"

Alvina Haines smiled and selected an equally succulent fruit for herself. "If I might join you."

"Now," Riggs said, and bit into the peach. The juice flowed down his short beard, and he ducked his head forward, flailing with the napkin. "Oh, my *God,* Gerty," he breathed. "Where ever did you find these?"

"Mr. Lindeman had them. He said they were from Sequim." Gert had reentered the dining room to finish clearing plates. When the talk turned medical, Horace had ducked his head and excused himself. "Don't you be slobbering on my clean tablecloth now," Gert said sternly, and Riggs waved a hand as she left the room.

"My," Riggs said. He took another bite, releasing yet more juice. "Even if we imagine that this peach has no pharmaceutical or medicinal value at all, it does me good, does it not? Beyond its simple pleasures that boost my morale, beyond driving away the dark storm clouds of depression, as a nutritious fruit it bolsters my entire system. Now how does it do that? Of course you know that the answer is marvelously simple."

He held up first one finger and then more as he counted. "It helps the bowels. Its sugar powers me. Why, its juice soothes the throat, the stomach. We might even argue that its wonderful bouquet helps open the sinuses. And one can argue that a veritable wave of pleasure sweeps through the body as we consume it." Juice running down his wrist, Riggs held the half-eaten peach toward Thomas. "What doctor on the planet is to gainsay the claim that these magic pills enjoyed twice a day will help maintain and support the constitution?"

Thomas grinned, delighted with Riggs's performance. "Of course. *Helps.* But only in a most general way."

"Granted," Riggs responded. "Granted." He held up a stubby finger. "And if you have a patient dying of tuberculosis, is not maintaining and supporting that fragile constitution the very task of the physician? And don't we use *any* means at our disposal to accomplish that task? Of course we do. Something that helps *in a general way* is to be embraced."

"You offer a most eloquent argument."

"Our Universal Tonic, Thomas. You asked a moment ago how it could be efficacious in the treatment of so many ills." He held up the peach again. "Like this wonderful fruit, the Universal Tonic is *supportive.* In every way. It is formulated for that very purpose." He carefully placed the peach pit on the side of his plate. "Now, can it be abused?" He let that provocative question linger for a moment as he wiped his mouth. "Suppose I were to grind up this rather homely pit, Thomas. Suppose that."

"The pit is known to be poisonous."

"Oh, indeed it is." He reached out and chose another peach, hefted it, then replaced it. "Even something this wonderful has its dark side. We all agree to that."

For the first time during the conversation, John Haines stirred. He had listened with obvious pleasure as his associate laid out the case for the tonic, but had interjected nothing. Now he said, "As I told you earlier, Thomas, imagine the results if *every* patient could be persuaded to follow a healthful regimen of nutrition. Imagine something as simple as airing out the sickroom. If the environs could be kept *clean* and aseptic. If the morale of the patient could be kept positive and constructive." He waggled his eyebrows. "You must agree that the ravages of disease would be lessened."

"Of course."

"A worthwhile tonic helps with much of that," Riggs said. "What we have developed . . . what John has developed . . . has proven itself over and over again. We would be remiss if we did not bring the tonic's supportive properties to every patient's attention."

Thomas nodded, but before he could make a comment, Riggs added eagerly, "And in your reading, you will have noticed—what do we exhort patients to do when it is known that they suffer one of the great maladies? Suppose we suspect"—he shrugged, pulling a disease from the air—"scarlet fever. What do we tell them? Seek a physician immediately. *Seek a physician immediately*," he repeated. "Short of that, the patient must be encouraged to maintain strength and support a positive outlook." He eyed the peaches and, unable to resist, selected another.

"I must admit, the clinic's pharmacy is most impressive," Thomas said. Engravings in the book had shown rooms lined with enormous vats reminiscent of a winery, while chemists labored in a well-equipped laboratory.

"Think forward," Riggs said. "Think always about what *will* be. That gives our work direction and purpose, my good man. No matter how busy one might become with the daily rigors of our profession, we must never lose sight of the greater picture. Simply put, where will we be in one year's time, five years' time, ten years' . . . even *fifty* years' when it will be up to the next generation to continue what we have started. That is the only way to build an empire."

Thomas felt a chill of anticipation and eagerness. "I confess that your inspiration makes me feel all the more useless."

"Nonsense, Thomas. You've had an unfortunate accident, but your recuperation is astounding." He reached out and slid the bowl of fruit toward the young man and grinned widely. "Have a miracle pill. It can only help."

"I had the opportunity to converse with Mr. Lindeman today at some length," Thomas said. "He said that the tonic is well received."

"Indeed it is," Riggs said. "You would be astonished to hear the number of prescriptions sold, all over the world."

"I was struck, however . . ." He hesitated, loath to insult his gracious hosts. "The new book seems somewhat . . . evasive? About the ingredients of the tonic—and other treatments as well."

"There again," John Haines said, selecting his words carefully around the haze of too much wine, "ask yourself what good it does to inflict a long litany of incomprehensible terminology on the sick patient. We must remember that the *Universal Advisor* is intended for the *patient*, not the physician."

"Yes," Riggs interjected. "The patient doesn't *need* to know. Now, if on the other hand, a physician writes to us in good faith, documenting a troublesome case, and then inquires about the nature of the tonic and its properties, and how it might be of benefit to the patient, then, in most instances, we will supply the information requested."

He pushed himself back from the table. "I could use the peach again," he said, and snatched up a fruit. "Give me a list of chemicals that make up this heavenly thing. Can you do that?"

"Of course not."

"There you have it."

"But, Dr. Riggs, I didn't *compound* that fruit. I didn't mix ingredients to create it. It is not the product of chemists in a laboratory."

"True enough. But as John points out, what benefit to the patient by listing a paragraph of incomprehensible Latin or German?"

"I understand that as well," Thomas persisted. "But suppose I were to ask you, as a *physician?* What would you say to me?"

"I would say," Riggs replied without hesitation, "that the tonic has undergone nearly a decade of intense scrutiny by our staff. We have *seen* its amazing results with our own eyes. In addition, we have *hundreds* of personal testimonials from physicians and patients alike about how the tonic has changed lives for the better. We can warrant, as independent laboratories have, that *nothing* in the tonic is dangerous, or deleterious to health in any way, when it is used as directed."

"Ah," Thomas said. He shifted in his chair, the effects of too long in one position sending pangs through his joints. "But you wouldn't tell me the ingredients."

Riggs regarded Thomas with amusement, and after a moment leaned closer. "Do you have any idea how many *thousands* of dollars we have invested in the development of the tonic?"

"I confess I don't."

"Exactly. No one asks that. But it is *thousands*. Perhaps *hundreds* of thousands. If we were to publish the ingredients, then what's to stop the copyists from taking advantage? Some of the ingredients are so rare, so dependent on the perfection of weather and circumstance, that they are not easily obtained. To open our enterprise to every get-rich-quick entrepreneur is to defeat our commitment to purity and professional standards. Open our files to rascals and snake-oil salesman, and you *would* see abuse, sir. And whose name would be blackened by that?" He lifted his eyebrows.

"Jealousy," Haines mumbled. "That's all it is."

"Indeed," Riggs agreed, and drained his glass. "When one is successful, the vultures descend. It's human nature."

"Suppose a patient has a sensitivity to a particular substance?" Thomas posed. "What then? For example, my father is sensitive to something that occurs in ocean fish. Eat a sardine, and his mouth feels as if he's consuming burning matches. Eat two, and he will become short of breath as well."

Riggs held up a hand. "And if your father's physician should write to us and ask if the tonic . . . which will surely calm his digestive processes, by the way . . . contains fish oil, or seafood products, we would reply instantly. Indeed, the tonic does contain an extract of ocean kelp, but no animal matter. Not a trace." He held up both hands. "So you see."

"But to work at the clinic, to be able to answer just such questions, I would have to know the analysis of each compound," Thomas persisted, and Riggs laughed.

"Of *course,* Thomas. Of course. By the time you have learned the processes of our pharmacy inside and out, you may well plead for mercy. But I hope you understand that I'm not simply being obstinately evasive. We want you to understand why we do as we do. The *why* of it all."

Thomas thumped a hand on the arm of the wheelchair. "I feel as if I've been consigned to prison."

"Patience is not one of your virtues," Alvi remarked. "Scarcely a week, remember. Charlie Grimes tells me that you've ordered ice for the morning?"

"I have," Thomas said eagerly. "I have made arrangements for its delivery each day. I have a hypothesis, but I must admit it is not original to myself. Harvard's Professor Palmer has talked much about the effect of alternating hot and cold on injuries, particularly those areas where joints are involved and blood supply is not marked."

"First one, and then the other?" Riggs asked. He leaned forward, both beefy arms on the table.

"As cold as the patient can stand, then as hot as can be tolerated without injury," Thomas said. He watched as Riggs clenched his hands together, and then relaxed them. The man understood perfectly. "Exactly," Thomas said. "Repetition produces an action not unlike a pump, forcing blood through the injured tissues."

"Fascinating," Riggs said. "I wonder how that action might be multiplied by application of our Journeyman's Extract. The success we've had in subduing inflammation has been remarkable." He nodded as if reaching a sudden decision. "I'll make sure some is delivered, if you don't have any on hand?" He looked at Alvi, then patted his napkin. "Anyway, it's been a long day. John, a few moments?"

"Indeed, indeed," Haines said. Thomas watched the older man close his eyes as he pushed himself up from the table. "Alvina?"

"I think not," Alvi said. "There is some reading I wish to do."

"Thomas, some brandy to settle your dinner?" Haines asked, in no hurry to release his grip on the back of his chair. "Zachary and I have been discussing strategies for transporting you to the clinic."

"I would be eager to hear those," Thomas replied. "More eager than you can possibly imagine."

16

Thomas awoke to a barrage of pounding, thumping, and cursing outside his window, interspersed with shouts and laughter. This time, instead of trying to leap from bed, he lay quietly, listening. Within ten minutes, he was sure that someone was building a house squarely in the center of Gambel Street, in the mud trap between 101 Lincoln and Lindeman's store. Then he remembered Haines's plans that they had discussed the previous evening.

The room was warm, and he didn't bother with his robe when he maneuvered over the edge of the bed, balancing now deftly on his right foot as he turned to settle into the wicker chair. He wheeled to the window and pulled the curtain aside.

Outside, half a dozen men were clustered, with two heavy freight wagons drawn up in the street, both laden with lumber and supplies. Considerable discussion appeared to center on a plumb line drawn tight between a stake driven into the mud half a dozen feet in front of the corner of the Haines's porch and another point more than a hundred feet farther north along Gambel Street.

Two men were industriously engaged in mucking out a posthole.

"Morning to you," a voice said, and Thomas started. One of the workers approached along the side of the house and looked up at Thomas. His pleasant face was familiar, bright blue eyes peering out from under a narrow cap. "We met a few days ago," he said. "Right before you and the mule went into the bay. You look like you're gettin' on with it."

"Ah," Thomas said. "Yes. How are you this fine morning?"

"Well, *I'm* fine. Name's Jake Tate, by the way. We don't mean to be disturbin' you, but we got orders to get this done, here."

"No disturbance," Thomas replied. "And is this the new boardwalk?"

"It is that. The doc's finally decided on it. Clear on down to the corner of Gambel and Grant."

"Well, my word," Thomas said. "That's a bit of an undertaking."

"We'll be finished with this little section this morning. Then you can have your peace and quiet." Jake pushed his cap back on his head. "Got to turn that corner and run 'er on up past the porch steps. Make kind of a landing, you know."

Thomas looked at the load of rough-cut lumber whose weight sank the wagon wheels deep into the mud. That freight would have been a stout pull up the hill for the two large Belgians in harness. "You work for Mr. Schmidt, then? All of you?"

"We do. Me and the boys here."

"Alvina tells me that things didn't turn out so well for your companion. I was sorry to hear that."

"Yep, well, these things happen sometimes. But, say, I need to get back at it." He repositioned his cap. "Sorry for the disturbance."

He trudged off toward one of the freight wagons, and Thomas's attention was drawn across the street. Alvina Haines had appeared in the side door of the Mercantile with an impossibly thin young man in tow. Probably in his late teens, Thomas guessed, the lad carried what appeared to be a wooden bucket with a towel draped over the top. Alvina slipped her right arm with casual affection through the boy's left elbow, and as they stepped off into the street, she reached across and rested her left hand on his shoulder for support.

Alvina Haines had not impressed Thomas as the sort of young lady who would need help with something as simple as crossing the street. As he watched their progress, Thomas reflected that if anything, it was more likely that she would be the one to pull the skinny youth up out of the mud. The sharp bones of his shoulders hunched forward as if he had no clavicles.

As they neared the workers by the porch corner, Alvi paused, her bright smile including all of the men. Caps doffed from heads, and the boy with the bucket managed to look a touch

88

more important. They disappeared around the corner of the house, and Thomas drew back from the window, remembering his lack of clothing. At the same time, he saw the boy recross the street without the bucket. One of the workers said something to the boy, who ignored him.

Before Thomas could wheel his chair across the room, knuckles rapped on his door. Alvi pushed it open without waiting for a reply. "I thought you might be up," she said, and wrinkled her nose as she regarded him. He reached for the robe, making a mess of it around his shoulders. "I have enough ice to start our own glacier," Alvi said, and set the bucket on the floor. "I told Charlie that after this, just a small pan would do. Now," and she stopped, hands on hips. "Let's get you back in bed and see if this works."

"I can manage," Thomas said.

"That's what you keep saying, and I'm sure you can. Here." She steadied his chair as he eased himself up on one foot. "You're getting pretty good at that. I can see that before you wrecked yourself, you were something of an athlete. You're downright shapely in the parts that haven't been mashed."

His face burned, but he ignored the unnurselike remarks. "I was watching the workmen outside," he said. "It seems we're to have a fancy boardwalk sooner rather than later."

"You'll be able to wheel your chair in grand style—unless it gets away from you on the hill, and then we'll be fishing you out of the inlet. Of course," and she smiled sweetly, "you've been there before." As she turned toward the door, she added, "I have a washed flour sack for the ice." She left the room and Thomas arranged himself in bed, pulling the sheet up to his shoulders. In a moment she returned. "This will work, I think," she said, holding out the sack. In the other hand she held a stout wooden bowl and an ice pick.

"Don't stick yourself with that." He laughed, and she raised an eyebrow at him.

"That's why I'm not giving it to *you*, Dr. Thomas. Now," and she knelt to attack the ice, first jabbing large pieces, and then expertly shaving off fine flakes until she had perhaps a pint of ice slivers in the bowl. "We don't want frostbite," she said. Deftly scraping the ice into the flour sack, she stood up and folded it, mashing the pillow of ice this way and that.

She advanced to the bed, and Thomas reached out a hand for the ice.

"Just lie still," she snapped. "Stop getting in my way." Her stern expression softened and her eyes twinkled. "Let's try it with you flat on your back first. Is that what you were thinking?"

"Yes. Maybe."

She flipped the sheet to one side, just shy of indecent. "You are *such* a mess," she said. Her fingers were cold, and he watched as she ran a feather-light touch down his hip, tracing the outline of the bruise. "Huh," she muttered. Slipping her left hand under his knee, she cupped her right hand over the hollow of his hip joint, just below the crown of the ilium. "When I pull up," she said, and he felt the gentle traction on his leg.

"It hurts," he replied.

"But where? Deep inside, or more . . ." The twang of pain lanced sharply enough to draw a gasp. "Right there, then," she added, and gently relaxed his leg to the horizontal. Mashing the bag again, she then placed it so that it draped across his hip, pillowing into the hollow. "Let me fetch a warm towel," she said. "In about ten minutes, that'll feel *really* good."

She left the room again, and Thomas exhaled a deep breath. He pulled the sheet back to cover himself, and a helpless laugh bubbled up. He could remember half a hundred times when he and his classmates had remarked on the various comely nurses who worked and studied at St. Katherine's Hospital in Philadelphia. Although some—perhaps many—had been more striking than Alvina Haines in appearance, and several had been more than willing for periodic recreation that would have sent their fathers searching for the shotgun, he could remember no one who so controlled a room when she entered it.

For a few minutes, the cold felt wonderful, but then the sensation turned into a deep, heavy ache. He shifted the ice pack several times until he could no longer endure it, then slipped the pack off, letting it lie across his left wrist and thumb.

About the time that the wetness soaked through the flour bag, Alvi returned with a bulky towel. "There are hot pebbles in this," she warned. "Gert is baking bread, and I shared the oven for a few minutes." She removed the sopping bag and regarded him expectantly. "Did it help?" she asked.

"It will in time," he said.

She positioned the hot pad. "I don't know if you're going to want the weight of this."

"It'll be fine." It was more than fine, the delicious warmth spreading across his pelvis and down his left leg. He closed his eyes, forgetting for a moment that she stood beside his bed.

"And you have something going on here," she said, and he opened his eyes and saw only the top of her head. She was bent over the left side of his chest, her nose inches from the dressing. "When did father look at your ribs last?" she asked, straightening up. She wrinkled her nose in a most fetching fashion.

"Yesterday morning, I think."

"Did *you* look at it then?"

"No. It's hard for me to see."

"Not even with a mirror?"

"No."

"Then let's do that," Alvi said. "The dressing is starting to turn." She left the room abruptly and returned with a small pair of scissors. "You might have noticed that Father doesn't see so well anymore," she said as she manipulated the dressings away.

"I had wondered. I thought perhaps it was merely an over-abundance of brandy."

"Hmm," she said, and shot him a glance of impatience. The last of the bandage came away, and she straightened up, regarding the enormous field of color that washed across the entire left side of his chest from armpit to waist, punctuated here and there with cuts, scrapes, and darker patches of hemorrhage. He started to reach for the patch of dressing that covered the open wound on his fifth rib, but she pushed his fingers away. "Let me."

The dressing was discolored and pulled sharply as she pealed it back. "Not good," she said, and straightened up. "Let me fetch a proper glass." She returned with a framed mirror that had been standing on the bureau, and held it so that he could view the damage. Cocking his head so he could focus his good eye, he could see that the wound was angry and inflamed. The irregular lips of the original ragged tear were swollen and dark. Alvi circled the bed and turned the gaslight up far enough that it hissed and spat. "Tell me what you think, Dr. Thomas."

"I think," he said, trying to duck his chin far enough for a clear view, "that there's still something lodged there. Give me the scissors." He held out his hand, but she hesitated. "I'm going to use it as a pointer only," he said. "That's all." With the tip, he indicated a particularly livid, inflamed spot between the fifth and sixth rib, two inches to the left of his sternum. "Explore right there," he said.

"Well," Alvi said, taking the scissors. "Let me find a few things."

Thomas lay still, listening to the construction outside, and after ten minutes, Alvi returned with a small pushcart laden with supplies. "How stalwart are you?" she asked.

"Just use a spritz of ether to deaden it," he said. "It looks like just a little flap of skin that's in the way."

"A little one." She smiled. "This might hurt *a little*," and she paused, ether bottle in hand. "Isn't that what the physician always says when he's about to inflict torture on the patient?"

"A small price to pay," Thomas said, but he could feel his spine tightening in apprehension. She took a deep breath. "My father drinks too much," she said, and the sudden change of subject took Thomas by surprise. "I know that. Part of it is missing my mother. They were deeply in love, for a long, long time."

"How long has she been gone, then?"

"Six years now. She died on my nineteenth birthday."

"That's hard."

"Certainly," Alvi said. "Hold still now." The ether spray made him wince. "And your mother?"

"She died when I was not yet two," Thomas said. "She and my infant sister."

"Ah. Your father never remarried?"

"No."

"Nor mine." She sprayed the ether again, draping the area with a light towel to trap the fumes. "He always drank heavily," she said. As she spoke, she traced the various bruises and nicks that decorated Thomas's torso, her brow furrowed in thought. "But after that . . ." Shrugging philosophically, she added, "Still, that's not the only excuse. His eyesight *is* deteriorating rather quickly, I think. He won't discuss it, but I see it in the way he holds his head, in the way he sometimes loses his balance when something in his path takes him by surprise."

"The alcohol would make that so much worse," Thomas said.

"Of course it does. But by the end of the day, I'm not sure that he particularly *wants* to see straight anymore." A little smile touched her even lips.

"He's sixty-five?"

"Six," Alvi corrected. "Soon seven."

"That must make it difficult for you, then. For you and Zachary."

"In what way?"

"I mean the clinic and all. That endeavor is obviously growing. It must be something of a burden for your father. The effort he has expended in the finishing of his book, the myriad patients . . ."

"Well, we help where we can. The faster *you* recuperate, the better. We expect an influx of patients when the book is circulated. My father's name carries considerable weight."

"I should think so."

She lifted the towel. "Now you can hold this." She busied herself at the cart. "Let me have it now." She blew another mist

93

of ether across the wound and quickly wiped the area clean with a gauze pad soaked in carbolic acid. She selected a bistoury from the small copper box.

"Don't jump around now," she said, and Thomas froze, neck aching from the tension. "Well, no wonder," she said almost immediately. From the copper box of sterile instruments she selected a delicate forceps. Applying pressure below the wound with the antiseptic pad, she grasped and pulled, and the sting turned savage.

"Good God," Thomas gasped between clenched teeth.

Another spritz of ether, and then Thomas became aware that Alvi was holding her breath as she worked. A final tug, and she let out a soft whistle. "Now look at this," she said, and held the forceps up. Captured was a shard of amber glass nearly an inch long, tapered to a fine point. "I think that's it," she said triumphantly. "On top of everything else, when you fell you managed to find a broken bottle." She clanked forceps and souvenir into the pan and maneuvered a clean gauze pad over the wound, wiping up the rivulet of blood that tracked down his ribs toward the sheets. "Let's debride a little of this dead tissue, and then we're all set." In a moment, she had a clean dressing in place over the wound.

"You really should have those ribs bound," she said. "I know it's going to hurt, but let's do that. It'll be easier for you if you swing your legs over the side of the bed."

After removing the hot towel, she maneuvered him into place, hands amazingly strong and sure, and by the time she had replaced the wraps around his ribs with clean linen, he was light-headed.

"I think that if you're going to do the ice, you should try it more often. Once a day seems insignificant to me."

"I don't want to be a nuisance," Thomas said, and Alvi laughed abruptly.

"Too late," she said, and patted his knee. "Rest until lunch. We'll do the ice and heat again then."

As he watched Alvi gather up her paraphernalia, Thomas felt only admiration. "Where was your schooling?" he asked.

Alvi, about to push the cart out the door, stopped and looked at him. "I spent almost two years at Grace Normal, over in Seattle. The first year, I couldn't believe how bad it was, so I went back to make sure." She smiled. "It was. I left."

"Your medical training."

"Father knows enough for any ten people. A little rubbed off on me, I suppose."

"Is that your ambition, then?"

"What, medicine?"

"Yes. There are women in the profession now."

"Oh, indeed there are," Alvi agreed, and let that suffice as an answer.

17

Two afternoons later, Thomas stood on the front porch, judging the five steps that led down to the fragrant, rough-cut fir of the new boardwalk. Propped uncomfortably on his crutches, he looked down Gambel Street. The workers' voices were muted by distance.

Thomas had deliberately chosen a quiet moment for this experiment. He didn't want hands on his elbow, or words of encouragement, or warnings of disaster. Gert James was busy in the back with laundry, and Horace was off fishing. He hadn't seen Alvi or Dr. Haines all afternoon.

Moving close to the right-hand railing, he took his weight on his right foot, easing the crutches down to the first step. Balanced with his right hip braced against the railing, he paused, considered, and took a slow breath. He shifted his weight, knuckles white on the crutches. The jolt as his right foot found the step was more than he had expected, and set off a wave of fireworks.

"You given any thought to how you're going to get back up, Doctor?"

Thomas looked up to see Lars Lindeman standing on his own step across the street, one hand cupping his bristly chin thoughtfully.

"No," Thomas said truthfully. "I confess that I haven't. Maybe I shall never return."

"I got me a wheelbarrow, I suppose," Lindeman said. "Me and the kid could haul your carcass back up."

"I'm hoping that won't be necessary," Thomas said. "I'm just seeing if this is possible."

"Don't look like it is," Lindeman observed. "Don't see the point, anyways. There isn't anything at the bottom of the steps that you need to fetch just yet."

With considerable effort, Thomas turned back, discovering that a mere eight inches could be a daunting precipice.

"I got some news for you," Lindeman said, raising his voice a notch instead of crossing the street.

"What's that?" Thomas leaned against the railing once more, breath coming in short stabs.

"You want the good news first, or the not-so-good." Before he could choose, Lindeman continued, "Your steamer trunk arrived this morning. I was going to send Charlie over with it."

"Ah, that's wonderful," Thomas cried.

"That's the good part," Lindeman said. "The steamer got here. Unless you meant to ship an empty chest, then a few things went astray somewheres between here and Connecticut."

Thomas's heart sank. "What are you saying?"

"I'll fetch it," Lindeman said, and turned back into his store.

Thomas stood rooted. The old man wasn't going to carry his steamer trunk. The thing weighed more than a hundred pounds.

In a moment, Charlie Grimes appeared, the large trunk on one skinny shoulder, and Thomas's heart sank. Lindeman trudged behind the boy, and stamped his boots on the new boardwalk.

"Pretty fancy," he said. He beckoned Charlie. "Up on the porch, son."

Charlie swung the chest down with ease. He glanced at Thomas, then quickly looked away as if this whole mess might be his fault.

"Surprised you didn't have a lock on it," Lindeman said. "Or did you?"

"Most certainly I did," Thomas groaned. Not only was the padlock missing, but the trunk's ornate hasp was twisted and bent, torn from the steamer's own less substantial lock. Someone had thoughtfully rebuckled the heavy leather straps that held the cover in place.

"You want Charlie to open 'er up?"

"Yes." Thomas already knew the answer before the eager youngster had wrestled the baggage open.

"Fella could fit a lot into a trunk that big," Lindeman observed helpfully as the steamer yawned open.

Thomas sagged against the railing. "Son of a bitch," he breathed. He glanced up at Lindeman. "Why was it shipped to you?"

"All freight for this end of town comes to me," the old man said. "I'm the terminal, and don't *that* sound important, though." He shrugged.

"What can I do?" Thomas said, more to himself than to Lindeman.

"Not a hell of a lot," the old man replied. "No way of telling where it all went. Three thousand miles offers up a lot of opportunity." He nudged the steamer's address plate with his foot. "Dr. Thomas Parks, MD," he read. "Might have been better to leave the 'doctor' off. Gives folks ideas. Anything gone that can't be replaced?"

"My books, for one thing." He tried to tally the various titles that he had packed, books that would take months, maybe years, to replace.

"Doc Haines has enough of them, I would think," Lindeman said helpfully.

"I suppose he does. All my clothing, other than a change or

two that I had with me in my travel bag. My father's pistol." He grimaced. "Most of my medical instruments. A very fine microscope that my father gave me when I graduated from medical school."

"All things that a little money can replace," Lindeman said. He lit his pipe. "Now a man could say that you're free to travel light. Something to be said for that."

Thomas laughed hopelessly. "Very, very light."

"How's that ice working, by the by?"

"It's working wonders," Thomas said. "I'm in your debt."

"That's okay. Lots of folks carry a tab at the Mercantile." He grinned. "And by the by, you're dead on right about that mutt. He's got something festering back there at his ass end. Won't leave it alone."

"We need to do something before it kills him," Thomas said.

"Wouldn't be much of a loss," Lindeman said, and Charlie frowned at the remark. "Want the boy to take this inside for you?"

"I'd appreciate that. Not that an empty trunk is of much use."

"You never know." The old man turned abruptly and started back across the street. "You need clothes, whatever," and he waved a hand at the Mercantile. "We either got it, or can get it."

"Thanks, Lars." Thomas followed Charlie and the steamer trunk toward his room. As the boy was turning to go, he held up a hand. "Charlie, surgery is the only thing that's going to give that dog any comfort. Can you help me with that?"

Grimes looked apprehensive. "Wha—," he began, then stopped as Thomas shook his head.

"Before I do anything, *someone*," and he emphasized the word, "needs to clean him up. I would think a good bath down at the shore would be a start. Do you think that's possible?"

"I . . . I . . ."

"If you could do that without being bitten to pieces, then I could do a proper examination," Thomas said.

"H-h-he won-won-won't let you," Charlie said.

"I intend to put him to sleep," Thomas said. "He'll have

98

pleasant dreams about biting people, and when he wakes up, he'll be back together." *And I traveled three thousand miles to perform my first operation on a mangy dog,* he thought. "We'll do the surgery down at the clinic. In the meantime, if you can do what you can to clean him up, it would make things easier."

"I-I-I'll d-d-do it."

"You better get back to work before the old man docks you an hour's pay. Thanks for lugging that steamer for me." Charlie nodded, looked like he wanted to say something, but then abruptly turned and headed back to the Mercantile. He crossed the street in a few nimble bounds.

18

Restless after too much dinner and not quite enough brandy, Thomas stared up at the dark ceiling of his room. He had written a lengthy letter to his father, then torn it to pieces, impatient with the letter's tone of self-pity and its casual criticism of John Haines's evening habits. After all, hadn't he imbibed nearly as much as the older man? Hadn't he let the warm buzz of liquor silence the demons in *his* joints, just as Dr. John Haines might find relief from the ravages of old age?

Thomas heard the clock strike midnight, and then the quarter hour, and eventually, half past. The night noises continued, including one dog whose bark reminded him of a metronome, a steady, deep four-quarter time of relentless impatience. He counted the beats—*whoa, whoa, whoa,* pause *whoa, whoa, whoa,* pause, on and on without hesitation.

The barking was nearby, and Thomas guessed that the gimpy Prince was standing in the middle of Lincoln Street, not far from the front steps of 101.

Somewhere in the house, he heard movement and muttering, and then the clock struck 12:45 A.M. Thumping steps, this time with no effort to keep them quiet, were followed by another door closed none too stealthily. Now Thomas heard urgent voices that must have originated from the front of the house.

The walls of the house blocked the conversation, and Thomas found himself straining to hear. The dog continued its cadence, but the voices fell silent.

In a moment, his door opened so quietly that he wasn't sure whether it was a breeze or a person.

"Thomas?" Alvina's voice was husky.

"I'm awake." He felt her hand on his right arm and could smell her fragrance.

"Can you get up? Charlie's hurt. Here, I'm turning on the lamps." The flash of a match was jarring, and as the light flooded the room, he saw that she wore only a flannel nightgown, her hair in disarray down below her shoulders.

Feeling the strength of her hands on his arm, in a moment he was upright. She threw the robe over his shoulders and pushed the chair closer.

"What happened?" he asked. "You said it was Charlie? The boy from across the street?"

"Yes, and I don't know what happened," she said. "I think he may have been stabbed."

"Is he conscious?" His chair was already in motion.

"I think so." Alvi pushed him down the hallway, then turned abruptly through the parlor toward the front door.

"Did you wake your father?"

"That's not possible. You can tell me what to do."

"My medical bag," he said. "I don't have that. You said that the nurse—"

"I don't think that's going to do you much good," and she didn't explain why. They rounded the corner to the foyer. Horace was kneeling on one knee, and Charlie Grimes was stretched out on his back on the carpet, his feet just inside the front door.

The young man drew up his left leg and then stretched it out, then again, a rhythmic motion as if he were trying to walk away. His left forearm was raised, hand clenched in a fist hovering in the air. He wore a scruffy homespun shirt above muddy woolen trousers. His shirt was unbuttoned and his long johns torn open. Horace held a folded towel against Charlie's white chest.

"This is impossible," Thomas said, flustered by the awkwardness of the wheelchair. He looked frantically around the room. "Can you lift him onto the divan? I can't reach down to the floor."

Horace reached out, took Charlie's left hand, and brought it down to press on the towel.

"I got his head." He rose and Alvi moved quickly to take the victim's legs. Together they half-lifted, half-dragged Charlie to the couch. Horace let out a loud grunt as they lifted the boy up. Charlie's legs pumped, and his eyes were wide and staring, his mouth trying to form words.

"Does he have family?" Thomas asked and took the stethoscope from Alvi.

"I don't think so."

"Then Horace, will you fetch Mr. Lindeman? We may need his wagon."

"That dog's out there."

"Oh, for God's sake, man. Just tell the dog to shut up. He won't hurt you."

His left hand with its bandaged thumb was awkward, and it took him a moment to find a way past the bandages around his skull for the stethoscope's right earpiece. With the instrument settled, he pulled himself as close to Charlie as he could. Easing the boy's hand away, he lifted the towel and frowned. A single small wound, perhaps a centimeter long and the width of a small knife blade, punctured the left side of Charlie's pigeon chest, the slice just touching the inside margin of the nipple.

"He's been stabbed," Thomas said. A quick survey showed no other blood, no other injuries. Eyes closed, Thomas roamed the bell of the stethoscope across Charlie's chest. The heartbeat was irregular and feeble, almost panicky, an odd muffled sound as if someone had wrapped the heart tight in a piece of flannel.

"Charlie, can you hear me?" Thomas said, and saw no

answering flicker from the patient. "Alvi, help me roll him a bit. Onto his right side."

That accomplished, he listened with the stethoscope down the boy's side and across the back.

"All right," he said. Taking the instrument out of his ears, he glanced up at Alvi. "What do we have that's sterile? I need to follow the wound track to see if the blade actually damaged the heart. If not, we may be able to aspirate some of the pericardial blood for some relief. Otherwise . . ." He held up his hand with thumb and forefinger spread far apart. "A slender Nélaton probe, if John has one here. Otherwise, a blunt, slender probe of any kind."

"It will be a few minutes," Alvi said. "We have only the one small gas sterilizer here."

"Then do it," Thomas said. "Then we can see about transporting the boy to the operating theater at the clinic."

The young woman hesitated, and Thomas turned to look full at her. "Well? I need that probe, Alvi. And sterilize a Robert's pericardial trocar at the same time."

"I'll see to it."

Thomas turned back to his patient. The wound bled scarcely at all, just a little, nasty slit in the pale skin. A quick survey showed no other obvious injuries. The boy's hair was filthy, but no blood was crusted, no goose eggs betraying a blow to the skull. The knife wound, as insignificant as it might first appear, had been enough.

Bruising around the edges of the wound showed where the handle of the knife had impacted the flesh, the bruise of the blunt trauma marking the outline clearly. The weapon had been small, with the sort of handle one would expect to see on a folding Barlow or similar efficient pocketknife—not the large guard found on a hunting knife. One side of the wound was sharply cut by the edge of the blade, the opposite side blunt . . . the typical wound from a single-edged weapon with a slender blade, driven in hard to the hilt.

"Charlie, look at me."

Thomas used his right thumb to lift first one eyelid and then the other. The boy's eyes were glassy and unresponsive. His legs stopped walking. With the stethoscope once more in place, Thomas strained to hear the faint pulse. If the pericardium had been cut, or a nearby vessel, the blood would fill the sack around the heart, suffocating it to a standstill. If the heart itself was cut, then everything depended on the nature of the wound to the cardiac muscle.

Like any muscle, the heart could heal from minimal injury, given time. A wound that actually punctured any of the heart's chambers would be invariably fatal in all but the rarest of circumstances.

Thomas sat back, resting his hip. It was so easy to slice open the thoracic cavity of a cadaver, resecting the ribs out of the way with a careless crunch of the shears, opening the way to examine the organs that lay underneath.

"How did this happen?" he murmured, but Charlie Grimes had settled into a coma, his heart fluttering in protest as the flood closed around it, his breath coming in shallow jerks, his chest shivering rather than rising and falling in regular breaths.

Footsteps thumped on the front porch, and Horace James appeared. "He's on his way," he announced.

Even as he said that, Alvi reappeared.

"We need one of the clinic's ambulances," Thomas said to Horace. "Can you arrange that?"

"An ambulance?" the handyman said, puzzled.

"It'll be faster to use one of Lindeman's buckboards with a hair mattress in the back," Alvi interrupted. "The probe and aspirator will be ready in five minutes. It's not a Roberts, but I think it will work."

Thomas thumped his fist on the arm of his chair in frustration, and as if in response, Charlie's eyes snapped open and he rose partially on his elbows, mouth open wide. Easing him back down, Thomas once more adjusted the stethoscope. The rattle of the lad's breath was loud, and for a moment his heart sped up, strong but irregular, to 160 beats a minute, then faster, impossibly fast. It stopped, missing ten or fifteen beats, then surged again for as many, then stopped. This time, it did not kick again.

Charlie managed one more choppy breath and then his body sank into the divan.

"Any wagon will do," Thomas heard himself say. He continued to listen, astonished, as his first patient in Port McKinney expired under his touch.

"He gone?" Horace asked.

"Yes, he's gone." They heard footsteps on the porch, and Lars Lindeman limped to the door, opening it slowly as if he might disturb them.

"My God," he said, "what happened?"

"Charlie was stabbed," Alvi said. Her face was a mix of emotions.

Lindeman advanced to the divan. He looked down at the boy. "Stabbed, you say?" The Mercantile owner's face was pale, and he held his hand over his mouth as if trying to catch a burst of words that he regretted. "Where'd you find him?"

"Right smack on the front step," Horace replied. "I got up to see what that damn dog of yours was yammerin' about, and there Charlie was. He was sittin' on the top step."

"Well, I don't know . . . ," Lindeman started to say. "Christ, this is . . . ," and his voice trailed off.

"What is it?" They turned to see John Haines, hair disheveled, dark velvet gown bunched around his ample paunch.

"Charlie Grimes has been killed," Alvi said. "He died before we could do anything to help him."

Haines shuffled across the room, adjusting his glasses as he did so. At one point he appeared to lose his balance, and took a short step sideways to steady himself.

Thomas removed the cloth, and Haines glanced at the wound, cocking his head sideways and holding his glasses for a better view. He shook his head and straightened up. "Damn shame," he muttered and turned to his daughter. "Did you send someone to fetch Eastman?"

"Not yet."

"That needs to be done before the body is taken to Winchell's. Horace, will you see to that, please?"

"I want to do a postmortem," Thomas said quickly as Horace left the room. "If the remains can be removed to the clinic . . ."

"Good God, man," Haines said testily. "Whatever for? A single knife thrust to the heart. That's fairly obvious, I should think. And autopsies are Winchell's province, not ours. He's the county coroner."

"Then I need to speak with him about that," Thomas said. He looked at the small pan where the instruments waited. "If we could have treated him sooner—"

"Sooner would have made no difference," Haines said. "You could have been standing beside Mr. Grimes at the moment he was wounded, and there would be nothing you could do." He sighed. "But suit yourself." He regarded Thomas critically. "Don't misunderstand me. We have no problem removing the body to the clinic, Thomas—if that's what Winchell wants to do. It's *you* that is at issue."

"Me?"

"You're hardly ready to stroll about town."

"But the boardwalk is nearly finished," Thomas persisted. "And if not that, then a wagon."

"I see." The corners of Haines's eyes crinkled a bit. He watched as Alvi spread a blanket over Charlie Grimes's corpse.

"With your permission, I'll be happy to remain at the clinic until I'm fully ambulatory."

"Oh, come, come," Haines said with a dismissive wave of his hand. "Hardly that. Besides, I don't think we want to miss your company at the dinner table, or during our evening sessions in the library." He took a deep breath and removed his glasses, holding them up to the nearest gaslight. "We'll see what can be done. Now, tell me how this all happened."

"We don't know," Thomas said. "Horace found the boy on our front steps. The dog's barking awoke us."

"I never heard him. You're telling me that young Mr. Grimes was not brought here by companions, or the like? He stumbled here unassisted?"

"We don't know," Alvi offered.

"He could have been . . . well, hell. He could have been any-wheres in town," Lindeman said. "Got himself a taste for the bottle, I'm afraid. Always was a scrapper. Him stammerin' didn't help none. My guess is that he got himself in a scrap downtown, maybe. Someone stuck him there, or followed him back up the hill, maybe. I didn't hear him one way or another. Didn't hear nobody cry out. Didn't hear no argument."

"Well, Eastman can sort it all out," Haines said. "Damn unfortunate is what it is." He turned and peered at the large grand-father clock. "What time is it? My God, just after one."

Alvi touched her father's arm. "Go back to bed, Father. I'll talk with Butch when he rouses himself."

Haines nodded and shuffled closer to the divan. He reached down and pulled the blanket back to clear Charlie's face, stand-ing silently with the linen in hand. "Such a waste," he said. "What was he, all of seventeen or eighteen?"

"Would have been eighteen come Thanksgiving," Lindeman said.

"You don't say." He flipped the linen back and turned to Thomas. "You be careful, young man. You're not ready for any of this." To Alvi, he added, "See that he behaves himself, Alvina."

Voices outside announced visitors, and Haines grimaced with irritation. "I'm going back to bed," he said.

19

Zachary Riggs looked like Butch Eastman's little brother. As burly as Riggs might have been, he appeared almost slight compared to the enormous constable. Eastman hadn't waited for an invitation. He rapped a knuckle on the door and then en-tered with both Riggs and Horace James on his heels.

He stopped just inside the room, hands on his hips, canvas

coat splayed winglike. Thomas guessed the man weighed nearly three hundred pounds, standing well over six and a half feet tall. A tiny woolen pullover hat appeared ready to pop off the top of a round skull evenly cropped to resemble a ripe burdock.

"Well, now," Eastman said, his voice a light tenor that would have been expected from a schoolboy. His large, expressive brown eyes drew attention away from a badly pockmarked face. "You're the new fellow," he said. "I'm Edgar Eastman. Most folks call me Butch." He didn't offer his hand.

"This is Dr. Thomas Parks," Zachary Riggs said, stepping around the constable. "But what happened here? Horace told us that Charlie Grimes ran into a knife." Riggs started to move forward toward the corpse, but Eastman reached out a hand and stopped him.

"One thing at a time," he said mildly, but the command in his voice was certain. "Show me," he added to Thomas.

Thomas wheeled his chair back and drew the blanket down to the victim's waist. "A single wound," he said. "It appears to have been inflicted with a small knife. Perhaps a jackknife or some such. After the postmortem, I'll be able to tell you more."

"Is that right?" Eastman mused, and Thomas couldn't tell if he was actually interested or not. "There are a good many knives in town."

"I would imagine there are." Thomas wondered if the death of this young man was going to be dismissed with that vague statistic.

Eastman looked down at the young doctor for a moment, his eyes inventorying the bandages, the chair, the awkward posture. "Where did you find him?"

"The boy was sitting on our front step," Horace interjected, and Eastman turned slowly in place to regard the older man, his expression blandly skeptical.

"And you carried him inside?"

"Yes. Horace and Alvi did," Thomas said.

Up to this point, Alvina Haines had said not a word, but

stood in the entrance to the hallway, on the opposite side of the room from the divan. She had fetched a robe, and looked elegant, Thomas thought. Sadly elegant.

"Good evening, young lady," Eastman said. He turned his inventory on her, taking a long moment. "And who brought the body to one-oh-one?"

"We don't know that," Thomas said. "As Horace already explained, he found Charlie sitting on the porch step."

"He cried out then?" Eastman's voice sank to little more than a whisper.

"No. Not that any of us heard." Horace nodded in agreement.

"Now that's interesting, Doctor. Last I looked, it's well past midnight. If the boy didn't cry out, how did you discover his presence?"

"The dog, sir," Thomas said. "Prince set to barking, and it didn't sound like he was about to stop until someone went out to see what the trouble was."

"I done that," Horace said. "Damn dog was just going on. Like to drive me crazy."

"I see." Eastman sidled close to the divan and bent down, peering at the wound. His brow furrowed with concentration. After a moment, he looked at Thomas without straightening up.

"So tell me what you think, Doctor."

"What I think? Charlie was alive when I reached him. We were in the process of sterilizing some instruments when he died."

"About the wound. That's what I mean."

"He was stabbed once. I think it was a fairly small knife, most likely a folder. You can see the bruising around the wound caused by the handle."

"Stabbed hard, then. Right hard on the hilt."

"Yes."

Eastman straightened up, his spine letting out a loud pop. He arched his back, then settled his shoulders. Turning, he surveyed the room. "So . . . none of you saw this?"

Heads shook, and Eastman's eyes rested on Horace James.

"You went out to see what was fussing the dog. You didn't see anyone running away?"

"No, I sure enough didn't."

"No one was with Charlie at that time?"

"No, sir. There he set, back against the rail, head leaning back. I could see he was hurt."

"And what did he say to you?"

"Not a word, Butch. Not a word."

"No response at all? He didn't say who attacked him, or where the attack took place?"

"No, sir, not a word."

Eastman turned to Lindeman, whose face was still pasty gray. "You didn't see anyone on the street, Lars?" Lindeman shook his head. "You were asleep? They say the dog was barking."

"Oh, I hear him all the time, the damn mutt. I don't pay no attention."

"You knew that Charlie was out somewhere, did you?"

"He's out all the time, Butch. You know that. He comes and goes as he pleases from that room I give him. I ain't his mama."

"No, you aren't," Eastman said gently. The constable turned back and regarded the corpse. "Doctor Parker—"

"Parks."

"Parks," Eastman repeated. "Parks, Parks." He nodded. "You think he could have gone far with a wound like that?"

"There's no way to tell, Mr. Eastman. There have been cases of victims who suffered more devastating injuries than this who then walked a considerable distance afterward. There's no way to tell how far Charlie managed."

"All right." Eastman surveyed the room again and nodded at Alvi. "Your father's not home at the moment?"

"He's in bed," Alvi said. "I don't think he needs to be bothered."

"No, I guess he doesn't," Eastman agreed. "Did you see any of this, young lady?"

"I heard Horace get up to tend to the dog," Alvi said. "He came to fetch me when he saw what the trouble was."

"And then you woke Dr . . . Parks."

"I was already awake," Thomas said quickly. "But yes. She came and fetched me."

"Not much you could do in any case, it appears."

"No. It turned out that there wasn't."

Eastman heaved a vast sigh. "That's that, I guess. I'll have Winchell come and fetch the body."

"Actually, I want to do a postmortem," Thomas said.

Eastman raised an eyebrow. "You discuss that with Winchell. Then maybe I'll talk with you in a day or so."

"Certainly."

Eastman turned to Zachary Riggs. "You about ready?"

"I think I should tend to things here," Riggs said quickly. "We need to move the . . ." He stopped, and Thomas found his lack of words surprising. "I need to see what Dr. Parks wants to do."

"Well, then, I'll leave you to it." Eastman nodded politely at each person in turn, and offered his hand to Thomas. "I heard about your misfortune," he said. "You'll be up and around before long?"

"I certainly hope so."

"You need anything now, I'm just down the street. Any of these folks can tell you."

"Thank you."

The room seemed empty when Eastman left, and for a moment, there was silence. Alvi approached the divan and once more pulled the blanket up, taking a moment to stroke a strand of blond hair away from Charlie Grimes's face.

"Well," Zachary Riggs said. "This is a sorry state of affairs indeed. I really liked that boy." He looked down at Thomas thoughtfully. "You're hurting. Pale as that sheet."

"Just sore, Zachary. It's nothing. I want to know who did this."

"Of course. That's only natural. We all do, I'm sure. Unfortunately, such things are commonplace around the camps."

"I hadn't thought of one-oh-one as a camp," Thomas replied. "Will Eastman do anything about this?"

"Ah, don't underestimate Edgar Eastman," Riggs said. "He and I were just playing chess when Horace interrupted." He smiled tightly. "And I hate to admit it, but Butch was winning. When he says that he's interested in your findings, he means every word."

"Can I leave transfer of the body to you?"

"Of course," Riggs said. "Winchell will have two men come around first thing in the morning."

"I'd prefer now," Thomas said, and Riggs looked at him with surprise.

"Now? You're not—"

"If someone would carry my chair down the front steps, I can ride along in the wagon. I can't sleep anyway, and I need to know."

"Good heavens, man. Need to know what?" Riggs said.

"Just . . . I need to know whatever . . . there is to know," Thomas finished lamely. "That's all. Nothing is served by waiting."

Zachary Riggs thrust his hands in his pockets, frowning at the figure on the divan. For a long time he stood that way, musing, and Thomas wondered what the physician was considering.

"All right," Riggs said finally. "I'll rouse Winchell and see to moving the body." He turned his frown on Thomas. "But at least do us the favor of waiting for daylight before *you* attempt the trip to the clinic, Doctor."

"I won't sleep anyway," Thomas said. "I don't see—"

"No, you won't sleep," Riggs said, and he smiled. "But others might. You'll need help with the postmortem anyway. So do us the courtesy."

Thomas chaffed with impatience, but knew that Riggs was right. "That's going to have to do, then," he said.

20

The new boardwalk followed Gambel Street, and as it started to curve downhill, Alvi put both hands on Thomas's shoulders. "Let's give him a good shove and be done with it," she said to Horace, and the handyman mumbled agreement.

A stone's throw beyond Lindeman's Mercantile, Gambel Street turned right, the grade becoming precipitous. Jake Tate's crew had installed a step every twenty or thirty feet so that the boardwalk descended in a series of semilevel decks. Each time they reached a step, Horace tipped the chair back and eased the wheels down the vertical drop to the next section of walkway. The torture was mild, and Thomas knew that Horace was right— this venture was easier, all things considered, than trying to bundle him into a wagon for the short drive.

As the street turned left again to parallel the hill, Thomas saw they were approaching half a dozen frame houses, and the boardwalk came to an abrupt end, marked by a pile of lumber and four sawhorses where the workers had stopped for the Sabbath. A hundred yards of rutted mud faced them before the intersection with Grant Street.

"Let me fetch Mr. Winchell," Alvi said. "He's here already." She set off quickly before Thomas had the chance to ask where "here" was, striding toward a three-story brick building across Grant in front of which a black hearse was drawn, the two matching black horses motionless at the rail. In a moment she reappeared with Zachary Riggs and another man, short and brawny, with a roll to his walk.

"Had to come see all this for myself," the man said as he drew near. His laborer's garb surprised Thomas, who had a fixed notion of what an undertaker should look like. The man grinned, showing a set of astonishingly white teeth behind his full mustache. "I'm Ted Winchell," he said, before anyone had the chance to introduce him. "The county says that I'm the coroner. You're Doc Parks, I assume." His grip was fleshy and powerful, and as he shook hands, he tipped his head and surveyed the wheelchair—at a casual glance, it appeared stuck in the mud. "Hell of a way to start a Sunday, I must say."

"Good morning, sir." Thomas saw that wood shavings had embedded themselves in Winchell's flannel shirt and trousers. The coroner turned and surveyed the muck through which he'd just trekked. "Well, no easy way, is there. Zachary?" And he motioned toward the other side of Thomas's wheelchair. "Let's deliver the goods." The two men lifted the chair as if its occupant were a child.

They crossed Grant Street, and the wheels touched down on a well-worn boardwalk in front of the building. Thomas looked up at the lintel over the front door, the marble carved in tombstone script, MCKINNEY MERCHANTS' BANK AND TRUST. Below that, gold-leaf paint on the front door's glass pane announced DR. JOHN L. HAINES, MD., with 601 GAMBEL STREET centered under his name.

Supposing this to be an auxiliary office of some sort, Thomas looked on down Gambel Street to catch his first sight of the massive clinic. He was taken by surprise as Alvi opened the door and the two men lifted his chair and hoisted him over the single step.

"Your offices are separate, then," Thomas said, rolling forward a bit on the polished wood floors of 601 Gambel. The foyer included several benches and two heavily padded chairs, a single long table against one wall, and two massive bookcases loaded with impressive volumes. Near one of the leather chairs, a grandfather's clock marked the time. Four doors, one to his left and three ahead and to the right, were all open, but the morning light was so dim that Thomas couldn't see what lay beyond. Alvi shut the front door, closing out the rush of raw coastal air.

"Home away from home," she said with a tight smile. She beckoned and he followed her through the door on the left, leading to a narrow hallway with windows facing Grant Street on one side and a stairway rising on the other.

"Ted, I'll speak with you later," Riggs said. "I'll be interested to hear what you find out." He nodded at Thomas. "I'll be upstairs should you need me."

Thomas watched him disappear up the stairs, footfalls echoing. Nothing he saw fit the image he'd built in his mind of the Haines Clinic and Vital Research Center—and certainly nothing in this modest building resembled the engraving in the *Advisor.*

The hall turned the corner through a wide archway. "When this building was first constructed," Alvi said, "it was to be a bank, but that didn't work out. Then the owners got caught up in a Seattle fire and went bankrupt." She lowered her voice. "My father had wanted to move his practice out of our home for a long time. So." She stopped in front of a door and tried the knob. "Let me go fetch the key," she said, and disappeared the way they had come. Thomas pivoted the chair in place. He could see four more doorways leading from the hall, all unmarked.

"First visit to Port McKinney?" Winchell asked pleasantly as they waited. "I hear it was something of an ordeal for you."

"Indeed," Thomas replied, and laughed helplessly. "From the ship straight to the rocks to this marvelous chair." He thumped the wicker arm.

"Eastman tells me that he doesn't know what happened to the boy," Winchell said.

"None of us do. Except that he died before we could help him."

"Sad thing. He never had a chance to say a thing, I'm told."

"True."

"What is it that you aim to find out with all this?" He stepped aside as Alvi reappeared, key ring in hand. The door yawned open, the room beyond pitch-dark. The motion of the door fanned the characteristic odor of the newly dead. The question, coming as it did from a coroner charged with performing autopsies in questionable cases, surprised the physician.

"I want to know everything there is to know," Thomas replied. A match flashed, and Alvi lit four gas fixtures. Thomas stopped in the doorway. "Operating theater" were the two words that came to mind from Dr. Haines's monumental new book, and they didn't fit this room. A slightly tilted table of heavily varnished wood dominated, the legs at one end raised by wooden blocks. The sheeted corpse of Charlie Grimes appeared pathetically small.

Glass-doored cabinets lined one wall, and below the table, a series of buckets were lined up, ready and waiting. Over the table, a chandelier of six gas lamps hung, and Alvi had lowered them, lighting each in turn until the room fairly blazed. Thomas turned in place, surveying what apparently had once been a small conference room. "Ah," he said, spying his black medical bag on one of the shelves. He wheeled over and looked inside. Everything was neatly arranged, the instruments dry and polished, each tiny bottle neatly stowed in its own boot.

"Everything should be in order," Alvi said. "Bertha fussed over it for some time, Dr. Thomas."

"I'm in her debt."

"I still don't see how you're going to do this," Alvi said. She touched the side of the table. "This is much too high for your chair."

"I think I can stand," Thomas said. "With the crutches, I mean. Did Zachary want to assist? He left before I had a chance to ask him."

"He's working in his office upstairs, Dr. Thomas. Mr. Winchell and I will certainly be able to provide you with whatever you need."

The closed atmosphere of the room pressed in. "There should be some kind of ventilation in this room," Thomas commented, swiveling to survey the chamber again—the room was little more than that.

"Yes, there should," Alvi said. "We don't use it often. Mr. Winchell takes care of things like this."

"Ah, but don't hesitate on my account," the undertaker said.

"Well, we'll make do." Thomas backed his chair against the table, leaned his crutches on the edge and pushed himself upward, pulling at the same time. Balanced with his right hip against the table, he considered the crutches. "This is going to be very, very awkward," he muttered. But standing beside an operating table, no matter how crude, with a patient before him, no matter how dead, quickened his pulse. For the first time since arriving in Port McKinney, he felt of some use. "Let's see how much information we can discover for Mr. Eastman." He bent down as Alvi slipped the straps of a rubberized apron over his head.

"You just tell me what you want me to do," Winchell offered. He watched Thomas thoughtfully. "Been here often?"

The young physician hesitated. "I just arrived last week."

Winchell smiled with genuine warmth. "No. I meant knife in hand at the operating table."

"No," Thomas answered truthfully. It was hard to put Charlie Grimes in the same category as the medical school cadavers, over which Thomas had spent hundreds of hours. But other than the cadaver's mummylike weathering and the reek of embalming fluid, how much difference could there be, Thomas thought. Exploration of the human body, if it was not to be repaired and returned to service afterward, required few specialized tools, and it was only the very first incision through the cold, stiff, alabaster flesh that made Thomas pause. This was not Charlie Grimes anymore, after all, but simply an anatomical puzzle.

"No matter," Winchell said cheerfully. "I can tell you what killed the boy."

"Yes, but we want to know more than that," Thomas replied.

"Don't know how much more there can be," Winchell said. The body bore no bruises, no bashing or battering from a saloon or street brawl. Other than a smashed little toe that had started to repair itself, it appeared that Charlie Grimes had been in average health before his final misadventure.

The fatal blow had come as a single, hard thrust from the victim's left, as if his attacker had been right-handed, facing him.

As Thomas worked, he saw that the blade had been plunged straight in, angled toward the center of the thoracic cavity, and then yanked straight out. A movement in his peripheral vision drew his attention, and Thomas realized that Alvi was standing quietly at the head of the table, watching.

"You don't have to endure this, you know," he said.

"I know," she replied quietly.

"Do you suppose you could find me a notebook of some sort?"

"Of course." She opened one of the cabinets and removed a slender bound volume, along with a pencil. "May I record for you?"

"Certainly." Moments later, he had confirmed what the initial probe had indicated—a wound slightly more than ten centimeters deep. The blade had punctured the heart's left ventricle, passed through the chamber and nicked the back wall, burying itself halfway through the tough heart muscle.

"Such a simple cut," he murmured.

"Killed him dead as dead, just the same," Winchell observed.

Thomas straightened up a bit, feeling the deep ache in his own ribs as he leaned on the crutches. "A suture or two and this wound would have been closed," he said. "Dr. Roberts lectured to us about this very thing. The heart has been successfully sutured in some of the lower animals. Did you know that?"

"No, I didn't know that," Winchell replied soberly, and Thomas noted the twinkle of amusement.

"It has, indeed. Dr. Roberts said he would not hesitate with the human heart, should the circumstances dictate." He frowned, turning the probe gently in the heart wound. Just a little slice, so easily sutured. Yet with every beat, a jet of blood flooded the pericardial sac, with some leaking through the pericardium itself into the thoracic cavity. Not a swift death, but a sure one.

"Don't know this Roberts fellow," Winchell said. "He one of the profs at the university?"

"Yes." With the heart itself laid open, Thomas explored the

wound in the rear ventricle wall. The knife's blade had been sharpened to an acute angle, with the cut in the posterior heart wall no more than a half centimeter wide at entry, narrowing to a pinprick deep in the muscle.

"And there's an interesting conundrum." Thomas motioned for Winchell to step closer. "Had the knife remained in place, the bleeding might well have been stanched somewhat. But with each contraction, the heart would cut itself against the blade in situ, creating more damage."

He glanced first at Winchell and then Alvi. "The war taught us a great deal," Thomas said, and he realized instantly that he had sounded as if he'd been there. "What I mean to say is that the writings about the war have made it abundantly clear that the more prompt the treatment, the better the odds are that the patient will survive."

"That's not the case here," Winchell said.

"No, I suppose not. But had Charlie been brought *immediately* to surgery, then perhaps . . ."

Measuring meticulously, he was able to render a fairly accurate depiction of the knife blade—he imagined a common, hefty pocket folder with a four-inch blade—and an anatomical drawing of the weapon in place in the wound. The bruise at entry indicated that the weapon probably featured a handle stout enough to house two blades.

Ted Winchell cocked his head and regarded the rendering. "Nine out of ten men who walk the streets or work the timber carry something like that," he observed.

"I would think so," Thomas replied. "Still, it's more than Constable Eastman had before."

Heavy, methodical footsteps approached down the hallway, and Thomas glanced up to see John Haines appear in the doorway.

"Good morning all," he said gravely. "Ted, how did you get yourself roped into this?" The question was asked in jest, and Winchell held up both hands in surrender.

"Learnin' more'n I need to know," he said.

Haines cocked his head and looked at the drawing Thomas had just finished. "Remarkable," he said, "and a goddamn shame. Poor Charlie Grimes." He stood for a moment, hands thrust in his trousers, lower lip pouched out, regarding the corpse.

"I'm about to close," Thomas said.

"All right," Haines said. He reached out and squeezed Winchell's biceps. "Thanks, Teddy." He winked at Alvi, and then hesitated. "When you're finished here, Thomas . . . may we speak?"

"Of course, sir." Haines left, and it took Thomas only moments to close the yawning incision with large, utilitarian sutures.

"Guess he belongs to me now," Winchell said philosophically as Alvi pulled the sheet up to cover the corpse. "Don't think Charlie had relatives, so the county will take care of him. I'll get Riggs and have him help me load." He extended his hand, not appearing to mind the gore that covered Thomas's own. "We'll be seein' each other," he said. "When you have a minute or two, stop by my place. Got some interesting things to show you."

"I look forward to that," Thomas said.

"Miss Haines, always a pleasure." Winchell nodded at her and shot a last glance at the corpse before he left, perhaps measuring and weighing.

Alvi helped Thomas shed the apron. "Father's rather proud of you for making the effort to come down, you know."

"And I can just stay here," Thomas offered. He looked hard at Alvi. "I confess that I'm more than a bit puzzled, Alvi. This is the clinic, then? This single building?"

"For the present it is," she said, and offered no further explanation.

"I see," Thomas said, although he did not. "Surely somewhere in this building you have a room where I might lodge? Zachary stays here?"

"He does, but on the third floor. As far as you're concerned, that might as well be Chicago." Alvi laughed. "Unless we hire two manservants to lug you up and down the stairs."

"I did five steps this morning," Thomas said gamely. "Seven tomorrow, then eight . . . in no time at all, two flights."

She smiled affectionately at the young man. "We'll see. Actually, Father had an idea for you."

21

John Haines settled into the huge leather chair behind an equally impressive desk. Thomas wheeled across the room so that his back was to the window and marveled at the impressive office—shelves heavy with the finest volumes, various surgical tools, some for show and some for use. A narrow door led to a lavatory.

"So," Haines said. He folded his hands in front of himself on the walnut desk. "Tell me about the boy. What did you discover?"

"A single powerful thrust, sir. Directed ever so slightly upward, and from the victim's left to right. A direct through-and-through laceration of the anterior wall of the left ventricle, and the tip of the blade passed through the chamber and lacerated the posterior ventricle wall."

"And death was sure, but far from instantaneous," Haines mused. He rubbed his face and then let his head rest in his hand. "Fascinating how these things work sometimes. Did Eastman happen to know where the crime was committed?"

"No, sir. All that is known is that young Grimes traveled some unknown distance to our front step, maybe without assistance. We can't be sure of that."

"Remarkable." Haines pushed away from the desk and leaned his head back against the chair. He closed his eyes. "But not altogether unusual, is it? As your studies in Philadelphia no doubt revealed, the heart is a more resilient organ than we once supposed. You attended Roberts's lectures at university, did you not?"

"John Roberts? Yes. I was most fortunate to know him well."

"I've read that he suggests that surgery on the heart may be possible, after all."

"I agree." Thomas leaned forward eagerly, and the sudden motion drew him up abruptly. "That very thought occurred to me as I explored the wound, sir," he continued. "The puncture of the heart was . . ." He stopped and smiled. "I was about to say 'a trifle,' but that's not quite true. A serious wound because of the complications, but had I been able to instantly stitch it up to stop the bleeding, Charlie Grimes would be alive. I'm sure of it."

"Circumstances made that clearly impossible," Haines said.

"Indeed they did," Thomas agreed. "But such a wound, say, into the hand, thus," and he marked an incision at the pad below his right thumb with the tip of his left index finger, "requires only a few quick stitches. Healing will be perfect."

"Interesting."

"But forgive me for prattling on," Thomas said. "I need not explain surgery to you, sir."

A slight smile touched John Haines's face. "Well, yes. I've had my share, haven't I? Nevertheless, all this is very sad. To waste the young . . ." He turned his chair and gazed out the window. "It's really quite magnificent when the sun breaks through, isn't it?"

"Indeed, it is, sir." Thomas waited politely, hearing the touch of melancholy in the older man's voice.

"I've lost the sight in one eye," John Haines said abruptly, and for a moment Thomas sat without breathing, unsure of what to say, unsure of what Haines might *want* him to say. Haines opened his eyes without moving his head from the pad of the chairback. He looked sideways at the younger man. "You could tell?"

"Only that you were having some difficulty," Thomas said. "I noticed that, yes, sir. The right eye."

"You're observant. I had suspicions, you see. The last time I visited San Francisco, only two months ago, I took the opportunity for an examination by a certain Dr. Dwight, a man of considerable renown who surrounds himself with the most magnificent machinery and gadgets. The examination was of excruciating thoroughness, I might add." He shrugged. "Nothing can be done. Were it something as simple as a cataract, or even the ravages of glaucoma, there might be something, but not in this case."

"I am genuinely sorry," Thomas said. "The nerve itself has failed?"

"I would suppose so. Or the retinal complex. Whatever it is, it's surely beyond the surgeon's scalpel, or for that matter, homeopathy. Even my own extensive study of alteratives has yielded nothing." He heaved a sigh. "And the left eye shows signs . . ."

"What does Dr. Riggs have to say on your behalf?"

"Ah, well," Haines said, and stopped, gazing out the window again. "Mysteries of the eye aren't his specialty, I'm afraid."

"Nor mine," Thomas said quickly. "But I look forward to being of any assistance that I can manage."

"Let me tell you, young man, your arrival has been a ray of sunshine for us. A certain delay has been thrust upon us . . . well, upon _you_ . . . but this, too, shall pass. I see your condition improving daily. I hope you see that as well, and do not grow too impatient."

"Most certainly. I'm grateful to you all."

"Alvi tells me that I missed a sliver of glass." He touched his own ribs.

"A trifle. Apparently along with my other accomplishments, I fell upon a broken bottle caught in the rocks."

Haines grimaced. "I didn't see that. I'm sorry. But you see what I mean."

"It's on the mend," Thomas said. "As is the hip. And the head."

Haines laughed gently. "You are a mess, most certainly. Most important, Alvi tells me that you are keen to begin work . . . right here at the clinic."

"As soon as possible, sir."

"I would much prefer that you stayed at the house, with us. I enjoy Zachary's company of an evening, but sometimes I have the impression he is most careful to tell me only what I want to hear." He grinned broadly. "I take that as a compliment, of course. But yours is a fresh voice."

"It's just that I don't want to be a nuisance when—"

"Please, Thomas. What little we expend in your care will be returned many times over, believe me. You know, I thoroughly enjoyed the stroll on that new boardwalk this morning, but I can see that my original thought—that it would be easy for a wheel-chair—was not carefully thought out. The slope, the steps." He held both hands up in surrender. "You could stay here, of course. We can certainly arrange something. Still, it would be easier for everyone if you'd consider our hospitality at one-oh-one. That way, Gert can keep an eye on you. I'll make arrangements for transportation. Alvi says that you believe you could rest on the back of a low wagon."

"Most certainly."

"Well, we'll find a way. But listen, what I wanted to discuss with you is your position here, relative to myself and Zachary. We haven't spoken of that." He frowned at the desktop. "I have no desire . . ." He paused, frowning harder, then reached out and straightened an elegant pen that had listed a couple of de-grees in the ink pot. "I don't wish to be one of those despots who refuses to acknowledge his own failings, stumbling on until he becomes nothing but an old fool."

"Hardly . . ."

Haines held up a hand abruptly, and then leaned forward, both elbows on the desk. "Thomas, let me be blunt. Will you al-low that? As a favor to an old family friend?"

"Certainly, sir."

"I am soon to be sixty-seven years old, Thomas. I am blind in one eye, and God only knows what the fate of the other eye shall be. I cannot see properly for the surgery, and already am in the habit of referring cases to St. Mary's that only last year I would

123

have taken on here without hesitation. As the fragment of glass buried in your rib so aptly illustrated . . ." He shrugged. "So," he continued before Thomas could reply, "on top of all this, I am just *weary*, Thomas. One of the joys of age, I suppose. The old bones don't want to rise from bed in the morning, and start yearning for repose by early afternoon."

He barked a short laugh. "You have all this to look forward to, in years to come, but enough of that." He rose from the desk with an impressive popping of joints, and stepped to an elegant cabinet near at hand. Removing a bottle of brandy, he poured first one generous tumbler for himself, and then held the bottle toward Thomas. "Too early?"

"Yes, sir," Thomas said.

"Good man. As you can see, a fine brandy is one of my more significant failings." He put the bottle back and sipped the brandy with his eyes closed. "But it helps. Now," and he returned to his seat. "This is what I propose. As soon as you're able, I wish to turn over my patient load entirely to you. During the next few weeks, as you regain your strength, working here each day as best you can, you will be introduced to my patients. They will be most impressed with you, I'm sure. Alvi knows each and every one, and will be of great assistance."

"I look forward to working with you, sir."

"Ah, more than that. I don't intend to look over your shoulder, my good man." He laughed again. "For one thing, I can't see a damn thing, so what good would it do?"

"But what about Dr. Riggs? I confess, I don't understand."

Haines leaned back in the chair and inspected the brandy tumbler for a moment. "What Zachary Riggs brings to this practice," he said carefully, "is an amazing talent for business. An absolute genius in that regard. Let me tell you, I could cease practice immediately, this very moment, and we would continue to enjoy a level of wealth I couldn't imagine just five years ago."

"He seems eager," Thomas said. Although from the first meeting, he had found Zachary Riggs a likable soul, he had also been impressed with how deftly the man parried questions that should have simple answers.

"'Eager' is an understatement," Haines said. "To be sure, I owe him an immense debt. And at this stage of my life, I have no intention of going to a poorhouse, blind and useless. Work with us, Thomas, and Zachary Riggs will make us all wealthy far, far beyond our needs."

Thomas could not contain his puzzlement. "I suppose I don't understand yet just what the business *is*," he said. "Beyond ministering to the needs of the community's sick and injured."

"Well beyond," Haines said. "Well beyond. Port McKinney is a tiny spot on some maps, and not at all on most. What Zachary has done is to take my medicine, my practice, far beyond this clinic. As he implied the other night at dinner, we have patients who correspond with us from practically every corner of the nation. From several foreign countries as well." He held up his glass, letting the light catch it. "This is the simple plan that we've discussed at length before your arrival. Although I shall remain the titular head of this practice, you will take over my patient load. Not tomorrow, of course, but as you recover. For their part, Zachary and Alvina will continue to organize the financial ways and means. Now, should you need anything, anything at all, for your practice, you have but to mention it to Alvi or Zachary." He grinned. "I'm sure you're developing a list already, given the carelessness of the shipping industry."

"Surely."

"Beyond that, Alvina takes care of the staff for me. The young women who work upstairs, and of course Bertha. My God, where would I be without her. You haven't yet met Bertha Auerbach." He sipped the brandy. "Even I'm afraid of her, but, thank God, Alvina isn't."

"I haven't had the pleasure," Thomas said, "but I'm already in her debt. She rescued my medical bag from the tide, it seems. Everything once more clean and neatly stowed. I need to thank her for that."

"Ah, you will have the chance. Bertha makes my day bearable. Now, upstairs, that's another matter. Perhaps six or seven young women work for Zachary in that enterprise. The correspondence and shipping is a veritable avalanche, rest assured. But you have no reason to concern yourself with that. What *you* will do is run the walk-in medical practice, with any assistance I can give you. Fortunately for us, that's entirely on the first floor. Later, we'll see about the other. I'll show you the examining room in a moment. The community will greet you with open arms, I'm sure."

"I look forward to it. But correspondence?"

Haines waved a hand dismissively. "Zachary's world. Now, I want to make myself clear." He leaned forward again. "I want you to take charge of the local medical practice. Just as soon as you can. I am here to help *you*. Not vice versa."

"That's very generous of you, sir."

"It's necessary, is what it is, Thomas. With your arrival, I see a chance here, and by God, I'm going to take it. When your father told me that you were considering my offer, it was as if a heavy cloud lifted from my shoulders. And then I spoke with John Roberts—"

"Professor Roberts?"

"None other. I'd allow you to read his recommendation, but I'm afraid it might drive you to the city, where you could earn far more than I can pay."

"Thank you, sir. But I'm capable of earning my way."

"I know you are, and so you shall. But as you're working here, as part of the clinic, there is a foundation salary that will keep the wolves from the door. The clinic is prepared to establish your partnership at one thousand dollars a month, to be increased on a regular semiannual basis as the practice builds."

Thomas's jaw dropped. He had grown up far, far removed from poverty, but this offer was beyond his expectations. "A thousand?" he managed to gasp.

"A month," Haines added. "Come January, we'll review that, if you're agreeable." He chuckled at Thomas's discomfiture. "Don't worry, young man. We'll work it out of you, to be sure.

But it's important work we do here at the clinic, with commensurate income. We don't want our staff worrying about where their next meal might be coming from."

He pushed his chair back and rose, not releasing his grip on the edge of the desk until he was sure of his balance. "While you're considering the offer, let me show you the basic examining room so that come tomorrow, you'll know where things are." He pulled out a gold watch and snapped it open. "Bertha normally opens the door at eight o'clock, although Zachary is in business upstairs long before that. Mrs. Cleary will be here by two minutes after the hour, and you need to be ready for her."

"Mrs. Cleary?"

"Just one of the patients who will convince you that you're vastly underpaid, Thomas."

"That's hard to imagine."

Haines laughed again as he held open his office door for the wheelchair. "You'll want a good night's sleep, young man."

22

Elated, even overwhelmed, with John Haines's generous offer, Thomas Parks could easily picture himself operating from this modest clinic, even though he saw nothing of the enormous hospital promised in the *Universal Medical Advisor*. He saw no enormous laboratory churning out barrels of drugs. He saw no patients strolling the manicured grounds—in fact no patients at all, strolling, supine, or otherwise. That made him a little uneasy, since the number of patients that Port McKinney could produce on a regular basis could hardly support such a munificent salary.

He wheeled behind Dr. Haines, listening intently. Haines started with the examining room immediately beside his private office.

The room where patients would first seek medical care was modest in every aspect, with two comfortable chairs for interviews and a central examination table. Tidy and clean, it boasted nothing out of the ordinary beyond an elegant little enameled steel cart made in Paris. The cart secured two open-topped glass jars of perhaps two gallons capacity each on an upper rack, the jars' contents piped via coiled rubber tubing to dual spigots over a recessed enamel sink. The small sink drained into a utilitarian bucket with leather handles.

"During the day, Bertha will keep this full of hot water." Haines proudly patted the storage jar. "I'm spoiled by such conveniences, I must say." He turned to the gas-fired autoclave that rested on one marble countertop, with a tilted rack of implements and steel pans beside a deep marble sink. "I purchased this in San Francisco just last spring," he said. "You're familiar with its operation, of course."

"One very much like it," Thomas allowed.

Behind the examining table, itself blanketed first with a heavy rubberized cover and then a clean linen, the pharmacy included vast rows of drugs arranged alphabetically. Thomas scanned the rows, seeing emphasis on alteratives, including labels that bore Dr. Haines's name.

Bottles of the Universal Tonic touted in nearly every chapter of the *Advisor* were clearly available in sizes from a few ounces to dark liter-sized bottles with rubber corks.

"Let me show you the ward," Haines said, slipping past Thomas. He stopped, nodding at the drugs. "If you have favorites that aren't here, you have but to mention them to Bertha or Alvi."

"Incredible," Thomas said politely. He wheeled after Haines. A double door opened from the foyer to the ward.

"At the moment, we have no patients admitted," Haines said. "That's something of a blessing just now."

"Earlier, Alvi mentioned that there was an injured laborer in the ward," Thomas said. He waited while Dr. Haines pulled the drapes, and the flood of daylight revealed a modest, narrow room that included eight beds, four on each side.

"Was," Haines said. "As I said, enjoy the peace and quiet while you can. It won't last. We tend to acute cases as best we can with the facilities that we have. The chronic ones, or the seriously ill, we transport to St. Mary's down in Pesqualmie. It's better for them, and allows us to focus our efforts."

"I see."

Haines lifted an eyebrow at the expression on the young man's face. "It's really quite adequate for our needs," Haines said. "But you appear surprised."

"Well," Thomas said, choosing his words carefully, "it's just that the clinic was presented in the *Advisor* as somewhat . . . as a bit . . ."

"More grand in scope?" Haines finished for him.

"Exactly, sir. Like the salary you offer me, I must add. Port McKinney is not a large city. It's hard to imagine how it might support—"

"A moment, please," Haines interrupted. He left the ward, returning with a wrapped volume. He removed the oil paper and for a moment regarded the book. "One of the advance copies of our magnum opus," he said and opened the volume. He smoothed the pages, finally arriving at the passage he sought. He held the book so Thomas could see the pages. On the left was the full-page engraving of the enormous Clinic and Vital Research Center, the same rendering that appeared on the title page.

"This confuses you," Haines said. He cocked the page, lifted his head, and peered through his spectacles at the print. " 'A model medical facility and surgical center,' " he read, and looked up at Thomas. "A *model*." He directed his attention to the next page. " 'Within five years' time,' " he read, " 'The Haines Clinic and Vital Research Center will be the focus of medical research and treatment that encompasses the best as practiced both in this country and abroad. Attending to patients in the facility as illustrated here by our architects, noted physicians from a dozen countries will provide the most skilled, prompt, and professional services on earth.' "

He looked up. "Zachary has a way with words far beyond my

poor attempts," he said. "Anyway, think *projection*, Thomas. What *will be*, given time and energy. Think well beyond the admittedly limited opportunities in Port McKinney."

"You're saying that this section of the *Advisor* presents what lies ahead," Thomas said.

"Exactly." Haines turned another page and held the book up so he could see the fine print. " 'Only physicians who are recipients of the most thorough and erudite education have been chosen to work at the Clinic, including men from the major centers of America as well as the continent.' " He closed the book, using his thumb as a marker. "That's you, Thomas. And Zachary, whom I must say has made so much possible for us. With the income he has secured from our various endeavors, we project that construction on the major clinic building will commence as early as next summer."

"Remarkable," Thomas said. "I wonder . . ." He wanted to ask what percentage of readers would notice the careful prose of the *Advisor*. What percentage of them would skip the nuances and assume that the facility already existed as vaunted in the text?

"Zachary worked with you on this project, then," he said.

"Oh, certainly," Haines said quickly. "Worked is an understatement, Thomas. He *slaved* on it." He held out both hands like a preacher holding a Bible before his congregation. "Left to my own devices, I wouldn't have finished a single chapter."

He snapped the book closed. "There are patients, Thomas, who need this. They need the comfort of an *Advisor*. In that, I completely agree with Zachary's logic. There is nothing in that text that is counter to good medicine, Thomas. Nothing. Although it promotes the use of various alteratives—especially the ones that are sold by the clinic—none are promoted for uses beyond their limitations."

"I recall the peach," Thomas said with a smile.

"Exactly so, and most apt. You know"—Haines relaxed with his back against the wall—"sometimes just knowing that someone else cares, that someone else is ready to provide a modicum of comfort, is sufficient to ease the burden of chronic disease.

That's something we should never forget in our rush to bring the huge, complicated battery of modern science and medicine to the patient's bedside." His eyes crinkled with amusement. "You know as well as anyone, after your own misadventure, how a quiet hand, or a bit of hot food, or even a few chips of ice may provide comfort and relief."

"Or a good jolt of fine brandy." Thomas laughed.

"Exactly so." Haines patted the cover of the heavy book. "That quieting hand is what this volume provides. In just a matter of days, we shall have literally thousands of copies of this fine text to dispense to patients worldwide. For but four dollars, they gain a valuable, wise friend in their time of need." He fell silent, watching Thomas.

"Zachary actually wrote most of this? That's quite an undertaking."

"Yes. He actually did. A remarkable talent, that man. And I must say, I have come to cherish our evening sessions in front of the fire. He questions, I respond. Sometimes the two of us pore through other texts for just the right answer or organization. But most of the material is the compilation of my own forty-year practice."

"An interesting fellow," Thomas said.

"I hope you two will come to work effectively side by side," Haines said. "You both have a good deal to offer, and there's much to be done. I want you to feel perfectly comfortable to poke about the place, Thomas. My office, the examining room, this ward. Every drawer, every corner. I think you'll find all the equipment you'll need, but as I said, if you should find some shortage or lack, you have but to make a list for us, and it will be ordered immediately."

"That's most generous, sir."

"Practical, Thomas. Practical. I want you to be content and challenged here. I'll do whatever I can to accomplish that." He pulled out his watch. "I want you to work as long as you like, and when you're ready for some rest, Alvi will arrange for you to ride back to one-oh-one."

"I can take a bed right here," Thomas said, nodding at the ward.

Haines laughed. "Certainly not, young man. I won't hear of it. For one thing, I'm selfish. I wish to pick your brain, and the best way to do that is over a glass of brandy in front of a roaring fire. I hope you'll humor me."

"You spoil me, Doctor," Thomas said.

"I certainly hope so. When your father demands an accounting, I would hate to come up short. And as I said, it's in my own best interest."

23

For some time, Thomas regarded his reflection in the small mirror. He unwound the bandage from his head and turned the bathroom gaslight up full. The colorful bash and laceration would be partially hidden by his thick brown hair. He touched a lock tentatively. He would allow that to grow a bit longer, but still, there would be no hiding the scar that arched around his right eye, giving his face a piratical cast . . . or the look of one who narrowly escaped scalping.

Taking more time than usual, he washed carefully, enjoying the sting of the cold water. The deep gouge between his ribs was now scabbing properly, but the torn muscles and fractures would tolerate not the slightest pressure. He had become adept at shallow breathing, but even the simple task of unwrapping the bandage had prompted a yelp.

Thomas knew that he was not giving himself enough time to heal properly, but rationalized that none of his injuries would heal any faster with bed rest. He braced against the sink pedestal and tentatively swung his left leg. He could manage a few degrees of movement forward and back, but nothing laterally.

"Would you like some hot water?" the voice outside the door asked, and Thomas startled, reaching for his robe.

"You must sleep with both ears open," he said to the closed door, and was rewarded with Alvina's easy laugh.

"I do," she replied. "My mother used to say that I was afraid I was going to miss something." She tapped on the door. "May I?"

"Of course," Thomas said. He opened the door and she held up the white enameled pitcher.

"I can't imagine scraping my face with a razor under any circumstances," she said, "but hot water must make it more bearable."

"Indeed it does."

She poured the water into the small basin, then set the pitcher on the table just to the left of the mirror. "Let me see," she said.

He pivoted toward her while she stood on her tiptoes, examining his face. Her fingers were gentle as she turned his head first one way and then another. "Hold still a minute," she instructed, and she dipped the corner of a small face cloth in the hot water. "Right in the corner," she added, and with one hand eased his swollen eyebrow upward as she dabbed with the cloth. "Perfect." She stepped back.

"Far from that," Thomas said.

"You should consider growing one of those wonderful mustaches," she said, spinning fingers out from either side of her nose. "You'd look elegant."

"That's not the word I would have chosen for this battered face."

She laughed again. "How are the ribs?"

Lying in bed and being examined in a semiprofessional manner was one thing, but pulling aside his robe in the bathroom seemed somehow inappropriate, and Thomas felt the flush creep up his neck and cheeks. He was surprised at his own prudishness. "Slow progress, but progress nevertheless." His tight grip on the front of his robe apparently wasn't lost on her.

"You're an amusing one," she said. "Inflammation?"

"No more than I would expect," Thomas replied. She reached out and touched the robe, and he slid his hand down out of the way, trying to maintain some modicum of decorum.

For a moment she scrutinized the bashed ribs, then stepped back. He pulled the robe together.

"That's not good, you know," she said. "You shouldn't be out and about. If you should fall . . ."

"I won't fall. Other than wrapping myself up in a torso plaster cast like some odd cocoon, there's nothing to be done about it other than to just let it heal."

"You're still going to the clinic this morning, then? We can't change your mind? Another week won't hurt, you know."

"Yes . . . and no. After another week of being useless, I'll be stark raving mad." He grinned, then his expression sobered. "Your father told me yesterday about his deteriorating vision." Alvi nodded and said nothing. "I can imagine nothing worse," Thomas added. "With this . . . ," and he indicated his own battered eye, then stopped, not wanting to compare his own bruises with something far more serious, far deeper. "It's obvious that he is relying heavily on you and Zachary. I must say that his offer to me was more than generous, and anything I can do to help him now . . . and you . . . I'll be happy and honored to do."

"Thank you." She nodded and touched the side of the enameled pan. "Your water is cooling," she said. "When you're finished, Gert has breakfast for you. Then we'll see about fetching you down to the clinic." She reached up with both hands, and Thomas assumed that she was repeating the examination of his eye. To his astonishment, she rested one hand on his left cheek, the other gently but firmly on the back of his head well clear of the ragged wound, and stretched up, kissing him full on the lips. The moment was so brief that in his astonishment he had no time to figure out what to do with his hands. And then she was gone.

"My word," he breathed finally, and took a long, slow, deep breath, just to the point when his ribs awoke. *A most forward young lady*, he thought with approval, unsure of whether the gesture of affection was simply that of a sister, or something more.

The first aromas of breakfast jolted him out of his reverie. It took a half hour to dress. Something as simple as slipping into a fresh white shirt brought sweat to his forehead. Arranging his black tie around the stiff collar with only one thumb to manipulate it prompted a string of colorful curses. On the other hand, the tight vest actually became a comfort, providing some gentle support for his ribs, and he buttoned it to the top.

For days, he had been wearing a pair of black slippers belonging to John Haines, but now, with everything but his coat in place, Thomas stood leaning against his bed, trying to imagine a strategy where he could pull on proper shoes. He had managed to shuffle his feet into his trousers as they lay crumpled on the floor, then pulled them up with the crook of the cane that rested in the corner by the door. That was not going to work with his stockings, and it wasn't going to work with his boots.

He was still standing, mulling his options, when Alvina tipped open the door of his bedroom.

"Don't you look nice," she said as if they had not yet spoken that morning, and Thomas saw that, in her own perceptive way, she took in his circumstances instantly. "You're going barefoot?"

"I was thinking of it."

"You wore the slippers yesterday," she said. "They won't serve?"

"Not if I'm seeing patients," Thomas said.

"Oh heavens, no. We can't have them thinking that you're recuperating," Alvi said, but she managed to make it sound fetching rather than acid, and Thomas laughed. "Let me help you."

"I—"

"No, you can't. And we don't want to waste half the morning fussing over a simple pair of stockings while the food goes cold." She moved to the wheelchair and spun it toward him. "Now sit," she commanded, and he did.

She knelt and shook out a stocking, rolling it expertly in her fingers before slipping it over the toes of his left foot. "My, you have elegant feet," she said.

"I didn't think that was possible," Thomas said. " 'Elegant' feet. You like that word, don't you. I should have an elegant mustache to go with elegant feet. I would have said 'functional.' "

"Oh, both are possible," Alvi said, and pulled the stocking up around his calf. "Boots or shoes?"

"The shoes," he said, and watched her manipulate the laces through the endless eyelets, loosening the shoe and spreading it wide so she could slip it on without a jolt of effort. In short order, she arose, regarding her work with satisfaction, bending down to adjust his trouser cuffs over the high shoe tops. She was most attractive, he had to admit, and for a brief moment wondered what her reaction would be if he took *her* head in both hands.

She straightened up and reached out for his coat.

"I wasn't going to wear that," he said quickly. "One nuisance too much."

"Well, regardless, you look very nice." She stepped back as he turned the chair toward the door. "Gert wants to make sure you have a proper breakfast, Dr. Thomas. After all, you may not see a crumb until dinnertime. Our days can be like that, you know."

"I'm hoping so," he said fervently.

The aroma of breakfast, including a strong fishy fragrance, wafted through the house. As he wheeled toward the dining room, he tried not to watch Alvi's every movement. Her starched white dress with high collar flowed in all the right places, long enough to reveal only the tips of polished patent leather shoes. Her apron was spotless.

If Gert James was an employee, there was no hint of it. Treating the older woman as if Gert were a cherished aunt, Alvi was quick to lend a hand, first tipping the heavy enameled coffeepot to fill Thomas's cup.

"Start with that," she said, and in short order a plate followed, laden with eggs, potato wedges, and a generous slab of fresh salmon, its skin charred just so. Another plate with dark flapjacks appeared, along with a small flowered pitcher and a slab of butter.

"That's huckleberry syrup," Gert instructed in the same tone that she might have ordered, *Use it.*

The two women joined him with equally heaping plates. "John will join us?" Thomas asked.

"He arises late," Gert said with disapproval, then added fondly, "There appears to be no breaking of bad habits. Maybe you can be of influence. *We* certainly haven't been."

"I'll do my best."

He tried a mouthful of the salmon, could not catch himself before wrinkling his nose, and followed it with a large forkful of hotcakes and syrup to drown the fishy flavor.

"It's an acquired taste," Alvi observed.

"What, you don't care for the salmon?" Gert said. "*That's* not possible. There's no better way to start the week."

"And celebrate the middle and the end as well," Alvi added.

"But you're from Connecticut, young man," Gert added as if that were an illness that plenty of salmon might cure.

After working his way through most of the breakfast, Thomas finally gave up and pushed his plate away. "I'm ready for anything," he said. "As long as I don't have to move from this spot. Mrs. James, you're a wonder. Thank you."

"It's Miss," she replied. "And Gert will always do. And you're welcome. You've given up this notion of staying the night at the clinic, I hope."

"Apparently I have." Thomas laughed. "I just wanted to avoid inconveniencing—"

"Stuff and nonsense. We're all family here."

If Zachary Riggs kept an apartment at the clinic, so could he, but he let the matter drop. He didn't mind the notion of Alvi Haines knocking on his door in the wee small hours of the morning—or any other time for that matter.

24

A tiny woman was busily engaged dusting bookshelves in the clinic's waiting room when Thomas arrived. She stopped and watched as Horace James and Alvi lifted the wheelchair over the last step, and then as Thomas followed on crutches.

"Good morning, all," she said. Thomas sank back into the chair.

"Thomas, this is Miss Bertha Auerbach," Alvi said. "Dr. Thomas Parks."

Bertha Auerbach folded the damp dust cloth neatly and placed it in a metal basin that rested on the windowsill. Folding her arms across her thin chest, she regarded Thomas critically.

"So . . . here you are," she said. "I've heard much about you, Doctor."

"Some of it good, I hope," Thomas said. "And I am in your debt, Miss Auerbach. Thank you for tending to the wreckage of my medical bag. You certainly didn't have to do that."

"My pleasure. We don't know when you might need it." The light of the window illuminated her face, and Thomas saw that Bertha Auerbach was actually younger than the stern voice made her out. A collection of flat planes with high cheekbones and full lips, her face was the sort that badly needed a smile. Were it not for the voluminous folds of her dress, her figure would have appeared childlike. Barely topping five feet, she wore the same style white dress and apron that Alvi had adopted, but with a small white cap that sought to capture the abundant black hair pinned high on her skull. Her large, deep blue eyes fixed on Thomas's face. He felt like a bacterium trapped on a microscope slide. "You're going to be staying here at the clinic as well?"

"Apparently not," Thomas replied. The nurse had made it sound as if he'd need her permission to do so. "I thought that I might, but now it appears that I'll be lodging at one-oh-one for a while."

"Just as well, I suppose. The elevator was never installed in this building, more's the pity. Now that you're here, how do you propose to reach the second floor?"

"I—"

"He's not," Alvi interrupted. "He'll be working with father tending to patients. At least until he's completely recuperated."

"I see." Bertha's gaze roamed down Thomas's figure. "And how's that progressing, Doctor? I'm to understand you nearly killed yourself."

"A bit of a bang," Thomas replied. "But I'm mending."

She nodded once. "I've worked for Dr. Haines for eight years." Thomas wasn't sure how he was expected to respond to the announcement, but she added, "Perhaps you'll instruct me on your preferences." She tucked a strand of hair back over one shapely ear. "When you're ready, of course."

"Yes. Where to start," Thomas said. He turned his chair in a circle, regarding the waiting room. All the medical offices he'd seen as a boy, especially the ones in rural Connecticut and even what private practices he had seen in Philadelphia, combined all activities in a single room. Patients waited their turn, their business with the physician as public as a town meeting. Here, Dr. John Haines had provided a waiting area with benches and even a comfortable chair or two, examinations and treatments remaining discreetly behind closed doors.

"I'm impressed with this, I must say," Thomas said, although he couldn't help comparing the reality of the clinic with the imaginary presentation in the new *Advisor*. "I could become spoiled very quickly."

"Where was your practice before this?" Bertha asked, and Thomas felt that cursed blush rise up his neck and touch his cheeks. Surely Dr. Haines had mentioned Thomas's circumstances to nurse Auerbach—fresh out of school, with no clinical or practical experience of his own.

"I assisted Professor Wilhelm in his work in Philadelphia," Thomas said. "During my last two years in school there."

"I see," she said, and Thomas saw that figuring out just what Bertha Auerbach was thinking was going to be a challenge. "Well," she said and turned away, "we shan't be ready for anything, standing about yakkety-yakking. If you have instructions for me?"

Her retreat to the examining room required that Thomas follow along if he wanted to converse with her, and he glanced at Alvi, who smiled sweetly.

"I've work to do upstairs," she said. "I'll be in and out, if you have questions."

"I shall have an unending list," Thomas said.

"In most things, Berti will guide you," Alvi said. "She's most efficient. And father will be here by ten o'clock, regardless of his promises."

Thomas glanced at the clock and saw that it was seven-thirty. He felt as if he had already wasted half the day. Wheeling into the examining room, he arrived in time to see Bertha empty the contents of a steaming kettle into one of the washstand's reservoir bottles.

"I did have one concern," Thomas said. "I wanted to discuss the gas clave system with you. Yesterday, I noticed that it wasn't operative."

"Of course not, Doctor. Yesterday was the Sabbath. Normally, no one is here at that time. House calls, perhaps. But not here."

"Well, you see the problem is," and Thomas pushed himself more upright in the chair, leaning on his good right arm, "we don't know when we're going to need sterile instruments, Miss Auerbach."

"I don't understand what you're asking of me," Bertha said flatly, and her tone cut through Thomas's efforts to be tactful.

"What I'm asking," he said, "is that at any time, day, night, Sabbath or not, I may have sterile instruments in my hand for the asking. Without delay. Without confusion."

"How will I know what you require?"

"A commonsense selection," Thomas said. "Nothing un-
usual. I shall draw up a list for you if that's necessary. But it's the
notion of everything at the ready that's important, Miss Auerbach. Ready and sterile."

"Sometimes we make do with what we have," she said, and she
might have added *and that's that.* Her tone softened a bit. "I heard
about young Charlie," she said. "Such a shame."

"Yes, but more than a shame. A crime, in fact. And that's my
point. Before we leave the clinic for the day, I'll have such a kit
in the pan, already claved, simply left inside the machine where
it will remain sterile," Thomas said. "I'd like you to see to that
each day. It's easy to become busy, I imagine. But that needs to be
done."

"I see."

He smiled at her. "Do we *have* such a selection at hand at the
moment, Miss Auerbach? That's sterile, I mean?"

"Indeed not. No."

"Then perhaps that can be your first chore," he said. "A scalpel or two, forceps large and small, sutures of varying sizes,
probes, the hypodermics. Whoever arrives first in the morning
will resterilize the kit as a double precaution." He pivoted the
chair so that he could survey the examination room again. "If
there's one thing that the War between the States taught us, it is
that *prompt* medical attention, coupled with aseptic conditions,
contributes to effective care."

"The war was forty years ago," the nurse replied.

"Indeed. Before either of us was born. I don't mean to be pe-
dantic, but it is also my observation that the lessons from that
war are slow in taking root. Please don't misunderstand me,
Miss Auerbach. I mean in no way to be critical of what is done
here. My particular interests have led me to believe that nearly
any injury may be satisfactorily repaired by prompt treatment,
including aseptic instruments, gentle surgery, and intelligent
therapy afterward." He realized that he had launched himself on
a sermon, and cut himself off abruptly. "That's all I'm saying,"

he said. "Where did you complete your training, if I might ask?"

"At St. Vincent's in Portland," she replied. "I went there directly from Macy Normal."

Thomas had heard of neither, but nodded as if he had. "May I ask what prompted you to move to Port McKinney?"

"An ill relative across the bay," she said tersely. "Since passed on."

"Ah, I see. I'm sorry. Other family here?"

"I have a brother who works for Mr. Schmidt."

"Really," Thomas said. "As does Mr. Tate, whom I've met already. He led the charge into the surf to rescue my carcass."

"Jake Tate is a good man," Bertha said. "You'll find that many of Mr. Schmidt's workers pass through here for one reason or another."

"I would expect so. It surprises me that the ward is empty today. Is that the usual state of affairs?"

"We transfer any patient who will need extended care to St. Mary's, Doctor."

Although he had been told that by both John and Alvina Haines, Thomas still found the notion incredible. "We do? All?"

"Yes."

"And that's a trip of some thirty miles?"

"Yes."

"My God, Miss Auerbach, whatever for? Thirty miles there and thirty back?"

"Yes."

"While we have a ward with eight beds? Good heavens. You have assistants? Am I understanding that correctly?"

The nurse looked sideways at Thomas. "I have no assistants, Doctor. There are six girls who work upstairs with Mr. Riggs and Miss Haines." She glanced at the clock. "They will arrive shortly, although most often, they use the back stairway. I don't want them clumping through the waiting room, you see. Down here, it is Dr. Haines and myself. And often, just myself."

Thomas gazed at her thoughtfully, interested to hear her version of Zachary Riggs's endeavors. "There are patients upstairs?"

"My heavens, no."

"Then I'm confused. What do eight people do all day long on the second floor, while you and Dr. Haines struggle with the community's medical needs here?"

"There is much correspondence," the young woman said, and Thomas heard the discomfort in her voice.

"There must be," he replied. "With whom are we corresponding at such a pace?"

"I was under the impression you would know about that aspect of the practice."

"Apparently I hadn't appreciated the magnitude of book sales," he said.

Bertha Auerbach's lips compressed a bit, and she raised an eyebrow as she stared at the floor. "I think it best that you discuss that affair with Mr. Riggs," she said after a moment. "Or with Miss Haines. Or with the good doctor." The *mister*, rather than a physician's title, was not lost on Thomas.

"I shall. But tell me . . . when you transfer a patient to St. Mary's, who drives the ambulance?"

"Normally, Mr. Winchell will do that."

Thomas laughed. "Having the coroner and undertaker at the reins must inspire the patient's confidence, I'm sure."

"Mr. Winchell uses his white team for ambulance duties," Miss Auerbach said. "The blacks are reserved for the hearse."

Thomas caught himself when he saw that she was serious. "We have no ambulance routinely at hand. That's what you're telling me?"

"Mr. Winchell has one. Or hearse, depending on its need."

"And when Mr. Winchell is transferring a patient, we are left with no ambulance at our disposal for at least two days?"

"We are a small village."

Thomas leaned back in the chair, resting his chin on his right fist. "That puts us at a serious disadvantage," he said. "Earlier you asked my preferences. Well, one of them is an ambulance at hand, here at the clinic, fully prepared with a driver of our employ. If we must purchase an ambulance or two, we'll do just that. I'll speak with Dr. Haines about it today. This isn't a matter for next year, Miss Auerbach."

"That's a considerable expense."

"Indeed," Thomas said. "I'm sure he is as eager as I am to make progress here. I hope you'll join with me in this."

"Of course," she said. A ghost of a smile touched the nurse's face, and Thomas saw that she was really quite pretty.

"This morning I'd like to examine the daily journals," Thomas said. "Dr. Haines said that he keeps a narrative?"

"Of course. They're shelved in his office. It is his habit to make notations after each patient he sees. There are times, certainly, when he is much pressed, and I'm sure some time passes before he makes an entry. But he's really very organized in that regard." She paused. "Would you like to see them now?"

"If you please."

He wheeled after her to enter the quiet sanctum of Haines's office. Bertha Auerbach opened the glass doors of one of the cabinets and slid out a heavy, leather-bound volume. Opening it, she turned to the last page of writing, and as Thomas wheeled behind the desk, she rested the book in front of him.

The doctor's hand was fine and angular, the entries in black ink as easy to read as a printer's copy. No scratch-outs marred the page.

"You'll see that he makes an entry for each date," she said. "A diary, more or less."

"I see that," Thomas said, reading down the page. "He assigns a case number for each visit, or for each patient?" He leafed back through two pages.

"That would depend," Bertha replied.

"On what?"

"It is my understanding that each *separate* incident or illness receives a fresh case number," she said.

"Ah, here I am," Thomas said. He grinned. "I'm Case Number

144

43,731, entered September 12, 1891." He turned the book slightly so that light fell more clearly on the page. "'Thomas Brian Parks,'" he read aloud, "'age 27, the victim of a riding accident, brought to this office via Schmidt's freight wagon, found to be in a semiconscious state, suffering from multiple injuries.'" He looked up at Bertha.

"I have read that entry," she said.

"Really?" He skimmed the lengthy list of injuries that the physician had enumerated. "He's most complete."

"I would imagine so."

As the dates progressed down the pages, Thomas saw himself mentioned several times, interspersed with other patients. In the course of the past week, Dr. Haines had seen thirty-seven different cases, with complaints ranging from slivers to abscessed teeth to fractures, lacerations, and other interesting wounds, to cases of debility, dyspepsia, tuberculosis, and influenza. One patient had eaten raw fish and nearly died, while number 43,760 had tried to shoot himself in the head, changed his mind at the last moment, and managed to blow off only a portion of his left ear.

The treatment for each patient was recorded and in a final column, the fees charged. At those rates, Thomas reflected, a new clinic would be long in coming—as would his first paycheck.

"If you have nothing else for me?" Bertha Auerbach asked, and Thomas looked up with a start.

"I'm sorry. No. If you have time to tend to the instruments, I would be grateful."

"I'll let you know when patients arrive," she said. "Since it's Monday morning, we might expect Mrs. Cleary promptly."

"Ah, Mrs. Cleary. Dr. Haines mentioned her."

"Every Monday morning," Bertha said. "She begins her week with a visit to the physician."

"Whether needed or not?"

"As regular as the clock in the waiting room."

"How interesting. She would be in here, then." He patted the book.

"Number 21,210." Her smile was tight, as if she feared that she might burst into laughter.

"My word," Thomas said, and looked down at the book. He flipped back to the previous Monday, and sure enough, the first entry was

Number 21210, Mrs. Robina Cleary, a 71 year-old woman of impressive stature. Complains of a ringing in the ears. Advised to exercise (again) and to avoid rich foods (again). Accepted Universal Tonic. $2.00.

The week previous, the entry read

Number 21210, Mrs. Robina Cleary. Claims that the spate of hot weather has caused some discomfort. Suggested lighter clothing. Universal Tonic, $2.00.

Thomas paused and looked up. "Is this sort of thing common, Miss Auerbach?"

"Common?"

"We have a number of patients who take up space and time without any specific complaint?"

"I'm sure we do."

He fanned some of the journal pages. "I had an elderly aunt," he said. "A wonderful woman whom I loved dearly. As my father would say, Aunt Ethel enjoyed nothing as much as a good ailment. Something to discuss with neighbors. Mrs. Cleary reminds me of her."

"Be kind, Doctor."

The comment surprised Thomas. "Of course," he said, and patted the book. "I'll be prepared."

25

Doctor?" Thomas Parks looked up with a start. He put a finger on a name in the journal to mark his place. "The constable is here to see you, Doctor," Bertha said.

Edgar Eastman's towering, broad figure appeared in the office doorway. "There you are," he said, as if Thomas might have been hiding.

"Come in, come in," Thomas said, although Eastman already had. The constable closed the door a bit, nodded at Bertha as if accepting her permission, and then shut it the rest of the way. He turned and surveyed the room, in no hurry to engage the young physician in conversation.

"I thought to stop by." He scanned the spines of books on the top shelf that were at his eye level. He pulled one book partially out, cocking his head to better read the inscription. "You read Latin?"

"Some," Thomas replied, impressed that the constable recognized the language in the title.

"I don't."

"I wouldn't think Latin of much value in your line of work."

Eastman turned and looked at him. "You never know," he said. "We can't always tell what's going to be of value, can we?"

"I suppose not."

"I came by to see what you found out." Eastman turned one of the heavy straight-backed chairs and sat down on it backward, then dug in his pocket, eventually pulling out a large pocket-knife. Sliding it across the polished surface of the desk toward Thomas, he waited while the physician pried out the blade and examined it.

"I have my notes," Thomas said, and reached for his own medical bag that now rested on the floor beside the desk. He handed the open journal to Eastman.

"As you can see, it would be most difficult to say that this is the knife," he said. "This blade is more blunt than I would expect, and there is only one." He folded the knife and ran his finger along the front of the handle near the base of the blade. "This is not as wide as the bruising around the wound."

"You're sure?"

"Reasonably, yes."

Eastman turned the page that included Thomas's drawing of the bruise and squinted at it. "This?"

"Yes. The boy was stabbed so hard that the handle of the knife bruised the skin around the entry wound. And in my view, that bruise . . . that mark . . . is not consistent with this particular knife."

"Interesting. And this?" He pointed at another sketch.

"That's the shape of the wound in the posterior wall of the heart."

"Huh."

"That's where the blade actually came to rest."

"So *that* shape would be fairly accurate?"

"I would say so."

"And it matches this?" Eastman held up the pocket knife.

"Not at all. As you can see, that blade in your hand is quite rounded, almost blunt. The knife that caused that fatal wound was sharply pointed, an acute shape. As you can see by my notations, the angle of the tip was approximately twenty-five degrees. That's a very pointed blade, sir."

"*Approximately* twenty-five degrees." Eastman grinned, looking ten years younger when he did so. "You're a man of exact science."

"It's a relatively simple task to measure an incision in tough muscle," Thomas said.

Eastman opened the knife blade and laid it on top of Thomas's drawing for comparison.

"As you can see," Thomas said.

"Huh." The constable refolded the knife, slipped it in his pocket, and pulled out a second one. "And this?"

Much heavier, this knife featured two blades, and as Thomas opened the first, he felt a chill of apprehension. Fully four inches long, sharply pointed, and razor sharp. He knew before he overlaid it on the journal drawing that it would match.

"Now this one." He looked up at Eastman. "It could match easily." He laid the blade over the drawing of the heart wound. "If not a match, then an amazing coincidence. Both the wound itself and the bruise on the skin."

"Well, well," Eastman said, and accepted the knife back. He opened and closed the knife several times, brow furrowed in thought. Thomas heard voices out in the waiting room, and then sounds as if a herd of elephants were crossing the floor. The door to the examination room closed with a bang, and through the thin wall, he could hear the voices continuing. Eastman ignored the ruckus, and Thomas forced himself to relax, knowing that if he was needed, Bertha would feel free to interrupt.

"You know to whom the knife belongs?" Thomas prompted.

"Yes."

"I should say *both* knives," Thomas amended. "The first is not the murder weapon, I'm sure of that. The second may certainly be. It, or another knife exactly like it."

Eastman rested his chin on his crossed arms, and for a moment it appeared as if he were going asleep. "All right," he said after a moment, and it was little more than a murmur. "Irwin Pedersen. You've met him yet?"

Thomas laughed. "I've met very few people, thanks to my circumstances. He's the owner of the knife?"

"No." Eastman pushed himself upright. He turned the chair carefully, arranging it just so. "Pedersen is the prosecutor who will handle this case. He'll want to talk with you in the next few days."

"Anything I can do to help," Thomas said quickly. "I can't imagine the circumstances that led to the boy's death, but if the perpetrator is to be found, then by all means—"

"You may be called to testify."

"Absolutely," Thomas said. "Against whom?"

"I have arrested Ward Kittrick," Eastman said quietly. He glanced at the doorway as if someone might be standing there listening, then looked at Thomas. "Kittrick is brother to Harvey, the man killed last week in the scuffle with Charlie Grimes, one week ago. I took the knife from Ward at the time of his arrest."

"You don't say. He was after revenge of some sort? I had heard that the man's death was more an unfortunate accident. A drunken brawl."

"That we'll never know. Ward tells me that he had nothing to do with Charlie's death. He claims that he wasn't in town when it happened . . . that he was out in the timber. But a dozen others say differently."

"Well, obviously his *knife* was in town," Thomas said.

"Kittrick is lying," the constable said. "There were no witnesses to the stabbing, and he thinks to get away with it. Your testimony is important, you understand. We can prove he was in town that night, and those drawings can convince a jury."

"As I said, you have my complete cooperation."

Eastman moved toward the door, reaching out for the knob. He didn't turn it, but stood there silently for a moment, deep in thought. "You'll keep our discussion to yourself," he said.

"Of course."

"Will you make a copy of your drawings for me?"

"Take the journal with you. The drawings and figures are the only things in it at the moment." He closed the journal and held it out to Eastman. "I hope it helps." The constable nodded. "The first knife you showed me? Whose was that?"

"My own," Eastman said. He smiled at the look of surprise on the young physician's face, and opened the office door. Thomas saw that his day had truly begun, and wheeled after the constable.

"Mrs. Cleary." Eastman greeted a voluminous woman who sat in one of the leather chairs as if she were royalty. "Good morning to you." Before the woman could respond, Eastman turned away and nodded at a much younger woman who sat with her arm around a ten-year-old child.

Robina Cleary saw Thomas and her face lit up with interest.

"Doctor?" Bertha Auerbach interrupted, her tone sharp and imperious. She held the door of the examination room open. "We'll need to attend to Mr. Doyle immediately," she said.

"You have a good day, Doctor," Eastman said. As the huge constable headed toward the door, Mrs. Cleary reached out a hand toward him, her face full of questions. Eastman skillfully ducked around her, nimble as a dancer, and with only a polite touch of his hat brim, left the clinic.

26

G ood morning, ma'am." Thomas greeted Mrs. Cleary heartily, but steered his wheelchair toward the mother and child. At the last minute, he swerved abruptly, halting directly in front of the little girl. He leaned on the arm of the chair and frowned at her, lifting his free eyebrow so the bandage bobbed up and down. He knew he looked comical, and was rewarded with a tiny smile from the child.

"I'll be with you in just a minute, all right?" he asked. "Will you wait for me?"

"Are you . . . ," the child's mother started.

"Dr. Thomas Parks," he said, and held out his hand. The woman's grip was bony and listless.

"Is Dr. Haines . . ."

"He'll be along in a few minutes," Thomas said. "I've joined the practice, so"—he leaned toward the little girl—"you'll probably see a lot of me. But excuse me for a moment. There's a gentleman who's injured himself." He reached out and touched the girl's chin, the hot skin feeling like fine silk held in direct sunshine.

"Young man," Mrs. Cleary called, and the command in her tone was unmistakable. Her hands clasped over the head of her black cane. Thomas flashed a cheerful smile her way. "We'll be with you directly, ma'am," he said, and before she could reply, wheeled to the examination room.

"Sorry," he said as he closed the door. "But the little girl looks miserable."

"Doctor, this is Mr. Doyle," Bertha said. She didn't rise from her position, kneeling with both hands holding a bandage on Mr. Doyle's left leg just above the knee. The fisherman—the smell said he had to be that—was thin to the point of emaciation, his clothing soaking wet. The fingers of one hand were wound in his long, unkempt hair as if he was trying to pull it all out by the roots. "He slipped down on the wharf." Thomas now recognized the man as one of the fishermen he had greeted when he first disembarked from the *Alice*.

"Mr. Doyle," Thomas said, and extended his hand. The fisherman hesitated, eyeing the wheeled apparition in front of him. Doyle finally untangled his grip on a shank of hair and took the proffered hand.

"I heard about you," he gasped. His face was gray and sweaty, eyes wide with pain. "Name's Jimmy. Everybody calls me Jimmy." The hand strayed back to grab another hank of hair as he sucked in a breath, close to panic.

"Fair enough. Let's have a look."

Thomas maneuvered his chair with an impatient shake of his head, and Bertha Auerbach saw his exasperation. "Let me move out of the way," she said. "Mr. Doyle, I want you to lean back. Just relax."

The moment Bertha released her pad of bandage on Doyle's thigh, a flow of dark, venous blood leaked down his leg. A nasty splinter of wood smelling like a not-so-fresh seaside had skewered the scrawny muscle of Doyle's lower left thigh. He jerked and gasped with pain as Bertha shifted her hands.

"A quarter grain of morphine," Thomas said, and glanced up at Bertha, accepting the scissors that she handed him. "Mr. Doyle, I'm going to remove your trouser leg, so hold still, if you please. The nurse is going to give you an injection that will ease the pain."

"I don't need nothin'," Doyle said, but his teeth were clenched so hard that it came out a slur. "You cain't take my leg!"

"Oh, yes, you do need something," Thomas said congenially. "And I'm only taking your trousers. Your leg will be fine." He cut the filthy, wet trouser fabric, removing the legging far up on the thigh. He grimaced at the odor. Jimmy Doyle was as much a stranger to the bath as he was to the barber. With the blood slowing, Thomas pulled away the strips of cloth.

"My God, man. How did you do this?"

"Slipped on the wharf," Doyle said. "Tried to catch myself, but damned if I didn't fall down the piling. Thought I was like to drown."

"My word." The fragment of wood that projected from the skin was roughly oval in cross-section, like the heavy blade of a weapon, broken off by the man's weight. Four inches above the knee, the splinter had driven upward, ripping through skin and muscle as it plowed under the flesh of his thigh. The man's own weight had broken the wooden spear free from one of the wharf's pilings, twisting the weapon in the wound in a hideous fashion.

"What's that?" Doyle asked, sounding like a frightened child. He eyed the hypodermic syringe in Bertha Auerbach's hand.

"That will help you forget your troubles, Mr. Doyle," Thomas said. Ignoring the man's mumbled protestations, they managed to maneuver his right arm sufficiently for Bertha to find a target. Doyle let out a squeal.

"Now, lie back and count the planks in the ceiling," Thomas said, "or dream about all the fish you're going to catch."

Doyle mumbled something, but it wouldn't be long before the drug dispersed through his system, dulling all the edges.

"We'll want to wash this entire area with sublimate," Thomas said. "And shave from here to here." He touched the leg well above the projecting spur of wood, running his finger down to immediately above the kneecap. "The splinter has been driven into the deep tissues. If we don't excise the entire wound, it will infect with certainty."

"Ether?" Bertha said quietly.

"Absolutely." He lowered his voice to a soft whisper. "If I just pull this out and bandage him up, he'll be dead in a week. Wood is host to all kinds of particularly nasty things." If Doyle heard the pronouncement, he made no sound, off as he was on the soft cloud of morphine.

"Clean, shave, clean," Thomas said. "I want at least ten minutes for the morphine to work before we start the ether." He pushed back. "The kit in the sterilizer is finished?"

"Yes."

"That's good then. Immerse the kit in a pan with beta-naphthyl," he said.

The bleeding had slowed, and Thomas wheeled so that he could converse with the patient who lay now with a fresh pillow under his head and his lower legs hanging off the end of the table.

"Mr. Doyle, are you feeling some relief?"

"I guess so," the man murmured. "They call me Jimmy."

Thomas watched the pulse ticking away in the man's temple. "Did you pull on that splinter after you fell, Jimmy?"

"Couldn't get it out," Jimmy replied. "Couldn't get old Bob to touch it."

"Bob is your companion?"

"Yep."

"He's a smart man. And where is he now?"

The words came slowly, with a slur. "Him and Dennis brought me up here. They went back down to fishin', I suppose."

"I see. Well, we'll take care of you. You'll be taking some ether, Jimmy. Have you ever done that before?"

"No. Heard of it."

"It will make the surgery painless for you. You'll wake up, and all will be well. But we want this to go smoothly, so I'm going to ask you to help me a little." Thomas looked up as the door of the surgery opened. Dr. John Haines hesitated a moment, then closed the door behind him.

"Sir, would you hand me two of those small towels?" Thomas asked, and Haines did so without comment. The younger physician hesitated, loath to defer to the other now that a patient was at hand, now that he had thought through the procedure and was confident of a successful outcome. But Haines lifted both hands palms up, offering that Thomas should continue.

"Jimmy," Thomas said, turning back to the fisherman, "I'll be putting this over your face, covering it with another small towel over your nose and mouth. I want you to breath easy, just in and out, as deeply as you can without straining." He folded the cloth and held it so that the patient could see it. "This is nothing but dry cloth," he said, "and I'm going to ask you to practice the most even, deep breathing that you can." He gently covered the man's face. One of Doyle's hands flailed, and Thomas could see that the man was holding his breath.

"Just relax back now," he said. "Breathe deeply. Let's try it. There is no drug yet. Just clean cloth. It can really be quite comfortable. Very peaceful. Think of a sunny, windless day with every fish in the world going for your bait."

"I'll do this," Haines whispered. He moved to the other side of the chair, one huge hand resting on Doyle's forehead like a gentle father, the other manipulating the cloth.

"Jimmy," Haines said, "easy now, in and out. In and out." Haines turned and snapped his fingers once at Bertha, then pointed at the shelf. She reached for a small brown bottle and handed it to him. "Now Jimmy," Haines said, "you're doing fine. Just relax back. Don't fight it."

In another ten minutes, the surgical kit was in an enameled basin at Thomas's elbow. His sleeves rolled to the elbow, his hands still tingling from the scrub in hot water, then the sublimate, and finally a rinse in dilute carbolic acid.

"I think we're set," he said. "Jimmy, are you comfortable?"

"No," the voice mumbled.

"Well, I'm not surprised. But we'll have you up and around in no time at all." *Just no time at all,* Thomas thought to himself. Haines opened the small bottle and poured a dollop into the cloth, then covering it with the second towel. As deft and quick as he was, the odd, cloying aroma of ether filled the room.

"Now Jimmy, I won't lie to you," Haines said in the same comfortable tone. "This stuff smells worse than rotting otters. But just relax and let it work." The moment Haines laid the cloth over Jimmy Doyle's face, Thomas could see the man's body stiffen, and his hands flopped.

"Just relax," Haines crooned. "Just close your eyes and breathe nice and deeply. There now. That's fine." Other than the older physician's continued lullaby, the room was silent. In three minutes, Thomas could see Jimmy's body relax, his left hand opening.

In another minute, Haines said, "The conjunctiva, now."

There was no reaction when Thomas reached across, lifted a corner of the towel, and stroked the corner of Doyle's eye, producing not a flicker. From under the cloth came a regular snore, and Haines nodded his satisfaction.

"Bertha, let's get the rest of the trousers out of our way," Thomas said. He watched, keeping his hands clear of the contaminated clothing. In a moment, the remains of Jimmy Doyle's trousers hit the floor, along with underclothing so rank it could have walked out of the office by itself. When the patient was draped for some semblance of modesty, Thomas nodded. "If you please," he said, and he watched as the woman industriously scrubbed the wound, then shaved it, then scrubbed again. Jimmy Doyle snoozed on, unaware.

The wound oozed around the wooden shaft, and as Bertha prepared the site, Thomas sat back, regarding the leg, imagining the damage the wooden spear might have done, planning his incisions. No major arteries had been severed or lacerated, but the wound was both large and filthy.

At last Bertha finished by draping clean towels around the site. Thomas wheeled the chair until he was snug against the patient. He scrutinized the wound. "All right," he said at last. "The best little bistoury we have."

Bertha started to reach, and he held up a hand. "You need to wash your hands again, Miss Auerbach. Let me." She offered the small pan, and he selected the bistoury that appeared new and winked a reflection at him. "We're just going to see what we have," he murmured. By the time he stopped his first stroke, the incision was nearly a dozen inches long, running along the ridge of swelling above the imbedded wood. For an instant no blood appeared, as if he'd merely scratched the skin with the back of the blade. But then blood welled up along the incision.

"We're after the very tip," Thomas whispered, and as he manipulated the small, sterile gauze pads from the brass sterilization box, he cursed his clumsy left hand. "You see what I'm doing?" he said, a little louder as Bertha returned to his side.

"Yes," she replied.

"Then follow along with me. This damn thumb . . ."

In a moment, as he cut delicately into the muscle, spreading aside the upper layers, the enormous splinter was laid bare, ragged and foul from its years in and out of the tide. Before he asked for it, a hemostat appeared, and he clamped a large torn vein.

"Now the largest forceps we have," he said. Holding his breath, he retracted as much tissue as he could as she lifted out the splinter. He looked at the wooden dagger for a moment, amazed at its heft. "Let's irrigate this with sublimate and then beta-naphthyl."

For the better part of half an hour, Thomas worked, until satisfied that the wound was clean down to the very depths reached by the splinter's ragged point and beyond. He sat back with a loud sigh, hip, ribs, and skull pounding.

"Nicely done," Haines said.

"We're lucky," Thomas said. "We have silk?"

"Indeed, Doctor," Bertha said. Again she presented the brass box, and he selected a long coil of black silk that she threaded for him. Haines remained at Doyle's head, minding the effects of the ether, although he had removed the pad for several minutes. Haines did not offer to assist in any other way, but Thomas knew he was being observed—and with a flush of pride now welcomed the opportunity. While many of his classmates had struggled with the intricacies of sutures, especially the finest ones of slip catgut deep in the viscera, Thomas had discovered that his fingers seemed to have minds of their own, judging the tension of the silk against tissue, the roll of the knot under the pad of the finger.

Now, with underlying layers of muscle sutured with gut, he used a neat, continued suture with the silk, applying only enough tension to bring the lips of the wound together. He kept the stitches as close as he would for a facial wound where appearance would matter—here just a matter of pride that this incision would heal to a mere white line down Jimmy Doyle's thigh.

In due course, he reached for one of the cotton sponges soaked in carbolic acid. With gentle strokes away from the incision, he cleaned the wound once more.

"I think that gets it," he said at last. "Now we have but the challenge of moving Mr. Doyle to the ward," he said. "May we request some assistance from Alvina and Dr. Riggs for that?"

"You're going to use the ward?" Haines asked. He tossed the ether soaked towels into the small wicker basket below the water cart. "In a few moments, he'll be alert and free to go."

"A day of rest would be better," Thomas said. "I don't want to create a drug addict, but a few hours of quiet rest would be efficacious."

"Efficacious," Haines repeated, as if he was impressed with the word.

"I need to make it clear to Mr. Doyle that cleanliness and rest will assist greatly in the success of this surgery," Thomas added. "He needs to be clearheaded for that."

"Well, certainly. Bertha, will you fetch some assistance?"

"Thank you," Thomas said.

"I examined Louella," Dr. Haines said. Seeing the puzzled look cross Thomas's face, he added, "The little girl waiting outside with her mother. Louella Unger."

"Ah. What do you think? She appeared to be in some distress, but listless, I thought."

"A gastric upset," Haines said. "She's tender around the umbilicus and the right groin. I suggested to Mary that the child should
go to St. Mary's," Haines said. "The Ungers have the wherewithal
to make a speedy trip, since he owns the livery. Better to go now,
should the condition be appendicitis in its earliest stages."

"I'll see her in a moment," Thomas said. "Let me clean up a
bit."

"They've left already."

"I beg your pardon?"

"I thought there was nothing to be gained by waiting," Haines
said.

Thomas felt a flush of irritation. "I wish that I had been able
to see her."

"Thomas," the elderly physician said, and gently shook his
head. "If it *is* appendicitis, and I think that surely it will continue to that, I lack the ability to operate." He smiled at Thomas.
"And so do you, at the moment."

"I—"

"Deep abdominal surgery with a broken thumb isn't the road
to successful treatment, Thomas. You'll have ample opportunity
to prove yourself, never fear."

"I wasn't thinking to prove myself," Thomas said, realizing
that he was being less than truthful.

"Well, then, you understand me," Haines said. The door
opened, and Bertha and Alvina maneuvered a narrow rolling
bed from the ward.

"Will you need me further?" Alvi asked, and the question was
directed at her father.

"We may," Haines said. "Thomas wants Mr. Doyle to be our
guest at least for the day. Can you see to that?"

"Certainly." In a moment, the snoring Jimmy Doyle had been
transferred to the bed and whisked away.

"Would you like to visit with Mrs. Cleary?" Haines said.
"You're looking a bit taxed at the moment."

"No, I'm fine."

"Then please . . . Use my office while Bertha tidies up here.

I'll make sure that Alvi has all that she needs, and I'll tend to Jimmy. Sometimes coming out of the ether is the worst part of the experience."

"Thank you, sir."

Haines offered a broad smile. "Oh, don't thank me. Notice that I cheerfully pass the good lady on to you, young man. You might as well experience baptism by fire early on."

"I have read your notes on patient number 21210."

Haines laughed loudly, his head thrown back and beard bobbing. "Oh, my word. That's rare." He dabbed at his eyes. "Then you're prepared."

27

Thomas glanced at his watch and saw that only forty minutes had passed. During the surgery, the rest of the world could have stopped. Now, he took a deep breath, determined to face Mrs. Cleary with a cheerful, attentive demeanor.

He wheeled out into the waiting room and saw Mrs. Cleary locked in conversation with another young woman holding an infant. Both women looked up as he wheeled toward them, and Mrs. Cleary bent closer and whispered something in the young woman's ear, who in turn nodded vigorously.

"Mrs. Cleary? Would you come in?" Thomas said. He held out his hand indicating Dr. Haines's office. "A moment, please?" he said to the young mother and watched as the elderly woman heaved herself out of the chair. Robina Cleary was heavy, but not ponderously so. Her steely gray hair was bound in a tight bun under a small, simple black hat, and her voluminous black dress touched the floor. As she pushed herself upright, she jerked to the side slightly, and a gnarled hand shot out for balance, gripping the back of the chair. For just a moment she remained frozen, and then, ever so gingerly, straightened up and released her grip on the furniture, transferring her weight to the cane.

"My," she said, and shook her head. "Now don't you ever grow old, dearie," she said, and the young mother responded with a tight-lipped smile.

Mrs. Cleary did not walk directly across to where Thomas waited. Rather, she maneuvered around the perimeter of the room, now and then reaching out for balance with her right hand, the same hand that held the cane. Her left hand appeared ineffectual.

"Young man," she said, "I've heard so much about you." She looked at Thomas with bright blue eyes that still managed to twinkle in the midst of a sea of wrinkles deeply caked with fragrant powder. "You had a surgery this morning."

"Yes, ma'am," Thomas said. "But how are *you* feeling this fine day, Mrs. Cleary?"

"Well, now, I'm ailing. There's no doubt about that. But I'm vertical, and that's something. What did young Mr. Doyle managed to do to himself?"

Auntie Robina, Thomas wanted to say, amused by the hallmark of the true busybody. Without replying, Thomas held the door for her, and she managed her way past his wheelchair, trailing an atmosphere of half a dozen fragrances. Thomas recognized perfume, a complex scent that argued with facial powder, various other lotions and potions, and the unmistakable intrusion of urine. She paused halfway through the door to catch her breath.

"Where do you live, Mrs. Cleary?" Thomas asked, unable to imagine the elderly woman walking up Grant or Gambel Streets.

"An absolutely charming little cottage on Bryan's Bay," she said wistfully. "My sister and I make do with very little, I assure you. But then again, when you reach my age, what all do you need?" She reached into her voluminous bag and brought out an empty Universal Tonic bottle and placed it gently on the desk in front of her. "Doctor Haines always appreciates when I bring the bottle back," she said.

"She's with you now? Your sister, I mean?"

"Oh, she's at the Merc," Mrs. Cleary said. "She drops me here, and then goes to the Merc and has a time with Mr. Lindeman. She's nearly twenty years younger, you see. She has energy for that sort of thing."

"Ah. That's convenient, then. Won't you have a chair?"

"Oh, with pleasure," Mrs. Cleary said, and with a sigh settled into the chair in front of the desk.

"I apologize that the examination room is unavailable at the moment," Thomas said. "We had something of a go first thing this morning, as you know. Now, I'm to understand that you've suffered the gout recently." He watched the elderly woman's face, watched how, when she first launched into a sentence, she struggled to bring the words to the surface.

"Most certainly," she said. "Dr. Haines has had me under treatment for just weeks and weeks. I'm really . . . really *quite* used to speaking with him, you know."

"I noticed that three weeks ago, Dr. Haines made note for the first time of a certain recurring vertigo? That was the word you used when you spoke with him at that time?"

"He's discussed me?"

"Indeed he did. As his associate, that's entirely proper, Mrs. Cleary. I've also read his journal with special interest," Thomas said. "In particular, I'm struck by your general good health up until about three weeks ago. Just short of your birthday, I noticed."

"*Good* health? My heavens, I'm a wreck," she said, and the generous wattles under her chin shook from side to side. Her mouth attempted a smile, but it was a crooked grimace. "You talk to Dr. Haines. He'll tell you. And *birthday*? Lord, when you have as many as I've had, what's the difference."

You've had but seventy-one birthdays, Thomas wanted to say, *two husbands, and five children.* He thought better of it and gently allowed his body to sink back into the wheelchair. With his elbows on the arms of the chair, he steepled his fingers in front of his mouth.

"I think a complete examination would be in order," he said carefully.

"Oh, you do," Mrs. Cleary replied. "I have a grandson who is no older than you."

"Yes? He's well, I trust?"

"I *really* think this is all a matter for Dr. Haines," she added. "If *he* thinks an examination is called for . . ." Her right hand strayed up to the top button of her dress, buried under the white lace of her collar, as if protecting herself from this mere child. "And I've talked to Alvina. She's such a dear. Although"—Mrs. Cleary tried to lean forward slightly, glancing sideways conspiratorially at the door—"I find that I have *great* difficulty talking with the good doctor's nurse. Miss Auerbach?"

"Really? Now why would that be?"

"Most assuredly, I do. I find that she seems . . . now how can I put this?" She curled a finger across her lips, gauging the best way to reveal the secret. "I often feel that she doesn't believe a word I have to say."

"I'm sure that's not the case," Thomas said. "It's clear that the patient is the best barometer of his own health. But do something for me now. Lift your left arm, if you will. As high over your head as you can."

"Lift my arm?"

"Only that. Can you do that for me?"

"Young man . . ."

"Yes?"

"I'd really prefer to discuss my condition with Dr. Haines, if you please."

Thomas sighed and raised his left eyebrow, regarding the elderly woman with good-natured impatience. "When Dr. Haines sees you," he said, "I'm sure that he will ask the same thing of you. I suppose that if you wish to wait, I can find you something to read." He started to turn his chair. "The young woman and infant outside need attention as well."

"It makes me ache to watch you," Mrs. Cleary said unexpectedly. She reached out with her right hand, touching the desk.

"Do I understand correctly that the mule you were riding fell directly on top of you? Down in the rocks by the water?"

"Well, *in* the water," Thomas said with a crooked smile. "I've had my fill of kelp and seawater, let me assure you."

"Will you walk again?"

The question was full of both sympathy and, Thomas knew, the search for delicious tidbits to pass on.

"Most assuredly. I'm walking short distances now—more each day. And yourself? I couldn't help noticing that you tend to become short of breath easily."

"Oh, that's the old lady in me," Mrs. Cleary replied. "I must say, the tonic is a *great* help." She reached out and nudged the empty bottle toward Thomas. "As a restorative, it really has no equal. I should be quite lost without it."

"Does the vertigo accompany those same moments when you're trying to find your breath?"

"Well, yes."

"When the pain strikes your left arm and shoulder, it travels all the way down to your fingertips?" He didn't add that he had merely read Dr. Haines's notes, not made a miraculous observation on his own.

"My word, yes. That's exactly what happens. But the tonic brings almost instant relief."

Alcohol is a wonderful elixir, Thomas thought. "And your left arm. Does it pain you now?"

"Well, no. But I confess to a certain weakness that's alarming. That's why I came by today."

"This weakness . . . is it slow in coming, or sudden in onset?"

"It's been with me, I would say."

"For how long?"

Mrs. Cleary closed her eyes, tipping her head back in thought. "I lost my balance two weeks ago," she said, as if revealing a deep, dark, ugly secret. "Something so simple. I turned from the stove with a pan, and my word." She opened her eyes and looked at Thomas. "I went *flying,* simply *flying,* across the kitchen. I have a bruise on my hip that's a wondrous, livid thing."

"Vertigo then?"

"Oh, my, yes. I had to sit down, or I surely would have fallen. I could not quiet my breathing for some moments."

"And the left arm?"

"An odd tingling, young man. And just no strength at all."

"This was two weeks ago?"

"Yes, very nearly."

"And has the strength returned? The strength in your arm?"

Mrs. Cleary bit her lip and looked down at her left hand, now quiet in her lap. "I must confess I have no strength. Not even to brush my hair or fasten a button."

"Will you raise your arm for me now?" He saw her left hand move, a little jerking motion to one side.

"I . . ." She looked puzzled, at the same time reaching out toward the desk. "Oh, my," she said. "I just . . . ," but a knuckle rapped on the office door, interrupting her.

"Yes?" Thomas called, and the door opened a few inches. John Haines peered into the room.

"May I?"

"Of course, sir."

"And how's my favorite young lady this morning?" Haines asked.

Before she could reply, Thomas interjected, "It is my belief that she has suffered a cerebral episode of some sort, Doctor. There's a loss of tension in the fine muscles of the face on the left side, along with uneven constriction of the pupils. Her left arm continues to be weak."

"You spoke of vertigo last week," Haines said. He looked down at Mrs. Cleary, who gazed up at him with adoration. Reaching out, Haines placed two fingers on her right carotid artery, then reached across and did the same to the left.

He made a face and picked up her left arm at the wrist.

"Does that cause you discomfort?"

"My, no."

Raising her arm little more than horizontal, he watched her face. "Can you hold that for me in that position?"

165

He released his grip and her arm sank back into her lap.

"Aha," Haines said. "My dear lady, your sister is up the street?"

"Yes." This time, a small note of fear had crept into her voice.

"Then we must fetch her," Haines said. "Are you comfortable now?"

"Yes, I suppose so," Mrs. Cleary replied. "But my sister?"

"My dear young lady," Haines said, and perched on the corner of the desk, hands clasped in his lap. "The sharp, discerning eye of my associate has given us early, fair warning. It is my belief, and please," he said, twisting to look at Thomas, "interrupt me if I'm wrong. It is my belief that you've had a small cerebral hemorrhage. I would call it a *minor* one, but nothing in the brain is minor. If treatment is to be successful, your sister will need to cooperate in your care. She must understand, along with you, what is necessary and what is counterproductive. It makes sense to explain all that once, to both of you." He turned to look at Thomas again. "You agree, Dr. Parks?"

"Absolutely."

"Let me have Alvi fetch your sister," Haines said. "In the meantime, Dr. Parks, while I continue to chat with Mrs. Cleary," he reached out a comforting hand to her shoulder, "perhaps you would speak with the young lady? I know what she wants, but I think she might benefit from a discussion with you."

"Of course." Thomas moved his chair, but stopped and reached out to take the elderly woman's right hand. "All will be well," he said, but he could see the fear in the elderly woman's eyes, and felt a pang of sympathy.

As he wheeled out of the office, he heard the physician's comforting voice. "My dear, let me find you a little restorative." Thomas glanced back to see Dr. John Haines pouring two shots of brandy, one more generous than the other.

28

From the memorable, nervous moment three years before when he had examined his first newborn patient under the watchful eye of Dr. Warren Wilhelm, Thomas had harbored a deep distrust, even a dread, of tiny patients who could not discuss their ailments with anything other than a heartrending cry. He had never felt so clumsy as he had when he'd picked up that first infant. The little limbs pumped every which way, defying a secure grip, sort of like trying to hold on to a large, loose-skinned grape.

That first experience, reinforced several more times, had prompted Thomas to promise that, were he presented with a choice, he would leave treatment of infants and tiny children to those physicians and nurses who treasured such an experience.

"Come in, won't you?" He tried to sound more confident than he was. "I'm Dr. Thomas Parks." The young woman, whom Thomas saw was really quite attractive in a harried sort of way, bundled her infant with practiced ease and rose to follow him.

Bertha Auerbach met Thomas at the door of the examination room. "Do you wish me to attend here?"

"Yes, I do," he said fervently. After Bertha's efforts, the room looked clean and neat, but Thomas could smell the lingering odor of Jimmy Doyle. The young woman arranged herself daintily in one of the chairs.

"This is Mrs. Henrietta Beautard," Bertha said, and her tone softened. "With baby Henry."

"Good morning," Thomas said. It was difficult to sound convincingly brisk and efficient while crumpled in a wicker wheelchair. He smiled what he hoped was an engaging welcome. "Is your complaint this morning with yourself, the infant, or both?" All he could see of the infant was the swaths of blanket, but the girl looked at him steadily, and Thomas saw that her large, violet eyes were clear—gorgeous, in fact, set against flawless skin.

The surname rang a distant bell. Somewhere in the pages of Dr. Haines's journal, perhaps.

"I'm afraid I'm in . . ." The girl's voice was husky. Bertha reached over Mrs. Beautard's shoulder, pulled a small corner of blanket to one side, and stroked the infant's tiny forehead.

"In?" Thomas encouraged. He saw mistiness in the girl's eyes.

"In a way again," she added quickly and looked away, cheeks aflame.

"Ah." Thomas folded his hands across his chest. "You believe you may be pregnant? Is that what you're saying?"

"Yes." Her voice was tiny, barely a whisper.

"Some morning unease then?" She nodded, and Thomas rubbed his forehead thoughtfully, trying to visualize the pages of his new Saunders obstetrics text—one of the books no doubt dumped in a ravine somewhere when his shipping chest was ransacked. He listened for Dr. Wilhelm's sonorous voice, echoing somewhere far back in his mind.

"Well, Mrs. Beautard, this will be your second child? Little Henry is your firstborn?"

"Yes."

"I was about to say you've had some experience with all this. You've not had the regular flow?"

"No." The blush deepened.

"This month only?"

"Yes." The single word came out as a birdlike peep.

"So we're very early, which is good news. Any other discomforts? Passions for various foods? That sort of thing?"

Mrs. Beautard tried a game smile and showed beautiful, even teeth guaranteed to melt any man's heart. Perhaps she had melted the *wrong* heart, and now suffered the regret.

"Well," Thomas said cheerfully, "what we must do is tend to your general health in the coming months so our little Henry is rewarded with a healthy, bouncing little brother . . . or sister, as the case may be. Now—"

She took a deep, shuddering breath. "I can't have a second child," she said.

"What do you mean, you can't? Did you suffer in the delivery of Henry? He's what, six months old or so?" Again, he rummaged through his memory for the proper journal entry. The book belonged in his lap, not in Dr. Haines's office.

"Four months."

"His birth was normal in all respects? You appear to have recovered fully."

"Yes. That's not what I mean. If his father . . . my husband . . ."

The light gradually began to dawn. "Your husband is who?"

"Lawrence Beautard," the young mother said. "He works in the mill for Mr. Schmidt."

Thomas glanced up at Bertha. "It seems everyone works for Mr. Schmidt, and I have yet to meet him."

"Mr. Schmidt is a good man," Mrs. Beautard said quickly. "He's a good, fair, honest man."

"I've heard that. Your husband is not enamored of the idea of a second child? Is that what I'm to understand?"

Mrs. Beautard closed her eyes. "He has little enough patience with this one," she said, and looked down at the tiny face. "If the child cries while Lawrence is home . . ."

"My heavens, Mrs. Beautard, that's what infants *do,* isn't it? Cry and eat and make interesting smells? And in between times, enthrall us all? Surely your husband realizes that. And surely *he* knows what causes pregnancy?" Immediately he regretted the levity, seeing no humor in the girl's eyes.

He reached out and stroked the corner of the blanket to one side. Henry Beautard was a well-formed infant, raven black hair across his forehead, fine features that he might have inherited from his mother. The baby lay listlessly, and when Thomas hooked his right index finger through the tiny hand that rested in the folds of blanket near the infant's mouth, the infant's grip didn't respond.

The half-lidded eyes puzzled the physician, and with his right thumb, he gently eased one of the eyelids upward. The pupil was tiny in the muted light, a mere dot of black surrounded by the wonderful violet coloration that the child had inherited from its mother. The other eye was equal.

Thomas motioned with his hand. "Let the child lie on his back on your lap, if you please," he said. Little Henry showed no response during this maneuver, and lay limp, eyes staring sightless at the ceiling. Thomas took his time adjusting the earpieces of his stethoscope, then slid the bell across the tiny chest. The cool touch brought an oddly disjointed, uncoordinated thrashing of the infant's limbs, as if the little boy was trying to swim through mud. At first, Thomas counted without his watch, then frowned as he pulled the gold-cased timepiece out of his vest pocket. He sat for some time, listening, his eye locked on the second hand.

"He needs changing," Mrs. Beautard said as he pulled his stethoscope from his ears.

"Yes, he does," Thomas agreed. With the gentlest touch, he explored the infant's abdomen. Such tender tickling should have produced a gurgling response of delight from the infant, but again, nothing.

"Doctor," Bertha said, and ran her hand down the infant's tiny left arm.

"I saw that," Thomas said. The elbow was swollen, and as Thomas stroked down both sides of the infant's forearm, he felt the unnatural curve of the bones and the warmth of inflammation. Using an index finger on either side of the arm between wrist and elbow, he explored the bone's shape. After a moment, he straightened up in his chair.

"On his stomach, if you please?" he said, and Mrs. Beautard deftly turned little Henry over so that he lay on her arm face-down. Again using just the index finger of two hands, Thomas felt across the silky skin of the shoulders, then down the tiny rib cage and spine, finally across the pelvis.

"What happened?" he said as he sat back. "His left arm is broken—a greenstick to be sure, but broken nevertheless. The elbow is inflamed and swollen."

"He fell . . ."

"Please, Mrs. Beautard. Infants who cannot yet crawl cannot yet fall. Have you given him medication? He should be a healthy, responsive child. Yet he clearly is not."

"No. I mean, only a little syrup now and then to ease his fussing. My husband . . ."

Thomas leaned back in his chair, leaning his head on his fist. He regarded the young woman until she looked away.

"Mrs. Beautard, you must talk to us," he said. Henry uttered a tiny wail, his first sound since arriving at the clinic. Thomas reached out and pulled down the back of the infant's diaper, trying not to recoil at the curdled soiling. "He takes nursing regularly?"

"I am most careful," Mrs. Beautard replied.

"'*Careful*' meaning what?"

"I sterilize the milk, just as I should."

"You don't nurse the child?"

This time, the flush was deep and lasting.

"Please, Mrs. Beautard. Let's not be ridiculous. We're talking about what has been done since the dawn of time, and what shall *continue* to be done until the world ends." His tone was sharper than he intended, and he leaned forward and lowered his voice to a near whisper.

"You must talk to us. You *don't* nurse this child yourself?"

"Yes. I mean no, I do not."

"Why ever not? Are you productive?"

This time, the reply was a short little nod, her face flushed bright. Bertha's hand slipped forward and rested on the woman's shoulder.

"The mother's milk is far superior to anything else. That is not open to debate," Thomas said gently.

"My husband . . ." She stopped, and Thomas waited. The room fell silent, so still that Thomas could hear the muffle of voices in Dr. Haines's office next door. "My husband does not want me to nurse the child," the young woman said finally.

"Why ever not?" She didn't answer, and after a few seconds Thomas repeated the question.

"He says that . . . He says that I will lose my shape."

For another long moment, Thomas could do nothing but stare at the woman in disbelief.

"And so you have been using cow's milk?"

"Yes. But he seems to tolerate it well. Still, when he cries and fusses, my husband loses his patience."

"I see. And what do you give Henry to soothe him?"

"Just some of the syrup."

"The name of it?"

"I have the bottle here," she said, almost eagerly. "I thought to obtain another today from either Mr. Lindeman or Dr. Riggs."

From her apron she produced a small, blue bottle. Thomas turned it toward the light so he could read the label: Sorrel's Soothing Syrup, packaged by Dr. Peter B. Sorrel, of Port McKinney, Washington. The syrup that soothes fretful teething infants and toddlers, producing the habit of peaceful, uninterrupted rest.

Uncorking the bottle, he found just enough that he could wet the tip of a finger, tasting sweetness with the tang of alcohol, other lingering flavors that he could not identify, and an odd tickle on the edge of his tongue.

"Mrs. Beautard, did Dr. Riggs tell you what the ingredients of this syrup were?"

"No. He said only that it *might* ease the child's fussing. And really, Doctor, it does."

Thomas looked down at little Henry, the child lost somewhere in his own private fog of opiates. "It must be hell to pay when he wakes," he muttered to Bertha. "Mrs. Beautard, you *must* not administer medications that contradict what nature is trying to accomplish." He realized that he was repeating a lecture he'd heard Dr. Wilhelm give several times. "Mother's milk exists for a good reason," Thomas continued. "When a child frets, it's for a reason. It is a call to attend to discomfort, or for affection, or simply for company. We do not give medications unless there is something actually *wrong* that the medication might correct."

"My husband loses patience when the baby frets," Mrs. Beautard responded. "And now, if there is a *second* child in the house . . ."

"I see. He strikes the child?" Thomas asked. "Is that how the arm was broken?"

"I'm sure he didn't mean it," Mrs. Beautard whimpered.

"When did this happen?"

"Saturday last. In the evening. My husband came home in foul temper. There had been a bad accident at the mill."

"What was the cause of that?"

"I don't know," she replied. "But he had been drinking, I know. Maybe he . . ." She shook her head. "I don't know."

"This happens often?"

She nodded. "But he's a good man," she said.

"I'm sure he is," Thomas said. "This is what we must do, Mrs. Beautard. First, Bertha will help you clean up little Henry. He'll be happier when he's presentable, I'm sure. I think that his system will purge the medications in due course, but it is absolutely essential . . . *absolutely* essential, that you give him no more of Sorrel's. Do you understand me?" She nodded. "If there's anything further we need to do other than letting nature take its course, I'll let you know. Now, when little Henry is cleaned up, we'll see to fashioning a little splint for that arm."

"I can't . . ."

"I beg your pardon?"

"If my husband sees a splint, he'll be furious."

"Why would that be?"

"For one thing, your fee."

Thomas looked up at the ceiling hopelessly, then at Bertha, whose face remained a mask. "Mrs. Beautard, the arm must be splinted. Further, his elbow must be tended, first with a warm pad—not hot to blister, mind you—then with cold. For that, Mr. Lindeman has a supply of ice that you may crush, a little at a time." He touched the infant's elbow. "If we don't help the healing process, he's apt to be lame in that joint."

"For how long must this be done?"

"Until the elbow is back to normal," Thomas said. "Three times a day, for ten minutes each time. That's where we'll start. I want to see young Master Henry in two weeks' time." He smiled at the young mother. "We can only hope that the joy of impending motherhood will make your husband more reasonable," Thomas said. "In fact, in two weeks' time, when you bring Henry back so that I may examine his arm and elbow, might I suggest that you bring your husband as well?"

Mrs. Beautard laughed shortly, a sudden exhalation loaded with derision. "If he knew that I was here, it would be *my* arm that was broken," she said.

"The offer stands," Thomas said. "If you would like me to talk with your husband, I will." *After all, what more can be done to me,* Thomas thought. "But will you return in two weeks' time?"

"Yes."

"Good. Then let's tend to this young man," Thomas said, and backed his chair out of the way. In half an hour, Henry Beautard was clean, powdered, and sporting a tiny splint on his left forearm that Thomas fashioned out of two pieces of clean lath stripping that Bertha produced from upstairs.

"And no more Sorrel's," he admonished. "He must have the breast, and I don't care what your husband says. The more you hold little Henry, the less he will fuss, I'm sure. In between times, show your husband how to hold the child so that no injury occurs. And tend to your own nourishment during the next few months."

The woman nodded wearily, and Bertha accompanied her to the front door. When the nurse returned, she closed the door of the examining room.

"Opiates," Thomas said before she asked. "I'm certain of it. Can you imagine?"

"It is a common thing," Bertha said.

He looked at her in astonishment. "A *common* thing? How is that possible?"

"She would be rid of the pregnancy," Bertha said quietly, ignoring his question.

"Rid of it? I think not," Thomas said vehemently. "I would like the opportunity to talk with Mr. Beautard."

Bertha shook her head. "No, Doctor. I don't think you would."

"You know him?"

"Only in passing. But I know that there are limits to what is our business."

Thomas looked at her quizzically. "Whatever affects the health of our patients is our business, Miss Auerbach."

She reached out to pick up the empty bottle of Sorrel's, but Thomas held out his hand. "I need that," he said.

29

Dr. Haines disappeared at lunch, and shortly afterward, Gert James arrived with a picnic basket laden with fresh bread, thinly sliced chicken and beef, carefully wrapped fillets of the ubiquitous smoked salmon, and a potpourri of fruit and vegetables.

A squat Mason jar held fresh buttermilk, a drink that Thomas detested but that Bertha cherished.

Between a fisherman's inflamed throat and a young lad whose mother was sure that his deafness was the result of self-abuse rather than earwax, Thomas managed to sample Gert's food. Jimmy Doyle was not conscious enough to partake, but Thomas could see that, were the ward to fill with patients who needed continuing care, both a nursing staff and a cook—not to mention a kitchen—would be necessary.

The smells lingering from the various patients dulled his appetite, even though he retreated to Haines's office. He managed to relax for ten minutes before five men arrived, four carrying the fifth, and Thomas found himself glad that Dr. Haines had returned promptly.

Thirty-six-year-old Howard Deaton, ashen, sweating, and wide-eyed with shock, had slipped at the wrong instant, and the back wheel of a loaded freight wagon had crushed his lower left leg. After his four companions had been ushered outside and a generous injection of morphine quieted the man, Haines examined Deaton's boot, pointing out the crease from the wheel rim.

"We'll cut it right down the back and the side," he said. "That way we can slip it off without doing more damage."

"Them are new boots," Deaton moaned. He lay back on the table, an arm over his eyes. "You can't be cuttin' 'em."

"My good man," Haines said, "trust me on this. A new boot is far less expensive than the alternative. Just lie still and let us do what we have to do."

Deaton mumbled something incoherent. The scalpel opened the leather as if it were paper, and while supporting the leg with his left hand, Haines slipped the boot off, prompting Deaton to jerk violently, back arching, gasping, his eyes rolling back in his head.

"I think this stocking is welded to the skin." Haines raised his voice a bit. "Howard, you might consider walking through the surf now and then," but Deaton didn't respond.

With the stocking peeled off and the trouser leg sliced off at the knee, they could clearly see the displacement of both lower leg bones, three inches above the ankle. "Simple enough," Haines said, and moved to one side so Thomas could wheel closer. He closed his eyes as he ran his fingers down both sides of Deaton's lower leg. Despite the morphine comforter, Deaton groaned, his upper body still stiff as a pine plank. Bertha wiped his face with a warm towel and murmured motherly things in his ear.

"He's lucky. Had he not been wearing those stout boots, the steel wagon rim would have sliced through his leg," Haines said.

As it was, the bruising was horrendous. "Both bones," Haines added. "That's what I see. The ankle isn't involved. Bertha, we'll want to wash this grimy limb from knee to toe. How's the morphine holding?"

"He's nodded off," Bertha replied. Sure enough, Deaton's body had sagged and his jaw hung slack.

"Good. Then let's see what's what."

Thomas nodded, his fingers telling him that both bones had snapped sideways, like sticks of firewood propped against a chopping block and stomped in half. "I don't feel any large fragments," he said.

"Nor I, but there are bound to be chips. Still, if he's lucky, we may see success with the fracture box. That will ease his trip to St. Mary's tomorrow."

"But for this?" Thomas said. "St. Mary's? Certainly, the fracture box is the place to start, but if there should be surgical intervention needed? He'll be about on crutches in three or four weeks with plaster, barring complications. On the other hand, such a trip now . . ."

"You believe there may be more internal damage than what we see here?"

"Well, no, I think the fractures are relatively straightforward. There is no joint involved, which puts luck on our side. It seems to me that a full day in a jouncing ambulance makes for a pointless risk at this early stage."

"Thomas," Haines said, and gently pushed the young man's wheelchair away from the drugged patient. He lowered his voice to a gruff whisper. "At the moment, we are not staffed to care for patients in the ward. "One night, we can manage, I suppose. But not as a general course of things. If you're thinking that Mr. Doyle should remain for the night as well . . ."

"Someone needs to tend Mr. Doyle for the night, without a doubt."

"But whatever for? Your surgical wound is as neat as I've seen. It's near no major arteries or veins, and certainly you've done all you could to assure asepsis."

Thomas hesitated, thinking the answer obvious. He glanced across at Bertha, who appeared to be entirely preoccupied with Howard Deaton. "A few extra hours tending his surgery will certainly ensure a successful result," he said. He slumped back in his chair, suddenly exhausted. "John, please. Let me offer a suggestion. I know it's only a quarter mile back to one-oh-one, but to me, at this moment, that distance seems like a transcontinental venture. I would look on it as a great favor if you would agree to let me remain here tonight . . . in the ward. Its convenience is a powerful attraction."

"Oh, good heavens," Haines protested.

"Please," Thomas said, and he knew that he sounded like a boy trying to talk his parents into allowing a dangerous trip into foreign lands. "There is food enough for a week just in what Gert sent down for lunch," he said. "Instead of the struggle up to one-oh-one, I plan to remain here. I shall keep an eye on Mr. Doyle and Mr. Deaton." He pulled out his watch. "By the time we have this leg sorted out, it will be after three, and I can only imagine that the day is yet young. By the time we're finished, I'll be comatose."

"You're holding up?"

"Well," Thomas said. "After a fashion. Collapsing on a bed in the ward would be a luxury for me."

Haines smiled and looked at Bertha. "Now we're having patients tending patients," he said. "But if that's what you want, young man, so be it. I'll inform Zachary that you'll be staying here tonight. We don't want him thinking there are intruders. He might shoot the wrong person." He smoothed the front of his vest over his belly and rolled up his sleeves. "But now, Bertha, let's clean up this broken man and put him back together. The smell of those feet is making me faint."

In an hour, Deaton lay flat on his back in a ward bed, the Stimson fracture box encasing his leg like a small wooden coffin, supported by a clever rack that included four legs easily adjustable for height. Pillows took weight off the heel, and elevation relaxed the calf muscle. Small pillows were bound in place by the wooden sides of the open-topped box, with the lateral pressure easily adjustable with cotton bandages.

Howard Deaton's leg was not the final case of the afternoon. As the afternoon progressed, a parade of patients passed through the clinic, including a ten-year-old who had managed to scratch a simple case of poison oak into a full-blown infection, a friend of Mrs. Robina Cleary's who had nothing wrong at all other than a deep, abiding curiosity, and a young man with an ugly boil on his neck.

Twice during the afternoon, Thomas wheeled into the ward and marveled at Jimmy Doyle, who continued his sleep with the peaceful countenance of a child. Howard Deaton, despite the morphine, was more restless, his lower leg swollen and discolored. The rest of the faces passed in a blur, and by six o'clock, Thomas was well aware that his decisions and actions were coming out of a fog of pain and fatigue. Haines remained close, never leaving him alone with a patient as he had tended to do earlier in the day.

At five minutes before six, Haines gathered together his medical bag. "I need to make a call," he said, without explaining what the call might be. "I'm going to lock the front door and pull the curtain. Now you, young man . . . We've both been adequately foolish today, allowing you to work as hard as you have."

"Well, I—"

"Well, you what," Haines said with a laugh. "Look at you. You can't even sit up straight in that damn chair. Your hands are shaking. Your left eye looks worse than an old drunk, and I venture to say that if I asked you to stand up right now, you'd fall flat on your face."

"Admitted, all."

"I've said nothing today because I've come to know a little bit about you, Thomas Parks. If left to your own devices, you would continue on until you drop. And then, who does that benefit?" Haines leaned back against the counter, regarding Thomas critically. "Let me tell you how highly I regard you, Thomas."

The young physician felt the damned flush on his neck. "But really—"

"No. Listen to me. I would rather have you, with your energy, your enthusiasm, your skills, even with your broken thumb and ribs, than half a dozen fit men. But now that you *know* your limitations, I want you to be patient, take your time, and allow yourself to heal. That's what I want. I want you to give yourself a chance."

"Thank you, sir," Thomas managed to say.

"I know that it's pointless to invite you for dinner and conversation," Haines said. "But I suppose that sleep will do you far more good. Still, I'll have Horace bring a basket of food down for you and your ward guests." He straightened. "If Mr. Doyle takes nourishment, be aware of the possibility of vomiting. We don't want him choking to death after all your hard work."

"You must have after-hours patients," Thomas said.

"Of course. They will come to the house, or pound on the door here until Zachary *sends* them to 101."

"He doesn't tend them?"

"On occasion. But a day-to-day medical practice is not Zachary's ambition, as I'm sure you've already observed. That's why you're here."

"I see," Thomas said, his head full of questions but his body too tired to pursue them.

30

Jimmy Doyle's snoring reminded Thomas of his berth mate onboard the *Alice*.

So tired that he couldn't sleep, Thomas lay back on the simple ward cot and listened to Doyle's symphony. Despite morphine, Howard Deaton slept fitfully. Occasionally the building would pop or creak. Earlier, in those first luxurious moments when he had stretched out on the cot in the rear of the ward nearest one of the windows, Thomas had heard footsteps on the floor above, but that, too, soon ceased.

He rested on his back, his shoes propped up on the end of the cot. The whole situation was ludicrous, he thought. He'd given no consideration to something as simple as undressing at the end of the day. He could no more remove his own high-laced shoes than Howard Deaton could run across the room. He had made no provision for a night nurse. The thought that John Haines was allowing him to learn from mistakes was little comfort.

He closed his eyes, letting the events of the day take curtain calls. A loud groan punctuated by a curse jarred him alert, and he realized after a moment of disorientation that he had been deeply asleep. One of the gaslights at the far end of the ward came to life, and for a brief, panicky moment, Thomas thought that either Deaton or Doyle had arisen, headed now toward disaster. A shadow moved about, certainly not one of the injured men. A soft, soothing voice mingled with impatient muttering, and after a moment, Thomas heard the distant but unmistakable sound of a metal bedpan in use.

The figure left the ward. Thomas shifted his legs off the bed, resting for a moment in the sitting position before reaching out for the arm of his wheelchair. With something akin to practiced ease, he swung into the chair.

Pushing up the center aisle, he paused first at Deaton's bedside, unable to see well enough in the shadows to ascertain whether or not the man was awake.

"Hurts like hell," a voice from the bed remarked, as if commenting on the weather.

"I'm sure it does," Thomas replied. He pulled out his watch and held it toward the gaslight. He frowned and brought the timepiece closer, astounded. Somehow, evening had faded into night. The watch announced twenty minutes after midnight. He'd slept like a dead man for more than four hours. Both of his patients could have expired, and he would have slept through their passing without a stir.

"We'll get you something," he said, tucking the watch away.

"I don't want no more of that addict stuff," Howard Deaton said. "Makes me feel like the walls are cavin' in on me."

"How are you feeling otherwise?"

"Like shit," Deaton said succinctly. "I was going to get up to take a piss and found things all bound up. Who the hell are you?"

"I'm Dr. Thomas Parks. Dr. Haines's associate."

"You're the one the mule tried to kill, ain't you."

"Yes. That would be me," Thomas said with a laugh.

"Heard about that. Hell of a stunt."

"Yes, indeed." Bertha Auerbach reappeared carrying a small enamel tray. "Ah, the ghost. I've very glad to see you," Thomas said to her.

"Well," Bertha replied, and let it go at that. She stopped at Jimmy Doyle's bedside. Jimmy snored blissfully.

"Mr. Deaton doesn't want an injection," Thomas said.

"It will help you sleep," Bertha offered, but Deaton shook his head adamantly.

"Nope," he said. "I'll sleep when I know what's what."

Bertha reached out and turned up the gaslight, and Thomas examined the position of the pillows in the fracture box.

"The wagon wheel broke your lower leg, Mr. Deaton. A nasty fracture of both lower leg bones, just a couple inches above the ankle." He reached out and indicated the spot with his finger. "Luckily, the joint was not involved. Now, this contraption allows us to both position the bones and keep the injury open for examination for the next several days."

"Several days? I can't be doin' that."

"You have no choice, sir. That's the best way to put it. The leg's properly and thoroughly snapped, both bones. Now, we're expecting an uneventful healing, *if* we can keep you quiet and cooperative. In two or three weeks, a gypsum bandage will allow you to start moving about cautiously in a chair, and then later with crutches."

"Good God. What do you think I do for a living, mister?"

"That really doesn't matter as far as the leg is concerned, although I'd be interested to know," Thomas said mildly.

"I'm a goddamn teamster, sir. I can't be 'moving about cautiously,' as you say, on no goddamn crutches."

"Well, your choices are fairly limited," Thomas said.

"Choices, shit. What's Doc Haines say?"

"The same thing I say, Mr. Deaton. If you want alternatives to think about, consider what we'll do if this injury deteriorates. Hemorrhage, abscess, gangrene . . . not a pretty picture I paint for you. Then we take your leg off right here," and he drew a line across Deaton's leg at the knee. "That's if we catch it in time. You think about that."

"Jesus."

"Exactly. That's why it's important that you remain quiet and do as you're told. You have everything to gain by being sensible."

"I don't want none of that," Deaton said, eyeing Bertha and the pan that held the hypodermic needle.

Thomas read the man's wide-eyed expression correctly. "Is it the morphine that bothers you, or the needle?"

"That goddamn thing is big enough for a horse," Deaton said. "You don't let her near me with that. Gimme a goddamn glass of some good whiskey."

"One of the problems is that alcohol tends to make you restless," Thomas said. "And we don't want that."

"Not if I drink enough of it."

Thomas laughed. "Well, that's true, sir. But there's the waking up, you see. Anyway, I gave an injection to a little girl earlier today, and she didn't mind at all."

"You're going to give me the needle? You are?" He glanced down at Thomas's bandaged hand.

"No, Miss Auerbach will do that. She's far more deft than I. You won't even feel it."

"You're a goddamned liar, Doc," Deaton said, but a trace of good humor crept in. "No offense, ma'am."

"Yes. She's the last person in this building you want to offend, Mr. Deaton. And a little stab is far better than what you're feeling now, believe me. We want that leg quiet." He nodded at Bertha. "Give her your right arm, and then look at me, sir," he said to Deaton. "From now on, we want that leg to rest peacefully. Let it knit without complication, and in six weeks you'll be happily on your way."

"Jesus, now it's up to six weeks," Deaton said, and grimaced as the needle slipped home.

"The morphine will give you several hours of rest," Thomas said. "You'll find that, in a day or two, the most acute pain will subside, and we can dispense with the drug. But the injection will help you until then."

"My arm's burnin' up," Deaton said as the hypodermic's plunger pushed the morphine into his vein.

"No doubt," Thomas said. "Relax and let it work." He watched Deaton's rugged face. "The more you can sleep, the better." He took Deaton's left hand in his, gave it a brief squeeze, and then backed away from the bed. Bertha turned down the gaslight to the slightest flicker.

"When did you arrive?" Thomas asked. "I didn't hear you."

"I came at midnight," she said. He wheeled after her as she left the ward. The gaslights in the examining room were ablaze.

"And you're sleeping in your clothes?" she said, eyeing Thomas critically.

"It turns out that I slept the evening away."

"No one can work all day, then sit up all night," Bertha said stiffly. "There's some sustenance in Dr. Haines's office, by the way. I brought down a meat pie my sister-in-law made. That and a bottle of fresh milk."

"You're both angels," Thomas said fervently. "Might we be able to find some coffee?"

"You need nothing that will keep you awake, Doctor," Bertha replied. "I'll return promptly at six. Gert will send coffee, I'm sure. Along with a substantial breakfast for your two patients

184

and yourself. With the effects of the ether and morphine, neither man should eat heavily just yet."

"Join me for some dinner?"

"No. I'll leave you to it, Dr. Parks."

"Don't tell me that you walked here from your home at this hour? How far is it?"

"It's not far, but I most certainly did not walk. My brother waits out in the buckboard."

"Well, good heavens, why doesn't he come in?"

"He loves his cigars, doctor. And they're best left outside."

Thomas laughed. "Well, I'm in his debt. And yours. I obviously hadn't thought this night through very carefully."

"Well, you're tired, Doctor."

"It's a good tired."

"Yes." She nodded curtly. "If there's nothing else?"

"A complete kit is in the clave?"

"Of course, Doctor. As you requested."

"You're irreplaceable," Thomas said. He held out his hand, and Bertha Auerbach hesitated for just a moment before taking it. Once again, Thomas was surprised by how small her hands were.

"Thank you," he said. "This is an awkward time. And I'm afraid it's of my making."

"You're welcome," the young woman replied. "One day at a time." She paused at the door. He had rolled his chair after her, out into the waiting room. "Good night, then, Doctor."

"Good night. And thank your brother for me. I look forward to meeting him."

She turned the knob. "I'll lock this as I go out," she said. "Dr. Haines showed you the key? In case someone comes in the middle of the night with an emergency?"

"It *is* the middle of the night, Bertha, and no . . . he didn't show me."

Bertha reached up along the doorjamb where a skeleton key hung on a small nail well out of Thomas's reach. She handed him the key. "All the locks are the same," she said.

"Thank you again." He slipped the key in his vest pocket. Bertha opened the door and the air was wet, the night too dark to see beyond the front step. Thomas thought that he saw the glow of a cigar, but then the front door closed.

The clinic settled once more into silence, and Thomas sighed. He found himself wishing that Bertha Auerbach had remained for a bit. If pressed, she would speak her mind, and Thomas wanted to hear her opinion on several matters.

He wheeled into the office, and groaned at the aroma from under the towel. There was enough meat pie for two meals. He eyed the bottle of milk and weighed the benefits of that against the brandy that he knew was in the cabinet beside the desk. Despite the wretched taste, he drank the milk as he ate what must have been a full pound of meat pie.

The struggle to use the small lavatory awoke the demons. By the time he finished pumping the toilet reservoir full from the cistern, his forehead was beaded with sweat.

He wheeled out of the office, leaving the light a tiny sputter and then turned all four gaslights on in the examining room, feeling more comfortable with that room at the ready.

The wheelchair was silent on the carpet, and he glided across the waiting room, feeling the cool draft that managed to find its way around the locked front door. He paused there again, his chair against the wall, his head leaning back against the wainscoting, letting his mind roam. The building creaked again, and he looked down the long, dark tunnel of hallway that led past the stairs.

Curiosity powerful, he considered a strategy. Retrieving his crutches, he parked his chair at the bottom of the dark stairs and calculated the venture. With the chair once again wedged against the wall, he rose, balancing on the crutches. A single gaslight decorated the dark wall near the foot of the stairs, and he took one of the friction matches from the sconce and lit the gas, stuffing a dozen matches in his shirt pocket as well.

The gaslight illuminated sixteen stair treads that led upward to a closed doorway. The banister was stout and he leaned his rump against it, putting just enough weight on the crutches that he could hop his right foot onto the first tread. The soft thump of his boot on the carpeted tread marked nine inches of vertical progress.

"Fifteen," he whispered aloud, and hopped again. Standing on the ground floor, the adventure had seemed tame enough. But as he made his way laboriously upward, to a point where the stairwell passed through the first-floor ceiling, he saw that a misstep now would cost him a devastating tumble.

With a flush of apprehension, he realized that returning to the blissful, restful haven of his ward cot required descending whatever he ascended. Six treads lay ahead. And suppose the doorway was locked? Bertha had said the front door key fitted all the locks, but did she mean interior doors as well?

His ribs told him loudly to do *something,* rather than hanging from his crutches half up or half down.

Clenching his teeth, he heaved himself up three more, stopped, and regarded the doorway ahead. The knob was one tread out of reach, and he hunched up that step. Back pressed against the wall, he reached out and tried the knob. It turned, but the door remained secure.

Thomas retrieved the key from his vest. It turned the lock effortlessly, and his pulse quickened. The door opened inward, revealing only darkness. The air itself told him that the room was large. This was no closet he had opened.

He navigated the final step and leaned against the wall, ribs shrieking, hip throbbing. After a moment he fumbled a match from his pocket, closed his eyes, and snapped it with his thumbnail. The head broke off and sailed away. The second match he raked across what felt like a plaster wall, and then flinched at the flare of light. Logically placed, a gaslight was mounted just to one side of the stairwell, and he lit it, turning it up full.

"My God," he breathed as he turned to face the room.

31

The light threw shadows around two rows of ceiling supports. It appeared to Thomas that the major portion of the second floor was included in this single room.

To his right, the banister continued, taking another flight upward to the third floor.

He counted seven desks, one near each ceiling support and gaslight. Along the back wall a huge pigeonhole cabinet reached to the ceiling, most of its bins heavy with paperwork. Framing the cabinet were two doorways toward the back of the building.

Thomas pushed away from the wall, heading through the center of the room toward the first desk. He paused and lit another gaslamp, then settled into the comfortable swivel chair, much like the furniture one might expect to see in a bank office.

Turning to face the desk, he admired a Remington visible writer, one of the newfangled, latest generation of machines that produced typed figures the equal of a print shop. Around the machine, the desk was a model of organization.

On the left was a pile of correspondence, and as Thomas leafed through the missives, he saw that the envelopes were addressed to various iterations of Dr. John Haines's name and the clinic's title and address. The postmarks and return addresses represented a scattering of states in the southern midwest. On each envelope, a large, bold number was written and circled with heavy grease pencil. The majority were number 1's, with a scattering of 2's, 3's, and 5's. Each envelope had been opened, the included letter turned slightly sideways to peek out of the top.

To the right of the Remington a wooden box contained a supply of clinic letterheads, the impressive engraving of the planned clinic building gracing the top of the printed sheets. Another wooden box labeled R & S included apparent correspondence printed on clinic letterheads. Yet another was marked File.

Thomas reached out and picked up the top letter from the R & S collection, to which was pinned a carbon copy of the clinic's response, as well as the original correspondence and envelope marked with a circled number one. Also attached was a blank version of a lengthy questionnaire that appeared to explore a patient's symptoms.

The clinic's letter was addressed to Mrs. John Henry Tyler, and Thomas saw that it was Mrs. Tyler's letter that was pinned to the reply.

Being careful not to smudge the fragile carbon of the clinic's response, Thomas slipped Mrs. Tyler's original letter from the envelope. It was dated the eleventh of August.

Dear Sir,

I write to you in hopes of recieving one of your dianostic insturments. I have been troubled of late with sleeplessness, irritabilty, and other signs of feminine weakness. As we have no doctor in our village, and am not able to travel distance, your assistance would be appreciate.

Thomas frowned and read the letter again. The "dianostic insturment" must refer to the voluminous questionnaire attached.

The typed letter of response from the clinic, as yet unsighed, was brief and to the point:

My dear Mrs. Tyler,

I am glad to acknowledge receipt of your letter of 11 August requesting assistance with diagnostic procedures. Please be aware that because of our enormous case load, we have found it necessary to reserve our services for only the most troublesome, acute cases. However, you mentioned that medical care was sadly lacking in your area, and it is our hope to be of some assistance. Enclosed is a diagnostic questionnaire prepared by our medical staff. Please address each question completely, as every individual's case is certain to include details unique to itself. Omit nothing, allowing neither false modesty nor self-consciousness to come between you and effective diagnosis and treatment. The sooner your reply is received, the sooner we

may analyze your condition and recommend prompt treatment. We urge
you, if unwilling or unable to travel to our clinic and research center, to seek
immediate and comprehensive medical treatment from a trusted physician
near your home. Still, because our treatment regime has enjoyed such
tremendous success, we urge you to act promptly. Your patient profile and
diagnostic questionnaire are the first step, without which we can do nothing
for you. To further assist you toward health without delay, we are sending,
by separate package, a sample of our patented tonic, which you will find
most efficacious.

The letter, neatly centered on the letterhead's sheet, bore the closure "Dr. Zachary T. Riggs, M.D., Director of Clinical Research and Operations." The reply seemed eminently sensible and medically cautious.

He restacked the various documents, laying them back in the wooden tray. The selection of typed responses apparently awaiting signatures was nearly two inches high. Being careful not to dislodge anything, he slid the tray toward himself so he could pick up one corner of the bundle. The stack easily included two dozen responses, each similar to the one typed to Mrs. Tyler. In each case, a diagnostic questionnaire was attached. All of the letters in the 'R & S' tray were number 1's. A sheet of foolscap was folded around each bundle.

The file tray included only carbon copies of clinic letters, each with one of the handwritten numerals circled in the top left corner.

Thomas saw that the topmost copy was numbered 2, and he picked it up gingerly. The letter was addressed to Mr. Burton Roman, with only the address, *Paris, Illinois* given.

My Dear Mr. Roman:

   As you know, because of a vast patient load spurred by the success of our
treatment regimes, we have strictly limited the number of new patients added
to our practice. Still, the contents of your letter of 13 July, and the answers
provided on your diagnostic questionnaire, have prompted me to forward
your case to Dr. Herman Tessier, formerly of Betil, Austria, but now on our

staff. Dr. Tessier has agreed to take on your case, a most perplexing and challenging one.

In just a few days time, Dr. Tessier will be in correspondence with you. However, because of the gravity of your situation, Dr. Tessier has authorized and directed us to send you a temporary supply of the clinic's Universal Tonic, enough to build your strength prior to treatment. The supply is sent free of charge. If you experience an increase in vitality, as most of our patients do, you may order additional supplies of the Tonic, at the price indicated on the included advertisement.

Once again, the letter was signed by Dr. Riggs.

Thomas frowned and replaced the letter. Tessier? Who was this new doctor? He thumbed the pile of correspondence until he found a number 5, the highest number he had seen, this time with a large capital letter T added after the numeral.

Five-T was addressed to the Reverend Clark Nolan of Clemson, Tennesee, and Thomas settled back with it in hand.

My dear Reverend Nolan:

You cannot imagine our delight to reserve your letter of 23 July indicating that Dr. Tessier's Metabolic Oil has effected a complete cure in an otherwise debilitating case of cancer of the esophagus. As we have related to you in the past, there is no "magic" in Dr. Tessier's formulation; only a most fortunate discovery that certain vegetable oils, when working in combine and when taken as directed, produce a rapid and miraculous result. In regards to your own case, we both congratulate you on health attained, and encourage you to continue a strict regime of Dr. Tessier's. The 16 ounce bottle you requested is being shipped promptly. If there is undue delay, or if the medications arrive in anything but perfect condition, please do not hesitate to contact us. Time wasted is health lost.

Dr. Zachary Riggs had signed this letter also.

"My God," Thomas whispered, uneasiness replacing his earlier admiration. "Dr. Tessier . . . I should like to meet this fellow." He replaced the letter. Taking his time with each pile, he counted the correspondence. The documents that covered this first desk included the names of fifty-seven patients. Growing more curious by the moment, Thomas struggled to his feet, leaning his right hip against the desk so he could reach each pile of documents. Of the fifty-seven patients, thirty-nine were either outright requests for the "diagnostic questionnaire," or were vague medical complaints first answered by sending the questionnaire as a reply. Four were testimonials similar to Reverend Nolan's. Eleven of the fifty-seven were number 2's, letters that included a referral to Dr. Tessier based on the questionnaire. A bottle of tonic was always included. Thomas found three number 3's. In each case, he saw that a 3 included a reply from Dr. Tessier himself. Selecting one, Thomas relaxed back in the chair. His left eye burned from reading the letter, written to a man in Dundee, New York.

> Dear Mr. Murtaugh,
>
> It is with interest and, I confess, some grave misgivings, that I read your profile. It appears that at this time you are suffering from a severe sarcoma, or cancer, of the lip. From your description, the cancer may have spread to your soft palate, tongue, and salivary glands. At the same time, it is apparent that the surgeries you have endured have provided you with no relief. In the vast majority of cases such as yours, my Metabolic Oils have provided prompt, permanent relief, with the cancer driven from the system by the combined action of the essential, natural oils. While I am relieved that the trial prescription of Metabolic Oils sent to you by my assistants has provided some measure of relief, you are wise to continue, even intensify, the treatment. As per your request, we are sending you the 32 ounce quantity of Metabolic Oils. Take as directed, increasing the original prescription to six doses each day, rather than four. With confidence that you will soon enjoy perfect health, I am,

Tessier had signed over his typed name with a great flourish. Thomas dropped the letter back in the tray, his gut clenched in a tight ball. "Dr. Wilhelm, I wish you were here," he said aloud. He could picture his favorite professor and mentor at the university standing in the auditorium, cigar clenched between yellow teeth, forefinger wagging toward the heavens as he faced the students. "Beyond any doubt," the eminent physician had shouted, "any and every advertisement for a cancer cure cloaks a swindle. There is no disease more dreaded, more lethal, and more perplexing to the physician. There is no disease that so effectively destroys the patient's hope as it destroys the body. Charlatans and swindlers know that as well as we do. It is that very hopelessness on which they prey."

Thomas turned, pushing the chair in a circle so he could survey the room. He had stopped at the first desk, and now saw that each of the others was equally awash in paperwork. Of the seven desks, six included Remingtons. The last did not; it held a mound of newspapers and what appeared to be a row of textbooks propped up by the wall against which the desk was nestled.

He stood up again, one hand on the desk for balance. Making his way toward the back, he approached the desk with the newspapers. Sinking into the chair, he was immediately struck by the aroma, more a bouquet, that he had come to associate with Alvina Haines.

32

Three grease pencils lay neatly arranged at the front margin of the desk blotter. On the floor to the left of the desk, pushed up against the wall, was a bin of mail—a bushel of letters in all shapes and sizes.

"My God," he breathed. None of the letters were yet opened. He turned back to the desk and rested his left hand on a low pile of neatly folded newspapers. The top edition, the *Weekly Courier and Express* from Mount Payson, Kentucky, was folded to expose the masthead. On the desk blotter, what appeared to be a design for an advertisement was in progress. The advertisement, sized for a half page, touted Dr. Tessier's Metabolic Oils as well as

Dr. Haines's Universal Tonic. An inset box at the bottom of the ad also featured an engraving that advertised the *Medical Advisor*. The book was available for $4.25.

Thomas read the advertisement carefully, noting the sidebar that presented the testimonials of satisfied patients . . . patients like the Reverend Nolan. A flowery description of the clinic included mention of Dr. Herman Tessier, recently arrived from Austria, Dr. Zachary Riggs, lately of Cincinnati Eclectic College of Medicine and Surgery, and, of course, Dr. John Haines, founder of the clinic and Vital Research Center. The center of attraction, presented in an ornately bordered frame, was an announcement for the diagnostic questionnaire, sent free of charge to patients who "suffer from ills, disease, afflictions, and general debility, as the first step down the path to glorious and perfect physical and mental health."

Most of the advertisement had been clipped from another publication, but Alvi—Thomas assumed it was her work—had penciled in various additions and deletions. "No other medications work so completely, thoroughly, and gently," the advertisement claimed. "Because of our exacting standards of laboratory and clinical procedures in the manufacture of our preparations, we can guarantee complete relief and cure for any ills for which we prescribe medication and dosage. Do not be misled by imitations."

Thomas leaned back and rubbed his eyes. He could imagine the process. Sitting at this desk, Alvina opened the mail, extracted any money orders that might be included, then passed the letter along with appropriate instructions to be answered by one of the six young ladies.

He turned and surveyed the wall cabinets. If the pigeonhole system organized and stored the original letters and the copies of their responses, it must have included thousands of documents.

But what of Zachary Riggs? He swiveled the chair, regarding the two doorways in the back wall. Perhaps. The first door opened to reveal a dark hallway leading to an outside entrance.

The second door was locked. Thomas still had the skeleton key in his pocket, and he fished it out. It slid into the lock easily enough but refused to turn. Wiggling it this way and that didn't help.

"We find you in the most intriguing places," a gentle voice behind him said, and Thomas startled so violently that he felt as if he'd been stabbed in a dozen places. He gasped and staggered sideways, his right shoulder smacking into the wall.

"My God, man, I'm sorry," Zachary Riggs said. He reached out and took Thomas by the left elbow. "I didn't mean to startle you." Thomas struggled to catch his breath. He wasn't about to argue the point, but the thought occurred to him that had Riggs *not* meant to startle him, the big man wouldn't have padded across the floor as quietly as a cat.

"No, I'm . . . ," Thomas whispered, seeing spots before his eyes. He bent over, trying to take the weight off his ribs. He saw then that Riggs was in stocking feet and wrapped in a great, red robe tied at the waist with a gold sash, the outfit accentuating his considerable bulk.

"Were I not seeing you standing here, I would find it impossible to believe that you negotiated those stairs unaided," Riggs said. He reached out and pulled Alvi's chair close. "Here, sit before you fall on your face. You know, I *thought* I heard something . . . Perhaps it was your crutches thumping on the stairs. I imagined all variety of intruders."

"I couldn't sleep," Thomas said, maneuvering into the chair. "And I confess, my curiosity won over. Here I am, pottering away downstairs while the wheels of commerce turn up here." He tried for a light tone, as if he actually believed what he read in the newspaper advertisement on Alvi's desk. "I hadn't seen you or Alvina all day, so busy were we with patients."

"Your first day was something of a trial for you," Riggs agreed. "Although John tells me the day was really quite serene." His neatly clipped beard bobbed as he nodded vigorously. "He already values your assistance, you know. He spoke of some really quite impressive surgery." His face suddenly growing sober,

Riggs frowned at a new thought. "He's losing his sight, you know."

"Yes, he told me. In his right eye."

"Well, in both, now."

"He spoke of that."

"He's a proud man." Riggs sighed. "I can only imagine how hard it is for him. We would have everything to gain if you would consent to examine him."

"I have only a rude foundation in ophthalmology, nothing more," Thomas said.

"But you've attended the best schools, and are bright and ob-servant. He . . . *we* . . . would value your opinion."

"Have you examined him, then?"

"I have," Riggs replied. "But I am no surgeon, sir. I know of no relief for his retinopathy, and was hoping that you would bring some new techniques that might benefit. Both his case and with others."

"I doubt that I can provide anything that the specialists haven't considered," Thomas said. *What does Dr. Tessier think?* he was tempted to ask.

"Ah, you're too modest," Riggs said. He had pulled a small ring of keys from the left pocket of his robe, and now turned to the locked door. "You're curious enough to climb your way up a mammoth flight of stairs, so forgive me if I appear to boast a bit. What you see around you is a thriving concern that is bringing relief to literally thousands of souls," he said. "I presume that you've perused some of the correspondence?"

"Yes," Thomas said, trying to sound impressed.

"We have discovered—and it's really nothing more than common sense—that many, many people live well away from any kind of formal medical care," Riggs said. He opened the door, but made no move to pass through. "What we provide is the best medical care and support possible via the mails. As I'm sure you're aware, recent advancements in the rails alone have made the post a vital resource for us. It no longer takes two or three months for a parcel to reach any spot in the country . . .

merely a week, maybe two. Sometimes just days. We depend on that."

Thomas nodded toward the large wooden box—much like a firewood box—that held the as yet unopened mail. "You have an impressive response."

"Oh yes," Riggs said proudly. "And what we have learned is that in order for us to address the concerns that literally flood in daily via the post, we must divorce ourselves from the day-to-day workings of the medical clinic downstairs. It is impossible to do justice to both concerns."

"I would suppose."

"By facing the challenges downstairs, Thomas, you're taking a considerable burden off John's shoulders. Now, he is free to advise us in operations here. Even to dictate responses to troublesome cases." Riggs lowered his voice and his hands folded over his belly. "John can do that, even though his sight is failing, Thomas. Being *able* to do that gives him purpose, allows him to pursue the work that keeps him vibrant."

"Of course."

"Good. Good." Riggs nodded enthusiastically. "My God, man, what time is it?" He peered at the small pendulum clock on the far wall. "Ten minutes after one, and here we are, blathering away." He smiled engagingly at Thomas. "Let me show you the rest, if you've a mind."

"I would appreciate that."

"Good. And then after that, I really must convince you to get some rest. Dawn brings another full day, you know. Now," and he pushed open the door. "The pharmacy is located here, along with a considerable effort to keep up with the massive shipping that we do." He grinned and held the door for Thomas. "I must say, I sometimes feel as if we are the sole support for the United States Post Office."

The back room actually included a full third of the second floor. Maneuvering through the doorway, Thomas saw that a large office was enclosed by a waist-high partition. The huge desk was an incredible clutter—newspapers, correspondence, clippings of various sorts, a large glue pot, another Remington typewriter, and several advance copies of the *Advisor*.

"My cubbyhole," Riggs said. "Alvi has given up with my housekeeping. Perhaps that's the reason I'm banished back here. I don't know."

Large shipping cases cluttered the floor beyond Riggs's office. He bent down and pulled some of the excelsior to one side, revealing the tops of small empty brown bottles. "All the way from San Francisco," he said. "I am continually astonished at the number of bottles we send in a month." He patted the excelsior back in place, straightened up, and swept his hand to include the various crates that were warehoused. "Each medication has a characteristic bottle design," he said with pride. "Over here," and he stepped through a passageway between crates, "is where I apply appropriate labels." He pulled a large printed sheet from a flat packing case. Thomas saw hundreds of small labels for the Universal Tonic. "We keep our printer very busy."

"And he is located . . ."

"In Bellingham," Riggs replied. "He is slower than I would like, but his business is growing as well. So we must be a little patient with him."

"You have assistance with all this?"

"No," Riggs said quickly. "The day will come, I suppose. But this is where I spend my time, Thomas. Alvi and the six young ladies take care of most of the correspondence, with help from John if need be. That frees me to work back here. Come, let me show you."

Along one wall, a row of sixteen wooden casks rested on a sturdy bench. "This reminds me of a winery," Thomas said and Riggs laughed, nothing evasive or furtive in his manner. He reached out and patted first one and then the other of the two largest casks. "The brandy can be an attractive nuisance," he said. "Miss Haines is not driven by temperance, but she sees that her father is coming to depend more and more on spirits for relief of his ailments." He grimaced. "One must embrace moderation, and as I'm sure you've observed, that isn't always the case with John, God love him." He sighed. "Anyway, this is the center of the pharmacy." He walked along a series of shelves that included several hundred bottles of various shapes and sizes, along with an equal collection of small wooden boxes.

"The raw materials," Riggs announced. "We expend considerable energy finding the various ingredients. You know, I sometimes think that the alterative approach to medicine has been much ignored in some of our colleges and universities. Do you agree?"

Thomas thought carefully. "I would think that in the most stubborn cases, the physician is advised to consider the entire arsenal," he said.

"The arsenal," Riggs said enthusiastically. "That's *exactly* right." He waggled a finger. "The physician's arsenal must be varied and creative, including the alternatives."

He stood with his hands on his hips, surveying the vast store of bottles, boxes, jugs, and crockery that lined the wall above the oaken casks. "There are people," he said quietly, "who would pay large sums of money to know what is in this room, Thomas. The world is full of imitators. 'If he can make it, then so can I, and for less, too.' That's what the imitators think. And so they use ingredients held to no quality standard. Or worse, they *guess* at what the ingredients might be."

"People are easily fooled," Thomas said.

"Indeed they are, sir. Indeed they are. The world is full of charlatans."

33

Thomas chose his words carefully. "I don't understand attempting to treat patients without actually examining them. Think of the possibility of mistakes, or of missing a condition that's obvious to the physician, but not to the patient."

Riggs nodded. "But, Thomas, please . . . Remember how many people cannot actually visit a clinic while ill. People with no physician within reasonable distance."

"A substantial number, I would suppose."

"Most certainly, a substantial number, Thomas. Now we provide an alternative. Not a perfect one, by any means, but an alternative. By applying reasonable standards and methods, backed by science, we can recognize the symptoms and signs of particular illnesses. You know that." He paused, and Thomas waited for him to continue.

"For instance, if a patient comes to you with tuberculosis, you are sure to recognize it, are you not?"

"I would hope so," Thomas replied.

"Now, suppose you receive a carefully written questionnaire—you've seen our document?"

"Yes."

"Well, then. The patient tells you that he is debilitated, losing weight no matter how much he eats, is coughing blood, suffering both sweats and chills . . . is in fact, in general decline." Riggs held up both hands. "If such a patient sat before you, you would listen to the complaints, then listen to the lungs, would you not?"

"Of course."

"And if sufficient tubercles existed in those lungs to alter the sound during auscultation, you might feel for tenderness in the hollow behind the clavicles. You might examine sputum under a microscope. You might perform a test with the spirometer. But you would know, would you not, in your heart of hearts, that the patient sitting before you was suffering tubercular consumption. Simply by hearing his complaints."

"I suppose so."

"If we receive such a profile in the mail, from a patient in"—he threw his hands up—"it doesn't matter where, but picture her sitting in front of a dwindling fire, her family wringing their hands hopelessly, her children petrified as they see their mother coughing blood into a kerchief. We receive her profile, and is there any doubt? Do we have to see her pathetic figure through our doors to know that the dread specter of consumption has yet another victim?"

It wasn't hard to see where the florid style of writing in the advertisements had its origin, Thomas thought.

"And so we recommend treatment. It's that simple."

"But no specific drug has shown promise in the treatment of tuberculosis," Thomas persisted.

"True enough," Riggs agreed readily. "But what *does* show promise in treatment?"

"Rest. Change of climate perhaps. Proper nutrition. Some symptomatic relief. Helping the patient maintain his strength."

"Exactly so," Riggs said triumphantly. "That's exactly right. Perhaps you recall my sermon about the marvelous peach? The human system is resilient, when given half a chance. If a few ounces of Universal Tonic each day help nature resume its course upward to perfect health, then we've done our job. If a few ounces of Dr. Tessier's Metabolic Oils reduces the tendency to hack the lungs out, so be it. Cannot we do all of this without seeing the patient?"

"I would suppose so."

"And if the patient is suffering not the ravages of consumption, but instead a cancer of the vitals—for which there is also no promising cure—then have we done harm in supporting his general health and well-being? No, we haven't."

Thomas heard the words in a blur. "It seems to me," he began, then started again, "It seems to me that such false hope is counterproductive. I—"

"We *raise* hopes," Riggs interrupted. "There is nothing *false* about that. Hope supports the patient's will to *fight*, Thomas. Look to yourself as an example."

Thomas surveyed the pharmacy behind him. "Perhaps . . . ," and he stopped. He had no desire to make an enemy of Zachary Riggs, but the examination of the tiny Beautard child remained etched in his mind. "I wondered about Sorrel's Syrup, for instance," he said. "I ran across that today."

"In what way?"

"A mother giving her four-month-old son the syrup to ease his fretful moments."

"My God," Riggs whispered. "Really so?"

"She said you gave it to her. That you prescribed it for the infant."

"Then she misunderstood me, I'm sure. Sorrel's relieves the discomfort of teething, no more."

"The child is a bit young for that."

"Of course."

"What are the ingredients of this concoction?"

"Of Sorrel's? We continue to evolve and change," Riggs replied. "As with all our medications. Not one or two ingredients, but a careful balance of a dozen or more. And again, I assure you that there are people out there who would pay dearly to know the specific formulation." He smiled. "I suppose I should be flattered by their attention."

"But the primary ingredient?"

"Again, the formulation is evolving. For teething, a small percentage of anodyne is almost immediately effective, touching the gums and mucous membranes of the mouth. I use Carlisle's preparation, for its purity."

"You have a veritable crowd of people working on your behalf, Zachary. Dr. Sorrel, Dr. Tessier, now Carlisle and his anodyne." "Anodyne" referred to no particular pain reliever, but Thomas decided that the middle of the night wasn't the time to pursue the issue.

"Well . . . ," Riggs said, and gazed around the room. "It's a large operation, Thomas."

"The correspondence appeared to advertise Tessier's compound frequently."

"Just so. We have found that if we can reduce the patient's coughing, Thomas, reduce some of the damage from that, then rest and recuperation so often follow."

"So, by weight?"

"Well," Riggs said slowly, "I would suppose that by actual *volume*, the liquid substrate is the foundation on which the tonic is built. I have found nothing that works any better than a particularly fine brandy. It both soothes, especially when supported with various herbs and vegetative preparations, and is a restorative. Nothing provides more immediate nutrition. By including careful instructions for dosage, we can make the most of its qualities."

"Along with a cough suppressant?"

"That's correct. I have discovered that a simple infusion of red clover is a gentle means to that end, especially with the Carlisle's. It is a fine balance, you see. Without the cough, we have nothing to purge the diseased lung tissue from the body. With an excess of violent coughing, as you know, much healthy tissue is torn and destroyed. But I don't wish to simplify."

Thomas pointed at a considerable selection of small wooden boxes with one crutch. "And these?"

"I have contracted with a mill up the coast to provide cedar shipping boxes," Riggs said.

"An amazing operation," Thomas said. "I would suppose a fair income from this enterprise?"

"In proportion," Riggs said easily, and let it go at that. "By the way, Dr. Haines informed me of his arrangement with you. Would you prefer a bank draft, or cash?"

Thomas found that he was hugging his arms around his ribs, and tried to straighten up. "At the moment, my world includes one-oh-one and this clinic. I have not even toured the village, and I've met only a handful of people. Visiting a bank or even Mr. Lindeman's Mercantile would be a keen adventure, Zachary. So . . . I don't know. I suppose it might be best to simply keep the money on account? Will that suffice?"

"Well, of course. Should you need anything, however, you will not hesitate to let one of us know?"

"Yes. And we *do* need something, without delay." Riggs's eyebrows raised in anticipation. "We must have additions to our nursing staff that allow patients to remain in the ward," Thomas said. "I know that it has been the policy to remand patients to St. Mary's, but we will no longer do that. Not when we can treat on the premises."

"I see. What have you in mind? Miss Auerbach isn't adequate in some way?"

"She is wonderful, Zachary. But we can't expect Bertha to work all day long, and then during the night as well. We need nursing staff who are fresh and alert."

"You have two patients in the ward now, I understand."

"Yes. Our two left legs, as Bertha calls them. One will leave us in the morning, the other with a serious fracture of the leg that must remain in a fracture box for as much as two weeks."

"And he wouldn't be better off at St. Mary's?"

"Indeed not. First of all, a trip of some thirty miles would likely kill him, or at least ruin what progress we've managed so far. All it would accomplish is removing the patient from under our roof. That's neither necessary nor prudent."

"Well, then," Riggs said. "Will you take care of this? Finding staff, I mean? Let me know and we'll add them to our books. I trust your judgment in this. Someone discreet, ambitious, industrious." He grinned. "In short, another Bertha or two would be nice. Is she paid adequately, do you think?"

Thomas laughed. "I have no idea *what* she's paid, Zachary."

"Ah, well, of course, there's that," Riggs said without providing a figure. "We want anyone who works for us to be content," he said. "So whatever that takes." He regarded Thomas. "Yourself included."

"Dr. Haines's offer was most generous," the young man said. "And on top of it all, we simply must have some way to prepare meals. It is cumbersome to have to bring food down from one-oh-one."

"Ah," Riggs said good-naturedly. "I can see a flood on the horizon. We'll see about it all, to be sure. Make a comprehensive list so nothing is forgotten." Riggs stood up and stretched, pulling his robe tightly across his barrel-like torso. "Now, if you please . . . You've exhausted me. And yourself, I'll wager."

"Your quarters are on the third floor?"

"Yes. A fine view of the harbor and the hills." He stepped to the doorway and beckoned the younger man. "I can assist you down."

"That won't be necessary." As they made their way forward, Riggs turned off each gaslight until the second floor was pitched into darkness behind them. Thomas opened the door, and the steep decent that yawned ahead of him seemed a dozen times longer than when he'd made the climb.

"How can I help?" Riggs said. He held out a hand, stopping just short of taking Thomas by the elbow.

"Really, I can manage," Thomas said. "I have this technique, you see." He once more rested his right hip against the wall, and gingerly lowered first one crutch and then the other to the first stair tread. He eased his right foot down and held his position there, looking back at Riggs, who watched with bemused concern.

"You see? It's just a matter of patience," Thomas said. He moved the crutches again, but this time the foot of the crutch caught ever so slightly on the tread, and he staggered. Riggs reacted instantly, catching the young man deftly by both shoulders.

"Patience and balance," Riggs said, laughing. "We can't have you landing at the bottom in a heap. Allow me." Together they made their way down the sixteen steps, and as he finally sank into the wicker wheelchair at the bottom, Thomas was faint, even slightly nauseous.

"You'll be all right now," Riggs said. "And I see yet another reason why we need to finish the installation of the elevator. Or we could stuff you into the dumbwaiter, I suppose." He held out his hand. "Good night, Doctor."

34

His conversation with Zachary Riggs had left a myriad of questions, and Thomas was irritated with himself for not pursuing answers more forcefully. Still, he found himself drawn close to these people who had welcomed him into their home with such hospitality. Dr. Haines, so close to the Parks family for so many years—now a dignified man facing his own demons. Alvina, a delightful young woman whose presence in the room Thomas had already begun to anticipate. And Zachary Riggs himself—assured, charming, bright, inventive—Thomas had liked him immediately.

Still, although Riggs's arguments were compelling on the surface, it appeared that the business they were building was based in large part on deception. Little Henry Beautard shared his listless behavior with some of the opium addicts whom Thomas had seen in the slums of Philadelphia. Riggs had sounded knowledgeable enough; could he actually be ignorant of the drug's effects?

Out in the waiting room, the clock chimed four o'clock, and Thomas heard it against the steady drumming of rain outside. The window near his bed was open only an inch, but he could feel the cool elixir as the storm moved through. At the other end of the small ward, his two patients lay like dead men. As long as they weren't, Thomas was thankful. He had not the slightest inclination to move an inch.

A small, cool hand rested on his forehead, and Thomas started, sucking in a quick breath that he regretted.

"I didn't mean to wake you, but you were restless," the voice said, and for a moment Thomas was so disoriented that he knew neither where he was nor whose shadow bent over his cot. The hand stroked across his forehead and stopped with the back of her fingers resting against his cheek.

"Alvi?"

"It's Miss Auerbach," the voice said.

"My word," he murmured. "It's that late?"

"Just after six. I gave both Mr. Deaton and Mr. Doyle injections."

"Thank you. Otherwise, they're resting easy?"

"As can be expected. I brought some breakfast. You should eat while it's still hot." The gas lamp above his cot flamed bright.

"You're never going to heal without a proper night's sleep," Bertha said stiffly. "My word, you didn't even take off your shoes."

"I *can't* take them off," Thomas whispered.

She bent down and peered more closely at him. "You're drenched with perspiration," she said. "You shouldn't have this window open. You'll catch your death of cold."

Slowly, moving like an old man, Thomas sat up, swinging his feet to the floor. His left hip now allowed him to sit reasonably straight, and he leaned cautiously forward until he could rest his elbows on his knees. "This is progress," he said.

"The night was quiet after I left? With the other two, I mean?"

"Yes. I heard not a word from them. What I really need is a hot bath."

"Well, you won't get it here, Doctor."

"That's something else that we need. If we must bathe a patient, how are we to do it?"

"With a sponge and pan, as always," Bertha replied. "Besides, Dr. Haines is adamant about sending patients to St. Mary's."

"I know he is . . . or was. We're going to have a proper ward here, Bertha. And staff to go with it. I mentioned that to Dr. Riggs last night."

"Oh. Mr. Riggs paid a visit, did he?"

"I went upstairs."

Nurse Auerbach stood up straight, tiny hands on her hips, riveting Thomas with the kind of stare that a schoolmistress might use on recalcitrant youths. "However did you manage that?"

"Well, one step at a time is how," Thomas said. "I was curious."

"I see. And your curiosity was satisfied?"

"I'm not sure what to think." He eased forward, and reached out to pull his wheelchair closer. She turned it for him, and braced it as he struggled from the bed. "I have a question or two to ask you, if you don't mind."

"I just do my work," Bertha said, "and that's that."

He wheeled after her. Jimmy Doyle was obviously sound asleep. Howard Deaton lay staring at the ceiling, his eyes half-lidded, mouth forming a silent conversation. For a moment, Thomas watched the pulse in Deaton's temple.

"A slight fever," Bertha said.

"To be expected. As long as it remains slight." He lifted the light towel that lay across the fracture box and examined Deaton's bruised and swollen leg. "I wish I felt more confident about this," he said. Bertha made no comment, and they left the ward. Both the examination room and the office blazed with light.

The delightful aroma emanated from the office, and Thomas found a towel-covered plate with biscuits, ham, and a mound of scrambled eggs. Bertha appeared with an old steel coffeepot that looked as if it had spent a lifetime in a prospector's camp. "The sterilizer serves admirably," she said, and poured a cup for Thomas. "You could have fallen, you know."

"I suppose. In point of fact, I almost did. As I was leaving, and on the very top step." He savored one of the buttered biscuits. "Zachary caught me."

"You just keep it up," Bertha admonished, and nodded toward the ward. "You'll be number three in there."

"I can't lie about useless anymore," Thomas said. "Yesterday was exhilarating, Bertha. I finally felt as if I was earning my keep."

"Patience is not your strongest virtue."

"True enough. But last night I decided to see for myself what it is that keeps Miss Haines and Dr. Riggs so busy."

"And what did you see?"

"You're aware of their enterprise?"

"Only in the most general way. I keep my nose out of other people's business."

"Do you know Dr. Tessier?"

"Only by name."

"You've never met the gentleman?"

"Hardly."

He slipped the small brown bottle from his pocket and held it out to her. "And Dr. Sorrel?"

She slipped her hands into her apron pockets as if she might be tainted by touching the bottle. "That is a common treatment," she said. "And you saw the infant yesterday. So you know."

"Am I correct to suspect opium poisoning?"

"Of course you are, Doctor." She took a deep breath and her black eyebrows nearly touched in the middle. "I have to say that I was most adamant with Dr. Haines some months ago about Dr. Sorrel's." She emphasized the name with contempt. "I was surprised yesterday to see that Mrs. Beautard had obtained a bottle."

"She said that she obtained it from Dr. Riggs, if you recall."

"Indeed she did."

"Well, he says not." Thomas watched her face and saw the tension there. "You don't care for him, do you?"

"What Mr. Riggs does is none of my business," she said.

"*Mister* Riggs."

"Yes. *Mister* Riggs. I have worked for *Doctor* Haines for eight years. In that time, I have *never* seen Mr. Riggs treat a patient . . . other than handing them the odd bottle of the nostrums that he peddles through the mails."

"Ah. So you know what the business upstairs is all about."

"How could one not," Bertha said. "This is a small town, but the fame of the Haines Clinic has spread far and wide."

"I want to send a bottle of this to the university, along with a sample of Universal Tonic. For analysis."

"And then?"

"Well, and then . . ." He stopped as he heard footsteps on the stairway. In a moment Zachary Riggs strode into the office looking fresh and energetic, stylish in a brown tweed suit and bowler hat.

"Morning, all. You're up and about. No ill effects from your journey last night?"

"Just aches and pains," Thomas said. He slipped the empty bottle of Sorrel's into his pocket. "It probably wasn't the smartest thing I've done lately."

"Well, we all make mistakes," Riggs said. He nodded at Bertha. "I was on my way down to the hotel for breakfast," he said. "When you're on your feet, you'll have to join me in that ritual. Although"—he peered at the plate—"it appears that you've done well for yourself." He consulted his gold watch. "Well, cheers. I must be about," he said. "A busy day ahead." He held up a finger. "Ah, I remember our discussion from last night. Be sure to discuss with Alvi about the nursing staff you anticipate hiring. We'll want to act on that sooner, rather than later. Miss Auerbach, how's that brother of yours?"

"Well, thank you."

"Good, good." He adjusted his bowler carefully as he regarded Thomas. "We expect great things from you, Thomas. May I make a suggestion?"

"Certainly."

"I hope you'll join us at one-oh-one this evening. I see that we have a number of things to discuss. And doing so over a nice brandy is so much the better, you agree?"

"We'll see what develops today," Thomas said. "At the moment, we have no one to stay with the patients."

"Alvi will find you someone," Riggs said. "Be assured of that." He pulled out his watch. "She'll be here momentarily. And I must be off."

He tipped his hat at Bertha and nodded at Thomas, then was gone, leaving behind a vapor of cologne.

"An accomplished liar," Bertha Auerbach said, and Thomas was surprised at the venom in her voice.

35

"Helen Whitman will attend the ward at night for us," Alvi Haines said without preamble. Thomas looked up from the nasty abscess that he was lancing deep in the crevasse between the cheeks of Pastor Roland Patterson's emaciated buttocks. Patterson didn't complain. A flow of nitrous oxide kept him blissfully unconscious.

"I haven't had the pleasure," Thomas said. "And good morning to you."

Alvi took a couple of steps into the examining room so that she could close the door, tilted her head, and looked critically at the mess on the preacher's posterior. "I've known Helen for years," Alvi said. "She was employed at St. Mary's, and welcomes the opportunity to return."

"You must have spoken with Zachary already this morning," Thomas said.

"Yes."

"When will Miss Whitman start with us? Yesterday is good as far as I'm concerned."

"As early as next week."

"No sooner?"

"I'm afraid not."

Thomas glanced around at Alvi again, sensing that her tone was a bit more clipped than usual. But she was watching the surgery with interest. "You'll return to one-oh-one for dinner tonight?"

"Yes," Thomas said. "But I plan to return here afterward." He leaned forward and squinted at the wound. "This is a bandaging challenge," he said to himself, and he looked up at Bertha, who so deftly managed the cylinder of nitrous oxide. "It would be advantageous if Pastor Patterson can remain with us for the rest of the day. We need to keep this wound open and dry."

"His wife is adept," Bertha said quickly. "She has served as midwife any number of times in the parish."

"She'd be willing, you think? This must be kept absolutely clean and dry. The opportunities for infection are legion with a surgical site such as this."

"Of course she would be willing," Bertha replied. "Shall I fetch her? They live just down the hill. Right beside the church."

"She's not waiting outside?"

"No."

"Does she know that her husband is here?"

"I suppose not."

"Good heavens, how odd. Then of course we'll need to fetch her promptly. I want to talk to him when he's sensible. It would be helpful to talk with her at the same time."

He pushed himself away, wheeled to the water cart, and washed his hands.

"Why did you risk the stairs?" Alvi said. She remained by the door, watching.

"Why? Well, I awoke at midnight after sleeping like the dead, and was so hungry that I thought about gnawing at the wainscoting. Who should come to my aid but nurse Auerbach, carrying with her the most wonderful meat pie you ever tasted. After eating like a glutton, I was so energized that I felt in the mood for an adventure." He turned and grinned at Alvi. "I discovered that I could manage one stair at a time, the whole sixteen."

"I hadn't counted them."

"Well, *I* did, believe me. Anyway, call it curiosity. And I was amazed by what I saw. However"—he dried his hands thoughtfully—"that's a voyage I don't plan to make again any time soon, I can tell you." He hung the towel on the cart's rail. "I have a number of questions, Alvi. They all can wait for this evening, at our leisure. You'll be there, surely?"

"For dinner, yes. For brandy and cigars in the library afterward, no. That time belongs to my father and Zachary." She nodded curtly. "I can see from the waiting room that it's going to be a busy day." She stopped at the door, hand on the knob. "Father probably won't be in this morning at all. Maybe after lunch. He was called out sometime after ten last night."

"Ah. I'm sorry. What was the nature—"

"Robina Cleary. Father said it was a stroke. There was nothing he could do except try to keep her comfortable. A very sad time."

"Mrs. Cleary?"

Alvi nodded.

"She passed away?"

"Yes. You'll need a hand with Mr. Patterson?" Alvi asked.

"As a matter of fact, yes." Stunned by the news of the woman's death, Thomas could only watch as Alvi and Bertha made short work of the transfer to the wheeled cot. As they maneuvered the cot out of the room, she added, "Constable Eastman would like a word with you, if you'll take the time."

"Of course. And that's another thing," he said. "I don't like taking patients, especially the indisposed ones, through the waiting room. What's everybody's business is really nobody's business, if you know what I mean."

"Certainly," Alvi said. "We'll talk about that." Thomas rolled his chair to the door, nodding at the collection of strange faces. Every seat in the waiting room was taken, and a woman had taken to the floor in one corner, playing with two small toddlers.

"We'll be with you all in a moment," he said cheerfully. "Constable Eastman, if you please?"

Eastman, who had been standing by the door talking to someone outside, ducked his head and plodded across the room, ignoring the seated patients.

"I won't be but a minute," he said, and made sure that the examining room door was closed behind him. "Ward Kittrick got away from us early this morning," he said, his voice not much more than a whisper. "Before dawn."

"I confess that I don't recall—"

"Kittrick. The man who killed Charlie Grimes."

"My God. He escaped, you say?"

"He did. My jailer has a sore neck and a lump over his left ear the size of a goose egg. Damn lucky not to be dead, or stretched out on your operating table."

"However—"

"I'm still workin' on that. I wasn't there, nor Aldrich. Jailer was by himself. Could have happened any number of ways, not that it matters now."

"Where did Kittrick go?"

"If I knew that, I wouldn't be here, Doctor. I just wanted you to know. You'd best keep a sharp eye peeled."

"Why would he come here?" Thomas asked. "Is he hurt?"

"Wish to God that he was. But I did a stupid thing."

"How so?"

"I've known the Kittricks for years. Hardworking boys. Tend to enjoy the bottle, but I can't hold that against 'em. Like to fight, but there again. Anyways, I was talking to Kittrick last night after I arrested him. He didn't fight me, and I appreciated that. I told him so. But I told him that it was a stupid thing he did to kill the Grimes boy, and then to go and boast about it to some of his drinking buddies."

"I still don't see."

"He said I wasn't about to prove anything against him, and *I* says just wait. We can prove that it was his knife did the cutting. See," and he looked apologetically at Thomas, "I figured maybe he'd see the way of things, and say why he done it. Go easier for him."

"Ah."

"So now he knows you're the one that can put the rope around his neck, Doc. I knew the minute the words came out that I shouldn't have let it slip. But I did, so there we are."

"Surely, you don't think he'd come here."

"I don't know what he'll do. I don't know where he'll go, except he's got kin down in Tacoma. Or maybe north. On into Canada. He knows I can't comb the timber for him." Eastman heaved a sigh. "But he'll show his face sooner or later. I just wanted you to know."

"Well, thank you, Constable. If he walks into this room ten minutes after you leave, I don't know what I propose to do about it."

Eastman grunted a laugh. "Nope, you sure as hell ain't run-nin', and I doubt there's much fight in you at the moment. A good poke in the ribs would do you in." Thomas winced at the thought. "You own a gun?" Eastman asked.

"Well, I did," Thomas said. "I had one in my shipping chest. That and everything else is being enjoyed by someone else at the moment."

"Then stop by Lindeman's and buy you another," Eastman said. "Couldn't hurt."

"I'll think about that," Thomas said. "Of course, he's not go-ing to try anything while I have a waiting room full of patients as witnesses."

"There's times when the waiting room is empty," Eastman said. "You plan to go to one-oh-one this evening?"

"I had planned so."

"Then fetch me or Aldrich. We'll make sure you get there."

"That's hardly necessary."

"Well, you can't be too careful with a man like Kittrick, des-perate as he is now. And I've heard stories about you already, Doctor. We'd kind of like to keep you around for a while, now that you're here and getting on."

36

The drive of a few blocks from the clinic to 101 had been a revelation to Thomas when he discovered that he could sup-port himself on his crutches and swing his right foot up to the step, then push up and pivot to land on the cushioned seat with his right hip. Immediately, visions of something as simple as a hot bath and then drives around Port McKinney had swirled in his head—until Horace had snapped the reins. The carriage's hard narrow wheels jounced through the ruts of Gambel Street at speeds no more than a sedate stroll, all of it torture. Once back at 101, the idea of a hot bath was more appealing than the reality of achieving it. Determined to shed clothing that now felt like a second, smelly skin, Thomas eschewed offers of help from Horace, from Dr. Haines—even from Alvina. The high-laced shoes were the most frustrating impediment, but Thomas stubbornly fussed and fumed until he discovered that he could actually flex his left knee sufficiently to reach the laces with the tips of his right fingers.

Finally he stood naked beside the tub, his body a spectacular array of colorful bruises. Laying the crutches across the tub, one behind him and one in front, he sat gently on the rim between them, put his weight on his right arm with his elbow resting on the rear crutch, and maneuvered his right leg over the rim.

He gasped as the water touched the sole of his foot, then shifted his weight until he could balance, right foot on the bottom of the tub, both hands holding his weight on the crutches.

Holding his breath, he lowered himself until his knees touched the bottom, and stopped, head pounding. For several minutes he knelt, arms folded on the crutch in front of him. By the time his rump hit the tub bottom and he could sit with legs stretched in front of him, he was panting from the exertion . . . and was thoroughly impressed with himself.

A knuckle rapped on the door, and Alvi Haines didn't wait for an invitation. She cracked open the door, and Thomas groped wildly for the towel. It was out of reach.

"You're all right?" she asked.

"I am," Thomas said. "And indecent."

"Oh, good," she said, and Thomas heard none of the reserve that had marked the young woman's mood earlier.

She opened the door and slipped into the room. "Gert wants to know if you need more hot water."

"I don't think so. I don't want to get the dressing on my ribs wet."

"It would be best to remove that so you can wash the rest," Alvi said. "Then we'll fix you up a fresh one. Let me get a scissors."

She disappeared before Thomas could protest, and he took the opportunity to reach out for the nearest towel with the crutch. He hadn't managed the task when she returned. She cocked her head.

"The towel?"

"Yes. Please."

She handed it to him. "You're really rather beautiful, you know. In an artist's palette sort of way." She laughed gently and watched him spread the towel across the platform of crutches.

"The whole town will talk," Thomas joked. He lifted his arms so she could unfasten the rib dressing.

"Do you think so?" she said. "Are they all lined up outside the window, watching lasciviously?"

"Watching me get into this tub would have made a side show, I suppose."

"Which brings to mind another question," Alvi said, unwinding the bandage. "Hold the dressing for me, please." As her arms encircled him, Thomas breathed in her unique fragrance, and wondered what it was that *she* bathed in. "How are you going to get out?"

"I prefer not to dwell on that," Thomas said. A fraction of an inch at a time, she pulled the bandage loose from his ribs. Without being asked, Alvi handed him a mirror, and he carefully inspected the wound. It appeared to be scabbing well, with only a small halo of inflammation around the deepest gash.

In a moment the head bandage was removed as well, and Thomas held up the mirror. His eye was bloodshot, the lid swollen and grotesque, and the stitches along the wound pulled a little at the swelling.

"How is the vision?"

Thomas closed his left eye and peered through the swollen window of eyelids. He looked around the room, and then at her. One long strand of her auburn hair curled down past her left eye, touching her cheek. "Fine enough."

"You're really going back to the clinic this evening?"

"Yes. I have to. We have patients in the ward. I'm not about to ask Bertha to remain all night. It's enough that she agreed to remain at the clinic until I return."

"I was surprised to see you in the carriage," she said. She reached down and swirled an index finger in the water, chasing a soap bubble. "We haven't had a chance to talk about last night," she said.

"Nor anything else, for that matter."

Alvi nodded. "Zachary says that you may have reservations."

Thomas mulled several ways he might respond. "I find it difficult to obtain straight answers from him," he said. Alvi withdrew her hand and folded her forearms on the edge of the tub, staring at Thomas. Her eyes roamed his face, and she tilted her head and examined the way the long row of stitches curled up into his hair, then looped back down to his right ear.

"Answers to what?" she said at last.

"Well, for instance. Tell me about the two physicians I've never met. Doctors Tessier and Sorrel."

"What would you like to know about them?"

"Let's begin with the most simple thing. Do they exist?"

A slight smile touched her mouth. "In the minds of desperate patients, they are as real as you or me."

"So they're inventions, then."

"I prefer to call them advertising techniques," Alvi replied.

"Techniques? Like the book's engraving of the enormous clinic that exists only in our dreams?"

"Think about what *can* be, Thomas."

"Oh, I am, I am. Right now, we have a solid three-story building—I haven't found my way to the third yet—and not a proper ward for patients. Not a proper surgery. We wheel patients from the treatment room through the waiting room, no doubt to the horror of those waiting. With Bertha, we do have more staff than a country doctor, but hardly that of a grandiose clinic and 'research center.'"

He stopped when he saw that Alvi was smiling at him.

"What? You find all this amusing, I take it?"

"I find your umbrage amusing," she said. "How long have you been seeing patients at the clinic?"

He didn't reply, unsure of what she meant. She outwaited

218

him, however, and he finally said, "I have completed my second day." That sounded foolish, and he felt the cursed blush wash up his neck, knowing exactly what she meant.

"We have an additional nurse who will arrive in a matter of days," Alvi said. "Jake Tate agreed to work for us if need be to renovate the clinic to suit you. Mr. Schmidt has given him permission." Her eyebrows rose as she reached out to push a strand of his hair away from the stitches. "Those are things that not only *can* be, but *will* be. And sooner rather than later."

"I fail to understand how letters from fictitious physicians who promise the heavens with their personal and prompt attention constitute merely an advertising 'technique,' Alvi. The patient must read those and believe that the entire resources of an enormous clinic and its distinguished staff are working on their behalf."

"There's something wrong with that surge of hope?"

"Certainly there is. It's all illusion. What do the world-renowned physicians actually *do* for the patient?"

She didn't answer, and Thomas nodded. "Just so. A bit of patent concoction, no doubt laced with opiates to keep them coming back for more. Their hopes are raised, only to be dashed."

"If anything dashes their hopes, Thomas, it is the dreadful disease—not anything we do." Her gaze was unflinching, but no smile now softened her features.

"Let me ask you something," Thomas said. "What does your father think of all this? I mean what does he *really* think?"

"You would have to ask him," she said with a sigh. "I know that he thinks highly of Zachary, as we all do. Zachary's work makes many things possible, Thomas. Like your nurses, and the carpenters, and everything else you're planning to ask for in weeks to come." She nodded at him. "Think on that." She pushed herself to her feet. "In point of fact, *without* Zachary's efforts, you *would* be but a country doctor, with the country doctor's limited resources."

She walked behind him. "Now let me wash your back so we can get to dinner. If Gert's roast grows cold, I'll never hear the end of it."

Thomas started to protest, but the young woman ignored him. In a moment, he had to admit that the attention felt wonderful. Halfway down his spine, she paused. "Are you going to do something about the dog?"

"The dog? You mean Prince? You know, I didn't see him when we drove up from the clinic."

"That's because he can hardly get up, Thomas. I stopped by the Mercantile and saw him lying by the stove. A pitiful wreck, Mr. Lindeman called him."

"He has an abscess on the inside of his leg that's going to kill him," Thomas said. "I must find a way to take him down to the shore so he can be cleaned up a bit. Charlie Grimes had agreed to do that."

Alvi was silent for another few swipes of the cloth. "A horse trough won't do?"

"Better than nothing, but I thought the salt water might be soothing . . . and far easier just to walk the beast into the water and have at it."

"And then?"

"Then the ether," Thomas said.

"He'll let you do that? The smell is awful."

Thomas flinched as her strong hands scrubbed the small of his back, working too close to his left hip. "With enough morphine, I think he will," Thomas said, gritting his teeth. "I can see it in his eyes."

She laughed and stood up. "I'll see to his washing," she said.

"Be careful."

"Oh, I shall," she said. "But he'll let me do it." She smiled again. "I can see it in his eyes, you know."

She left the bath, and once more Thomas had that odd sensation of being in a room far emptier than before.

37

Dinner presented a succulent pork roast with small potatoes, late garden greens, biscuits that sopped up butter like small sponges, and copious wine so dark that it appeared black in the crystal glasses in the gaslight. Thomas did the meal justice, all the while a bit uneasy.

As if sensing his discomfort, Zachary Riggs was at his most charming and solicitous. He poured wine for Gert and Horace James as if they were visiting royalty, was unfailingly differential and courteous to the rest of them—and playfully flirtatious with Alvi.

His mood was in sharp contrast to Dr. John Haines, whose fatigue was tempered with intoxication.

"My apologies for never making an appearance at the clinic," he said at one point to Thomas, and Alvi reached over and rested her hand lightly on the elderly physician's forearm.

"I was distressed to hear about Mrs. Cleary, John," Thomas said. "A formidable woman."

"Oh, my," Gert James said. "Such a sadness."

"Well, one in, one out," Haines muttered. "She was a re-markable woman in many ways. We'll all miss her. On the other side of the balance beam, little Heather Thompson has come into the world, all six pounds seven ounces of her."

"Oh, my," Gert said again, and clasped both hands together over her bosom. "And little Janey?"

Alvi leaned toward Thomas and said softly, "Jane Thompson is the mother."

"Janey is fine," Dr. Haines said. "A *long, long* and difficult birth. I really do think that little Heather didn't want to have anything to do with this world. But we forced the issue. Now Bruce, on the other hand . . . he's *not* fine."

"Oh, dear," Gert breathed. "He's such a sensitive boy."

"Bruce is the father," Alvi whispered, her breath wine-sweet on Thomas's ear.

"Yes, well, Bruce managed all right, with the help of a bottle of spirits," Haines said. "If Janey had let out one more scream, I think he would have walked into the sea and not returned."

"Oh, but he'll dote on his new daughter," Gert said.

"I hope so. That's child number three, and I told him that if he wants to lose his wife, having another child is apt to accommodate the matter."

"Did he hear you?" Alvi asked. "Sometimes men don't, you know."

"I doubt it," Haines said glumly. "Anyway, Thomas, that's been the sum and substance of the last twenty-four hours for me . . . one into the world, one out of it." He sighed and sipped his wine. "I understand from Zachary that you had adventures of your own last night."

"I admit so." Thomas hesitated, unsure of how to proceed. "I confess, my curiosity got the better of me. At first, sixteen steps didn't seem insurmountable."

"Your hip is showing marked improvement, at least," Haines said. "We've been a bit concerned about that."

"Much improved," Thomas said. "And then Zachary was good enough to give me a tour, so to speak. Quite an undertaking, I must say." He tried to sound offhanded. "I'm of mixed minds about attempting to treat patients without meeting them face to face."

"The questionnaire is thorough," Riggs said.

"That it is. But the issue is simple, it seems to me. Can a patient be trusted to describe his own illness? Will the questionnaire be a fair and true reflection of what is actually wrong? We know how one pain may initiate another, referring to some other part of the body."

"Of course," Haines said. "That's an issue even when the patient is sitting in front of you, true?"

"I suppose so. But my observations might reveal what the patient fails to tell me. That's not so with the questionnaire."

"Well," Riggs said with some resignation, "what it allows is treatment where none is possible otherwise. Or all else fails, and the patient has nowhere to turn. And I think we may assume further that in such cases, the patient has heard enough about his condition, has discussed it sufficiently with various physicians, that he has a fair notion of what his ailments might be. We may assume that what is reflected in the questionnaire is fair and true. And then we act upon it."

"But there is nothing . . . There is no *drug* or medication that is known to treat cancer, for instance. Much less cure it," Thomas interjected. "To promote some patent medicine as a cure is to raise false hopes."

"We have countless testimonials that support the treatment," Riggs said.

"That's human nature," Thomas replied. "When someone has lost all hope, is truly grasping at straws, there is a surge of desperate optimism when something new is offered. For a time the patient is convinced that this new thing has worked miracles for them."

"You've seen that happen often enough, then?" Riggs commented. His tone was not derisive, but Thomas, who was acutely aware of his own lack of experience, understood him clearly.

"No, sir, I haven't. But I've studied. I've read. I've listened to the most eminent professors in the field. Nostrums build false hopes. A bit of alcohol, a pinch of opiates to dull the pain . . ."

Horace shifted uncomfortably, and Thomas bit off what he was about to say. "I apologize," he said instead. "I'm tired. I should make my way back to the clinic."

"I'll drive you when you're ready," Horace muttered.

"Thank you." He smiled at John. "Now that I've survived my first ride, I anticipate being able to explore the environs. If the people I've met are any indication, the country has much to offer." He watched his wine catch the gaslight. "And I'm intrigued with some I *haven't* met as of yet."

"Really?" John prompted. "For instance?"

"You mentioned Bruce . . . Thompson was it?"

"Indeed."

"I had an infant patient today suffering a broken arm, compliments of his father. The arm of a four-month-old. Can you imagine that?"

"Unfortunately, I can," John said sadly. "You refer to the Beautards?"

"Yes. The same. The mother is absolutely charming. And pregnant for the second time. She's fearful of what her husband will say—or do—when he finds out."

"I know Lawrence," John said slowly. "He works at Schmidt's mill. The mother is fearful, you say?"

"Decidedly so." Thomas cleared his throat. "So much so, in fact, that she won't nurse the baby."

"May I take your plate, dear?" Gert said, rising suddenly and reaching out for Alvi's plate. "Honestly," she added, but let it go at that.

"That's not unusual." Haines ignored his housekeeper's discomfort at such risqué conversation. "People harbor these odd ideas."

"The child cries, and the father loses his temper at the disturbance. Now with a second child coming, Mrs. Beautard is distraught. She was feeding the child teething syrup to quiet his fussing. I told her no more opiates. Can you imagine? Opiates with an infant?"

"There are no opiates in the tonic," Riggs said pleasantly. "Perhaps she should try that, in judicious amounts."

"Brandy with an infant? Hardly."

"What did you suggest?" Haines asked.

"That she feed the child in the natural way. That she attend to the child's general health, and that she reason with her bone-headed husband. Perhaps teach the man how to hold the infant. I said that I'd be pleased to speak with him myself."

"Most—," but Riggs was interrupted by the bell on the front door as someone twisted the thumb crank.

Haines reached out and set his wineglass down, practically in slow motion. "Almost," he sighed, and flashed a grin at Alvi and then Thomas.

"Let me," Riggs said, already on his feet. "Enjoy your dinner." He strode out of the dining room, and Thomas could then hear an agitated voice on the front porch. In a moment, Riggs reappeared.

"Nathan Unger, John."

"Nathan? I instructed him to drive his daughter to St. Mary's."

"It appears that he didn't," Riggs said. "What would you like me to tell him?"

"Good God," Haines muttered, and pushed himself to his feet. "Thomas, I may need you."

38

With the scalpel tip, Thomas scratched a faint line on the pearl-white skin of the child's lower abdomen, a scratch perhaps three inches long just outside of the right semilunar line, ending an inch above Poupart's ligament. He hesitated, heart pounding. That was the location the textbook had outlined, but . . .

"Let the appendix itself be your guide," Dr. Roberts had lectured at the university, exhorting his students to avoid a standard "one incision fits all" mentality. Thomas's mind raced. He had actually *felt* an inflamed appendix only twice in his student career, and neither time had he been sure of himself. This time, the patient's small body was so slender, so entirely lacking in adipose padding, that the swollen organ presented itself as the slightest imperfection, so painful that even the gentlest touch caused distress.

He glanced over at John Haines, who raised an eyebrow as he

moved around the small patient's head. The little girl lay under the ether now, quiet and relaxed.

Thomas swallowed hard and looked up again at John Haines, who appeared serene and confident. "I have assisted once and observed another time," Thomas said.

Haines nodded enthusiastically. "Well, that's plenty, then. You're an old hand at it. I did my first on a kitchen table with everyone watching, including the damn dog. I think he was waiting for scraps. Haines stroked the girl's forehead. "Just take it one layer at a time, just as the books say. That's all there is to it. You know that. The young lady and I are both ready when you are."

Thomas glanced across at Bertha Auerbach, who tended the generous selection of accoutrements arranged in neat order on the small, linen-covered table. She was either confident or an accomplished actress. Out in the waiting room, Mary and Nathan Unger sat with hands entwined and frightened black-hollowed eyes. Alvina Haines kept them company.

They needed encouraging, Thomas had reflected. They might not have known that John Haines was half blind and more than half inebriated, but they could hardly fail to notice the bandaging that encircled the young surgeon's left hand and skull. Facing the knife was a fright in the best of circumstances, he knew, let alone in the middle of the night with two cripples wielding sharp instruments.

"Simply know what you're going to do before you do it," Haines said easily. "That's the trick."

"Indeed," Thomas said. Adjusting his stance once more to take his weight entirely on his right leg, with his hip braced against the side of the table, he bent slightly at the waist, took a long, slow breath, bit his lip, and drew the first incision. The skin split like that of a peach, blood welling up as Bertha's deft fingers worked the gauze sponges.

The moment the bistoury parted the skin, Thomas's pulse slowed, and the rest of the room ceased to be. He deepened the incision to the first mass of abdominal muscle below the skin and fat. He worked with restraint, since the bands of muscle weren't the tough, clearly defined layers of a lumberjack or sailor. This child patient, not yet eleven years old, was not simply an adult in miniature. The muscle masses were still developing, without the definition that marked a fit adult.

Bertha sensed when Thomas might struggle. They worked together, even their breath in synch, she with forceps and Thomas with the scalpel turned so that he could employ its polished handle to compress the thin layer of the peritoneum away, freeing the thin, elastic layer from the tissues of the intestines that lay underneath. The extra set of hands worked as if they were linked directly to his own mind.

Fortune was with little Louella. The appendix itself, swollen and inflamed, had not ruptured, and was easily separated from mesentery. When he was satisfied with the clamp around its base, he tended to the fine ligatures. By the time he was prepared to tackle the appendix itself, he could feel the sweat running down into his eyes, and he straightened for a moment so Bertha could mop his face.

"Splendid," Haines said, and Thomas wasn't sure what the older man was referring to, since Haines was staring off into space as if communing with spirits. Little Louella slept on, her respiration strong and even.

With another ligature around the base of the appendix, he deftly tied the purse-string sutures.

"A moment," Bertha said, and nestled another layer of sterile sponges around the area.

Confident of his ligatures and sutures, Thomas excised the diseased appendix, then spent several minutes disinfecting the area. In another moment, the stump of the appendix was invaginated back into the wall of the cecum.

Retracing his steps for closure, he took extra time with each layer of sutures, making them as elegantly small and neat as he could.

When he finally straightened up as Bertha swabbed the area around the tiny line of fine stitchery that now marked the lower right quadrant of the little girl's abdomen, he felt as if Horace's wagon had rolled back and forth over his lower back and hip.

"A wonder," John Haines said. He had capped the ether bottle a few moments before. He stifled a belch and looked at Thomas with affection. "Why don't you talk with her parents?" he suggested. "You'll want her in the ward for the remainder of the night?" He pulled out his watch. "It's just after eleven."

"Yes. We'll see her through the wake-up. That can be terrifying for children." He blushed when he realized what he had said, since he had never actually *seen* a child awaken from anesthesia. But the books said so.

"Not just children," Haines said. "Well, if she's staying, we'll figure out something. You're staying the night?" he asked Bertha.

"I think I should," she replied.

"Thomas is staying. One or both of her parents may decide to be with her as well."

"If you don't think it's necessary . . ."

Haines shrugged. "It's just that tomorrow is another day, Bertha. Someone in this outfit has to be clearheaded come morning." He grinned lopsidedly. "*I* won't be, that's certain."

"Then after the little angel is situated, I'll be off," Bertha said. "And return promptly at six."

Thomas settled into his wheelchair and pushed open the door. The parents looked up as if for a moment they didn't know where they were.

"Oh," Mrs. Unger managed. "How is she?"

"She'll be just fine, ma'am," Thomas said. "There were no complications. The appendix had not burst, so there's little danger of peritonitis. Still, coming out of the ether is always something of a trial. It would be a benefit if one of you were to remain with her for the night?"

"She can't go home?" Nathan Unger asked. He was a tiny, angular man.

"No. That is to say, she *could*, I suppose, but subjecting her to a wagon ride in the middle of the night would be a pointless risk.

She's going to be very sore for a day or so, and then for several days, excessive movement will be a trial. Tonight, the nurse will administer an injection that will help her rest, and tomorrow we'll see what can be done. I'd prefer if you can give us two or three days, to make sure."

"Can we see her?"

"Of course you can."

The couple rose, leaving Alvi sitting on the bench, and made their way with obvious trepidation to the surgery. Thomas heard John Haines greet them.

"You look exhausted," Alvi said.

"I confess I am."

"It went well, though?"

"Perfectly. I couldn't remember where the appendix was, so I just started at the neck until I found what I thought was it."

Alvi nodded soberly. "Sometimes that's the best way." She turned as the front door opened. Zachary Riggs stepped inside. He closed the door quickly to shut off the rush of sodden, cold air.

"Ah," Riggs said. "Here we are."

"We just finished the surgery," Thomas said.

"Good. Everything is well?"

"Perfectly."

"And good again. You look a wreck, my friend."

"It's temporary."

"Of course. Of course." Riggs drew his watch out of his vest and regarded it thoughtfully. "Well, tomorrow is another day. I think if there's nothing more I can do, I'll retire for the night." He pointed upward. "You'll visit later? You never did have the chance to enjoy your brandy this evening."

"Ah, no," Thomas said with a smile. "I'm not ready for the stairs again, thanks just the same."

"Well, imagine that," Riggs said, and laughed. He winked at Alvi. "Good night then, all. Good work, young man."

"Thank you." He watched Riggs stride off down the hall and listened to the rhythmic thudding of his boots on the stairs.

"Something bothers you," Alvi said softly.

"I'm just tired."

"When Zachary arrived, I could see the veil come down," Alvi said.

He found it impossible to dissemble with her. "I think that I will send a sample of each of the potions that he bottles for an analysis."

Alvi nodded but said nothing. Thomas found himself wishing that *she* was transparent.

"What would you do for the patient then?" she asked quietly.

"I can do nothing from a thousand miles away, other than advising them to visit a competent surgeon. If a cancer has progressed sufficiently, then there's nothing the surgeon can do, either."

"And if he is unable to visit this surgeon? What then?"

Thomas shrugged in defeat. "Then he makes his peace," he said. "He does what he can to bolster his body's systems."

"Just so," Alvi said. "The Universal Tonic does exactly that."

"But it is promoted as a *cure*," Thomas persisted. "It is not a cure. A palliative, perhaps. That's all."

"What are you suggesting?" Alvi asked. "That we advertise by saying, 'Buy our tonic and feel a little better while you wait to die'?"

"It would certainly be more honest," he replied. "How can he address the myriad questionnaires presenting all manner of afflictions?"

"He doesn't work alone."

"Obviously not. But Doctors Tessier and Sorrels are inventions. You're suggesting that your father has the energy to do so?"

"We had hoped that with your arrival . . ."

Thomas scoffed. "You expect I should spend my days reading the mail and writing palliative responses to be packaged with worthless snake oil?" His tone was sharper than he would have liked, but Alvi didn't flinch or respond in kind.

"And the surgery you just performed," she said gently. "Do you think that the thirty-five dollars we will receive from the

Ungers will pay for expansions to the clinic? For the new equipment which you will want to buy? For nursing staff? Even your thousand dollars a month stipend? Or Bertha's fifty dollars a week? Or the support of the household at one-oh-one?"

"Of course not," Thomas said. "But—"

"On the other hand, can you imagine how many people we have reached? How many we have helped? How much pain and suffering we have assuaged?"

"I think I can. Upstairs, I see six desks where the ladies work for you. Each is piled high with various correspondence. I looked at only the first."

"And mine."

"True."

She regarded him in silence for a moment, and Thomas could hear the hushed voices from the surgery. Bertha appeared, and nodded at the two of them.

"We'll move her now," she said, and vanished into the ward.

Thomas started to turn his chair, but Alvi reached out and rested her hand on his right arm.

"Three thousand, four hundred and sixty-five dollars, Dr. Thomas. And some odd cents," she whispered, and first clenched his arm for emphasis, then released him. "Think on that."

"The number means nothing to me," Thomas said.

"It means that you would have to put the knife to a hundred Louella Ungers to equal it," Alvi countered.

"This clinic has operated on three patients in the past twenty-four hours," Thomas said. "And seen a dozen more."

A faint smile touched her lips. "You are splendid," she said. "Imagine what you might do when you are on your feet."

"Just so."

She nodded and stretched, bracing her hands on her hips and arching her spine. "You need rest," Alvi said. "Let's get little Louella settled, and then do the same for you."

As he wheeled after her toward the surgery, she turned and bent down, blocking his path. Her lips brushing his left ear, her whisper husky.

"By the way, Dr. Thomas, that three thousand five hundred dollars represents one *week*. The income from only a single, average *week*. You think on that." She patted him affectionately on the shoulder.

39

M y, what a brave little girl," Bertha Auerbach reported. Thomas looked up from the desk where, without energy to do anything else at this hour, he had been recording the events of the day in his journal.

"The pain should not be great," he said, and then had second thoughts. Bertha voiced them first. "Well, perhaps not to you," the nurse admonished kindly. "But to a child, I suppose it feels as if large hands have been rummaging about in her insides, cutting and stitching and snipping. Most delicate and expert work, Doctor, but painful nevertheless."

Bemused, Thomas nodded agreement. "She's resting comfortably?"

"As much as can be expected."

"The acute pain should last only a few hours—perhaps a day or so at most. Warm pads over the area of the incision will be soothing." He sat back, realizing with a jolt just how easy it was to slip into the physician's efficient mode, assuming that pain was something the patient must endure.

"Her mother is with her for the night," Bertha said.

"Good. You're going home now?" Thomas stretched back. "You have an escort?"

"As it happens, Constable Eastman is outside. He will see me home safely. And you should go back to one-oh-one for some rest," she said.

"I'll be fine, really." He glanced toward the door and lowered his voice. "It would be convenient if Dr. Riggs would occasionally descend from his aerie. Does he ever? In an emergency, for instance?"

"No."

"If I had not been here, and if Dr. Haines had been unable to operate on the little girl, what would have happened?"

"She would either survive the carriage ride to St. Mary's, or she would not," Bertha replied. "Poultices might have helped."

"Poultices?" Thomas said incredulously. "I think not. Even in a matter of life or death, Dr. Riggs would not operate?"

"*Doctor* Thomas," Bertha Auerbach said, heavily emphasizing the word, "*Mr.* Riggs is no physician. Certainly he is no surgeon."

"I wasn't aware that I had voiced that opinion," Thomas said.

"You don't need to. Bandages over your face or not, poker should never be your game." She raised an eyebrow at him. "I had best not keep Edgar waiting."

"Thank you for all you've done." Thomas escorted her to the front door and, when he opened it, smelled pungent cigar smoke. A huge figure emerged from the shadows.

"All is well?" Constable Eastman asked.

"It is," Thomas replied. "Thank you." He watched Eastman offer his left arm and Bertha hooked hers through his, the size differential comical. "Good night, then."

Back inside, he returned to the office and spent half an hour finishing his journal entry. Finally, with eyes refusing to focus, he laid down the pen and wheeled into the ward. Thomas didn't feel confident about Howard Deaton. Once bones were shattered out of line, the natural pull of tendons and muscles made matters worse. A fracture box or a plaster cast, no matter how skillfully employed, most often produced cripples. If he was very lucky, Deaton would spend the rest of his life with a cane and an awkward limp.

The man appeared to be asleep, and Thomas passed by.

Behind the screens, Mrs. Unger was seated in a straight chair beside her daughter's bed. She looked up as Thomas approached.

"She is asleep," she whispered.

"Good," Thomas said. He wheeled close to the cot and reached out to touch the child's forehead. A degree or two, no more. No sign of bleeding marked the small bandage on her belly, and only slight swelling.

"Good," he said again.

"My husband says that you were nearly killed."

Thomas glanced across at the woman, noting the black circles under her eyes and the pale cheeks.

"It was not one of my more graceful moments," he replied. "It is of the utmost importance to keep her quiet and relaxed for the next few days," he said. "Is she normally a sprightly child? Active by nature?"

"Oh, a dervish," Mrs. Unger replied with pride.

"Well, the dervish needs to be harnessed for several days to allow the incision time to heal. Tomorrow and the next day, she will be allowed a thin, easy broth only. We have no kitchen facilities yet, so if you would arrange that? When she can sit up with only modest discomfort, she may start with the softest foods, in small quantities, still with a great deal of liquids." He saw her eyes shift as her gaze strayed past the corner of the divider, focusing toward the front of the ward. At the same time he heard footsteps.

He turned, pivoting the wheelchair in place, and saw a figure of medium build advancing down the ward. The man stayed away from the side of the ward where the two injured men rested. He wore a shapeless hat that obscured his features, along with what appeared to be a canvas coat that reached to his knees.

"Good evening, sir," Thomas said, pushing himself away from Louella Unger's bed.

"You're that new doc." The voice was raspy, low pitched, and carried an air of belligerence that raised the hair on the nape of Thomas's neck. The man stopped several strides from him.

Thomas continued turning his chair until he directly faced the man. "I'm Thomas Parks," he said. "How may I be of assistance?" Thomas still could not see the man's face, but he saw the man's head jerk in reaction.

"'How may I be of assistance?'" the man mimicked, mangling Thomas's eastern accent into that of a stage-show fop.

"You're Mr. Beautard?" Thomas guessed.

"Don't know what makes you think that," the man said. "And no, I ain't. You got somewheres we can talk?"

"Certainly," Thomas said. "Let's go to the office." He partially turned toward Mrs. Unger. "Excuse me for a few moments, will you?" She remained in the chair with both hands holding her daughter's. If she knew the man, she showed no sign.

"This way." Thomas pulled the office door shut behind them. The rich aroma of alcohol and tobacco assailed his nostrils. He wheeled over to the desk, pushed himself to his feet, and turned up the gaslight behind the desk. Settling back in the wheelchair, he regarded the man with interest. The man's coat gaped and Thomas saw that his rough shirt was soaked with blood, the dark patch extending down to his belt line and soaking his trousers halfway down his thigh.

"What—," he started to ask.

The man cut him off with a stabbing forefinger, making no move to seat himself. "You know who I am."

"We've never met. I'm quite certain of that." He nodded at the man's midriff. "You're hurt."

"That ain't none of your affair. The name's Kittrick."

"All right. Do you want to sit down, or are you content to just stand there bleeding all over my floor?" For a moment, Thomas was sure the man was going to reach across the desk and clout him. He found himself wishing that he had taken Constable Eastman's advice about a replacement revolver of some sort. But should he have had one, before he could manage to retrieve it from his waistband or a desk drawer, this man would be across the desk, breaking him into yet smaller pieces.

"State your business, sir," Thomas said, hoping he sounded authoritative.

"My business is simple enough," Kittrick snapped. "That fat bastard says you're claiming it was my knife that killed the punk."

Thomas leaned back. "Are there some names here? Who's the fat bastard?" Thomas asked, knowing the answer full well, but hoping to defuse some of the man's rage.

"Eastman," Kittrick said. "He says you claim my knife killed the punk."

"A knife wound *did* kill Charlie Grimes," Thomas said. "Of that I'm certain."

"'Of that I'm certain,'" Kittrick mimicked again. "Eastman says you claim it was my knife."

"Was it?"

"Don't matter if it was."

"Really. Now just how could it not matter?"

Kittrick eyed him sideways, and his left hand strayed to his gut. "You're a right smart-ass for somebody so busted up," he said.

"All I told the constable is that the knife *he* showed me is consistent with the blade wound in the boy's heart."

"Well, ain't nobody can say I did it, 'cause nobody saw," Kittrick said.

"How do you know that nobody saw? If you didn't do it, that is."

Kittrick ignored that. "And I'm here to tell you that it *weren't* my blade, and even if'n it was, *you* ain't the one to tell nobody. You ain't *going* to tell nobody."

"It's a bit late for that," Thomas said. "Eastman already knows. And without a doubt, he's already talked with the prosecutor. Or will, if he hasn't already."

"Don't matter now what that fat bastard thought he knew," Kittrick said. "You go shootin' off your mouth, fancy boy, and you'll join him."

Thomas's pulse pounded louder in his ears. "Now wait a minute. If you've hurt—"

"No, *you* wait a minute, fancy boy. You want to keep this fancy roof over your head, you want to keep all this, you just keep your opinions to yourself." The man patted his hand against his belly, and his palm made a wet smacking sound. "I ought to just put an end to it right here and now," he said. "But I know the Beau-tards, and I know you been looking after their little one. And that"—he leaned over the desk—"is the *only* reason." This time, Thomas identified the aroma of burned gunpowder that haloed the man like cheap perfume.

40

Kittrick left behind a trail of muddy boot prints and a lin-gering potpourri of sodden wool, coppery blood, and burned powder. Thomas sat motionless, listening to the beating of his heart, so loud that he didn't hear the front door close behind the man.

In his apartment on the third floor of the building, Zachary Riggs would probably have heard nothing of the rude visitation. John Haines would be home at 101, lost in a deep alcoholic slumber. Thomas pounded a short, frustrated tattoo on the arm of his chair, then swung around and reached for his crutches.

He wheeled to the front door, pushed the chair against the wall, and rose to his feet. Maneuvering outside to the front step, he stopped and listened. The rain was only a mist now. To his left, the street curved down, into what he did not know. Where did Bertha Auerbach live? She and the constable had headed down the hill. The night before, when Bertha's brother had brought her to the clinic in the wagon, she had said her home wasn't far. What did that mean? Two blocks? A half mile? A mile?

In the distance, a dog barked, a high-pitched excited yapping that certainly wasn't Prince. Thomas cursed his helplessness and turned back inside. He could not simply sit and wait. He first wheeled to the examination room and selected the largest scalpel he could find, then rummaged through one of the drawers until he found a large cork. After working the scalpel's blade into the cork, he slipped the weapon into his pocket.

The ward was still quiet, and he wheeled quickly down the aisle.

"I must find a way to alert authorities," he told Mrs. Unger. Her eyes were wide and frightened. "Do you know the man who was just here?"

"Yes," she whispered. "I heard that he had been arrested for the boy's murder."

"And now, we don't know," Thomas said. "I fear for Miss Auerbach. She was under escort by Constable Eastman, and now I fear this man and Eastman may have had a confrontation. If Nurse Auerbach was with them . . . I must have your help. I will stay here with your daughter, but I need you to go upstairs and fetch Zachary Riggs. He has an apartment on the third floor." He handed her the key. "This opens the door at the top of the stairs, just around the corner from the waiting room."

"Now?"

"Yes. This instant. I need help, and Riggs is capable. Please! Go now. I'll wait here."

He wheeled around the bed and took up her position. "The child is resting comfortably," he whispered. "Please go immediately. There is no time to waste."

He watched her hurry out of the ward, voluminous skirts swishing. Thomas could follow her progress as she reached the stairway, at first hesitant, then resolute. The footsteps paused at the top as she unlocked the door, and then faded as she continued around the corner to the second flight.

In a moment, he heard distant voices but couldn't determine whether they came from outside or upstairs. The little girl remained quiet, and Thomas pushed away. Mrs. Unger reappeared, this time taking care to walk gingerly.

"He's talking with Kittrick," she whispered, handing Thomas the key.

"What do you mean?"

"Just that. I could hear their voices. I'm sure it's him."

"Kittrick is confronting Riggs now, you mean?"

She nodded.

"The back stairway, then," Thomas said.

Mrs. Unger's attention was drawn to Louella, who shifted slightly in her sleep, one little hand coming up to curl under her chin.

What business did Kittrick have with Zachary Riggs? "Did you speak with Dr. Riggs?" he asked her.

"I did. I knocked on his door at the same time I became aware of the voices. He came to the door, and I told him that you needed to speak with him. I said nothing of the reason. I could not see Mr. Kittrick."

"Stay close to your daughter, then," Thomas said, relieved at her quick wit. He wheeled back through the ward and reached the waiting room where he stopped, hand in his pocket, feeling the corked scalpel. In a moment, he heard the purposeful footsteps on the stairway. Zachary Riggs appeared, his usual expression of bonhomie now grim.

"Thomas," he said quickly, and glanced toward the ward. "Mrs. Unger said you—" He bent close to Thomas, and the younger man could smell the brandy on his breath. "I may have done a terrible thing."

"Kittrick was here with threats," Thomas blurted. "He claims a confrontation with the constable. And now you as well? Upstairs?"

"No idle claim," Riggs said. "I feared the worst."

"Kittrick and you?"

"Yes. And I feared for my safety and yours, Thomas. When Kittrick heard Mrs. Unger mention your name, I don't know what he assumed, but he became as a wild man." Riggs took a deep breath. "I shot him, Thomas."

"Shot him? What do you mean?"

"Just that." Riggs reached into his pocket and drew out a stubby little pistol, its short over-and-under barrels revealing remarkably large bores.

"My God, man. I heard no shot. Where is he now?"

"By the back door. His body is on the stairway."

"His body? You killed him, you mean?" Thomas had visions

of the enraged Kittrick reappearing, leaking from yet another wound.

"Oh, yes. I'm sure of that."

Thomas felt a surge of relief, followed by another rush of concern. "But Miss Auerbach," he said quickly. "Constable Eastman came earlier to escort Miss Auerbach home. They left a short time ago, not long before Kittrick arrived. I fear for her safety. Kittrick said that he and Eastman came to account—whatever that means. If Bertha was with him at that time . . ."

"Bertha was to return here tonight?" Riggs asked.

"No. Not until six. I don't know what he intended," Thomas said. "He seemed a desperate sort, and was badly wounded somehow. He threatened me if I should testify against him in the Grimes matter. Obviously he *was* desperate, to threaten you as well."

"My word."

"Zachary, I am concerned about Miss Auerbach. If Kittrick set upon Eastman as the constable and Miss Auerbach were walking to her home, anything could have happened. We haven't heard from her. She might be lying injured or worse this very moment."

"I thought her brother drove her," Riggs said.

"Well, not this time," Thomas said impatiently. "Nurse Auerbach enjoys the constable's company, it would seem."

"Kittrick had nothing more to say to you?" Riggs asked. "Only the threat against you, and that somehow he had gotten the best of Eastman?"

"Only that. He said the reason I haven't met my maker is because of my patients. He claims to know the Beautards . . . and their child."

"Of course he knows them," Riggs said, "but I have heard no commotion outside."

"Nor I. Still, he was here. His threats were very real."

Riggs looked toward the front door, one hand holding his chin. The color had returned to his face, and he appeared his usual calm self again. Thomas scrutinized him intently. "You're unhurt?"

Riggs waved a dismissive hand. "I was fortunate," he replied. "I don't know where Miss Auerbach lives."

"On Chauncey, I believe. No more than a half mile."

"Then we must go there."

Riggs frowned with exasperation. "You can't go anywhere," he said. "Let me see what's what. I'll fetch the deputy constable. We can't leave a bleeding corpse on the back stairs. I'll find Aldrich, so not to worry."

Riggs buttoned his coat, opened the front door, and stepped out into the night.

As Thomas waited, the minute hand of the clock appeared brazed in place. He wheeled back to the ward, looking through the shadows at the silent occupants, then turned and went back to open the front door, trying to see through the wet darkness. The minute hand clicked so loudly that it startled him.

How could a village be this quiet? Was it possible for a couple to be accosted on the street, and no one notice? Of course it was. Riggs had just dispatched Kittrick on the back stairway of the clinic, and Thomas had heard nothing—no gunshot, no cry, no thud of a body. He thought of half a dozen scenarios, and all of them made him nauseous. There was nothing he could do about any of them. He would have to depend on Zachary Riggs.

41

Well, at least we know *you* didn't do it," Deputy Constable George Aldrich said. He stood in a puddle, rain dripping off the brim of his soft cap, as Thomas wheeled across the waiting room. Zachary Riggs entered behind the constable, with two other men on his heels. Thomas could see at least five others either on the clinic's front step or in the street beyond. Aldrich jerked his head at them, and the door was shut against all but the deputy constable and Riggs.

"So tell me," Aldrich said. He was a short man, rotund and ruddy-cheeked, the sort who would look perfectly at home serving drinks in a warm, dry pub. "What do you know about all this?" His accent was soft, almost melodic, reminding Thomas of some of the farmers in rural Pennsylvania.

Thomas took his time before answering, searching the constable's face for hints. "What have you discovered?" he asked. "Is Miss Auerbach . . ."

"She's home, Thomas," Riggs said quickly. "Home and entirely well. And we're all certainly relieved about *that*."

"But what about—"

Aldrich held up a peremptory hand. "When was the last time you saw the constable?" he asked.

"Midnight, at least," Thomas said. "What happened? Is he all right?"

"He was here?"

"Certainly. He came to the clinic to escort Miss Auerbach to her home."

"You saw him for certain?"

"Yes. He was standing outside, smoking a cigar. You must tell me what happened, for God's sake."

"You exchanged words with him?" Aldrich asked, ignoring the question with infuriating calm.

"Only the briefest of pleasantries. We were all tired. Miss Auerbach was anxious to be home."

"I see." Aldrich's frosty blue eyes regarded Thomas, and his heavy lips pursed, the lower one protruding like a pouting child's. "So Mr. Kittrick paid you a visit as well?"

"Yes."

"What did he want?"

"He threatened me."

"Is that so."

"Yes, that *is* so."

"And the threat?"

"Constable Eastman asked that I testify to the courts about the weapon that killed Charlie Grimes. A folding knife that the constable had in his possession was consistent with the weapon that could produce the wound. Eastman said the knife belonged to Ward Kittrick. I'm sure you know more about that than I do."

"I wondered about that knife." He drew himself up and rested his hands on his hips, coat flaring behind him. "How is it that you could tell that this knife—"

"The shape of the blade makes a characteristic wound," Thomas said. "Always. Especially with a single, hard, swift thrust. It's simple enough."

"I see. What did you tell Kittrick?"

"I told him nothing, sir. He said the only reason that he didn't kill me was because of the Beautard child. I had treated the infant earlier. But Kittrick also may have caught sight of Louella Unger and her mother. Perhaps that stayed his hand." Thomas turned and nodded toward the door. "They are here in the ward. I hope they won't be disturbed."

"Mrs. Unger saw Kittrick as well?"

"Yes, she did. He presented himself unannounced in the ward."

"Did she hear the threats?"

"No. Kittrick and I spoke in the office. I did not want the patients disturbed."

"I see. And then he left?"

"Yes."

"He made no move against you?"

"No. Only the verbal threats. Against me and the clinic. I assume he meant all who work here."

"You know where he went then?"

"No."

Aldrich heaved a deep breath and looked over at Riggs. "Very odd. What else did he tell you at that time?"

"He said that he and Mr. Eastman had reached an accounting. That was his word for it."

"You took that to mean?"

"That they had a confrontation. Kittrick was injured. If you examine his body, you'll see that. That's why I was concerned about Miss Auerbach."

"Explain it to me."

Thomas straightened in his chair. "Kittrick was bloody, here." He laid his hand on his own left flank. "The blood had soaked his trousers as well. But he wasn't interested in being treated. Eastman is badly hurt?"

"Kittrick did not come here for treatment?" Aldrich asked.

"I told you. He would not allow me to treat him," Thomas said again, "or even make a preliminary examination of the injury. It did not appear to impair his movements."

Aldrich laughed abruptly. "So then. He left here, and you did not see where he went."

"No."

Aldrich turned to Riggs. "But we know, eh?"

"Indeed," Riggs said, then added, "I confess that I'm flummoxed. It's clear the two men fought. Constable Eastman is dead, Thomas."

Thomas looked at him in disbelief. Surely a scuffle with a single foe wasn't enough to bring down the enormous constable.

"Indeed he is," Riggs added.

Aldrich once more held up a hand. "It would appear," he said slowly, "that they confronted each other in the alley beside the bank. Just down the hill. You heard no shots fired?"

"No. But I was occupied in the surgery."

"You heard not a single shot?"

"No. Please! Tell me exactly what happened."

"Well," Aldrich mused. "That's difficult to say, certainly. It appears there was a confrontation, yes. The chief constable was stabbed, so." He turned and jabbed a thumb into his own right kidney.

"And he's dead? He died on the spot? But what of Nurse Auerbach? She was witness to all this?"

"I think not," the constable said. "I believe that the constable had escorted her home, and was then returning to the office. It was at that time that the confrontation took place."

"And he was not able to resist Kittrick? I find that hard to believe."

"The element of surprise, perhaps," Aldrich said. "Maybe he managed to draw his revolver. One shot, only grazing, as you say. And then Kittrick comes here, to make threats. Or so we are led to believe. We may never know." He reached under his coat and pulled out an impressive hunting knife in a leather sheath. "Kittrick had this weapon, and as you can see, the blade shows use." He slid the knife out of the sheath. Blood smeared the eight-inch blade. He turned to look at Riggs. "You were lucky, my friend."

"He made sure I saw that," Riggs said. "And when he made to draw it out, I confess I acted."

"Well, sometimes it's good not to wait so much, you know." Aldrich turned back to Thomas. "And you say you heard nothing?"

"Nothing."

"They were between buildings, and that, I'm thinking, is why. Even *I* heard nothing." He regarded Thomas for a long moment, and then the crow's-feet at the corners of his eyes deepened. "You've had an interesting time of it."

"Memorable."

Aldrich laughed. "It's clear to me that Mr. Kittrick got exactly what he deserved." He raised his eyebrows at Riggs. "The bodies go to Winchell's now."

"He will do the postmortem?" Thomas asked.

"He would, if there was a question remaining," Aldrich said. "But there isn't so much now."

"What did Kittrick want from you?" Thomas asked Riggs, and the older man shrugged.

"I wish I knew. He made threats, just as he did with you. I presume that he might have been after money—Mrs. Unger interrupted him before he could make those demands."

Thomas nodded sympathetically, keeping his confusion to himself. Mrs. Unger had said nothing about hearing two men *arguing* when she reached the top of the third flight of stairs, or making threats. She had said, in fact, that she had *become aware of* two men talking. After she left, things had obviously escalated to a fatal result.

"Will someone stop by Miss Auerbach's to inform her? She should not have to wait until morning to learn from some passerby of Eastman's death."

"I will make sure of that," Aldrich said. "I will want to talk with her in any case. It is possible that she heard something, or saw . . ."

Thomas nodded.

"Are you remaining here, or returning to one-oh-one?" Riggs asked. His frown was one of concern.

"Here, I think." He turned to Aldrich. "Did Mr. Eastman have family?"

"A confirmed bachelor," Riggs said. "A brother, I believe. I have no idea where he might reside."

"Tacoma," Aldrich said. "It will be taken care of. Thank you, young man."

"Certainly. If there's anything else, here I am. I'm something of a captive audience at the moment."

"Yes," Aldrich said thoughtfully. "In some ways, that's good." He nodded at Riggs. "Should I need to speak with you, you'll be . . ." He glanced upward. "Until we know who Kittrick was dealing with, or why, it is best that you remain discreet, I think."

He moved to the door, and looked first at Riggs and then Thomas. "You both will be here now." It wasn't a question.

42

Bertha kinda had a soft spot for the constable," Harlan Auerbach observed after Thomas settled awkwardly on the wagon's hard seat. "Damn shame."

"An awful turn of events," Thomas said. "I confess I've never felt so useless in my life. If something had happened to her . . ."

Her brother had delivered Bertha to the clinic promptly at six. She had given Thomas a quick hug—the first time that had happened in the few days he'd known her—and then vanished without another word into the ward. Instead of intruding with some sort of commiseration, Thomas thought it best to let her have her own time.

Riding the few blocks to Winchell's was torture in the unsprung wagon, but Thomas braced himself and waited it out. The street angled down through a grove of runty evergreens that had sprung up after the timber had been put to the ax. Mounds of dirt lay here and there as new iron water piping expanded through the village, ending at a massive foundation that Harland said was the new post office building.

"How you gettin' back?" the young man asked as he pulled the wagon to a halt at Winchell's, a cedar clapboard barn of a building that displayed, in lieu of a business sign, half a dozen styles of tombstones erupting out of the mud by the front door.

"I hadn't thought about that," Thomas said, wrestling his crutches free from the welter of garden tools in the back of the wagon.

"I'll wait, then," Harlan said affably. "You ain't going to be long, I guess. You need help?"

"No. I can manage." He navigated to the spread of flagstones in front of the door. His first rap went unanswered, and then Ted Winchell appeared, looking as if he'd been up most of the night himself.

"Good morning, sir."

Winchell brushed a cloud of wood dust from his trousers. "Well, good morning yourselves," he said, and regarded Thomas skeptically. "I don't need more business, if that's what Harlan's bringing me." He craned his neck. "You got another one in there already, young fella?"

"Not this time," Harlan replied.

Winchell clapped the dust off his hands. "It's looking like a long day." He reached out a hand to Thomas's right arm. "Come in out of the weather. Harlan, you, too. Let the horse soak by himself."

"Thanks just the same," Harlan said a little uneasily.

"Suit yourself." Winchell held the door for the young doctor. "Well, sir, quite a time we had last night. You've come to take me out for a second breakfast?"

"Food is the last thing on my mind," Thomas said.

Winchell led Thomas down a narrow hallway and held open a door for him. The office was small, spare, and neat. "Coffee?"

"No, thanks. I came to ask a favor."

"Name it."

"Constable Aldrich says that no postmortem is planned."

"He does, does he?"

"Yes. Is that true?"

"No. Any time there's a homicide, there's an inquest. All a matter of public record. Now . . . in a way, he's right. If the cause of death is as obvious as a bullet through the heart, then what's the point? In the coroner's report that's filed with the county, we have to be able to say what the cause of death was." He stretched back and clapped more dust off his hands. "I guess it would be fair to say that we do what we need to do to satisfy the county and its newfangled record-keeping procedures."

"Aldrich says that Constable Eastman was stabbed in the lower right back, through the kidney."

"Indeed he was. I'd be surprised if he was able to take ten steps afterward."

"No other injuries?"

"Not that I saw. What's your concern, Doctor?"

"Ward Kittrick came to see me shortly before he was shot," Thomas replied. "He was hurt at the time, but it didn't appear to slow him down. Afterward he went upstairs to confront Zachary Riggs. That's when he was shot."

"That's the yarn, is it?" Winchell said, but his face was serious. He rose and beckoned Thomas. "You might as well satisfy your curiosity."

Ward Kittrick's body awaited its appointment with the earth and worms in a dark, plain room that included four flat, heavily

248

varnished work tables and a series of cabinets. Three of the tables were occupied by sheeted figures.

"This is the county room," Winchell explained. He snapped one of the sheets back, and Thomas exhaled slowly. Ward Kittrick, once so inflated with his own menace, was now not much different than any of the cadavers dissected at the university—just a little fresher.

"The gut wound must have been damned painful," Winchell said. "Another inch, and he wouldn't have felt like threatening anybody." The six-inch trough gouged by the bullet began an inch to the left of the umbilicus, ripping through skin, muscle, and fat. "Didn't find the bullet. The one in his brain is another matter."

He rolled the unyielding corpse so that Thomas could examine the skull. "Poked it right against his head," Winchell said. Sure enough, the little hole marked the middle of a scorched field, the hair crisped and flayed, with black powder dappling the scalp and the back of Kittrick's left ear. No exit wound was evident, but Thomas could imagine the catastrophic damage the little pellet would cause as it exploded through the thin bone of the mastoid process, scattering lead, bone, and powder grains through the brain.

Winchell watched Thomas examine the wound. "You have a probe?" the physician asked.

"Better than that. I have the bullet. It wasn't hard to fetch out of there. Let me show you." He stepped across to one of the cabinets and waited with one hand on the top drawer while Thomas maneuvered his crutches. "Little hobby my father started. I've been keeping it up."

He slid open the drawer.

"My heavens," Thomas exclaimed. Neat rows of curiously deformed projectiles lay in cotton-lined partitions.

"An old type font case I bought." Winchell patted the drawer. "Handy as hell." The collection wasn't limited to bullets. Tips of knife blades, spikes, even a short section of what looked like a saw blade were all carefully labeled.

Winchell selected the deformed slug that nestled in the slot marked 23 SEPTEMBER 1891, WARD L. KITTRICK, and held out the specimen. "Your man told Aldrich that he used his Remington derringer, and that's probably right. It's a .41 caliber." Thomas hefted the deformed slug. "Not much of a round," Winchell said, "except in a case like this, with the barrel held right against one of the thinnest parts of a man's skull." He clapped his hands, imitating the sharp report. "And down he goes."

"Immediately behind the left ear," Thomas said. "They were struggling, do you suppose?"

"Maybe."

"Riggs said nothing about that," Thomas added. "I sent Mrs. Unger upstairs to fetch him, and she heard men's voices. The final altercation took place shortly thereafter."

"When Kittrick was leaving," Winchell said skeptically. "And *that's* what fits. Picture Kittrick standing at the top of those stairs."

"I have never actually seen them," Thomas said. "The stairs, I mean."

Winchell's eyebrows shot up in surprise. "My, you *have* been caught in a deep rut, haven't you. Well, stairs are stairs. Aldrich says that Kittrick tumbled halfway down the first flight, until he got fetched up in the balusters. Does that sound like a struggle to you?"

"Certainly not. Riggs said that Kittrick either drew his knife or was in the process."

"While facing away, or while standing at the top of a deep flight of stairs." Winchell snorted. "We'll have to work on our imaginations."

"What do you think happened?"

The coroner shrugged. "I can imagine Riggs spooked by this gentleman. Kittrick was a rough and ready sort. Both him and his brother. If Riggs saw an opportunity to gain an advantage on a dangerous man, then more power to him. Whether you want to call it self-defense . . . Well, that's a point of view, I suppose."

Thomas handed the spent bullet back and straightened against his crutches. He looked across at the largest sheeted figure. "Eastman?"

Without a word, Winchell returned the specimen to its drawer, closed the cabinet carefully, and crossed to the second table. Eastman's corpse lay on its belly, and Thomas winced at the enormous wound a handsbreadth to the right of the spine, between the last two ribs.

"A powerful thrust," Winchell said. "Driven in and angled toward midline, then wrenched and twisted out. Done with a big, stout-bladed knife. If I had to guess, I'd say that it fairly split his right kidney clean in half."

"And still he managed somehow to fire off a shot," Thomas said.

"He would have a few seconds. That's all."

"Thank God that Bertha wasn't with him at the time," Thomas said.

"Auerbach? Why would she be—"

"The constable had escorted her home from the clinic. This happened after they parted, thank God."

"Ah. Well, she's a lucky one, then."

"Kittrick and Eastman struggled, do you think?"

Winchell held up his shoulders in a prolonged shrug. "I would guess not. In a fair struggle, Eastman could have easily managed a man like Kittrick. My guess is a quick ambush from behind. The knife was in before Eastman could flinch away. That would have been Kittrick's style."

Thomas nodded in question at the third corpse.

"That's Wiley Jonson. Got drunk and fell off a fishing skiff," Winchell said. "Last week sometime. They found him yesterday afternoon."

"This is a dangerous place," Thomas said.

"Well, it can be, if you're not careful," Winchell said. He thrust his hands in his pockets and regarded the floor, then nodded at a plain pine coffin resting on a pair of sawhorses toward the back of the room. "That's Charlie Grimes. He goes in the ground later this morning." He tipped his head as if he wanted to say something else.

"A sad thing," Thomas said.

"Indeed. But I just stick to business, recording the 'what' of it all. I leave the 'why' to fellas like Aldrich. He and Riggs will figure out how it all needs to be."

Puzzled by the undertaker's tone, Thomas was about to ask what he meant, but Winchell cut him off.

"How's Doc Haines doing?"

Thomas nodded noncommittally.

"Getting old, like all of us," Winchell said. "He and my dad are a pair, that's for certain." He held out a hand toward Thomas. "Anything else I can do for you?"

"Not today," Thomas replied. "I appreciate this."

"Certainly. You know, my term as coroner ends next year. You might think about it."

Thomas laughed. "I think I'd rather try and repair the living, sir."

"Well, wouldn't we all?" Winchell said. "But sometimes folks don't give us the choice."

43

We're now dispensing veterinary services?" Dr. John Haines asked as Thomas wheeled into his office. He waved off Thomas's question. "Alvina is in the back room with the canine royalty. Quite a transformation, I must say." He pushed himself out of his chair.

He glanced out the window. "Nasty night."

"Yes, it was. Both the constable and Ward Kittrick."

"My heavens. That's what Zachary was telling me upstairs just now. You've been with Winchell?"

"Yes."

"He's a good man, Thomas. One of the best. He's a valuable friend to have."

"That was my impression."

"Well," and Haines flashed a quick smile. "Alvi is anxious, so I'll not detain you further. I sent Jimmy Doyle home, by the way. Two of his fishing buddies came to help him. The wound looks fine." Seeing no point in arguing, Thomas simply nodded his thanks.

"I'll see what Alvi's planning," he said as he left the office. The door of the small room where he'd done the postmortem on Charlie Grimes was open.

Alvi was kneeling beside Prince, stroking his broad head and whispering who knew what to him. The animal sat awkwardly, obviously in great discomfort. "My God, Alvi," he exclaimed. "You are a worker of miracles."

"Well, hardly that," she said, straightening up. "But you must admit, he's rather handsome."

And he was, Thomas had to agree, in a gaunt, gangly sort of way. "How did you accomplish this transformation?" The abundant muck had been washed from the dog's coat, leaving him a uniform brindle, with the expressive long eyebrows of the wolfhound blood that lay somewhere in his lineage. He gazed at Thomas and sighed, then looked up with adoration at Alvi.

"We made a mess of one of Mr. Lindeman's horse tanks," Alvi said.

Thomas examined the animal critically. "I would guess seventy or eighty pounds?"

"Certainly every ounce of that. At *least* that. I had to boost him into the tank one part at a time. He was reluctant."

"I wish I'd seen that. Now the question is, Alvi: Once in and clean, how did you get him *out?*"

"In a very undignified fashion," Alvi said, smiling sweetly. "I hope no one was watching. Much like yourself and the bath."

He felt the dog's bony shoulders and slender neck. Prince smelled faintly of perfumed soap. "The problem here is that I've never experimented with morphine on an animal," he said. He reached out and stroked the wide dome of the dog's skull, running his other hand back along the dog's spine. When his fingers reached within inches of the abscess, Prince shifted away.

"Yes, it hurts," Thomas said. Then, to Alvi, "I think a half grain to start." "We want him far, far off in his dreams. Otherwise he'll take my hand off."

"A half grain? That's rather a lot."

"Yes, it is. But in order for the ether to take effect without him struggling?"

"I'll do it," Alvi offered. She rose, one hand on top of the dog's head. "I'll be but a moment."

When the door closed, the dog's head swung back to Thomas like an odd pendulum, and for several moments they sat quietly, the animal's head hanging, one shoulder heavy against the young man's leg, his posture one of complete resignation.

After a bit, Alvi returned with a small wheeled cart and an array of instruments, including a pan of hot water, shaving cake, brush, and razor. She nodded at the selection of steel instruments. "This is all that was claved," she said. "Bertha is restocking. She said to tell you that half a grain may be too much for a dog."

Thomas looked sideways at Alvi. "And how does she know this?"

"I have absolutely no idea," she said. "But she said it as if she knew. And if I recall correctly, that's what I said as well."

She raised her eyebrows at him, at the same time handing him his stethoscope. He took his time adjusting the earpieces, watching the big dog. The animal simply waited.

The dog's heart galloped along at 145 beats a minute, a good solid beat without additional sounds. He shifted the instrument's bell and listened. "Take a deep breath and let it out slowly," he said in mock seriousness. After a minute he straightened. "Well, I don't know what to compare him to, but nothing sounds as if it's leaking. No murmurs, no rales, no . . . What?" He frowned and the dog held his gaze without blinking.

"All right, let's try a quarter grain. His pulse is high, and there isn't a lot of fat on this old carcass." Alvi held out the charged needle, and Thomas looked at her in surprise.

"You didn't really want me to do it, did you?" she asked.

"Anyway, somebody has to hold him, and I *know* that he won't bite *me*." In a completely unladylike fashion, she swung a leg over the dog so she stood astride the animal at the shoulders. She buried her hands in the thick ruff high on his neck, and Thomas moved as quickly as he could, slipping the needle into the muscle of the dog's left haunch rather than searching for a vein. He managed to empty the dose before the dog had pulled completely away, despite Alvi's hug.

"That does it," he said. "No vein, but it'll find its way."

In moments, Prince's eyes drooped even more than usual, and he rested his head and shoulders hard against Alvi's knee. She continued cooing to him, stroking his face and muzzle as the drug took effect.

"Okay, he wants to lie down now," she said, and eased out of the animal's way. The dog uttered a mighty sigh, but Alvi kept her arms under him until, with an enormous grimace and grunt of effort, she caught him fully in her arms and stood up.

"My God, if I—," Thomas said, but she already had the dog up on the table, where the animal stretched out with another sigh and an odd smacking of his loose lips.

"Let's give him another few minutes and try it without ether," Thomas said. He wheeled to the end of the table. "I'll want him on his back." He tentatively lifted one of the dog's hind legs to measure a response, but Prince was somewhere else. Thomas pulled his crutches close, backed his chair against the wall, and rose to his feet. He swung to the table and in a moment, the two of them had the large dog stretched out on his back, his vast, narrow rib cage sloping down to a belly that hugged his spine.

Thomas splayed the damaged leg outward, and the dog shifted uneasily. "The other quarter grain, I think," he said. He pointed at one of the large veins on the inside of the leg. "Right here." The abscess appeared to surround a small wound about the size of a pencil, but the dead tissue and inflammation surrounding it was grossly swollen and foul.

He took his time with the razor, and Alvi watched critically. "Make sure he's not in danger of swallowing that big tongue of his," he said. He bent down, moving his head out of the light. The abscess was deep, pushing into the thick, ropy muscle, the necrotic tissue extending to within an inch of the dog's anus.

"Well," he said, and let his apprehensions go at that.

With the smallest scissors and bistoury, he excised dead tissue from around the rim of the wound. "Something poked him a good one," he said. With a probe, he began to explore the wound, but immediately released a purulent gusher of pus, blood, and fluid. The dog jerked, but Alvi remained at the animal's head, whispering nonstop assurances. Grimacing from the smell, Thomas cleaned the area again, liberal with the caustic disinfectant.

In a moment he tried to relax back. "This is deep," he said. "I'm afraid that I'll have to cut a fairly good-sized incision. Best to use ether, or he's going to thrash about."

With the stethoscope, he listened to the dog's heart as he dripped the ether into a small towel draped over the animal's muzzle. By the time he was convinced that Prince was thoroughly anesthetized, the dog's pulse had settled at eighty beats a minute, solid enough but sounding as if the organ was pumping molasses.

With swift, sure incisions, Thomas opened the abscess, cutting parallel with the muscle fibers.

"This animal has been shot," he said finally. "If I'm not mistaken, the bullet is lodged against the head of the femur." Five minutes later he held up the forceps clamped around a sizable chunk of gray lead. The nose of the projectile had mushroomed slightly when it struck the bone.

By the time Thomas was confident that he had removed all the dead tissue and cleaned out the wound to the bone, he had excavated an impressive crater.

He had settled back to relieve the ache in his lower back when he heard heavy footsteps in the hallway. In a moment, Zachary Riggs thrust open the door without knocking.

"Alvi," he said pleasantly enough, "are we to expect you upstairs shortly? Carlisle is here today, remember."

"When finished."

Riggs stood silently for a moment, regarding them. "Am I to assume that this is to become a regular service? Surgical services to the bestiary?" He chuckled with disbelief.

"When it's necessary," Alvi said, the same even tone offering no excuses, no apology.

Thomas glanced up at Riggs. "Someone shot the dog," he said, and held up the slug, now aware of the obvious similarities with the one lying in cotton padding in the Winchell collection.

"That's hardly surprising," Riggs said, turning to go.

"From your derringer?" Thomas said, and Riggs stopped, eyeing him thoughtfully.

"Of course it is," he said after a moment. "The choice open to me at the time was clear." He smiled and started to close the door. "You won't be long, I hope," he said to Alvi, and didn't wait for an answer.

"We ought to have a drainage tube in this, but I can't imagine the patient will leave it alone," Thomas said, breaking the uncomfortable silence. "The sutures will be enough of an attractive nuisance." He selected the first thread and began the laborious process of reassembly. He had finished only the first set of internal sutures when they heard loud voices, first outside, and then in the waiting room.

44

Thomas felt the change of air in the room as the door opened behind him, and he paused, fingers motionless, deep in the wound. He turned, half expecting to see Zachary Riggs again. But it was John Haines. "You're finished?" Haines asked, his voice husky.

"No," Thomas said. "Closing, but it's going to take some moments."

"We've had an ugly incident at Schmidt's mill, and one of the injured can't be moved. I'm riding out, but . . ." He hesitated, moving closer to examine the patient. "I'm not sure how much help I can be. I want you to go along, Thomas. If you're able. I know riding in the wagon is a trial for you, but if you think you can manage?"

Thomas looked across at Alvi, who nodded without hesitation.

"Go ahead, Dr. Thomas. I'll finish here."

"She can suture with the best of them," Haines said. "Horace has the carriage here, and Bertha is putting together your kit."

Thomas felt Alvi's small hand take the suture and needle from his fingers, and he moved out of the way. "Be careful that you—"

She interrupted him with a raised eyebrow. "I know how to suture, Dr. Thomas. You're needed elsewhere."

Haines waited at the door as Thomas dropped into the wheelchair and pushed himself out of the room.

"My horse is here, so I'm going on ahead," Haines said. "From what I'm told, time is of the essence." A trace of a smile appeared. "I've told Horace to drive carefully, Thomas."

"Riggs was just down here," Thomas said as he wheeled out of the room. "Surely he can be of help as well."

"Zachary is no surgeon," Haines said over his shoulder. "Let's not waste another moment." Haines's heavy medical bag was sitting by the front door, and with that he was gone. Thomas heard the creaking of a buggy just as the door closed behind Haines.

"This is all we have," Bertha said from the door of the examining room. She hurried toward Thomas with his medical bag.

"Do you know what I'm to expect?" he asked.

"No, I have no idea what happened. One of the workers who came to fetch the doctor said that a saw exploded. What that means, I don't know."

Heavy boots pounded on the porch, and Horace appeared, breathing hard. He held the door for Thomas, at the same time taking the medical bag from Bertha.

The partially enclosed buggy was more awkward than an open buckboard, but with his right foot on the steel step and a hand grasping the canopy uprights, Thomas was able to turn and find the seat. He braced his crutches between the footboard and the seat and gripped the fly upright with his right hand. Horace let the reins stroke the mare's back, and the animal stepped out smoothly.

The rain had stopped, the sky hanging gray and threatening. The horse obviously knew the way, and Thomas braced himself against the bumps and ruts. Horace took the main high road, a lane that wound north away from the coast and skirted a low bluff northeast of the village, country entirely new and breathtaking for Thomas.

"Can't take the shore trail," Horace explained. "Not with the buggy."

"Good," Thomas said, flinching from the jarring. Now, he saw that Port McKinney was smaller than he had first imagined.

The road turned to skirt another swampy inlet alive with waterfowl, but Thomas dared not take his eyes from the road, ready to brace himself every time the wheels found a root hidden in the muck.

By the time they drove around the bluff, Thomas could see the stretch of coastline again, denuded of timber, instead presenting vast stumpage that thrust up through a mat of emerald rhododendron, berry canes, and strangely contorted little trees that Thomas didn't recognize. Most of the shoreline was a mass of boulders, black and thrusting, decorated with swarms of waterfowl and curtains of white droppings.

His pulse quickened as he saw the complex of low, flat-roofed buildings ahead, a small, uniform village tucked in close to the shore. But in five minutes, Thomas discovered that what he had assumed to be buildings were in fact enormous ricks of lumber, marching in neat columns down toward the wharf. Great pilings jutted out of the water, and he saw the double masts of a schooner, its hull hidden behind the ricks.

The road swung sharply toward a large, pitched-roof building, the pungent aroma of freshly cut timber in concert with the tang of the ocean, mud, and horse sweat. Thomas saw Haines's horse tied to an upright by the open end of the mill, but Horace drove around the building and pulled the mare to a halt beside a single doorway. "Easier for you to go in this way," he said, and in an instant he was out of the buggy. "I have your bag. When we're inside, mind where you step."

Although he had but a dozen steps to maneuver on his crutches between buggy and building, he was breathing hard by the time he reached the doorway. The grasping, fathomless mud was replaced by a soft, fragrant pad of sawdust as he hobbled inside. As gloomy as it was outside, the interior of the mill was far worse, and Thomas stood for several seconds, trying to make out the blur of shapes.

Thomas's pulse raced as the size of the mill operation became clear. Massive iron wheels and heavily greased gears, open leather drive belts, logs that must have weighed tons, live steam apparatus, cables stretched tight as a giant's piano strings—his darting eyes inventoried those and more as he made his way through the mill, following closely behind Horace, who appeared intimate with the business.

Two men with their backs turned never heard them coming. Thomas saw others working in the shadow, and at one point thought he saw Dr. Haines's looming figure.

"What happened here?" he asked.

"We got a mess," one man said. He looked Thomas up and down, and saw the medical bag that Horace carried.

"Boss is over there." The man pointed toward a jumble of equipment. "In the sawyer's shack with Larry and the others. Mind your step around the carriage."

The wind through the open side of the mill was wet and cold, with the light muted enough that Thomas felt as if he were trapped under a dark blanket. He concentrated on following Horace. The "carriage" turned out to be an enormous version of the slick tracks Thomas had once seen in a small Connecticut sawmill. Here, the two mammoth parallel chains dogged the logs toward the saw, and then carried the cut slabs to the outside. The saw itself made no sense to Thomas. No blade was in evidence, and an enormous log lay on the carriage.

As they drew closer, he saw Dr. Haines straighten up. "For God's sake, man, find some light," the physician boomed to a stocky man barking orders. "Ah, good," he said when he saw Thomas. "Careful, now." The crowd of perhaps a dozen mill workers gave way as Thomas maneuvered his crutches. He could smell grease, hot steel, and both sawdust and wood smoke.

Thomas stopped short. In the tangle of broken framework, he could see the dim light glint off a great, gray curl of steel with teeth an inch long. He realized he was looking at the remains of a giant band saw, rather than the circular saw that he had expected.

"She just exploded, boss," one of the men babbled. "Hit something and just came a flinders. Old Larry, he was right in the middle of it."

Edging sideways, Thomas traced the path of the saw blade and saw that one loop had been stopped by the lower portion of what had been a standing wall. Like a great snake, the curve of the steel arched down to the floor and back up, passing diagonally across a man's body from right hip to left shoulder. The man's shirt had been cut away, and Thomas saw that the spine of the blade had actually plunged into the man's torso high up, under his left shoulder.

"Over here," Haines said.

Thomas could see that as the blade fragment hit the man, the teeth had been facing outward, raking across the inside of his arm, slicing muscle and bone. It appeared that the end of this section of blade had plunged to a halt in the wall behind them.

"Bring the lights in," Thomas snapped. Nothing he was seeing made any sense. Edging awkwardly along the remains of a back wall, Thomas made his way far enough that he could slide down and reach the man's head. Reaching over the curve of the saw blade—he saw now that it was nearly twelve inches wide and could only guess at its original length—he touched the man's neck. He could see no respiration, and the pulse was thin and thready, racing as if the heart was desperately trying to manufacture blood to pump.

"What's his name?" Thomas asked.

"Larry Beautard," the burly man said, and by the deference shown him, Thomas guessed him to be the mill boss. He held a lantern close, and Thomas could feel its heat on his face. As he counted the faint heartbeats, he tried to imagine the carnage the massive blade would have caused to fragile tissues. "How many minutes ago did this happen?"

"Be about twenty," a voice said.

"Had to be more'n that," another argued. "Closer to half an hour." Thomas recognized Jake Tate's voice.

Something touched his shoulder and Thomas turned to see his stethoscope dangling from Dr. John Haines's hand.

Slumping to his knees, Thomas worked the earpieces into place and closed his eyes as he placed the instrument's bell on the bloody chest.

The pulse was ragged, lopping, thin—but the respiration was worse, an airy gurgle as blood and air mixed in all the wrong places.

"My God," Thomas breathed. He snatched the earpieces out. "Let me have the lantern down low," he ordered. Taking most of his weight on his right knee, he braced against one crutch. Sure enough, the blade was crushing into the left shoulder joint. It had sliced into the man's chest at the third rib, ramming through muscle, bone, and then lung. At the same time, the giant's sword had slashed through the inside of the sawyer's left arm, chopping the upper arm bone, muscles, and nerves. With such a gash, the great arteries and veins of the shoulder and arm surely would have been severed. Beautard should have been dead.

Thomas sat back. By a quirk of fate, that very blade was responsible for Beautard's continued pulse and feeble breath. Had the blade flashed on through, leaving the man lying free, the massive wound would have bled him out in seconds. As it was, the blade's pressure acted as a clamp—a spring steel tourniquet. The huge blade had pinned Beautard against the floor and wall, crushing the blood vessels.

"If we move that blade now, he'll bleed to death," Thomas said quietly. "That's what's keeping him alive." He turned to find the man at his elbow. "How long is this thing?"

"Before it broke, fifty-four feet." The man bent over, hands on his knees. "Don't know how long this piece is. Maybe fifteen, eighteen foot, it looks like. You aren't going to move it without killing him . . . if he's not gone already."

"He's not gone," Thomas said. "I won't move the blade, but we'll certainly move *him*." He grimaced and looked at the worried faces, but Haines had evidently read his mind. "Let's move about a dozen of you out of here," the older physician boomed. "And then every light you have, Bert. That's what we need right now. Light. And put the two bags right here beside me."

Thomas pushed his head bandage upward, and then with a curse jerked it off altogether. The gauze yanked at several stitches, and he swore.

"You're able to do this?" Haines said, and Thomas could smell the alcohol on the man's breath.

"We have no choice," he replied. Saying it was one thing. His hip flexed enough that he was able to thrust his left leg behind him after a fashion, taking most of his weight on his right knee as he leaned forward.

By the time he'd managed a position from which he could work, Haines had sutures in the pan of phenol.

"The light," Thomas ordered, and someone maneuvered around the blade and the victim. With the lantern held so close it could make blood sizzle, Thomas first cut away the remains of the sawyer's clothing. He worked steadily, following the wound deeper and deeper, being careful not to nudge the steel blade.

After a moment he looked up, nodding at what had been the back wall of the shack. "Take out that wall," he said, and the man to whom he spoke didn't react.

"You're Mr. Schmidt?"

"Yes," the man said.

"Well, Mr. Schmidt, in order to move him out of here, you're going to have to remove that wall. Just the portion immediately behind him." He reached for another suture. "And don't disturb the blade. Not a fraction, not a hairsbreadth. Don't touch it."

"Jake!" Schmidt shouted, but Tate had heard the instructions and was already moving. In less than a minute, they could hear a crew of men outside the building, working on the slab wood behind Beautard's head. Nails screeched as they were yanked from the green wood. When one proved stubborn, the wall shook as Jake took an axe to it. A splinter of wood flew from the wall, glanced off the rim of the pan holding the sutures and landed on Haines's forearm.

"By God, pay attention to what you're doing!" the older man shouted. In another minute they felt the flow of raw outside air. Hands reached to remove the piece of slab wood behind Larry Beautard's head.

"Wait!" Thomas snapped, and six pairs of apprehensive eyes turned toward him. "When you move that, his body's going to shift. We don't want that yet, so I need some hands in here. About three of you, if that many will fit."

With Beautard's head and body supported to the physician's satisfaction, they watched as Jake removed the final small section of wall.

"I need more light," Thomas said, and another lantern moved in close. "You see how that arm is going to have to move?" Thomas whispered to Haines, but even as he spoke, he was watching one of the sawyers who knelt nearby. The man's face was pallid, his forehead soaked in sweat, his eyes about to roll back in his head.

"You're not going to be able to save it, Thomas," Haines said.

"I know that. But I want to amputate where we can see what

we're doing, and where we can keep the stump clean." He motioned with a free hand, his right buried in Beautard's armpit. "Just enough to clear the blade, now," he said, and then more to himself than anyone else, he added, "I don't want any tension on the axillary ligature after I stitch him up." His plan was to ease Beautard backward, away from the blade, working bleeders as they erupted.

All the blood and gore was too much for the faint mill hand, and he collapsed backward, flailing to keep his balance.

"Jake, get in there," Schmidt shouted.

When he was sure Beautard was supported, Thomas worked to draw the man's left arm up and away from his body, trying to place the arm as if the patient were reaching to scratch the center of his own back. Haines moved with surprising speed to offer his assistance.

"The bone's shattered," he breathed.

Thomas said nothing, but waited as Haines manipulated the arm. Like gaping shark's teeth, the blade's rakers appeared, along with a flood of black blood. A sheen of sweat broke out on Haines's face, and he bared his teeth. "Free," he said triumphantly.

"Bring it down and in," Thomas instructed. He held a compress against the wound, padding it closed as Haines brought the arm down, now under the blade, holding the man's forearm tight against his lower ribs.

Thomas wanted to stand, but found he could not. He looked up at Jake Tate. "He must be moved gently back toward you," he said. He held out his hands to explain, and Tate's eyes widened as he stared at the physician's blood-soaked fingers. "Do you hear me?"

Tate gulped and nodded, looking down.

"Slide him back away from the blade," Thomas instructed. "Two at his legs, and two of you at his head and shoulders. Gently now."

Working in awkward concert, the mill hands positioned

themselves and then waited in hushed silence as Thomas frowned. Then he held up his right hand.

"Wait. This isn't going to work," he said. He rummaged in the medical bag and came out empty.

"Do you have more gauze?" he said to Haines. His question was met with a blank expression. "More gauze?" he repeated and held out his hand to accept a large pad from the older man. In a moment, he had positioned the gauze deep in Beautard's body, underneath the blade. "Maybe now," he said, and nodded at Jake. "Easy now. Straight back."

At least three inches of the blade's spine was buried in Larry Beautard's chest, and after what seemed an eternity, the sawyer was free of the steel.

"He's clear," Thomas shouted. Both hands held the sawyer together, and the young physician let his own weight add both to the pressure on the gaping wound and relieve the shrieks of pain in his own hip and ribs.

"I'll need bandages, Mr. Schmidt," he called. "I don't have enough. Clean bed linens will do, torn into four-inch strips."

"We don't, ah . . ." Schmidt hesitated.

"Clean long johns then. Anything at all." Thomas could no longer see clearly, his own sweat stinging his eyes. "And a wagon with a mattress in the back." He turned to find Schmidt. "Something to protect him from the rain as well."

"He going to make it?"

"Most likely not," Thomas said sharply. "Certainly not if we all stand around dithering. Come on, now."

He almost lost his balance and floundered with his right hand as he maintained the pressure on the enormous wound with his left. He lowered his voice and said to Haines, "We must find a way for me to ride in the wagon with him. If we can hold him together . . ."

By the time Thomas and John Haines had prepared Beautard for the agonizing journey to Port McKinney—two miles as the crow flies, but three miles of jolting, rutted torture by road, a fresh team of mules stood outside the mill, harnessed to a heavy freight wagon. A tarpaulin had been tented over the bed of the wagon, each raindrop making a soft plopping sound as it struck the canvas. Two horsehair mattresses had been found, lumpy, hideously stained things that reeked of mildew.

"Nothing but the best," Thomas muttered, and frowned at Schmidt in exasperation.

"We didn't plan this," Schmidt said.

"No, we didn't," Thomas said. He maneuvered his crutches carefully, having unwillingly given up his post at the wounded man's side for the trek from mill to wagon. Haines took his place, clamping the injured man's arm against his ripped torso as Beautard was carried outside, a twenty-four-inch-wide spruce plank serving as a stretcher. "Someone must find this man's wife," Thomas said. "She should meet us at the clinic." He didn't wait for a response, but Schmidt caught him by the arm.

"You'll look at the other one?" Schmidt asked.

"Other one?"

"Over on the other side of the carriage," Schmidt explained.

The young victim rested against a wheel housing, pale and trembling, lips compressed white. Thomas crutched carefully around the debris, marveling at its immensity. The gigantic band saw's blade had tracked on the enormous drive and idler spools above and below the carriage. Part of the fractured blade had stabbed up through the roof and now hung above them, swaying gently. A six-foot long portion had snaked out and stabbed through the opposite wall. The remainder of the snarl of steel had lashed out at the sawyer's control shack.

The young man rested with a large pad of greasy, bloody rag pressed tightly against the back of his thigh. Thomas halted and stared. The remains of another sawyer lay in the sawdust where he'd been flung, slashed into two ragged halves, no doubt dead before he understood what had hit him.

"Your name, son?" Thomas asked, trying to keep the tremor out of his voice.

"Melvin Smith," the young man managed. He couldn't tear his eyes away from the corpse a dozen feet away.

"He might as well ride into town with Beautard," Schmidt said. "And for God's sakes, someone cover Skip," he ordered.

"I'm . . . I'm all right," Smith said.

Thomas leaned one crutch against the carriage and bent down, pulling Smith's hand away from the bandage. The wound, compared to a sawyer cut in half or another skewered, was a trifle, a mere eight-inch flick of the blade as it flashed past.

"We don't have enough sutures left to do anything here," Thomas said.

"Oh, I don't need to . . . ," the man stammered, and started to pull away.

"Oh, yes, you do," Thomas said. "If you want to save that leg, you'll do as you're told."

Leaning on companions, Melvin Smith hobbled out into the rain, hand still pressing the bloody cloth against his leg. He leaned his good hip on the tailgate of the wagon and rolled in, letting out a yelp as he skinned his injury against the wooden sides in an effort to avoid Beautard's silent form.

"One of you will ride with me," Thomas said. By the time he had the freight wagon organized to his satisfaction, Dr. Haines had already set out to Port McKinney on horseback.

Schmidt looked at Thomas with a mixture of apprehension and worry. The young physician had found enough room to lie beside Beautard, legs out straight, back propped against the wagon sides. He had instructed Jake Tate how to cradle Beautard's body so that Tate could provide additional compression and support.

"What else do you need?" Schmidt asked.

"Find Mrs. Beautard," Thomas replied. "Make sure someone is with her." Craning his neck, he caught Jake Tate's attention. "Careful now," he ordered.

The wagon eased forward in the mud.

45

Where the hours went, or what time of the day or night it might be, Thomas was unaware. At some point, he realized that it might be possible to save both Lawrence Beautard's life *and* his arm, and that notion consumed him. He tied off thoracic vessels, positioned a drainage tube in the pleural cavity after successfully reinflating a collapsed lung, and stitched so many sutures that Bertha was hard pressed to keep pace. All the while, a portion of his mind tussled with another challenge—the possibility of repairing the patient's mangled left arm.

Dr. John Haines had been assisting, and Thomas found himself minding his tongue when the older man's hesitancy got in the way.

"I need a piece of silver," Thomas said at last. An idea had hovered, despite the improbability of it all or the difficulty of the surgery at his fingertips. Haines looked up, eyes blurry.

"A what?"

"I need a small piece of pure silver, John. A bar perhaps a centimeter wide, perhaps ten or twelve centimeters long. Half a centimeter thick at least." He held up his fingers, illustrating what he wanted.

"I have no such device," Haines said.

"It can be made from the handle of a fork or spoon, I think," Thomas said. "A silver fork. Not a steel one."

"A fork."

"Yes. I should think that the handle could be easily fashioned. Surely Mr. Lindeman has a grinding wheel for sharpening axes. It would take but a few seconds to grind down the handle of a piece of silverware."

"My God, man," Haines said, an exclamation of wonder mixed with excitement. Thomas felt a chill of admiration that

269

Haines, weary and ill, still grasped the essential thought in Thomas's mind without further explanation.

"I'll talk with Alvi," Haines said, holding out yet another suture.

"Please impress on her the urgency, John. We have no time."

"Yes." Haines stepped away from the table and swept off his apron. On the table, Beautard stirred with a long, awful groan. Thomas knew that Beautard, young, strong, and fit, was nearing the end of his endurance.

"A quarter of morphine, please, Bertha," Thomas said. "If we must go deeper with the ether, we will, but I'd rather there was no added burden on his system."

"I have it ready," Bertha responded. Together they continued, and Thomas became absorbed in the laborious process of repairing the large brachial artery. What had saved Beautard's life was the very impact of the blade that had torn him apart. The major artery running down the inside of his arm essentially had been crushed shut, the flying steel becoming an enormous, violent arterial clamp, the hot steel macerating the tissue into an instant clot.

Thomas felt a hand on his forehead as Bertha reached across and patted the sweat away from his eyes. He had still not replaced the bandage on his head, and his eyes stung now from both concentration and perspiration.

"It was unpleasant after you left," she said, her voice no more than a whisper.

"How so?" he asked impatiently, not looking up.

"You left Miss Haines with the dog?"

"I had no choice."

"I could hear her arguing with Mr. Riggs."

Thomas glanced up at her. Under other circumstances, he would have been curious, but at the moment, such matters seemed ridiculously trivial. "He has an odd way," he said, dismissing the subject.

"Odd? That's a generous way to put it. He was issuing orders right and left, but I suspect that you've come to know enough of Miss Haines to know that most of them were ignored."

"Orders?" He found it odd that Bertha felt the need to keep up the constant chatter. Perhaps it was her way of trying to calm his nerves, strung at the moment as tight as a banjo string.

"Yes. The dog was to be out of the building instantly, he said. No more time wasted on such things. And on and on he went."

Thomas sighed. "He and I will have to have a talk."

"Be careful about that, Doctor."

"More sponges here," he said. "The dog survived, I hope?"

"He's asleep in the office," Bertha said. "On the old rug in the corner. I check on him from time to time."

"The more sleep the better," Thomas said. "If we keep him substantially lubricated with opiates, he may leave the stitches alone."

"One would wonder how an addicted dog behaves," Bertha said with amusement.

"We shall find out, won't we."

In a moment, or maybe ten, maybe more, he heard the clock in the waiting room chime, and ignored the number, then heard it chime again. As if the chimes were an announcement, he felt rather than saw an added presence in the room. He glanced up to see Alvi waiting at his elbow.

"This?" she said, and held up a small enameled pan. Lying in the pool of phenol was a highly polished sliver of silver, exactly the dimensions Thomas had imagined, but tapered gracefully to a point at each end.

"Perfect," he exclaimed. "My God, you're a wonder."

"My father had most specific instructions. I can't say that Gert was overly enthused about losing one of my mother's best, but father didn't stop to negotiate." Her eyes shone with excitement.

"I'll replace it if this doesn't work," Thomas said.

"Ah," Alvi said, stepping back from the table, "but it's *going* to work, Dr. Thomas."

"In which case, Mr. Beautard will replace it." Thomas turned his attention back to the sawyer's mangled arm. The humerus had been slashed in half ten centimeters below the shoulder joint. There was no logical way he could imagine to hold the two ends of the severed bone together, despite—or maybe because of—the reasonably clean cut. Under the best of circumstances, no plaster cast in the world would result in anything beyond a hideously contorted union, permanently weak and ill-formed. But held in place by a neat pin until true union could take place, that might be a different matter, Thomas speculated.

It seemed logical to the young physician that leaving the slashed ends of the bones somewhat rough might be preferable to a journeyman woodworker's approach where butted ends were trued and flat. Unavoidably, the bone would heal a bit short in any case. His proposed repair was simple. Just as the carpenter might drive a dowel into the two jagged ends of a broken chair rung, the silver pin could unite the two lengths of bone.

Holding his breath as if expecting an explosion, with the upper arm muscles separated and clamped, he gently tapped the pin so that one sharpened end sank into the bone marrow of the upper portion of the humerus. Aligning upper and lower portions was another story entirely, and it was only because Bertha's deft little hands seemed to read his mind that he finally succeeded with a union that satisfied him.

"We'll need a stout splint," he said between clenched teeth. "With the splint under a plaster, it might hold the arm secure if we cast from shoulder to wrist. But we'll have to leave a significant opening in the cast so that we can tend the wound's progress."

Keeping the wound clean had become Thomas's obsession from the first moments. The saw blade would have carried fragments of sawdust and who knew what else with it, as well as exploding bone chips throughout. Thomas had observed that nothing seemed to create sepsis quite as effectively as wood. Even a minor wooden splinter, let untended, festered. If Beautard's wound wasn't perfect in its cleanliness, all the clever surgery in the world would not save his life.

Beautard struggled again, a series of small jerks that appeared as if he was trying to flex his legs.

"Doctor," Bertha said quickly, and Thomas looked up to see Beautard's eyes wide open, although entirely unseeing. The man's breath came in swift little stabs, his lips turning blue.

"The ventilator," Thomas snapped, but before Bertha could prepare the rubber bag and bring it into position, Beautard had sucked in a great, shuddering breath, let it out, struggled again with a horrible gagging sound, and then the air in his lungs whistled out for the last time.

Thomas grabbed his stethoscope and heard the last feeble, struggling heartbeat and then profound silence. He looked across at Bertha in disbelief.

"A clot, maybe," Thomas said helplessly. "My God, we had him." He moved the bell of the stethoscope to a half dozen locations, as if a pulse might be hiding from him. Even at the side of the neck, the great vessels now felt as unresponsive as wood. Finally he straightened up, tossing the forceps that he had been cradling in his left hand toward the enameled pan. It missed and clattered on the floor.

"I'm so sorry," Bertha said. "You did everything you could." She picked up the forceps and then started to pull up a linen sheet to cover Beautard's remains. Thomas held up a hand. He took the forceps and with a wrenching flick, withdrew the silver pin and dropped it into the pan.

"Perhaps someone else can benefit," he muttered. Bertha drew up the sheet.

"Mr. Smith still waits," she said softly.

"No one tended him? In all this time? How long has he waited?"

"Long enough, Doctor. And no . . . No one has looked at him." She held the wheeled table with a hand on each side of the corpse's feet. "I think that Dr. Haines had to return home. He wasn't feeling well. Alvi mentioned that after she left the pin for you."

"I didn't hear her say that," Thomas said.

273

"You were involved," Bertha said, and favored him with a tender smile. "It will be thirty minutes or so until we have more sterile implements. Shall I have Mr. Smith come in?"

"Of course." He collapsed back into his wheelchair, watching Bertha Auerbach wheel the table out of the room. If she struggled with the weight, it didn't show. He closed his eyes, forcing himself to review each step of his procedures. In a few moments, Bertha's voice startled him.

"Mr. Schmidt would like to speak with you," she said. "Shall I show him in?"

"Certainly."

The burly mill owner appeared in the doorway and stopped, regarding Thomas. "You look like hell," he said.

"And feel like it," Thomas said. He saw now that Bert Schmidt was well beyond middle-aged, his close-cropped hair a uniform salt-and-pepper. "Before today, I'd heard so much about you that I was sure we'd already met," Thomas said. He held out a hand, then grimaced and started to pull back. "I should clean up."

Schmidt moved quickly and grasped the physician's gory hand with a powerful grip. "Thank you, sir," he said. "That's what I wanted to say."

"Well, we lost him," Thomas said. "For a few minutes there, I was hopeful. I'm sorry. I truly am."

"We've lost a good man," Schmidt said. "I valued Lawrence Beautard highly. But you did more than I could have asked of anyone."

Thomas pushed himself up a little straighter in the chair. "Someone needs to tend to his widow," he said. "She's with child again. This will be a difficult time for her."

"My wife, Carlotta, is with her now."

Thomas sat for a moment with his face cradled in both hands, and Schmidt waited patiently for him. The young physician straightened and shook his head. "You know, I've heard that Seattle has an entire telephone system, Mr. Schmidt."

"So it has."

"We should have one. If the mill could have placed a connection here, how much time would that have saved? Twenty minutes at the very least? Half an hour? That might have been enough. That and a proper ambulance, ready and waiting."

Schmidt watched Thomas in silence for a moment. "Your dejection is to be expected," he said. "Bertha says that a successful result was tantalizingly close."

"We'll never know."

"I've seen a good many injuries in a third of a century in the timber, Doctor. My guess was that Lawrence's number had been called the instant that saw shattered." He heaved a sigh. "When I saw you that first day, I would have guessed the same thing. And now maybe someday, we'll have that dinner together."

"I would hope so."

Schmidt nodded quickly. "Have you looked at Melvin yet? I saw him sitting in the ward. He's more afraid of you than that saw."

"I'm on the way," Thomas said, "and hope to God for no complications there. A fair amount of yelling, a few stitches, and a marked limp for some time. He'll not be eager to lift anything heavier than a whiskey glass for the next week or ten days."

"That will break his heart, I'm sure."

"You'll need someone to come by later this afternoon to fetch him," Thomas said. "He won't want to walk."

"Done."

"What caused the saw to explode, do you know?"

"Well," Schmidt said, his face taking on a determined set, "I haven't had time to look, but one of my men said that the blade struck something in the wood."

"Really. I wouldn't think a knot or whatever would make much of a difference to such a huge apparatus."

Schmidt laughed without a trace of humor. "Knots don't."

46

You'll have to shed the trousers," Thomas ordered, and pre-
dictably, the nineteen-year-old blanched and looked
around toward Bertha, whose back was turned to him. "I can't
treat you through layers of filthy cloth," Thomas said. "We'll
need the trousers off, the undergarments off, and you facedown
on the table. We'll clean out the wound and see what we have."
Bertha had the needle in Melvin Smith's arm before he knew it
was coming. The lad yelped and tried to jerk away, but Bertha
was ready for him, and moved in concert.

"What's that you're doin'?" he bleated. "Burns like hell."

"Some morphine," Thomas said. "You need to relax."

"I told you, it don't hurt."

"Well, of course it doesn't," Thomas agreed easily, "but it's
going to when I start stitching."

"You can't do that," Melvin wailed, but the edge in his voice
was beginning to dull. "Oh . . . ," he moaned, and shook his
head.

"Off with the shirt first, darling," Bertha said, and Melvin's
face lit up.

"She called me 'darling,'" he said to Thomas, with a silly
grin.

"You have her attention," the young physician replied. Bertha peeled the woolen shirt off, managing the buttons that the
morphine hid from the young man. In due course, the sawyer
was shed of every stitch of clothing and lying facedown on the
table, white skin changing at the wrists and neck to weathered
brown. Bertha covered him with a clean linen except for the
damaged leg, and Melvin's left hand snagged a corner and drew
it to his face, like a small child hugging his crib blanket.

Thomas stood for a moment, assessing the gash in the back of
the man's right thigh. With the capriciousness of fate, the ex-

ploding blade had spared young Melvin Smith. A fragment of steel had flicked out and slashed meat down to the bone, laying open a gash a full eight inches long. The bone lay untouched. Thomas leaned his own right hip firmly against the table, and began the tedious process of cleaning the wound. He had never seen the slash of a sharp cavalry sword, but imagined this to be nearly identical—clean and deep.

Even though Thomas and Bertha spread the wound wide, flushing the canyon in Smith's thigh liberally, the sawyer felt no pain. Time stopped as Thomas became engrossed in the challenge of reassembly. Repairing first the deeper and then the surface musculature took patience and considerable force. Once again, Thomas was soaked with sweat by the time the wound was closed, leaving a neat, lazy-S railroad track of sutures across the back of the man's leg.

"He can rest in the ward until he's fully conscious," Thomas said. "I'll want to talk with him before he leaves."

"Of course," Bertha said. "Always. Jake Tate said that he would stop by later this afternoon. I'll tell him to fetch Mr. Smith some clothing and a proper set of crutches."

Thomas pulled out his watch. "Do you know what time it is?"

Bertha laughed. "As a matter of fact, I do, Doctor." The laugh didn't erase the melancholy in her eyes. Despite the whirlwind of the day, Thomas knew that Bertha Auerbach was running on sheer nerves after the loss of Constable Eastman, forcing herself to carry on like the good soldier that she was.

"Three fifteen. How did that happen? We missed lunch." He wheeled to the doorway and pushed it open. The waiting room was empty. He started toward the ward, then changed his mind and turned to the office, opening that door just in time to see Prince bent in a horseshoe, his left leg lifted and nose embedding in his crotch.

The dog stopped his excavations and turned to watch Thomas, but otherwise remained frozen, left leg still high in the air.

"Stop it," Thomas said. The long, ropelike tail thumped

twice on the floor, but the left leg remained elevated until Thomas wheeled closer. With an enormous, heartfelt groan, the dog's head sank to the floor. The leg lowered. He didn't move as Thomas reached down and grasped his left foot, but the instant Thomas lifted the dog's leg, Prince's head snapped off the floor and, as if he'd been given permission, once more began investigating his surgery with tongue and nose.

"Stop it," Thomas repeated sternly. Bertha appeared in the doorway. "He's had food?" he asked, nodding at the enameled pan near the dog's head.

"Miss Haines brought pot roast down from the house." She smiled. "I would imagine that Gert meant it for you."

"I would have enjoyed some," he said. The pan was clean. "I think another quarter grain to keep him quiet for the afternoon. I'll tend to that." He pushed the dog's head away gently and examined the surgery. The area around the stitches was reddish, but Thomas saw no undue swelling or drainage.

"It's too soon to tell, but he's tough enough," he said, and dropped the dog's foot. The tail thumped again.

At the same time, the chime by the front door rang, and Thomas looked past Bertha. The man who had entered appeared vaguely familiar. Short of stature, tending to paunch, his florid face appeared as if he'd jogged up the hill through the mud. Dressed entirely in a neatly cut brown woolen suit, he carried a small valise. Inside the door, he stopped, set his valise on the floor, and industriously polished the rain off his spectacles.

"May we help you, sir?" Bertha Auerbach greeted him, but it didn't sound to Thomas as if she was greeting a complete stranger. The man beamed.

"I'm looking for Dr. Thomas Parks, Miss Auerbach," the man announced. "I'm told that I might find him here."

Thomas wheeled to the office door. "I'm Parks," he said, still thinking hard to place the man.

"Well," the fellow said heartily. "So you are. So you are. Some small misfortune, I'm told, but it appears you're healing nicely."

"Thank you. I fear you have me at a disadvantage, Mr. . . ."

"Carlisle," the man said, thrusting out his hand. "Efrim Carlisle. Your cabin mate aboard the *Alice* some weeks ago. Seems a lifetime, no doubt."

As the man's surprisingly rough, calloused hand clamped his in a viselike grip, the memory came back in a flood, memories in particular of Carlisle's snoring that had marked every night of the small schooner's passage.

"I hope your travels have treated you with better fortune. Come in." Thomas beckoned toward the office. "You look fit."

"Thank you, thank you." Carlisle entered the office with alacrity, valise in hand. Whether it was the bag swinging this way and that, or the new smell, or simply being taken by surprise, Prince's head jerked up as a bellow erupted from deep within his scrawny frame. His hindquarters remained as if spiked to the floor, but he lurched up on his forelegs.

Thomas quickly wheeled his chair between Carlisle, who backpedaled to the far side of the office, and the dog. The physician reached out a hand and rested it on the dog's wide head, but the animal's dark eyes tracked Carlisle.

"Come now, beast," Thomas said gently. "You're in no condition to take on anyone or anything." The dog gulped as if he'd tried to swallow something distasteful and glanced at Thomas. In a moment he collapsed back on the floor, eyes on the visitor.

"He's had a bit of surgery this morning."

"My word," Carlisle said. He sat gently in a chair on the other end of the massive desk, well away from the dog. "Run out of human patients, have we?"

Thomas laughed and wheeled behind the desk. "I think not. What can I do for you?" He glanced at the clock again.

"But a moment or two of your time, sir," Carlisle said. He opened the valise, withdrew a single sheet, and handed it to Thomas.

Let it be known to all and sundry, that the bearer, Efrim L. Carlisle, Esquire, is charged with conducting business on behalf of Pitt and Burgess Lumber and Mining Co, Ltd., headquartered in Denver, Colorado, with

279

holdings represented in Bellingham, Washington State, Houston, Texas,
and the Alaskan territories.

With this letter of introduction, we are pleased to present Mr. Carlisle to
you, and assure you that any negotiations he may undertake with you and
your firm are backed with the full confidence of Pitt and Burgess Lumber
and Mining, Ltd. Our firm appreciates any courtesy extended.

The letter was signed by Richard Culhane, President.

Thomas laid the paper on the desk. "Most impressive," he said. The elaborate engraving on the letterhead showed a collage of various industrial endeavors representing, presumably, the business of Pitt and Burgess.

"You may have heard of us," Carlisle said.

Thomas shook his head. "I mean no disrespect," he said, "but you must remember I'm an easterner until just a few days ago." He smiled. "In fact, I know little beyond the bounds of these four walls."

"Yet, word of your accomplishments has spread up and down the coast," Carlisle said.

"I find that hard to believe."

"You're too modest," Carlisle allowed. He glanced at the dog. "It's not every physician who willingly includes the veterinary sciences in his practice."

"Medicine is medicine," Thomas said. "But so . . . What may I do for you? Or"—he peered at the letter again—"do for Pitt and Burgess?"

"Shall I come right to the point?" He licked his lips as if hinting that an ounce or two of something might not go unappreciated.

"Please do," Thomas replied.

"My firm would like to offer you employment, Doctor."

47

Carlisle folded his hands over the top of his valise in satisfaction and smiled indulgently at the surprise on Thomas's face.

"My firm," Carlisle said, leaning forward now and lowering his voice in confidence, "is in desperate need of a director of medical services." He frowned. "Now, this is a complicated matter. We're looking for a physician who can coordinate not only his own successful practice, but provide medical services to our company development on Coues Island."

"I am not familiar with the country."

"Oh, there's no reason you should be, Doctor. But suffice it to say that our company operations in and around Coues Island, and Coues Inlet, produce more than most other lumbering operations in the area *combined*."

"I see."

"Our company clinic on Coues Island includes eighteen beds, with many more to come. A similar facility near Bartlesville has just expanded to thirty-two beds. We currently employ a nursing staff of twelve." He raised an eyebrow. "I dare say you could use some assistance here in that regard."

"Matters are in hand," Thomas said.

"In addition," Carlisle continued, a bit too smugly for Thomas's liking, as if what he really meant to say was, *Oh, I know that matters really aren't in hand, sir.* "we have perhaps the most comprehensive sanatorium in northern Washington, with particular emphasis on tuberculosis patients."

"Also on Coues Island?" Thomas had never heard of Coues, but then again, the northwest was full of odd corners he had never heard of, and certainly never visited. If it wasn't three blocks of Port McKinney or a narrow lane out to Schmidt's sawmill, he hadn't been there.

"Yes, indeed."

"It's surprising that with all the clinic work and expansion your firm has time remaining to cut wood," Thomas said. "You've spoken with Dr. Haines, I assume?"

"Oh, I know John well, believe me. But no, I haven't, at least not today. Strangely enough," and he suddenly hesitated, biting his lower lip, "we find ourselves in a similar situation as yourselves. Dr. Willette—perhaps you've heard of him?" Thomas shook his head. "Well, Dr. Willette—Maurice Willette—has headed our efforts for years. Unfortunately, the good doctor recently suffered an attack of some sort and is partially incapacitated. Now, for some time, he has been our medical director, in charge of all our facilities. But regrettably, we find that he is no longer able to carry on." Carlisle leaned forward again. "We are in desperate need, sir. The country is challenging, the task is in many ways daunting. The responsibilities are great. But," and he lowered his voice another notch, "the opportunities are tremendous for the right man—a young man such as yourself with imagination, ambition, the finest training from a leading institution, someone who will take the reins and provide quality service."

Thomas held up both hands, and suddenly the plaster around his left thumb appeared huge and ungainly. "As you can see, I'm not really in a position to go anywhere."

"Nonsense, man. You've had an accident, and a bad one. Nearly killed, I'm to understand. And yet look at you. You refuse to surrender. You wield the scalpel as if born to it. In a few weeks, all this will be behind you. Now, all I'm asking is that, when you're first ready to travel a bit, that you come to Coues Island and review my proposal in person. Tour the clinic. Meet the staff. Learn of our other facilities, and, I dare say, our other opportunities."

"It sounds interesting," Thomas said noncommittally. "Perhaps you should present your offer to Dr. Riggs."

"Well, I know that you don't practice medicine as a road to being a wealthy man," Carlisle said as if he hadn't heard the comment, "but at the risk of being indelicate, let me present the bones of our offer, so to speak." He sat back and opened his valise, leafing through several papers. Finally he found the one he wanted, consulted it, and then slid it back in the case without showing it to Thomas.

"Pitt and Burgess hope that their offer reflects the urgency of our situation, Doctor. I had no difficulty whatsoever in persuading them that your remuneration from our company must reflect the fact that you are a young, ambitious physician who would otherwise be expected to build an impressive private practice over the years. They understand that. However, at Pitt and Burgess, your first responsibility will be to the diverse and growing number of company employees and their families." He took a deep breath. "To that end, Pitt and Burgess Lumber and Mining is in a position to offer you the sum of three thousand dollars a month, with the express understanding that as the fortunes of our company continue to grow, so, too, will your remuneration."

"Three—"

"Yes. Three thousand a month. That would total thirty-six thousand your first year. That's entirely separate from expenses that you would be expected to encumber on behalf of operations, and in that respect, I've found our firm is most generous."

"My God . . ."

Carlisle pulled what appeared to be a bank draft from his briefcase and laid it on the desk. "Some funds in advance, of course. And rest assured that Pitt and Burgess will make your move from Port McKinney to Coues Island as effortless as possible."

"I have little to move," Thomas said, then frowned. "I have been in Port McKinney something less than two weeks . . ." He stopped as the door of the office opened abruptly. Alvi Haines's face was flushed, her eyes narrowed with obvious anger.

Prince shifted expectantly, but she ignored the dog.

"Mr. Carlisle," she said in greeting, and Thomas could see that she forced a smile, her lips tight, her jaw set.

"Ah, Miss Haines. How delightful." He started to rise, but she interrupted him.

"Oh, no need for the courtesies," she said. Her eyes shifted to the bank draft on the desk. "Dr. Parks is needed immediately in the ward. I do hope that your business is concluded?"

"Well, I certainly don't want to—"

"It's just that this is an extraordinarily busy afternoon for us, and several surgical patients are waiting," Alvi said. She smiled sweetly this time. "I assume that you've already concluded your business with Dr. Riggs upstairs."

Carlisle rose to his feet, tucking the leather straps of the valise through their buckles. He frowned at them, taking his time, as if they presented a problem about which he had to think long and hard. Prince watched him intently, shifting his gaze back and forth between him and Alvi. "Zachary and I spoke earlier, Miss Haines."

With a sigh of resignation, he pushed back the chair and held out his hand to Thomas. "Doctor, I expect to be speaking with you again, very soon. As I said, time is something of an urgency for us. I hope you understand and give our offer prompt consideration. Good day to you." He touched his forehead. "Miss Haines. As always." As he left the office, he gave the dog a wide berth. Alvi moved just enough that he could pass. As he stepped by, he lowered his voice, and Thomas, although the exchange was obviously not meant for his ears, clearly heard Carlisle say, "Be careful, my dear." He offered a cold smile and was gone.

"How very, very odd," Thomas said. Alvi turned and nudged the office door shut. "Mr. Carlisle sailed on the *Alice* with me. I hadn't seen him since then."

"And hopefully won't again," Alvi said.

"What did he mean by his remark to you just now? You two appear to be acquainted. Be careful of what?"

"Ah, well, that," Alvi said dismissively. She crossed to the desk and picked up the bank draft that Carlisle had made no effort to recover. Glancing at it dismissively, she handed it to Thomas. "Other than misspelling your name, Doctor Thomas *Park*, it's an impressive offer."

The draft was for six thousand dollars, and he stared at the figure. "Impressive indeed," he murmured. He looked up at Alvi. "How is it that this Carlisle chap has come to know Zachary Riggs?"

"He is a supplier of certain pharmaceuticals," Alvi said, and it was clear she didn't want to discuss it further.

Thomas sucked in a breath at the memory. "Carlisle's anodyne."

Alvi didn't respond to that. "Bertha asked me to remind you that Mr. Deaton is anxious. And Mr. Unger is here to fetch the child."

Thomas dropped the bank draft on the desk, and was surprised when Alvi picked it up. With exaggerated precision, she tore it into small bits and held the remnants out to him.

"Something to think about," she said, and then smiled in sympathy at Thomas's expression. "We need you here, Dr. Thomas. If Carlisle's check were an honest offer, I'd have done my best to talk you out of accepting." She smiled coquettishly. "Bribery, logical discourse, charming feminine wiles . . . anything it took."

"It's not an honest offer? Am I to understand that?"

"Not to worry," Alvi said, and then bent down to ruffle Prince's shaggy ears. "I want to talk with Father about this."

"Alvi," Thomas began, then stopped, choosing his words carefully. "I don't wish to sound ungrateful for all you've done for me—for all your father has done—but Carlisle made the offer to me, and it's my choice whether or not I accept." He saw her eyebrows knit. "Don't misunderstand me. It's not that I don't appreciate your concern. I'm most grateful for everything you've done for me. Truly I am."

"You would consider his offer?"

"Well, no. As a matter of fact, I wouldn't. I don't even know where Coues Island is, or Bartlestown, or—"

"Bartlesville," Alvi corrected. "It's a small village about a hundred miles northeast of here, near the border, but well inland from the coast. If it has a medical facility of *any* kind, I'd be much surprised. And the next time you speak with Mr. Schmidt, whose operation you have now seen in person, ask him about the company that Carlisle claims to represent."

"Pitt and Burgess?"

"Yes. I wasn't sure what company name he was using this time."

"Just what are you saying, Alvi? What am I supposed to believe? You're implying that Carlisle is an imposter of some sort? Why would he make a spurious offer to me? Am I supposed to jump at it, running off and leaving the clinic just when your father is less able—"

"A *spurious* offer. I like that, Dr. Thomas." She shook her head. "Let me tell you what my fear is, my friend. If you accept that offer and hie off to Coues Island, we'll never see you again. There will be no six thousand dollars waiting for you, no medical director's job. We'll never know what happened to you. Zachary Riggs will convince my father that he be allowed to hire another physician, and rest assured, it will be someone who is more compliant with Zachary's grand design."

"And what *is* that, Alvi? Just what *is* his plan, other than to make obscene amounts of money from snake oil? I haven't been able to ascertain what that might be. I never see Riggs down here with real patients. He offers no assistance of any kind, even when we're in sore *need* of another willing pair of hands. *You* have been helpful, I must say. Perhaps it is none of my business, but it is clear to me that Mr. Riggs is no more a physician than Prince here." At the sound of his name, the dog lifted his head a few inches off the rug, but his eyes remained fixed on the door. "And why a complicated conspiracy to get rid of me, if that's what he's about? Carlisle, I mean. Your father—or you, for that matter—have but to say, 'Thomas, you're not the man I had in mind. I'm hiring another.' "

Alvi smiled, but Thomas saw a touch of sorrow in her expression this time.

"I'll talk with you tonight, Dr. Thomas. Give me until then."

Thomas held out a hand, catching Alvi by the elbow, but she took his hand in hers. "Give me until tonight. And Mr. Deaton is most eager to see you, Doctor."

Alvi opened the door fully, sliding the stop under it. "Prince may have the need," she said. "A mess anywhere but my father's office." She smiled at Thomas once again, and he felt the warmth to the very core of his being.

48

Louella Unger's brilliant blue eyes, huge in her thin, pale face, locked on Thomas and grew even larger. She stared at the scar around Thomas's head, her lips forming a silent O of amazement.

"Does it hurt?" she whispered.

"Not anymore," Thomas replied.

"It looks *awful*," Louella said soberly.

"Child," her mother said, "mind your manners, now."

"And how do *you* look?" Thomas asked. He felt the gauze stick a bit, and the girl flinched. "You're going to be tender for several days, Louella," he said. He cocked his head, examining the small wound. "Does it pain you?"

"It aches a little," Louella replied bravely. "Just a little."

"Well, I should think so." Slight redness around the stitches, no swelling, no tenderness anywhere else in the abdomen—the child was well on the road to perfect health.

He replaced the dressing and sat back. The little girl was unable to take her eyes off Thomas's torn scalp. "I think you should go home," he said. He turned to Mary Unger and her husband, Robert. "Unspiced fluids for the rest of today and tomorrow, the lightest of broths without much seasoning. Nothing with vegetables, or anything hard to digest. And then by Saturday, mild foods that offer little resistance to the digestion. A nice stew with soft potatoes, perhaps."

"Ice cream," Louella chirped.

"That would be fine." Thomas held up an admonishing finger. "No nuts. Let's see. This is . . . What day of the week are we?"

"This is Wednesday, Doctor."

"Ah, thank you. Wednesday. I'd like Louella to remain quiet until Saturday, when I shall visit. And then short walks and quiet play. No sudden bending. No lifting. No straining. Activity increases after that, of course, when she feels no tenderness whatsoever in her belly. By next week, she'll be nearly good as new. A regular, healthful diet may replace soft foods by Monday."

"Daddy said he was going to take me fishing," the girl said. Her father smiled indulgently.

"That's perfect," Thomas said. "When you land the big one, you must remember to ask for help hauling him into the boat." He pushed himself upright, and found himself able to balance on his right leg without the crutches. "You've arranged something in the back of a buggy, Mr. Unger? Horsehair mattress, something like that?"

"Got a goosedown mattress," Unger said.

"Well, you'll ride in style then, Louella," Thomas said. He nodded and looked up the ward. Bertha Auerbach was bent over, listening to something that Howard Deaton was saying. "I'll be around to see you on Saturday. Until then, you behave yourself." He extended a hand to her father, who pumped it fervently.

"Who is taking care of you, Doctor?" Louella asked, brow furrowed with concern.

"Well, I'm taking care of me, sweetheart." He shrugged. "That's what mirrors are for, you know."

"May we pay you now?" Mr. Unger asked.

"Let's settle up on Saturday," Thomas said. "How would that be?"

He glanced toward Bertha again and saw her put both hands

on her hips, as if about to deliver a tongue-lashing to the teamster. "Excuse me," Thomas said to the Ungers. "Not all patients are as delightful as your daughter." He made his way to his chair and then wheeled up the ward.

"Doc," Howard Deaton whispered as Thomas approached. "Doc, you're a right proper wreck yourself."

"I'm considering hemorrhoid surgery with a rusty scalpel for the next person who tells me that," Thomas replied, and noted the dark circles around the man's eyes, the sunken cheeks, the pale lips. "The leg is a trial?"

"Pretty bad, Doc." The swelling had increased, and bruising near the fracture site was worrisome. "I cain't just lie here. This is like havin' a boat anchor tied to my leg."

"The bones must have time to knit," Thomas said. "If they aren't held in place properly, the leg will be crippled."

"Yeah. That's what you said, but it ain't gonna work, Doc. I can't just lay here for weeks. Christ, man, I'll go mad. And I tell ya, it hurts like bloody hell."

Thomas sat silently, regarding the leg. So much time had been spent learning techniques for the speedy removal of a damaged limb—perhaps he had only prolonged Howard Deaton's agonies by persisting with the fracture box. In less severe cases, in greenstick fractures, or when but one bone of the lower leg was affected, the technique was obviously proper. But here . . .

"I would not hesitate," he had heard Professor Roberts say. *I would not hesitate. Good enough,* Thomas thought.

"Nature must be helped," he said aloud, and surprised even himself at not only the remark, but also the accompanying wave of excitement that swept over him. Roberts had preached that. *Nature must be helped.* He swept the stethoscope from his neck, adjusted the earpieces, and listened to Deaton's heart—strong, steady, willing. "Breathe deep for me," he said, and listened to the air rush unimpaired through the man's lungs.

He sat back, removing the earpieces from his sore head with a flinch of relief. "Tomorrow morning," he said. "We shall repair that leg."

"What do you mean? What do you aim to do?"

Thomas held out two fingers of each hand, pointed toward each other, but an inch apart, like over-and-under derringers staring each other muzzle to muzzle. "Your leg bones are fractured, like so. In order to assist nature in reuniting them, so," and he pushed his fingers together, "we must lead the way. Give them guidance. It is a common procedure," he said, feeling the slightest flush at the falsehood. "What I propose is a series of silver pins, carefully inserted into the bone fragments themselves, arranged in such a way as to hold the bones in proper position until the bone heals around them."

"Jesus, Doc. You think that's going to work?" Deaton asked. "Course, it don't matter none. I got eyes. I can see. That leg is useless as tits on a boar hog the way it is. Fix it or take it. I guess my druthers is that you fix it."

"The recovery is still a matter of many weeks, or even months," Thomas warned.

Deaton fell silent, one fist thumping the bed. "That's what it'll be if you take it off, too," Deaton said. "I seen that a time or two." His face crumpled in a grimace, and Thomas saw moisture in the man's eyes. "I guess it's my time to pay the piper one way or the other, ain't it. I've been lyin' here, thinking about that most of the past two days. I don't figure there's much point in wasting time waitin', and then dyin' anyways . . . or end up with that leg all wadded up and crippled." He shuddered a deep breath. "How do you aim to do it?"

Thomas held his fingers together again. "It is possible to insert a pure silver pin in the bone," he said. "The pin will serve as reinforcement and keep the bone fragments in perfect position until healing union can take place."

"Knew a man who fixed a wooden axle like that," Deaton said. "He bored a hole in each piece, put a big old iron rod down the middle, and whanged the wood halves back together."

"In principle, exactly the same thing," Thomas agreed. "Silver will not react with the body's own chemistry." He smiled as if he knew that for sure. "I'm afraid if I made you out of iron, you'd rust."

"'Spect so. I asked the man why he didn't just make the axle out of iron in the first place. Save time and trouble. He said axles weren't made out of iron. And that was that."

"But his repair worked."

"Oh, hell, yes, it worked. For a while, anyways." He tried a smile. "With silver, I'm going to be worth a few bucks more, eh?"

"Certainly."

"Well, then," and Deaton covered his face with one arm, "have at it."

"Good man," Thomas said. "I shall make preparations." He saw that Bertha had moved around the bed and now stood with her hands folded.

"Tomorrow morning at ten," Thomas said, again feeling the surge of excitement, mixed with a trace of foreboding. He had sent home a widow the first time he'd tried the procedure. Deaton was strong, the injury was a closed fracture, and the growing inflammation could be managed.

"I shall need perhaps eight pieces," Thomas said, drawing Bertha to one side. "But I don't know how long. He thought for a moment, visualizing the bones of the man's lower leg.

"I shall make a list of a variety of sizes, and Lindeman can fashion them all."

"Out of . . ."

"The silver that Alvi used last time was ideal," he said. "I'm sure there are more forks to be had."

"Gert James is going to run out of patience with you, Doctor."

"I'll deal with her. Will you find Alvi? I'll give her the list."

Deaton watched Bertha Auerbach leave the ward. He sighed, and his voice dropped to a whisper. "This is going to be one of them things that either cures me or kills me? Is that about right?"

Thomas reflected for a moment. "I'm confident. That's the best I can do."

"That's something, I guess. How many others you done like this?"

Deaton's gray eyes assessed the young physician, waiting.

"None yet," Thomas said.

"Figured that, too," Deaton said. "I heard about Larry Beautard." He held out his hand, and Thomas wheeled forward to take it. The man's grip was damp from slight fever. "Proud to be the first," he said.

49

The more Thomas pored through the various volumes in Dr. John Haines's medical library, the more he felt the conflict of excitement and apprehension. With a messy compound fracture such as Howard Deaton's, every author chose amputation. The newest text in the library, written in 1876, showed only maps of the most expedient incisions for the knife and saw.

He found himself racking his memory, trying to recall the advice from the first edition of Dr. John Roberts's *Modern Surgery*, a text that he now so sorely regretted losing with his steamer trunk. He had read of attempts in Europe to join bones artificially, to "assist nature," as Roberts would say, when the very muscles, tendons, and ligaments surrounding those bones proved to be the enemy, pulling the fragments out of alignment.

He considered wiring Roberts at the university with a list of questions, but he knew that from three thousand miles away, the physician would be loath to recommend specifics without being able to examine the patient himself. Still, something might be gained, some little shred of advice to guide him.

With that in mind, Thomas set about writing a concise outline of his needs for Carter Birch, Port McKinney's telegraph operator. With any luck, some answer might be promptly received from Pennsylvania.

So intense was his concentration that when the knock came on the door jamb of the office, he bolted upright, letting out a cry as pain stabbed his ribs and hip.

"Didn't mean to set you off," the assistant constable said as Thomas settled back in the chair.

"My God, man, I didn't hear you come in."

"I'll be a little more clumpy next time," George Aldrich said. His eyes settled on the dog, who had not bothered to lift his head. "Not much of a watchdog."

"That's what he does, as a matter of fact," Thomas said, holding his ribs. "He watches. He seems to know who his friends are. Right now his best friend is morphine."

"You cut him up pretty bad?"

"His leg was badly abscessed. It appears that someone shot him. I removed the ball." He stretched carefully.

"That don't surprise me. Half the town he's either bit or tried to. Riggs let fly at him once, I know that."

"The same sort of ball that was recovered from Kittrick's brain," Thomas said. "Riggs admitted it."

"So there you are."

Thomas glanced at the clock and saw that it was approaching six.

"Interesting thing," Aldrich said, and without invitation settled carefully in the straight-backed chair on the other side of the desk. He bent far to one side and Thomas heard the jingle of metal. The constable pulled out what appeared to be half a dozen enormous spikes, square in cross section, polished off on one end, tapering on the other. He reached out and placed them on the desk in front of Thomas. From another pocket he pulled yet another, this one of the same general proportions, but badly mangled.

"Railroad spikes," the constable said, seeing the question in Thomas's expression. "Except the flanges have been ground off."

"So . . . ," the young physician said.

"And so this one here we took out of the log that broke Mr. Schmidt's saw—and killed two good men."

Thomas picked it up, feeling the heft of it. Nearly cut in half, the iron spike had bent and split.

"That saw blade is fifty-four feet long," Aldrich said. "A good foot wide. Only one like it in these parts. Schmidt tells me that when the saw's wound up, that blade is traveling a hundred miles an hour."

"Amazing," Thomas said.

"Meant to cut wood, you know. Now, you put iron in the way . . ."

"You mean someone drove one of these spikes into the log? Why would they do that?"

"To wreck the saw," Aldrich said calmly. "Shuts down the mill. Costs Schmidt maybe more than he's got."

"Wouldn't someone at the mill see it done? Good heavens, man, sledging one of those things into a log would take some effort, not to mention making a good deal of noise in the process."

"That it would. Unless done on the stump, out in the timber. Nobody to see or hear." He reached out and laid his hand on the six new iron spikes.

Thomas sat silently, staring at the spikes, not sure what he was supposed to say, or why the constable was confiding in him. "The obvious question is why," he said after a moment. "And who."

"The why is easy. There's a hundred reasons why somebody might hold a grudge against Mr. Schmidt. Anybody who runs a big operation has his share of enemies. Bound to, you betcha."

Thomas nodded at the pile of altered spikes. "Since you have these unused spikes in your possession, it would appear you also know the who."

"I found these in the Kittrick brothers' cabin."

"Really."

"Yep."

"But it was my understanding that Kittrick worked *for* Schmidt. Both brothers did, I thought."

"Did." Aldrich spun the mangled piece of iron in his fingers thoughtfully.

"Not long ago," Thomas said, and Aldrich looked up at him. "I mean, it couldn't have been long ago when that was pounded into the tree. There's no significant rust on the fresh iron, where the head was ground."

"Nope, there isn't." Aldrich frowned. "So, I come to ask you about last night."

"However I can be of assistance," Thomas said. Aldrich dropped the spike on the table and crossed his legs, folding his hands in his lap.

"Kittrick came to see you. That's what you were telling me."

"He did. He warned me to remain silent about the knife and the circumstances of the boy's murder."

"And then he left."

"Yes. It's my understanding that he went upstairs to see Mr. Riggs. Mrs. Unger heard them talking upstairs when she went to his door."

Aldrich frowned at his folded hands. "I'm just wondering why Kittrick would do that."

"Mrs. Unger reported that the two were engaged in conversation. Not an argument. You might ask her if she recollects differently now. Riggs claims that Kittrick threatened him as well as me. That he feared for his life."

Aldrich grunted something and made a wry face. " 'Claims,' you say. You don't believe him?"

"I don't know what to think, sir. All I know is that Kittrick was a ruffian, that he threatened me, and then went upstairs. Moments later, he was dead."

"Any number of ways it could have happened," Aldrich mused. "Hard to say now. Nobody saw. Well, except Riggs. Still," and he uncrossed his legs and stretched the left one, massaging his knee.

"Still?"

"I wonder why you shoot a man in the back of the head just when he's leaving. That's a puzzle."

"Maybe it's how Riggs claims. Afraid Kittrick would return, he saw an opportunity, and took it."

"Goddamn good thing he didn't miss," Aldrich said. "Otherwise Kittrick might have taken that little peashooter away from him and shoved it up his ass." He smiled at the image. "Then you'd *really* have work to do, eh?"

The front door chimed, and Thomas turned to see Alvi enter, carrying a large tray.

"I have to be going," Aldrich said, and stood, tipping the narrow brim of his hat as Alvi entered. At the same time, he scooped up the spikes and dropped them into his coat pocket. "Ma'am, whatever you have there smells mighty fine."

"You're welcome to stay. There's plenty," Alvi said. She set the tray on the desk. Prince lifted his head like an old drunk, his neck muscles sedated to flab. His thick, ratty tail rapped the floor a time or two.

Aldrich grinned, and switched an index finger back and forth between doctor and dog. "You feed him the same thing?"

"As a matter of fact, I do . . . except the dog doesn't get the peach cobbler."

Aldrich nodded, and once more turned to Thomas. "You think on all this," he said.

"I wish I could be of more help," Thomas said.

"Pleasant evening to you both now." The constable nodded at them again and left the office.

"Bertha told me that you needed more silver pins," Alvi said. "I gave your list to Lindeman, but the only silver we have at the moment is my mother's dinnerware, Doctor."

"I will replace it."

An eyebrow drifted up. "I wasn't concerned with that, particularly. A service for twelve leaves plenty of spare dessert forks." She smiled and removed the towel from the tray. Prince groaned pathetically, but didn't move. "I hope you don't mind stew again. This is elk. A couple weeks ago, one of the hunters south of here paid off a bill to father with a hindquarter. Gert canned most of it."

"It smells wonderful." His eyes widened at the pan of muffins. Alvi retrieved the dog's enameled dish and deftly selected out several large chunks of savory meat, along with two small potatoes and several carrots.

Approaching the dog, she paused. "You're probably too sorry for yourself to eat a bite, aren't you." The dog's tail flailed twice, and his jaw dropped open an inch, a long drool of saliva stretching to the floor. Alvi set down the pan, and the dog turned his head sideways without rising, reaching for the food with an impressively long tongue. In an instant, every scrap had vanished.

"If I can get him on his feet, we'll go outside for a few minutes," she said.

"Have you had a chance to talk with your father?"

"No. Perhaps at dinner. Perhaps we'll both take an evening stroll down here. It's really quite beautiful outside."

"I hadn't noticed," Thomas said. "Is there someone who can take a telegram to Mr. Birch for me?"

"I'll be happy to oblige," Alvi said. He handed her the carefully worded message that he had composed to John Roberts in Philadelphia, and she folded it up twice without looking at it. "May I send Horace down for you this evening if father isn't up to the walk? I'm sure he'd like to talk with you."

Thomas grimaced. "I can't, Alvi. Deaton is in a bad way, and no one else is here. He can't be left alone."

She nodded philosophically. "I'll see what father says."

They both turned at the sound of a carriage sliding to a halt in front of the clinic, and in a moment the door burst open. Horace James took no notice of the mud flinging from his boots as he hastened across the waiting room. Prince huffed a short grunt, but otherwise remained silent.

"Needja ta home," he said. "Gert went upstairs to fetch your father for dinner and can't rouse him."

50

When they reached 101 Lincoln, Alvi raced on ahead, carrying Thomas's bulky medical bag. She plunged up the stairs to the second floor where her father kept his bedroom and a private study, and Thomas had managed only three stairsteps before she reappeared and descended to meet him, a sudden, desperate hug telling all.

Alvi released him. "I don't think there's anything you can do," she whispered, and blinked back tears. Her eyes searched his as if she expected him to say, *"I know just the cure."* The twelve stairsteps were narrow, but he crutched up quickly, back against the wall. Alvi followed, a hand offering balance.

Dr. John Haines sat in a rocker by the window. The late afternoon light flowed in over his shoulder, illuminating the book in his lap. Nothing was out of place, no brandy tumbler knocked over to stain the carpet, no spectacles dropped in his lap—simply an old man deep in a comfortable nap.

For Thomas, the absence of struggle erased any vestige of hope. The older man's head had sunk to his chest, but his hands remained on the book, two fingers of his right hand still curled around the corner of a page, as if poised to turn it just as the flood of bursting blood vessels somewhere deep in his brain eclipsed his thoughts.

Thomas leaned his crutches against the wall and bent over as far as he could, one hand grasping the back of the chair while he manipulated the stethoscope. A pulse so faint as to barely disturb the great arteries in the old man's neck could be felt with a gentle fingertip. Haines's eyes were half-lidded, jaw slack, skin unresponsive and ashen gray. Lifting first one eyelid and then the other, Thomas saw that the pupils were dramatically unequal and unresponsive.

"Let's get him onto the bed," Thomas said. Gert James stood by the end of the bed, hands clasped at her bosom, face set in anguish. Alvi had stepped over to her, and stood with both hands on the older woman's shoulders. "Alvi," Thomas prompted, "can we do that?"

"I'll fetch Horace," she said, and enfolded Gert in another hug before leaving the room.

"I came up to fetch him for dinner when he didn't answer my call," Gert whispered. "I knocked, but . . ." She shook her head in misery. "He never closes the door unless he's ill."

"He might have known," Thomas said, more to himself than to the others. The heavy *Universal Medical Advisor* was open to the page featuring the engraving of the massive clinic, left thumb marking the spot. He took the book gently and placed it on the dresser. Haines's fingers never moved.

"Had you spoken to him this afternoon?"

Gert shook her head. "I heard him come in sometime—I don't remember just when. He said he wasn't feeling well." She pulled in a sniff and touched the end of her nose with her hankie. "He said he would take a little nap before dinner."

Heavy boots clattered on the stairway, and Alvi and Horace James reappeared, this time with Zachary Riggs in tow.

"Oh, my," Riggs said gently. As he advanced into the room, he reached out and squeezed Alvi's left arm in sympathy. "What may I do to assist?" he asked Thomas.

"I need to have him on the bed," the young man replied. That took but a moment, and Alvi began unlacing her father's black boots.

"A bit on his left side," Thomas directed, trying to turn Haines somewhat. "The stertor is from his tongue falling back." He looked up at Alvi. "Several pillows to keep his head up, if you please. We must make his breathing as easy as possible."

"Some venesection to lower the pulse tension?" Riggs asked.

"No," Thomas snapped. "He *has* virtually no pulse tension, Zachary. He needs to lose no more blood."

"Stimulant, then."

"Yes." He bent down close, smelling the patient's breath. "I'd like to see some calomel, if he'll swallow. Relaxing the bowels is only going to help. And Alvi, first some ammonia, to see if there's any response at all. We may be able to support the pulse with digitalis. I think that's the order of things."

"Brandy?" Riggs asked.

"No. He's had enough brandy." Thomas held up three fingers. "Ammonia, then digitalis, then calomel. We'll see where that puts us." He pushed himself upright. "Let's see no restrictions from clothing. That should be first."

A few moments later, any slight optimism prompted by their activity vanished. The pungent ammonia held directly under Haines's nose produced no reaction. The patient's bowels had released without aid of any drug, and it was Alvi who set about both preserving some small sense of modesty for the patient while at the same time removing the soiled linens and clothing. To that, Zachary Riggs reacted by backing toward the door.

"I think I'm only in the way," he said apologetically.

"I need nurse Auerbach," Thomas said before Riggs could disappear. "Zachary, will you do that?"

"You want her here, you mean?"

"No, at the clinic. We have a patient in the ward who shouldn't be left alone. Would you ask her to return to the clinic and remain as long as necessary?"

"Of course. I'll see to it, Thomas." Riggs took on the confident, officious tone that suited him so well. "Do what you can here." He left the room so quickly that he nearly ran over Horace, himself seeking a way to exit graciously.

In a few moments, it became abundantly clear to Thomas that there was nothing to be done, other than to keep the patient comfortable.

When he placed a small amount of digitalis extract on the back of Haines's tongue, the swallow reflex was feeble. He tried a tablespoon of brandy as well, and most of the liquor simply ran out of the corner of Haines's mouth, staining the pillowcase.

Something bumped the back of Thomas's leg, and he turned to see Alvi sliding a chair under him. He slumped down, and she rubbed the back of his neck briefly before turning away to sit on the other side of the bed.

They remained in silence for a long time, watching each of the patient's fragile breaths. Seeing nothing that needed doing, Gert James said softly, "Oh, my, you poor dear," and left. The house grew silent. Even the aroma of dinner, at first as welcome as the fire on the hearth, gradually died, and 101 took on a somber, musty chill.

"If he makes it through the night, then there might be some small hope," Thomas said at last. Alvi had been sitting with her elbows on the bed, her father's right hand held in both of hers.

"Do you believe that, really?" she asked.

"It helps to," Thomas said.

Alvi heaved a long, deep sigh and shook her head. "What will we do?"

"We can only let nature take its course. At this point, that's all that can be done."

"And then? Will you stay?"

Thomas looked at her in surprise. "Stay? Whatever do you mean?"

"Just that. Will you stay?"

"Of course," he replied, still unsure what she meant.

She lifted her father's hand, touched it to her lips, and then placed it gently on the coverlet. For a long time, she seemed content to sit, eyes closed, alone with her thoughts.

Thomas listened again with the stethoscope and detected no change, as if the powerful heart had simply not been told that its command center had abdicated. Respiration had become a bit more ragged, uneven, and shallow. He folded the instrument and stretched back. Thomas rose and made his way to the window. Darkness had settled over the village. From this vantage point, he could see the roof of the clinic six blocks down the hill.

"Do you suppose Port McKinney will ever enjoy a telephone

301

exchange?" he asked, and his voice sounded intrusively loud in the hushed room.

"By next year," Alvi said.

"Really." He turned to look at her. "You've heard that?"

"Yes. Zachary says it's coming. Seattle has enjoyed such a success, and other communities have followed. Mr. Birch agrees."

"Imagine if the workers at Schmidt's mill had been able to telephone for help. We could have saved half an hour. That might have made the difference."

"Right now, there's only one life I care anything about," Alvi whispered.

"Of course. I'm sorry." He turned away from the window, hearing the admonishments of Professor Roberts ringing in his ears.

"At this moment, you have but the one patient," Roberts would preach to the harried medical students, *"and you owe him your complete and unflagging attention."*

"And must I lose them all?" Thomas whispered to himself. To watch a patient simply fade away wrenched at him. The list was too long for so few days in this community, he thought glumly: Mrs. Cleary, Charlie Grimes, both Kittrick brothers, the constable, Lawrence Beautard and the other mill hand—and now John Haines himself was poised at the brink.

Thoroughly depressed, Thomas sighed and leaned on the bureau. He gazed down at the mammoth *Advisor* and then opened it to the fanciful rendering of the future clinic. Alvi was correct. The row of poles that walked along the water from the village to the imposing building carried the telephone or telegraph lines. Behind the clinic lay the last spit on land before the inlet, and from there a connection with the rest of the world. Regardless of how small and insignificant the village of Port McKinney might be, the clinic would be a beacon above the busy shipping lanes of Puget Sound, drawing patients from all over the world.

He turned and looked at Alvi, saw that she appeared to be whispering to her father, her face close to the old man's right ear. Thomas felt like an intruder. *Will you stay?* she had asked.

"What are you thinking?"

He realized that she was now looking at him, probing his thoughts.

"I . . . I don't know," he managed.

"Will you just sit and wait with me? I need that."

"Of course," he said quickly, realizing at that moment that there was nothing more difficult that Alvi Haines could have asked of him.

51

John Luther Haines, M.D., died at 5:17 A.M. on September 24, 1891, nine days before his sixty-seventh birthday.

Thomas and Alvi hadn't exchanged a word for more than an hour. The young physician was sitting with his head back, eyes closed, waiting for the clock downstairs to drag itself forward to chime the half hour.

Haines simply stopped breathing, and for a moment Thomas didn't understand the new silence in the room.

"He's gone," Alvi said. Thomas jerked upright. She rose from her chair as Thomas explored with the stethoscope, the small mirror, then felt the jugular with the tips of his fingers. By the time he finished, she had moved to his side of the bed, and he rose awkwardly to take her in his arms.

For a long time they stood thus, her face buried in his left shoulder, one hand holding the back of his neck in a vise. She said nothing, and Thomas did nothing to interfere with her thoughts. Her breathing settled, and for a time it seemed as if she had actually dozed off. But eventually she pulled back. She reached out and brushed his collar.

"I'm sorry, Alvi," he said, and the words sounded empty and foolish.

"Ah, we all are," she said wistfully. "Very, very sorry." She shook her head and patted his shoulder as she stepped away. She bent down and drew the coverlet up far enough to cover Haines's face. Without turning around, she added, "Mr. Lindeman promised to have the silver ready after breakfast this morning." She turned to face Thomas. "Father was excited by the prospect of what you proposed, Thomas. I wish you could have seen how excited he was."

"Mr. Deaton can wait," Thomas said. "Now, with this . . ."

"Don't be ridiculous," Alvi said with surprising vehemence. "Father would have none of that. His only worry would be that you might fall asleep at the knife halfway through the surgery." She smiled faintly. "With both Bertha and I there to prod you along, we'll get through it. And that would make father very, very proud."

"What are the arrangements to be?"

"Let Gert, Horace, and me worry about that, Dr. Thomas." She regarded the still form on the bed. "My father was most specific, and if I do anything other than what he instructed, I know he'll come back to haunt me. His wish was to be buried beside my mother, with only the simplest graveside ceremony. Nothing more." She drew in a breath and slowly shook her head. "Ah, me." Reaching an arm around Thomas once again, she drew him closer. "We all know these days will come, but somehow, we're never ready. I'm glad you're here, Dr. Thomas."

"Someone should tell Zachary," he said. She made no reply. "May I do that for you?"

"Of course. You're going to the clinic now?"

"Yes. I have two patients and no doubt a very tired nurse who awaits."

"Horace will drive you. Let me fetch your bag."

"I can manage, Alvi."

"I know you *can*. But don't be ridiculous."

He saw the hint of tears, but Alvina Haines had impressed him as the sort who would wait for a private, lonely moment to let her deep sorrow well unchecked to the surface. She packed the valise, and by the time Thomas had found his crutches, she was down the stairs. Thomas heard the yelp of grief from Gert, and the murmur of sympathy from Horace. By the time he reached the bottom of the stairway, Alvi and Gert were sitting together at the table by the kitchen range, arms around each other. Horace had retreated and now waited on the front porch.

"Damn shame," he said as Thomas maneuvered through the front door.

"Yes," the young man replied. "Yes, it is. Alvina is going to appreciate anything you can do, Horace."

"Somebody's got to tell Winchell."

"Alvi will let you know when she wants that done." Thomas struggled into the buggy. "Right now, I need to be at the clinic. Later this morning, Lindeman will have a set of surgical pins that you might pick up for me."

"Alvina told me about that," Horace said, and snapped the reins. He drove down the middle of the street where enough morning light filtered through to highlight the worst of the ruts.

"You got him movin' around, I see," Horace said, and Thomas was pulled out of his thoughts.

"I have what?"

"The mutt, there," Horace said. He pointed toward the clinic, still a hundred yards distant. "I guess that's him. No other dog so god-awful ugly."

Sure enough, the gray specter moved out of the side street beside the clinic and stopped in the middle of Gambel.

"Bertha must have let him out to do his business," Thomas said. As they pulled to a stop, the dog retreated a step or two and staggered to one side.

"If you'd check with Mr. Lindeman the instant he opens for business?" Thomas asked as he prepared to lower himself from the buggy.

"You bet," Horace said, but he hesitated. "What do you figure I ought to do?" From the troubled expression on the older man's gaunt face, Thomas knew that the question wasn't about surgical pins or the limping dog. He felt a pang of sympathy that this

305

taciturn man was now so lost that he felt the need to ask a comparative stranger what to do next.

"Alvi will need you," Thomas said. "She'll need both you and Gert more than ever. As will I." He reached out his hand, and Horace's grip was strong, his hand rough. "We'll work it out together, Horace."

He pulled his crutches from the buggy and saw that Prince had advanced a step or two.

"You aren't supposed to be out, old fellow." Thomas stopped abruptly. Blood seeped from an angry furrow that began on the top of the dog's round skull and ripped across to the base of his left ear. A portion of the ear hung loose. As if reminded of the wound, the dog tried unsuccessfully to scratch the ear with his uninjured hind leg, a move that caused him to stagger sideways.

Thomas turned to look at Horace, who held up both hands. "Don't know," Horace said.

"Did Nurse Auerbach go after you with a scalpel, old fellow?" Thomas asked, and made his way carefully to the front door. The dog followed, his right hind leg and now his left ear useless.

Thomas let himself through the unlocked front door. His office door was closed, the examining room open, one gaslight turned low. Crossing to his office, he opened the door and made his way to the nearest lamp. The dawn light was only adequate for counting shadows, and he turned the lamp up full.

"Stay put," he said as the dog found his rug. "I'll tend you in a moment." He closed the office door behind him as he hobbled out. As he entered the ward, he saw Bertha sitting beside Deaton's cot. Thomas stopped at the first gas lamp, and it hissed and popped as he turned it up.

"You've been here all night?" he asked.

"Since ten, perhaps," Bertha replied. "Mr. Riggs came to fetch me. I'm to understand that Dr. Haines is gravely ill?" As Thomas drew closer, he saw that Bertha appeared neat and prim, as if fresh from her rest. A knitting project occupied her lap.

"John had a stroke last night, Bertha. He died this morning."

"Oh, no!" Her shoulders slumped. "I'm so sorry to hear that. Alvi must be . . ."

"She's at one-oh-one with Gert and Horace at the moment."

"He died near dawn, you say."

"Just after five."

"Oh, my."

He bent over the teamster, who appeared to be sleeping peacefully.

"Mr. Riggs told me that you were going to transfer the patient to St. Mary's," Bertha said, and Thomas caught the disapproval in her tone. "I told him that I was sure he had misunderstood you."

"My God, indeed he has," Thomas said. "Why would he invent such a notion?"

Bertha took a moment to fold her knitting carefully, sliding it into a bag near her chair. "In preparation for your leaving for up north," she said quietly. "He says that you're likely to accept an offer from Pitt and Burgess."

"Oh, I think not," Thomas said angrily, and his face flushed. "Absolutely not. His friend Carlisle is a bit overeager." He rested his hand on Deaton's forehead. "We'll go ahead with the surgery this morning. Alvi was insistent, and she's right, you know. There should be no delay."

"Whatever I can do," Bertha said.

"And by the way, what happened to Prince? He was waiting outside, with his ear torn to pieces."

"Then he's come back," Bertha said. "All I know is that he most certainly was not on his rug when I came in during the evening. I assumed that you or Alvina let him out. And it's his ear now?"

"Yes. We didn't let the dog out, Bertha. And if Zachary did, he's most likely upstairs now, missing part of his leg," Thomas said.

"Surely . . ."

Thomas drew back from Deaton. "I'll need to take a look at it," he said. "The ear, I mean."

"They don't care for each other much," Bertha observed. "Riggs and the dog."

Thomas laughed. "That's an understatement."

The nurse looked carefully at Thomas. "You look tired, young man."

"I *am* tired. I've been up all night, as have you."

"How is Alvina taking her father's passing?"

"She's philosophical," Thomas replied. "At the moment, that is. I'm sure it will all sink in soon enough. I get the impression it wasn't altogether a surprise."

"No, I don't think it was. But she's a very strong young woman," Bertha observed. "Does Mr. Riggs know?"

"Not yet. He left one-oh-one early yesterday evening. After all, there was nothing he could do."

"Or would," Bertha said, and Thomas looked at her in surprise. "I'd be advised to keep my own counsel," she added, rising quickly. "I'll make myself useful. There will be a full complement by the time you're ready for surgery, Doctor." She left the ward quickly, as if loath to offer an opportunity to pursue her comment.

Thomas made his way back to the office, entered, and shut the door carefully behind him. The dog, sitting crookedly on his blanket, regarded Thomas expectantly. Leaning his crutches against the desk, Thomas relaxed into the wicker wheelchair, then rolled across to the dog, whose tail thumped once.

"Let me see what you've done," Thomas whispered. "You tried to court another man's wife, old boy? Or another bad shot?"

The wound was ugly, but an instant's examination showed that it hadn't been caused by flailing teeth. The single furrow tracked across the dog's skull as straight as a bullet.

He gently slid his hand under the ear and lifted upward. The bullet had torn the back margin free from the animal's scalp for the better part of an inch. Already heavily crusted, the wound had evidently bled profusely.

"I could stitch you back together," he said, "but you'd scratch it loose in an instant." He bent down and looked closer. "Maybe it's better if it just adds to your character, my friend. Let's leave it be and see how it heals." He brushed off his hands. "You have the habit of getting in the way of people's bullets."

Without warning he found himself nearly capsized from the chair as the dog exploded off the pad, deep, furious barks erupting. Thomas made a grab for the dog's thin neck. At the same time he heard the heavy footsteps coming down the stairs.

52

Y ou have that damn creature under control?" Zachary Riggs's tone outside the office door was that of a stern headmaster.

"A moment," Thomas answered. The dog trembled and his lips wrinkled back from chipped, yellow teeth. "We'll take care of this," he whispered as he coaxed the animal down on the blanket and stroked the undamaged side of his head.

"Shall I come in?" Bertha called, and the dog's one operative ear perked.

"Yes," Thomas replied, and she opened the door just far enough to slip through. Despite the young man's best efforts, Prince struggled to his feet, body tense. A deep *huff* issued from him, but Thomas could feel him relax with a shiver as Bertha closed the door.

"My, what a mess," she said, and the dog ducked his head.

He pushed away from the animal. "If you'd stay with him?"

"Oh, he'll be fine." She lowered her voice to less than a whisper, mouthing the words with exaggerated diction. "Mr. Carlisle is with Mr. Riggs."

"Really," Thomas said. "Now how curious." He paused with both hands poised above the wheels of his chair, a dozen thoughts whirling through his head at once. "Well . . . You have the dog?"

"I do."

Thomas wheeled to the door and opened it cautiously, keeping his chair so that it blocked the way. Zachary Riggs stood in the center of the waiting room, the fingers of each hand thrust in his vest pockets. Efrim Carlisle relaxed on the short bench by the window, legs crossed, arm casually on the sill, chin resting on his fist, as if he'd been there half an hour.

"Dr. Haines died shortly after five this morning," Thomas announced. He kept his tone neutral. He moved forward a little, since Bertha Auerbach appeared determined to leave the office with him, despite what he'd asked her to do. She pulled the office door closed behind them. Carlisle collected himself and rose from the bench, nodding perfunctorily at the young woman.

Riggs extended a hand to Thomas. "You did all you could, but that doesn't make it any easier, does it." He regarded the younger man thoughtfully, his expression sympathetic. "It's hard to lose family and old friends, just the same." He tucked his hands back in his vest.

"Doctor," Bertha interrupted, "I'm going to take a moment and fetch the pins from Mr. Lindeman now. Otherwise I fear we won't have them when we need them."

"Horace was going to do that, Bertha."

"I know he *was,*" Bertha said, frowning severely. "But I've had my experience with that man." The criticism of Horace James surprised Thomas, but Bertha didn't give him a chance to respond. Instead she nodded curtly at the two visitors and then bustled out of the clinic. Facing the door, Thomas saw that she immediately set out down Gambel, not uphill toward Lindeman's Mercantile.

"This is perhaps not a good time," Riggs said after the door closed behind Bertha. "But then, sometimes it's better not to wait."

"For what, sir?"

"You're intending complicated surgery on Mr. Deaton this morning?"

"Yes. At ten o'clock."

"My," Riggs said, his eyebrows raising in wonder. "Such an ambitious schedule." His face grew sober. "I want you to give that a second thought, young man. Especially in view of the circumstances." From John Haines, Thomas might have accepted such an ultimatum—or at least the tone of voice expected from an employer. But from Zachary Riggs, it rankled.

"I have given it nothing *but* thought," Thomas said. "The choices are simple. Either I amputate the leg, or I repair it. The injury could very likely kill Mr. Deaton unless something is done immediately."

"Indeed? You think so? It didn't look that critical to me."

Thomas's first inclination was to let the remark pass, but he understood clearly that, with John Haines now gone, his buffer had been removed. With John Haines alive and a vital force in the clinic's organization, Zachary Riggs had treated Thomas with deference, good humor, even patience. Now there was no reason for any of that. And sure enough, Riggs's tone carried ice that had never been there before. "I look at it as a physician," Thomas said evenly. "You don't."

A quick smile touched Riggs's face. "I discussed another possibility with Miss Auerbach last night, Thomas."

"She tells me that you did. I will have no part of it."

Riggs held up a hand, smiling benignly. "Hold on, hold on." With the hand safely back in the vest pocket, he continued, "I think we should employ the good Mr. Winchell's ambulance, and take Mr. Deaton to St. Mary's. Before his condition deteriorates any further."

"Nonsense," Thomas said.

Riggs's eyebrows twitched at the unpleasantry, but he otherwise ignored it. "Let me ask you. Should the surgery be a success— and we have no guarantees one way or another, do we?"

"It will be a success."

"Your optimism is commendable, Dr. Parks. Should the operation succeed, how long do you expect Mr. Deaton's convalescence to be?"

"Here at the clinic? Several weeks at best. Perhaps a month."

"That long here? In the ward?"

"Most or all of it, yes. When he can move safely on crutches or in a chair, then he might go home."

"With nursing care the whole time while he's here, I presume."

"Yes. Of course."

"That's impossible," Riggs said. "Simply impossible. We are not a convalescent's hospital, Thomas. I understand another nurse is coming into our employ shortly, but this is ridiculous. We are not equipped for such procedures."

Thomas felt his pulse racing. "We are . . ." He hesitated, choosing his words carefully. "We are what we need to be, Zachary. In this case, Mr. Deaton needs surgical intervention. That's *my* decision. *I* will decide what is best for my patient. He can't tolerate a rude trip to another facility. To subject him in his condition to a thirty-mile trek lying in the back of a wagon would kill him. You might as well just shoot him, too."

"Too?"

"I saw the dog."

"Ah. The beast." Riggs looked down, extending his left leg. "Somehow he managed to escape the office," he said. A tear marred one woolen trouser cuff. "But that's another issue."

"It is no issue," Thomas said.

Carlisle let out a long, impatient sigh. "So much for the smooth transition you promised," he said to Riggs.

"What's your business in all this?" Thomas asked as Carlisle stretched with exaggerated relaxation. "Other than as a supplier of certain pharmaceuticals for Mr. Riggs's enterprise upstairs."

"You're told that, eh?" Carlisle said mildly. He reached out and removed one of the new *Advisors* from the bookcase beside him, making a show of thumbing the pages. "Well, you're told what you're told, I suppose." He slid the book back with a thump, his interest in it merely as a means to keep his hands occupied.

"That's it, then," Thomas said, the full realization dawning on him. He wheeled across to the bookcase and removed the same volume. Flipping it open to the frontispiece, he once again looked at the engraving of the grand clinic on the page facing Dr. Haines's portrait. Fronting the water, imposing in every respect, the clinic could house an entire community—a grand illusion.

"This is Bert Schmidt's property," Thomas said, holding the book toward Riggs. "I see that now."

"Do you imagine so?"

"More than imagine. It's obvious. Although the art is fanciful, the building is prominent on the spit of land where the mill now stands. Do you deny it?" He held the book toward Riggs.

"And if it is?" Riggs made no move to take the volume.

"Pitt and Burgess would like to gain Schmidt's property, I'm sure—including his timber leases."

"What do you know of leases," Carlisle scoffed.

"Not a thing," Thomas replied. "Not a thing. Others do, of course." He turned the book and regarded the engraving. "With the leases, I imagine that this becomes more than just an advertising gimmick," Thomas said. "That's the promise, isn't it." Riggs regarded him with an infuriating amusement. *Now is not the time,* a voice in Thomas's head warned, but his hands trembled with his rising temper, and for a brief moment, he wished that Bertha Auerbach, his staunch ally, hadn't left the clinic.

"You help Pitt and Burgess with their interests, they help you with yours. That's reasonably simple." He closed the book. "I saw the spikes," he said, lowering his voice as if sharing a confidence. "I know what Kittrick was up to."

"Spikes?" Riggs's eyebrow shot up.

"Until recently, I didn't understand what Kittrick's business was with you," Thomas said. "The constable found a set of spikes in Kittrick's cabin. Just like the one recovered from the log that destroyed Schmidt's saw and killed two good men."

"I know nothing of that," Riggs said, but his eyes flicked toward Carlisle, his manner taking an edge.

"If you weren't so caught up in the business of peddling opiates, you'd know it," Thomas snapped, and immediately regretted his insult.

"How eloquent," Carlisle said quietly, and Thomas heard the danger in his voice.

"Say what you like," Thomas snapped. "I can't argue with your considerable financial success, if that's your purpose. Useful medicine certainly is not."

"And you scoff at that?" Riggs asked. "How much will Howard Deaton pay you, my good man? And Mrs. Unger? A fine bit of surgery on her daughter, I'm sure. For thirty dollars, perhaps?"

"That's a fair charge," Thomas said. "For a fair service. An *honest* service." He felt the smallest change of air in the room, and he turned quickly to look behind him at his office door, thinking that the dog had somehow nosed it open. The door remained closed.

"I think," Carlisle said judiciously, but his face was pale with anger, "that the time has come for you to consider my earlier offer, Dr. Parks. I would hate to see you throw such an opportunity away in a moment of pique—of minor disagreement over medical treatment."

"I have no interest in your offer." Behind Riggs, at the far end of the waiting room by the hallway to the stairs, Thomas saw the slightest displacement of shadow.

One of Carlisle's eyebrows shot up in surprise. "Is that right? No interest at all? That's foolish."

"No interest. Less than none."

"I would have thought that some three thousand dollars a month would have been *most* attractive for a young man such as yourself, just now setting out in the world." He smiled indulgently and touched his own right eye. "A young man who has had his share of bad luck. Even your steamer trunk with all your worldly possessions, gone by the wayside. Zachary told me about that. It surprises me that you'd reject out of hand an offer that is so generous. *Most* generous, in fact."

"Think what you like. I don't need your money, sir." To his surprise, he saw George Aldrich appear, moving close to the wall, his steps stealthy.

Carlisle's eyebrows gathered, and Thomas saw the flush run up the man's cheeks.

"Let's not be hasty here," Riggs said heavily, in the tone used by a man used to having the final word. "When John touted your background, your studies, Thomas, we both thought that you would be a valuable asset to our enterprise—and I still do."

"I will be no party to Mr. Carlisle's schemes," Thomas retorted. "Or yours."

"Now, I must protest," Riggs said, trying to sound reasonable. "Suppose—"

"Suppose nothing," Thomas said. "Mr. Aldrich will be most interested, I'm sure. I don't imagine it will take long to prove to his satisfaction who Ward Kittrick was working for. It doesn't take much imagination to figure out who profits from spiking a stand of timber. Or why Kittrick felt the need to talk with you after his visit with me. Someone has to be the local paymaster, I would suppose."

"Aldrich is a fool," Carlisle snarled, "and so are you, I'm beginning to see. You have no idea what you're talking about, or who you're dealing with. My firm—"

"Your firm," Thomas said. "Did your firm hire the Kittricks to spike trees, Mr. Carlisle? Someone who would take railroad spikes, and grind off the flange . . ." A sudden thought drew him up short. "Or perhaps hired Charlie Grimes to grind them? The Kittricks may not have a grinding wheel at their shack, but Lindeman's Mercantile certainly does. And what's to gain is obvious, isn't it."

He turned to glare at Riggs. "I suppose from your point of view, Zachary, a thriving medical practice is really a nuisance—nothing but an interference for your day."

"My God, you're a bit the smart one, aren't you," Carlisle said. He faced Thomas, feet spread wide, both hands on his hips.

"Then deny it all," Thomas said. "I'm told that your complex at Cous Island is fictitious. I must say, I wouldn't be surprised if the same enterprising printer who produced the fine artwork for this volume"—he held up the *Advisor*—"also drew up your fancy stationery. Alvina was right to tear up your check, worthless as it was."

He turned back to Riggs. "This is hardly the time, with John barely cold. But let's be clear. I don't intend to send my patients to a hospital a day's drive away."

"Now listen—"

"No, Zachary. I do not intend to spend one iota of time with your ridiculous questionnaires, or your nostrums, or with your mail order narcotics business. In that sense, your friend Carlisle here is correct, there is no room for us both under one roof." He stopped and found he was panting for breath, since now he had set the landslide in motion.

"Well," Carlisle said.

"I will also testify, sir," Thomas interrupted. "Kittrick threatened me about Charlie Grimes, and now I can only think that there may have been something more than a simple drunken brawl between a drunken brother and a boy who stuttered. It occurs to me that Kittrick could have simply let Constable Eastman pass by in the night, unharmed. He could have left the country, and never been apprehended. He didn't need to kill the lawman in such a cowardly fashion. That makes me think that the constable knew more than he ever shared with me."

"Saying it is one thing, proving it is another," Carlisle said easily.

"I suppose that's my job," Aldrich said, and the extra voice intruding on the tension was electric in its effect. Both Carlisle and Riggs turned, and Thomas slipped his hand into his coat pocket, gripping the corked scalpel. "So, I see it's a good thing I happened by," Aldrich continued pleasantly. *Happened by?* Thomas looked past him, searching for Bertha Auerbach.

"What do you want?" Carlisle said. His tone dripped with distain.

"If the saw broke, that's one thing," Aldrich said. "But when it breaks and kills two men, that's another. Don't you think so?"

"This is absurd," Carlisle said. "Zachary, if there's nothing else you need from me today, I'll be on my way. I'm not about to remain here and listen to all this."

"Oh, I don't think so," Aldrich said, his manner still so calm that Thomas marveled at his nerve. Physically, the constable was no match for Efrim Carlisle, and certainly not for Zachary Riggs. Carlisle shook his head in disgust, turning toward the door. With a sideways step that would have done credit to a dancer, Aldrich moved to block his way.

"You will stay out of my business," Carlisle snapped. "I don't know who you think you are, but this is none of your affair." Aldrich cocked his head quizzically.

"Is that so then?"

"Get out of my way."

"I think what we need to do is talk with Mr. Pedersen," Aldrich said. "He'll be interested in all this."

"Pedersen?" Carlisle said.

"The county prosecutor," Aldrich said. "He'll want to talk with you."

"Get out of my way," Carlisle whispered again. His hands rested on his belt. "Mr. Riggs," he said, and turned toward his partner. The turn was a feint, Thomas saw. The hand blocked by his twisting body from the constable's view manipulated a stubby revolver from his waistband.

Thomas drove hard on the right wheel of the chair, spinning it toward Carlisle, several strides away. At the same time, he heard Zachary Riggs bellow, "No!" and with astonishing speed, the burly fellow dove at Carlisle. The two crashed into the wall and then went down, Carlisle's shoulder hitting Thomas's chair and upending him against the office door. Inside, Prince erupted in a maniacal frenzy, and for a moment, as his face hit the floor, Thomas was sure the dog would charge right through the door.

Carlisle cursed, and the flail of limbs included an elbow in Thomas's face, smashing the bridge of his nose so hard that he saw stars and then tasted copper. Nothing was more important than gaining a grip on the revolver, but Thomas could no longer see to do so. Carlisle cursed again and then the explosion was so shatteringly loud that it produced an instant ringing in the ears, the cloud of smoke thick and acrid.

Riggs let out an oddly high-pitched little yelp and rolled to one side. Carlisle pursued his advantage, lunging to his feet before Thomas could grab him. He still held the revolver, but now he swung it toward Aldrich. The constable moved with measured determination, as if he were lining up for an Austrian sporting shoot. Carlisle's gun roared again, and Thomas saw the slug tug at the constable's coat sleeve. Aldrich didn't flinch. He fired five times with rapid but methodical precision. The heavy slugs smacked loudly as they connected, driving Carlisle back with a cry of surprise. The final three were unnecessary, since the first slug caught Carlisle squarely in the center of the chest, with the second striking an inch above. The shots battered the man against the wall, and with a final gurgling sigh he slid to the floor and slumped over on his left side, eyes staring into the distance.

For a moment Thomas lay still, tangled in his chair. A sea of blood grew around Carlisle's left elbow. A light ticking sound drew Thomas's attention, and he turned his head to see Aldrich, still rooted in his shooting stance, shucking the empty cartridges out of his revolver. With the five empties on the floor, the constable thumbed in fresh rounds, then with the gun casually at his side, he advanced across the waiting room. He didn't bother to inspect his target, but instead walked directly to Riggs.

"You had enough?" he asked.

"My knee," Riggs whispered.

"I see that," Aldrich said. "You have a gun?"

"Just this," Riggs said, pulling the little over-and-under derringer from his pocket.

"I'll take that," Aldrich said. He slipped the derringer into his own coat. "Until we see what's what. So, you can walk, you think?"

"I don't know," Riggs said. "I . . . I don't think so."

"Then maybe we find a doctor," Aldrich said, and chuckled at his own joke.

53

In an ungainly, uncollected gait, his back feet six inches out of line from his front, Prince trotted ahead a short distance and then turned to face the water, nose working. More than once, he gingerly waded out until the dark water lapped at his belly, soaking his hip. No matter how the gulls dived at him, or how curious the sea otters became, the dog never extended his explorations, staying always on the invisible thirty-foot leash that connected him with Thomas.

This particular section of shoreline had become a favorite of the young physician. Thomas remained on the narrow strip of damp, firm sand just above low water, where the footing required no effort. He avoided the jumbled rocks and tree stumps, picking his way deliberately, enjoying the smells, the show of wildlife, the soft language of the water. Although he could not kneel with either grace or comfort, he could walk, and walk he did, extending his explorations of Port McKinney and the water's edge.

On this particular day, he had left the clinic to find some relief from the incessant noise of the eager carpenters, who, led by Jake Tate, were transforming the building on Gambel and Grant. The new ambulance, driven by either Horace James or the gimpy Howard Deaton, could now drive under a protective portico on the Grant Street side of the building.

Inside, carpenters worked to create a clean, spacious surgery, a generously equipped kitchen, a second-floor ward for women and four private rooms for children. A laboratory and pharmacy had taken over several rooms on the Grant Street side of the first floor, not far from the most remarkable acquisition—a clanking, squeaking Otis elevator that Horace felt the continual need to "adjust" even though it had been in operation for less than a week.

Leaving the beehive of activity behind for a few moments was a relief, and with Prince always eager for a jaunt, Thomas had extended his walk long enough that he knew Bertha Auerbach would grow fretful. He continued to his goal for the day—the giant spruce log that lay beached and graying in the dark sand just before the shoreline started to curve out to the spit of land beyond Schmidt's mill.

He sat on the log for a moment, watching an otter tease Prince, then arose to set out for home. He did not need to call the dog. Prince immediately charged back and followed from in front, as Alvi was fond of saying. Leaving the shore, Thomas strolled up Lincoln Street that now, after a week of blazing sunshine, was baked to burnished bronze. He was exhilarated at being able to push up the incline of the street, the ache in his ribs settled now to a minor nagging.

The step up to Lindeman's porch was effortless, but the dog remained in the street, first visiting the horse trough for a noisy drink, and then sitting carefully in a patch of shade. Lindeman's new boy was busy with two women customers, and Thomas paused only long enough to purchase the latest newspaper newly arrived from New York, only three weeks past its publication date.

Eager for news from the east, Thomas settled in one of the rockers on the porch of 101 Lincoln, Prince in attendance. He had been engrossed in the newspaper for a few minutes when Alvi joined him.

"You need to see this," he said, and folded the paper so she could read it. The advertisement was enormous, printed in such a way that it resembled an actual newspaper article. "Oxypathy!" the headline trumpeted, and then proceeded to introduce the reader, in half a dozen different ways and by impressive testimony from physicians and patients alike, to the Oxypathy Electrical System, *absolutely* guaranteed to return vital oxygen to the body's fluids by a "continuous, soothing application of electrical current from the most natural of all sources . . . the earth's own carbon." By connecting the patient to two "comfortably applied" electrical leads, the article exulted, the system sped the gentle electromagnetic current to the body's ailing system. Even diphtheria, the scourge of children, was not immune to the power of Oxypathy. "Nothing can relieve the choking child as can the process of Oxypathy!" the article proclaimed, and then quoted numerous testimonials from patients, physicians, and research scientists.

"That's Father," Alvi said softly. Sure enough, the engraving that was captioned as representing the eminent Dr. Claude Lucier, recently returned to Philadelphia from Paris, was the same engraving that appeared in the frontispiece of the *Advisor* . . . Dr. John Haines.

"Indeed it is," Thomas agreed. "And Dr. Tessier is back as well." He reached across and tapped one of the sidebar articles.

Alvi's brow furrowed as she roamed the half-page advertisement until she had found what she sought. "He's in San Francisco now," she said, "and for only thirty dollars, you can have this device to heal all your patients, Thomas."

"I'd like to order one as a curiosity," Thomas said with a laugh. "To have in my office for impossible cases." He took the paper offered by Alvi. "In a way, I'm not surprised that Zachary is thriving. No doubt he's even turned his limp into elegant effect. I can see him with his fine suit, patent boots, and a silver-headed cane."

"I saw Mrs. Beautard on the schedule for this afternoon," Alvi said, eager for another topic of conversation.

"Yes," Thomas said, pushing himself to his feet. "I've asked Jake and his crew to go away this afternoon. We need some peace and quiet."

"Ovariotomy?"

"Yes. I'm afraid so. There's a tumor the size of an orange."

"Will there be trouble with her new fiancé? I met him yesterday, and I'm not sure she's any better off than she was with Lawrence."

"No," Thomas said. "I suppose not, but believe it or not, Howard Deaton spent a few minutes with him. I'm not sure what he told the man, but he does have an emphatic way of explaining things." He grinned at Alvi. "Both Bertha and Helvina are assisting, but I can always use more help."

"Maybe," she said, stretching back languorously. She rubbed her belly. "I was thinking I might go for a walk myself."

Thomas reached over and placed his hand on her abdomen, feeling only the slightest, most graceful curve. "Take Prince with you," he said. "He's going to have a lot to get used to, Mrs. Parks."